Just MURDER

Just MURDER

A MYSTERY NOVEL

Jan Rehner

SUMACH
PRESS

National Library of Canada Cataloguing in Publication Data

Rehner, Jan
Just murder: a mystery novel/Jan Rehner.

ISBN 1-894549-22-8
I. Title.

PS8585.E4474J87 2003   C813'.6   C2003-901592-0
PR9199.3.R4283J87 2003

Edited by Jennifer Glossop
Copyedited by Emily Schultz
Cover and design by Elizabeth Martin

*Sumach Press acknowledges the support of the Canada Council
for the Arts and the Ontario Arts Council for our publishing program.
We acknowledge the Government of Ontario through the Ontario
Media Development Corporation's Ontario Book Initiative.*

ONTARIO ARTS COUNCIL
CONSEIL DES ARTS DE L'ONTARIO

Printed and bound in Canada

Published by
SUMACH PRESS
1415 Bathurst Street #202
Toronto Canada
M5R 3H8
sumachpress@on.aibn.com
www.sumachpress.com

To my mother, Margaret Rea, in her stead

Acknowledgements

I want to thank my first circle of readers for their criticisms and encouragement: Janet Broomhead, Fran Cohen, Alan Davies, Kate Ney, Ellen Saslaw, Trish Swanson, Richard Teleky and Betty Tully. Thanks also to the women at Sumach Press for taking the risk. Most of all, and again, thanks to Arthur Haberman for Paris, for being the exception, and for those two words.

Prologue

Saturday, December 12, Toronto

The man beside her promised too much and listened too little. Amanda Martin tilted her head politely in the direction of his voice, but she was already planning her exit. A bar, she thought, is the loneliest place in the world after your friends have left.

"Sorry," she interrupted, "perhaps some other time."

The rakish air waned a little and the jaunty smile sagged at its edges, but he rallied. "You don't like dancing?"

"I do, but I've an early start tomorrow. Thanks anyway."

"At least let me buy you another drink. It's Saturday night. The holidays are coming. Let's celebrate."

Amanda wavered, but only for an instant. He caught the moment of indecision and leaned toward her, placing a hand over her own. "I'll bet you dance beautifully," he whispered.

The gratuitous compliment was merely banal, but the seductive tone was a fatal error. Amanda extricated her hand, and reached for her shoulder bag.

"Good night. I mean it. I'm sure you'll find someone else to celebrate with."

She was a step away when she caught the insult. She turned back slowly, astounded, and raised a black eyebrow. "Excuse me?"

"You heard me. Cockteaser. You accept a drink from me, invite my company, and then just walk away?"

"Forgive me," Amanda shrugged, not curbing the sarcasm. "I thought you were grown up." She fished in her bag for a twenty and flicked it onto the counter of the bar. Then she smiled her most radiant smile and turned away quite deliberately.

Outside, above the webbing of streetcar cables, the winter's night sky was clear and cold. Amanda shivered and pulled up the fur-lined hood of her long black coat. Despite the icy temperature, every stride away from the petulant drama of the bar cheered her. The downtown core of the city was festive, busy with people and softly lit by strands of tiny golden Christmas lights that looped around the trunks and bare branches of trees.

Peering out from under her hood, she scanned the street for a taxi, but was not really disappointed when she didn't see any. She was strong, a habitual walker, and she lived only two, perhaps three, miles away. She turned her steps in the direction of home, watching her warm breath frost the air. She knew a shortcut.

She walked for some time along College Street, lulled by her plans for the holidays and listening for the familiar refrains of carols that occasionally escaped into the night from the opening doors of record shops and computer stores. She passed the old fire station with its bell tower and the grey-stoned church of St. Stephen-in-the-Fields. The string of coffee houses, Portuguese, Italian, and Tawainese restaurants, all crowded side-by-side, had decked their windows with coloured lights and miniature Christmas trees. Outside the Salvation Army building, she stopped to listen to three trumpeters in their black and red uniforms drumming up money for their flock of the homeless. But it was too cold to linger. She made her donation and moved on.

When she reached the parking lot between the yellow-brick Employment Resource Centre and the glassy Ontario Hydro Building, she turned right, skirting the parked cars to the laneway beyond. She barely noticed that the night had fallen silent until she came to the top of Murray Street.

She stopped. She surveyed the length of pavement before her. The lights and the people were gone.

The street, dominated at one end by the back of Mount Sinai Hospital, looked narrower than she remembered. Night seemed to have shrunk it into an alley. The parking garage opposite the hospital looked cavernous and eerie. Most of the hospital's row upon row of rectangular windows were dark, but those that were lit threw a checkerboard pattern on the pavement below.

Unnerved, she was urged forward by the cold. She tucked her chin into the collar of her coat and, with head down, began to walk faster. She watched her feet move from the dark to the bright squares, step after step, from dark to light. Her footsteps echoed on the pavement. She passed the garage. She would be out of the alley soon. Once she made it to University Avenue, there would be people, noise, and traffic.

Closer now, she began to relax, mesmerized by the rhythm of her footsteps moving in and out of the squares of light.

A crackling, snapping sound froze her. She looked back quickly, her instincts for danger fully aroused. There was no one, nothing, just a stray sheet of newsprint being buffeted about in a gust of icy wind. She was only yards away from the corner.

She saw the shadow of her attacker behind her a second before her left knee and right arm hit the pavement. Her long indrawn breath of shock and fear was muzzled by an iron hand.

Amanda swallowed her bile. Her mind screamed and screamed, but she heard only his ragged voice chanting "Bitch, bitch, bitch" in her ear. She felt the spittle from the ugly syllables spray her face.

With a surge of adrenaline, Amanda tried to push him away, arching her back, kicking with her knees, shaking her head from side to side. Nothing worked. She heard the low laugh. His smothering weight shifted. He was on top of her, laughing and chanting. Her nostrils were filled with the pungent smell of whiskey from his breath.

Look at him, Amanda's mind screamed. *Look at his face.*

It was him. The man from the bar, his smooth features now distorted, menacing. Amanda went suddenly limp. Hope drained from her body like blood. She was only vaguely aware of the sound of her clothes ripping, his hands raking across her exposed skin.

He grabbed a fistful of her dark hair with his free hand and began banging her head against the pavement. The night around her blurred. She closed her eyes. *Let me be unconscious*, Amanda thought. *Let it be over.*

"Let her go. Now."

Amanda felt the weight upon her freeze.

"I said, let her go." The voice was soft, almost sad. It was a woman's voice.

The weight lifted. Pain flooded Amanda's body as the hand slid off her mouth and jaw. She groaned and opened her eyes.

She saw a figure standing above her, a young woman dressed in jeans and a black leather jacket, pressing a gun against the temple of the attacker. He was still on his knees, his head bent forward. Dazed, she heard the voice again.

"Are you all right? Can you move?"

Tentatively, Amanda stretched her limbs. She touched her own face and the back of her head. She could feel the swelling, but nothing sticky. No blood. She felt light-headed, but strong now, strong.

She wanted to run.

Amanda scrambled to her feet. Instinctively, she wrapped her coat around her ruined clothing. She could stand. She could get away.

She didn't even glance at the man, but fixed her gaze on the other woman. Who was she? Amanda studied her face, a pale oval in the dim light. She had never seen her before. She opened her mouth, she wanted to thank her, but no words came. Mute and shaken, she wanted only to flee.

"Yes," the woman replied to Amanda's wordless question. "If you can move, go now. Go quickly. Don't look back."

She reached out a hand to Amanda, lightly touching her shoulder. Then she gave her a little shove, as if to break the gaze between them. Amanda turned away and ran.

She reached the end of the alley in seconds. In minutes, she was on University Avenue, waving down a taxi. As she entered the cab, she was sure she heard the jarring blast of a gunshot. But when the cabbie blandly asked where she was going, she slammed the door behind her and drove away from the nightmare without looking back.

Thursday, June 24, New York

No one noticed her as she moved silently around the periphery of the room. Wearing a plain, starched black dress and black stockings, she was invisible as all domestics are invisible, a part of the decor, a mute accessory. Rosa, the maid.

Her skin was tan, her coarse, black hair pulled back tightly and tied at the neck. Her features were pleasant, her face expressionless. Though a bit thick in the waist and hips, she moved lightly, quickly. She freshened drinks, picked up glasses, emptied ashtrays. She kept her eyes lowered, but watched intently, anticipating her employer's needs. Listening and watching.

There were seven men seated in the living room of Peter Dexter's brownstone in Greenwich Village. Rosa had seen them all before — Dexter's lawyers and business partners. They had been summoned for a celebration of sorts.

"Hey, what d'ya call one hundred district attorneys at the bottom of the sea?" Peter Dexter's voice was raucous, his speech slightly slurred. "A good start, that's what! Four months with those bastards and they couldn't lay a finger on me."

The lawyers laughed on cue, perhaps less heartily than Dexter's partners. Rosa could tell the lawyers didn't like Dexter much. He was often loud and embarrassingly vulgar, but he paid well and money doesn't have a personality.

"Here's to the American justice system," Dexter gloated. "More Scotch, Rosa."

She circled the room with the decanter, while Dexter began to reveal plans for his next film. She listened to the outline of yet another crude plot: a male and female pair of teachers this time, doing sex education with a group of twelve-year-old girls. It made her feel slightly queasy, but her face remained blank, her hands steady. She couldn't afford the luxury of tuning him out. She couldn't afford not to listen.

"Got me a hot prospect," Dexter bragged. "A sweet little morsel. Maybe I'll audition her later tonight. You know, celebrate my creative licence."

A few of the men laughed. Some stared into their Scotch glasses. They preferred not to know the more sordid details of Dexter's lucrative business in porn videos. As long as he didn't break the letter of the law, they didn't much care what Dexter did. As far as they knew, though they didn't choose to probe too deeply, he never used girls younger than sixteen. Most were street kids, lured into Dexter's net by his partners, who were no better than pimps in Rosa's view. They cleaned up the girls, bought them pretty clothes, and dressed them to look virginal, though none were virgins after Dexter was through with them. During the futile investigation into Dexter's business affairs, there were rumours of drugs and intimidation. But those few girls who could be found once they had been discarded wouldn't testify. Nothing stuck to Dexter.

The party began to break up at about six. As the men drifted toward the door, no one said goodbye or even glanced at Rosa. She never minded. In fact, she depended on their oblivion. So when one of the newer lawyers paused with her in the doorway, she was caught off guard.

"How do you stand him?" he whispered.

For once, Rosa's face betrayed her disgust. "Same as you do, I guess. He pays well."

The man flushed and turned away quickly. The remark had stung.

From the living room, Dexter hollered at Rosa to clean up. She took a deep breath, her mask falling back into place, and closed the door softly.

The discipline required of her over the past five months had tested her to the limit — five months as a live-in maid, cooking and cleaning for Dexter, never betraying either her anger or her contempt. She'd followed the investigation avidly at first, filled with hope that eventually dwindled to resignation. The search warrants for Dexter's posh home and seedy Brooklyn studio turned up nothing. Witnesses vanished. Worse, she sometimes had to look into the faces of the young girls, hardly more than children. Their eyes haunted Rosa. Some pretended to be tough and street wise, as though they knew what was happening to them and could still control their lives. Others were star-struck with the sequined veneer of glamour and easy money. Saddest of all were those few who believed they had found someone who actually cared about them.

Now, at last, with the investigation clearly faltering, it was time for Rosa to act. She felt almost relieved, jumpy with pent-up energy.

She had laid her own plans, stealthily and carefully. It had taken her three months to find a conspirator, a woman who still had courage and the capacity to trust. Rosa had eavesdropped on Dexter's phone conversations until she had heard one woman's voice and a surname that surprised her, the name of a prominent New York family. She had followed Dexter in cabs until she had learned the woman's address. She had talked to the superintendent of the woman's building and had discovered that Dexter paid her rent in cash. But, at first, Rosa couldn't imagine why. The cliché of the hidden mistress didn't fit here: Dexter was too cold a fish and the woman was in her early twenties — used up, overexposed in Dexter's world. But he kept up the payments and occasionally bought her extravagant gifts.

Compliant and unobtrusive, Rosa had hovered at the edge of rooms, listened at thresholds and sifted through papers and files. She had made strategic calls from local pay phones to her Toronto contact and had learned about the woman's past, the rebellion of the rich wild child.

Finally, when the search warrants had failed to yield anything more incriminating than a stack of grainy videos in poor taste, Rosa guessed: the woman's apartment must be where Dexter kept the illegal videos, and the drugs that she knew he handed out like candy to babies. Dexter must be blackmailing the woman, not for money but for silence, no doubt with footage of her own naked body slithering over a male torso. She was the perfect blind for him, a link the investigators would know nothing about.

Rosa had to find that tape. With it, she could make a far better bargain than Dexter could. First, she eliminated both the brownstone and the studio from her consideration — Dexter would never have risked having the tape seized by the investigators. She pondered the problem for several weeks, but the solution, once imagined, seemed inevitable. She knew Dexter. She knew his habits, his arrogance, his small cruelties.

She'd gambled everything on the next step. She'd waited for Dexter to leave town on one of his weekend jaunts and she'd gone to the woman's apartment and told her everything she knew, everything she guessed, and everything she hoped.

"The tape's here," Rosa had insisted. "He wouldn't have left it anywhere else."

"That's crazy. Does he think I'm stupid?"

"Yes."

"Does he think I wouldn't even look?"

"Yes."

"There are tapes in the basement, in my storage locker. They didn't even seem particularly important to him."

"And the drugs?"

"There's a panel in one of the bookshelves."

"First, I'm going to help you find that tape."

It had taken them about two hours to spot the right footage, two hours of mind-numbing obscenity during which time they had hardly spoken, scarcely moved. Finally the woman ejected the tape.

"If you only knew," she whispered, "how loudly I was screaming then, inside my head. I never — "

"Don't. Let it go. Destroy it. Erase the others, too, if you have time."

"Time?"

"We're both going to disappear. Soon. Maybe a week, maybe less. Can you be ready? Do you have a place to go where Dexter can't find you?"

"I do now. Now that I have the tape. But what are we waiting for? Let's go now."

"First, the drugs. I don't want the police to find them here. I know Dexter and his stable of lawyers. They'll find a way to wriggle free. I need to construct a hiding place that the first search warrant might have missed, but that the next won't. When it's ready and the coast is clear, I'll call you. If Dexter contacts you in the meantime, you'll have to play along. Can you do that?"

"It'll be the best acting I've ever done. I promise."

"Show me."

The two women emptied the books from one of the shelves and removed its false back. The drugs were mostly cocaine, with a few bags of pills for exotic cocktails. Rosa smiled.

"Wait," the woman said. "There's more."

She handed Rosa a plain black notebook. "I kept records. Dates, phone numbers, drop sites. And whatever names I could catch. Guess I'm not as stupid as he thought."

That had been eight days ago. Rosa had found the right carpenter, smuggled him in and out of Dexter's house at opportune times, and paid him handsomely. But there were no charges pending against Dexter. The investigation had ground to a halt for lack of evidence, and even now he was planning to seduce yet another child from the streets.

It was time to act.

Rosa cleaned up from the afternoon and waited for her orders. She knew the routine. After a few calls, Dexter would head upstairs to shower. If things went her way, he'd want a quick nap before dressing to go out. And he always ordered a Scotch before his nap. Rosa felt lucky.

She waited in the kitchen until she heard Dexter shut off the shower. Then she took a bottle of sleeping pills from the cupboard, crushed two into the freshly poured Scotch and carried it upstairs to Dexter's bedroom.

"Your drink, sir."

"Oh. That's a good girl. I was just thinking I'd take forty winks."

Dexter drained the glass and handed it back to her, dismissing her with a wave of his hand.

Rosa returned to the kitchen, unclenched her teeth, washed and dried the glass and returned it to the cupboard. She flushed the remaining sleeping pills down the sink and slipped the empty bottle into her pocket.

Walking to the foot of the stairs, she cocked her head and listened. All was quiet in Dexter's bedroom.

She picked up the phone and dialled.

"It's time. How soon can you get here?"

"Forty minutes."

"You won't go back to your apartment?"

"No. I'm all packed. I'm picking up a rental car on the way."

"Okay, let's do it."

Rosa prayed the sleeping pills would be strong and fast-acting. She'd had to guess at the dosage: enough to keep him out, not enough to be dangerous, not enough to arouse suspicion.

So close to the end of her mission, she found the waiting almost as hard as the servility she'd paid to Dexter, but at last she heard the soft knock at the door.

The woman smiled and handed her two plastic grocery bags. They were heavy.

"I don't know how to thank you, Rosa."

"No need. I couldn't have set him up without you. Thanks to you, if the drug charges don't stick, maybe the suppliers named in your records will pay him a visit of their own. Now go. I can't be sure how long he'll sleep."

One last smile and she was gone. Rosa carried the bags into Dexter's study and removed the books from the recently altered book shelf. There was a certain poetic justice to the new hiding place.

When the drugs were safely in place, she went to her room at the back of the house and took down a small suitcase with a shoulder strap from her closet shelf. She threw the pill bottle into it and removed three 5"x 7" padded envelopes, each one bearing a different New York address. A second, larger suitcase was packed with her own clothes and toiletries.

Then Rosa sat down in front of her bureau mirror. She took off the black wig which always made her scalp itch, and smoothed cold cream across her face to remove the dark makeup and the black pencil from her eyebrows. Carefully, using the tip of her baby finger, she popped out the tinted contact lenses. She stripped off the generic maid's uniform and the dark hose. When she removed the padded girdle, she was fifteen pounds lighter.

Rosa stepped into her shower, shampooed her shoulder-length blonde hair and soaped her body all over. The makeup from her arms, hands and neck swirled around her toes like mud. She rubbed herself dry and left the towel in a heap on the bathroom floor. Someone else would have to clean it up.

She dressed carefully. Without the heels, she would be two and a half inches shorter. She put on a short-sleeved white linen suit and sandals. From the bottom of a dresser drawer, she removed a passport in the name of Eva Renault and placed it, together with the three envelopes, into a white purse. When she was ready, she scooped up all the discarded clothing that had helped to create Rosa the maid and dumped it into the shoulder suitcase.

A few minutes later, a blue-eyed blonde, about 5' 6", 120 pounds, wearing a white linen suit and sandals, carrying a white purse and two suitcases, left the brownstone in Greenwich Village and boarded a bus up Madison to midtown. She went into a post office and bought stamps for the three envelopes.

"How long will it take," she asked, "before these arrive?"

The postal worker shrugged. "Couple of days. You want express?"

"No, two days is fine. But could you put a 'Do Not Bend' sticker on them? They contain photographs."

There was one photo in each envelope. It was all that she'd been able to manage. Dexter had rarely brought any girls to his home and she'd had to take the snapshots when they were still asleep or too groggy from drugs to notice the camera. Even then, she had not always been able to discover the whereabouts of the girls' families or whether or not they wanted the lost girls back. But these three, at least, had families who still cared, who would be glad to receive the current addresses of their missing children. These three might have a chance and maybe, just maybe, enough support from reunited family to testify against Dexter. One of them, she knew, was only fourteen.

A few minutes later, she left the post office and hailed a cab to La Guardia. Once there, she walked to a bank of public phones and called the detective who had headed up the search of Dexter's home. It was a short conversation, one she had to make anonymously, but she was sure she'd made his day.

Her flight to Toronto was scheduled to leave in two hours. She was not particularly nervous about the wait. She was carrying nothing suspicious. She was using her own passport and had a ticket in her own name.

It was time to say goodbye to Rosa. She slipped into a washroom and took up a position in front of the mirrors closest to the waste bin, fussing with her hair and makeup until there was a quiet moment. When she emerged five minutes later, anyone watching carefully might have realized that she was without the shoulder suitcase. But no one was watching, and Eva Renault disappeared into the crowd.

Part One

THE HUNTER

Saturday, July 10, Toronto

The early evening sun cast golden shimmers across the calm surface of Lake Ontario. Lights were just beginning to shine along the sandy boardwalk that lined the shore. Lily Ross loved this part of the city, known simply as the Beaches. The area had been spruced up in recent years with trendy restaurants and shops, a new band shelter for outdoor concerts in the park, and a boom in the renovations business. Old homes that still bore the traces of cottage architecture now sported skylights, modern decks, and cathedral windows. Tucked here and there, where space permitted, were new, low-rise luxury condos and townhouses. There was too much traffic and the water was too polluted for swimming, but to Lily the Beaches still tasted of summertime, long twilights, and soft nights.

Lily looked through the viewfinder to compose the perfect shot. She wanted the model in the right side of the frame, where leaves from the maples lining the boardwalk would trace lacy shadows across her face. Over her left shoulder was the skyline of Toronto's downtown in the distance and the expanse of golden water.

"Okay, I'm set. Let's do this," Lily signalled.

Photographer and model began their slow choreography: Lily circling around, adjusting the focal length of the camera lens, recomposing, pressing the shutter release in rapid sequence; the model adjusting her facial expressions, turning her face away and toward the camera, lifting a shoulder, sometimes just laughing. Lily always got better shots when the beginning pose was broken and the spontaneous movement began. A special kind of magic occurred when the models were not self-conscious, when they saw her and the camera as part of a game not to be taken too seriously. Lily had never worked with this model before, but she liked her naturalness. Besides, with her black hair and creamy skin, she looked like a 1940s movie star. The pictures would be great.

"I'm almost done, Amanda. Want to go for a drink when we finish?"

Amanda Martin stared one more time into the camera. Lily thought she saw surprise in her eyes.

"Sure. I haven't been out in ages. But let's make it dinner. I'm famished."

"A model who eats," Lily gasped. "I'm shocked."

The last shot was of Amanda sticking out her tongue at the camera.

An hour later, seated at one of the sidewalk tables of a neighbourhood bistro, Lily watched in amusement as Amanda surprised the waiter by ordering her steak with a double portion of *frites*.

"How do you eat like that and manage to stay thin?"

Amanda raised an eyebrow.

"You're not doing badly yourself, you know."

Lily had to agree. She'd ordered mussels in a wine cream sauce and had already begun to eat her share of the bread basket.

"I exercise," Amanda grinned. "And for dessert I'll have the banana bread pudding with caramel sauce. Oh, and an espresso."

"I'll pass," Lily smiled at the waiter. "But we'll share a bottle of the house Merlot."

He hurried away and Lily settled back to enjoy the mellowness of the evening. The Beaches was enjoying a peaceful twilight, too late for the joggers and roller bladers, too early for the jovial bar crowds.

"So, Lily who-doesn't-exercise, what do you do when you aren't on assignment for companies selling shampoo? I mean, you were having too much fun to do this for a living. The photographers I work with are usually bored."

"You're right. I do freelance photography and some writing, too." Lily found herself glancing away from Amanda as she spoke. It was only a small lie, but she hadn't been able to write anything for months. Not since her last feature article, not since its devastating consequences. She shrugged. "It's okay — these odd jobs help me stay independent."

"Me, too. People think that all models lead glamorous lives walking down runways in Paris and New York. But most of us live and work on a much smaller scale. I may not see much of the high life, but I earn a living."

Lily said nothing. She knew Amanda was just chattering, just being friendly, but the references to the so-called high life of models, a life she had exposed in print as both shallow and dangerous, made her feel uncomfortable. The waiter rescued her, setting down the plates with a flourish. Amanda's conversation paused while she savoured the first bites.

"Sure you don't want some of these fries?"

"I'm tempted, but no."

"So, tell me about freelancing," Amanda mumbled with her mouth full. "It sounds almost as precarious as being a model."

Good choice of words, thought Lily — *precarious* — but her answer was casual. "It is, really. I worked for *Toronto Press* for a while and found it too confining. I like to choose my own stories. All I miss is a regular paycheque."

"Oh well," Amanda laughed. "If that's all. Have you ever thought about modelling yourself? You have great bone structure."

"Amanda, look again. My bones only stretch to five feet five — that's a midget in your world. My hair is hacked off like this so no stray ends will flit across the lens at an inopportune moment. And I don't know the first thing about makeup. Mascara smudges the viewfinder."

Amanda did look again, but thought her new friend was too modest. Her sandy hair was streaked with golden highlights, its shortness making her look impish, an effect heightened by the dark eyebrows, wide grey eyes, and the dimples that appeared when she smiled.

"No, I much prefer being behind the camera," Lily continued. "I'm a natural observer, rather than a performer. Not like you — you're such a natural, Amanda. Maybe we should collaborate. We could — "

She stopped talking in mid-sentence. Amanda was staring past Lily's right shoulder, her fork frozen in mid-air. Her eyes were huge with alarm and she looked shaken. Instinctively, Lily turned to look behind her to see what had so upset her friend. There was only a scattering of diners, a young couple entering the restaurant patio, two elderly men relaxing over a pitcher of beer, and a woman with sandy hair seated alone, reading the menu. A blues track played softly in the background. Lily could see or hear nothing out of the ordinary, nothing that telegraphed danger.

"Excuse me." Amanda abruptly left the table and approached the lone woman. Lily watched just long enough to see a similar look of alarm on the stranger's face. She turned away, not wishing to intrude on the encounter, but though she couldn't hear any words, she couldn't help but overhear the urgent tenor of their whispered conversation.

A few minutes later, Amanda returned to the table looking solemn, her creamy skin ashen.

"What happened? Who was that?"

"Forget it. Let's go."

"But you look terrible. Are you all right?"

"I said forget it."

The two women paid for their unfinished meal in uneasy silence, the comfortable intimacy that had grown between them over the last two days of the photo shoot seemingly shattered. Lily felt stunned by the rebuke of Amanda's sudden withdrawal. She was hurt, and more than a little concerned by Amanda's evident distress.

As they walked toward the parking lot where they had left their cars earlier that morning, the congenial laughter and chatter of other diners and evening strollers only made Lily feel worse. When they came to the park, softly contoured by the rising moon and smelling of freshly cut grass and summer leaves, she stopped walking. The night was too lovely to end this way.

"Look, Amanda," she smiled. "Thanks for dinner. I'm sorry it ended so badly for you. I'm going to sit in the park for a while. You can join me if you like. If not, well, maybe we'll see each other again sometime."

Without warning, Amanda began to cry.

"For God's sake, what's wrong? What have I said?"

"It's not you. I'm sorry. I can't ... I ... something happened to me six months ago and I can't — "

Lily took Amanda's hand and led her to a park bench under the canopy of a copper beech tree. She fumbled in her camera bag for tissues.

"Whatever it is, Amanda, I'm a friend. Do you want to talk about it?"

"No — yes. I — I haven't told anyone."

Lily sat and waited. She had interviewed enough people in her job to know when to be quiet. And since she didn't have the faintest idea what was going on, she had no questions anyway. She thought again about the last article she'd written. How sure of herself she'd been. She had stripped away the facade of glamour, revealing the reality of the models' world — amphetamines, bulimia, and relentless self-criticism. Nothing new, really, but she had named names. She had felt proud of her work, even a touch self-righteous, until one of those names was found dead, a needle in one arm and a copy of Lily's article in one hand. That the guilt she felt was irrational didn't make it less paralyzing. Lily needed to make amends. The least she could do now was listen.

After what seemed a long time, Amanda began to tell her story. Lily closed her eyes. She could see the narrow winter street, the ugly shadows against the harsh bands of light, and Amanda, vulnerable, head down, not paying attention, walking blindly into a cruel trap. Amanda struggling.

All around them, it seemed to Lily, the park had grown huge and unnaturally still. Eventually, Amanda stopped crying.

"Were you sexually assaulted?" Lily whispered.

"No, not quite. I — I got away. Someone, something happened to distract him. I ran away."

"Did you report him?"

"No. I just ran away. I don't know what happened. My head — when I got home my head was hurting. I stood in the shower, scrubbing and scrubbing, but my head still hurt. It was throbbing. I began to throw up. I threw away all my clothes, all of them, my coat, everything. I called 911 and told them I'd fallen in the tub. They took me to emergency. I had a concussion."

"But, Amanda, they must have suspected. Weren't there other marks, bruises?"

"They knew. They even sent in a sexual assault counsellor. But I just kept saying I'd fallen in the shower. Nothing happened, I mean there was no penetration, no internal exam or anything like that."

"Everything happened. You were attacked. I'm not judging you. I don't know what I'd do in the same circumstances, but if you didn't report it, if you don't report it now, he could still be out there preying on other women."

"No, I don't think so."

Lily glanced at Amanda's face. Her last words were whispered so softly, she had barely heard them. The two women looked into each other's eyes for a moment. Then, with a photographer's experience, Lily saw the subtle change in Amanda's expression, the openness vanishing like a veil slipping over her eyes. Amanda looked away first.

"Was that the counsellor, then?" Lily probed.

"What?"

"That woman in the restaurant who upset you, was she the counsellor they sent to you in the hospital?"

"Oh, her. No, she was just someone I thought I recognized, but I was wrong."

Lily gave up questioning. The veil had become a steel curtain. She knew that Amanda was lying. The woman in the restaurant had mirrored Amanda's expression of startled recognition. Whatever had passed between them it had been more than a case of mistaken identity. But Amanda looked uneasy now, the impulsive confessor who was wondering if she could trust her confidante. Lily thought she had cause to wonder.

"C'mon," Lily said. "It's still early enough to catch a movie. I think we could use a comedy."

Amanda's relief was palpable.

"Sounds great."

Lily hoisted her camera bag and the two women left the park, Amanda already outlining their choice of movies. The convenience of comedies, thought Lily, was that most of them did not require much attention. She wanted to think. She knew there was more to Amanda's story than she was willing to tell. The question was whether or not this was a story that Lily should tell.

Monday, July 12, Toronto

She'd spent much of Sunday trying to convince herself that there was nothing more to Amanda Martin's story than a frightened woman reluctant to report an attempted rape. It happened all too often — the silence, the misplaced guilt and shame of victims. The desperate need for privacy was something that Lily could understand, something that part of her wanted to respect. But she was also haunted by Amanda's impulsive confession, by her compelling need to tell someone what happened. And what did happen? This was the question Lily kept turning over and over in her mind. How did Amanda get away? Who was the woman that Amanda had recognized in the restaurant? Lily was convinced that that encounter had been the catalyst for everything that Amanda had told her, and not told her, afterward. And why was Amanda so convinced that the man who assaulted her would not prey on others?

Lily was stumped. Unreported, the assault had never officially happened. There would be no police reports, nothing in the newspapers, and Lily didn't even know which hospital Amanda had been taken to or who the counsellor was who had tried to help her. All she had from Amanda's story was a date and a street and an instinct that there was much more to discover.

Discouraged, Lily poured her third cup of coffee of the morning and sat staring out the window at the quiet, tree-lined street. She'd bought the narrow brick duplex on Birch Avenue, with its front stoop and pointed gable, just after her mother died three years ago. Most of her neighbours were professionals of some sort, or retired; most of the two- and three-storey houses were modern or newly renovated, with small, neat lawns and sometimes decorative urns or wrought-iron fences. Despite its proximity to busy Yonge Street, the avenue was seldom travelled except by children on their way to Cottingham Public School at the end of the park. During school term, she loved watching the youngest ones line up for the ice-cream truck, or play hilariously inept games of baseball. She was happy here, most of the time.

Not having a mortgage had made her choice to be self-employed possible. She was free to travel on assignments and arrange her own schedule, but she also felt the burden of freedom. Her days were often piece-meal. She worried over where she would find the next job, the next assignment. Eventually, she'd established that she could make a living with her photography and her articles for magazines, but money was scarcer now that she felt unable to write. She was drifting. She lacked focus. Most ironic, she thought, for a photographer. And now she was focused on Amanda and more questions. Was this the chance she was looking for to push past her fear and make amends for her earlier mistakes?

When she couldn't bear the thought of another sip of cold coffee, Lily grabbed one of her cameras, jumped on her bicycle and headed for Mount Sinai. Maybe her sensitivity to place would help her sort out her thoughts or simply give her an opening to resume a conversation with Amanda.

It was hot outside, one of those hazy, humid July days in Toronto when the air was thick and the pavement seemed to steam. Lily felt even more enervated when she reached the street behind the hospital. It was drab in daylight, with not even a whisper of the sinister drama Amanda had described. Just a banal strip of asphalt, with barely any grass and no trees. The north end was dominated by the back entrance to the hospital where staff and patients smoked furtively and visitors came and went, listless in the heat. Opposite was a huge parking garage, an architect's eyesore of climbing cement.

Lily dismounted and walked her bike toward the south end where Amanda had been attacked. At least there, where the alley opened out to a cross street, she could see older buildings in handsome red brick, the late morning shadows of awnings, the splashes of colour from hot-dog vendors, and sidewalk fruit-and-vegetable markets. She lifted her camera and began shooting — first, the banal stretch of concrete, then the surprising relief of a kindlier, more lively vista. In twenty minutes, she had seen enough. There was nothing more for her here, and nothing of Amanda's ordeal.

As she passed the parking garage for the second time, the attendant emerged from his glassed-in booth. He was sweating profusely, and wiping his forehead with a towel. *God,* thought Lily, *it must be over a hundred degrees in that garage.* She reached down to her bike, removing her fresh water bottle.

"Would you like a drink?" she offered. "You must be dying in there."

The man grinned, holding up his towel. "You are very kind, miss. But, you see, I have my own supplies. I come prepared."

Lily recognized the sing-song cadence of a South Asian accent, and smiled back, taking a drink of water herself.

"Well, good luck to you, then." She swung her leg over the bike and was about to push off when the man spoke to her again.

"You are a reporter, miss? We do not have tourists on this street and you take many photographs."

"Oh, no, not a reporter. I was just curious."

The man chuckled. "Ah, yes, many curious people come after the murder, but you see there is no sign."

"Murder?" The word reverberated in Lily's mind like a heavy stone dropped into water from a great height. "What murder?"

The man raised his eyebrows in evident surprise. "I am so sorry, miss. I assumed because of the photos ... yes, very sad. A man was shot, just there." He pointed to the south end of the alley. "About a dozen feet from the end of the street."

"When?" Lily demanded.

A small cloud of disapproval altered the man's expression. No doubt he found her urgency unbecoming. "Many months ago, now. In the winter. It was not a good thing to have happened on our street. And so close to hospital. I must go now." He turned away and walked back to his booth.

Lily stood rooted to the spot for a moment, her mind racing. She knew exactly when the murder had occurred. She knew it in her bones. She would bet her duplex on Birch Avenue that the date was December 12th.

Twenty minutes later, Lily popped her head around the partition of Ben Kelter's computer cubicle in the office complex of the *Toronto Press*. The ride to Front Street had left her hair spiky and her cheeks flushed, perhaps not the most promising way to approach an ex-lover.

"Hi, Ben. Got time for an old buddy?"

"Lily! You're a vision." Ben rose to give her a peck on the cheek and then held her at arm's-length. "A bit of a damp vision. What brings you back to these old digs?"

Lily had rehearsed in her mind exactly how she would approach Ben. She would be cool and casual, maybe invite him to lunch and then, ever so smoothly, introduce the murder and delicately pick his brain. All of her strategy flew out the window when she saw his unruly mop of salt and pepper curls, the half-glasses he wore perched on his nose, the rumpled jeans. He was huggable. His smile went all the way to his hazel eyes.

"Oh, Ben. You haven't changed a bit. I need your help."

"You okay?"

"Yes, I'm fine. Can you come for a walk with me?"

"You mean right now?"

Lily nodded and tugged on his arm. Ben laughed, hit a few keys on his computer, and swung his wrinkled sports jacket over his shoulder.

"As impulsive as ever, I see. Okay, let's go. I'm all yours. You haven't decided to accept my proposal after all this time, have you?"

"No — but I'm not sure I should have let you slip away."

"Truer words, Lily m'dear."

The two walked along Front Street, passing up the ubiquitous

Starbucks for a booth in an old diner with sticky plastic tablecloths and dusty fake flowers in recycled vinegar bottles.

"Nothing but the best for old friends," Ben joked. But Lily thought the place was perfect, deserted even at lunch time, either because of the heat or the *bas cuisine*. They talked about old times until the waitress brought their orders. Ben took a few bites of a limp cheese sandwich, and then pushed his plate to the side.

"You're on, Lily. What's up?"

"Ben, you have the best memory of anyone I've met, and I know you'll be totally discreet."

"Cut to the chase, girl."

"I need you to tell me everything you know about a shooting behind Mount Sinai sometime in December. December 12, to be precise."

"What, you don't read newspapers anymore? I wrote up that story."

"I knew you would have. But I was in Calgary last December. I promise to do my own follow-up research, but I need you to fill in the details that I won't find in print. Will you, Ben, please?"

"I'll give you what I've got, but there isn't much about the actual murder. The police haven't closed the case. The body was found at about six o'clock Sunday morning by an orderly leaving the hospital. The man had been shot in the head, one bullet. They figure he'd been dead about seven hours. Died instantly."

Lily ran her hands through her hair as if she could physically remove the pictures of Amanda flashing through her mind. *Is this how she got away? She couldn't have done it. She couldn't. She wouldn't have told me anything if she had done it.*

"That's it?"

"Well, like I said, there wasn't much about the actual murder. No witnesses, no leads. But the victim had an infamous past. His name was Roger Mahoney and he'd served two years in prison for sexual assault. He was out on parole. Are you sure you want to hear this, Lily? You don't look so hot."

"Sorry, Ben. Go on."

"It's the earlier story that I remembered when I saw Mahoney's name. His case caused quite a furor at the time. It was just after you left the paper. He allegedly raped and brutalized three women, but two of their testimonies were suppressed on some legal technicality.

Mahoney was a real-estate agent, very good-looking before he went to prison. He knew these women, and date rape is always touch and go with juries. The women went to his house willingly and then he assaulted them, repeatedly. The assaults lasted several hours, Lily. It was ugly stuff. But, with only one woman to testify, there were no multiple charges. No one in court could talk about Mahoney as a serial rapist. Even the cops were pissed off. They knew how dangerous he was. When he turned up in that alley with a bullet through his forehead, I can't say they were grieving."

"But he was sentenced to only two years?"

"Yeah, well, he probably wouldn't even have gotten that if it hadn't been for the woman who testified. I'll never forget her."

"What are you saying, Ben? Did you know her?"

"No. But I sat in that courtroom for three days looking at her. She was so — I don't know — dignified, I guess, and compelling. Her eyes were huge and dark and she looked right through you, unflinching, at that terrible hurt she'd suffered."

"Who was she? What happened to her after the trial?"

"Her name was Jeanine Forrest. She was an American student doing medical research at Mount Sinai. For a year or so after the trial, she volunteered to speak to women's groups and counsellors about the trauma of sexual assault and the legal process. I went a couple of times, and she was amazing. Unbroken, if you know what I mean. She talked a lot about the people who gave her strength — her brother, her parents. She grew up near Niagara Falls and she talked about her childhood memories, how calling them back could create a healing space. She felt that talking about what had happened to her, and trying to help others break their silence, was a way of humanizing the inhumane. Eventually, she left the country to study again at the Sorbonne in Paris. Her mother was French, I think."

Lily sat quietly, thinking.

"She worked at Mount Sinai?"

"Yeah. But the police remembered that, too, and checked it out. She really was in France. She lives there now."

"And the other two women?"

"I can't help you there. Their identities were kept confidential. Jeanine knew who they were, though. She spent a lot of time with them, even took them to meet her family. If the cops checked out

Jeanine, I'm sure they checked them out, too."

"What about Mahoney's time in prison? Any problems there?"

"Apparently not. Model inmate — blah, blah, blah — you know, all the stuff about having paid his debt to society. He was released about six weeks before his death. There was a blow-up with his former employer when the agency wouldn't give him his job back, but nothing serious. He still had money, and his house. He hadn't suffered much. He was apparently drifting, spending his time pretending to look for work, when he was killed."

"So, good riddance to Roger Mahoney, is that it?"

"Pretty much. Though the cops were puzzled by one detail."

Lily raised her eyebrows.

"The way he was shot," Ben replied. "One bullet through the forehead. Almost as if it were a professional hit."

Lily walked Ben back to the office, grateful that he was asking her no questions. She gave him a hug and began to unlock her bike.

"Thanks, Ben. You know I can't tell you anything yet. It's just a hunch, but I won't leave you out if it leads anywhere."

"No problem. Hey, Lily, does this mean you're thinking about writing again?"

He waited what seemed a long time for an answer, watching while she fiddled unnecessarily with her bike.

Finally, she looked at him and shrugged. "Maybe. I can't say yet."

"It wasn't your fault, you know. That model who died."

"Yeah. Well."

Ben sighed. It was still too soon to push. "Okay. Look, I did an interview with Jeanine about her work with women's groups. I'll fax it to you, if you like. Same number?"

"Yes. Are you sure you remember it?"

"Ah, Lily. How you wound me."

"You mean you haven't proposed to anyone else yet?"

"Not yet, but I'm working on it."

Lily laughed, promised to keep in touch, and headed for home. She needed to talk to Amanda as soon as possible.

If anything, the day had become even more humid, the sun scorching. Exhaust fumes from the downtown Toronto traffic lay smoke-thick in the air. Lily was drenched by the time she dashed through her front door and found Amanda's number. She dialled, her hands trembling, not certain of what she would say.

The phone rang once, twice ... four times.

"Hi. You've reached Amanda Martin's answering service. At the tone — "

Damn.

Lily hung up and raced upstairs to her office. In her files, she found the number of Amanda's modelling agency, and dialed again.

"Good afternoon. Model Fashion. May I help you?"

"Hi, this is Lily Ross. I've just finished a layout with Amanda Martin, and I'm wondering how I might reach her. Is she on an assignment? There's no answer on her home phone."

The receptionist hesitated.

"I'm sorry, Ms. Ross. We don't normally give out that information. I could take a message."

"Well, my problem is that I did some extra shots with Amanda for her portfolio. I promised them for this morning, but ran into some technical difficulties in my darkroom. I'd really like to get them to her today, though. She's a friend."

Silence on the other end. Lily crossed her fingers.

"Okay, Ms. Ross. If she gave you her home number, I guess I could look up her schedule for you. Can you just confirm that by repeating Ms. Martin's number?"

Lily recited the number. She waited what seemed an endless minute.

"This is odd."

"What's wrong?" Lily asked.

"Oh, nothing's wrong. But Ms. Martin left this morning for a long-term assignment in Mexico City. Her regular appointments have been re-booked with another of our models."

"But — but I'm sure she wanted these pictures. She would have told me if she was planning on leaving the country. Is there anyone else I could talk with who might know how I can reach her?"

"Well, I could put you through to her booking agent, Ms. Ellis."

"Please."

More waiting.

"Dianne Ellis speaking."

Lily repeated the gist of her fabricated story.

"So you see," she ended, "I spent all of Saturday and most of Saturday night with Amanda, and she didn't say a word about

Mexico. It's not like Amanda to have me waste my time developing these shots."

"Of course not, Ms. Ross. But Amanda didn't know about the assignment until late last night. She was probably so excited, the photographs slipped her mind. And she didn't have much time to pack and make arrangements. She was booked on the first flight to Mexico City this morning. It's quite a coup for her. The client requested her specifically."

"I see. Do you know where I might reach her?"

"No, I'm sorry. She'll be staying at a private villa, but I'm sure she'll contact you herself. You are, as you said, a friend."

"Y-yes. Just in case, do you know how long she'll be away?"

"Oh, several weeks I would think. It's a great opportunity for her."

Lily extricated herself from the conversation as soon as she could, and exhaled slowly.

A sudden trip to Mexico? How convenient. She didn't think Amanda would be calling her anytime soon.

In the meantime, she had research to do.

Monday, July 12, New York State

Marie stood in her kitchen with a large chopping knife. Methodically, she began dicing celery, radishes, and just the tiniest bit of shallot for potato salad. She made it the way her mother had over forty years ago in Provence when all her summers were drenched in golden light and you could taste the sun in the juice of a fresh tomato. She always used a homemade basil dressing, never store-bought mayonnaise.

Heading outside to her herb garden she paused to admire the river. It was ever-changing, deceptive, beautiful, carving a wide path between wooded cliffs and parklands, a liquid border between Canada and the U.S. Here, the currents were strong, but safe enough for anyone who knew the water. Just twenty miles or so downstream, the friendly Niagara would roar, churn, and plunge into the awesome fury of the Falls. Marie often imagined what the earliest explorers must have felt in their fragile canoes, and wondered whether the quickening speed of the currents and the rushing thunder warned them soon enough to jump for their lives.

Marie crushed the leaves of basil between her fingers and drank in the spicy fragrance, the smell of France, the smell of her youth. The twinge of arthritis in her fingers reminded her of how long ago all that had been, those heady times when she'd run off to waitress in the cafés of Aix-en-Provence and fallen in love with Jack Forrest. She was sixty-seven now, Jack seventy-one.

Marie glanced at her watch. Four o'clock. She looked again at the river, this time with a practical eye. There was still lots of traffic, sailboats bobbing like great white birds, water-skiers, paddlewheel cruise boats with tourists and jazz bands. The busier the better. As long as the river was filled with activity, the illegal crossings were made easier. A single boat among so many would raise no suspicion.

Marie hated the waiting. Jack would be back in an hour or so if all went well, and the runners would be hungry. She went in to finish preparing the salad and set it on the sideboard to rest. Even after all this time living in Little Falls, she still couldn't imagine why Americans ate their potato salad cold. She sliced some pressed chicken and tapped the baguette she had baked fresh that morning. The risks were minimal, she reminded herself, especially if the runners had followed instructions. She cut a wedge of brie, and spooned black olives, glossy with marinade, into a small dish. The police were seldom a bother, though crossing the once-porous border between Canada and the States was trickier now. It was the hunters, the men who sometimes tried to follow or track down the runners, who could be dangerous. The hunters were unpredictable.

Outside, Marie walked to the guest cabin at the edge of her wooded property. She and Jack had started the bed and breakfast about five years ago. It brought in a little extra retirement income, but mostly it was good cover. Folks in Little Falls never noticed strangers coming and going, especially in the summer. Jack had called their business The Lifeboat. Marie thought it a witty name.

She knocked at the cabin door, but there was no answer. Paying guests were usually out at this hour, enjoying the river or the hiking trails. She used her key, turned down the bed, and put out a dish of chocolates. The runners didn't use the guest suite, but everything was ready for them at the main house. They never stayed long.

Just as she was locking the door, she heard Jack's car; it was all she could do not to run to the driveway. She looked over at her husband first and felt weak with relief when he smiled at her.

"Marie, we have company."

She turned to welcome the woman and the child, just emerging from the car. The woman looked wan, with dark circles under her eyes that spoke of fear and sleepless nights. She was pretty — had once been pretty. But the child was beautiful. She had green eyes, a sprinkle of freckles across her nose, and long silky red hair that even in the late afternoon sun shimmered and seemed to flame. *People will remember her*, Marie thought, even as she took the child by the hand and led her guests inside. The little girl smiled up at her.

"I'm Suzy. I'm six and this is my — "

"I know. This is Suzy's mama, right?"

It was an old superstition, but Marie felt more comfortable when she didn't know the names of the runners. She led them inside and fussed around them, filling their plates and chatting. She even coaxed a few smiles from Suzy's mama. Slowly, she began to relax. When Suzy began to yawn, Marie took her guests up to their room. She hugged the little girl and took her mother by the hand.

"Come down for coffee when the little one's asleep. Good night, *cherie*."

Marie hurried back to Jack, who was washing dishes in the kitchen. She stood behind him, circling him in her arms, and laying the side of her face against his back.

"So, everything is okay? No hunters?"

Jack turned to his wife. "No, no hunters. But there was a small hitch."

"What happened?"

"They got to the gallery ahead of schedule. This woman is really scared, Marie. She drove too fast. She felt conspicuous sitting in the car, so she took her little girl inside."

Marie's arms dropped to her side.

"Jack, you didn't — "

"I had to. I found the rental car in the parking lot just as we'd planned, but it was empty. Anything might have happened to them. I had to go inside to check if they were there."

Marie went to the cupboard and took down a bottle of red wine and two glasses. The plan had worked a dozen times before. Drive to the parking lot of the Albright-Knox Art Gallery. Identify the rental car by its licence number. The runners would be in it. Give the signal. Greet each other like old friends, take a quick stroll down by the lake, pile into Jack's car and drive off. People outside were visitors. They came and went and wouldn't be around to answer questions if a hunter came asking. But inside the gallery was a different matter. People worked there, bored people who were sick of seeing the same paintings day after day and who watched the tourists instead.

"So why didn't she drive around for awhile, or go for a walk or do anything but go inside the gallery? How could she be so stupid?"

"I'm — I'm so sorry."

Marie and Jack turned toward the young woman standing in the doorway of the kitchen. She looked stricken. She began to cry, her body slumped against the door frame. Jack rushed to her side and led her to a kitchen chair.

"Marie, pour some of that wine."

Marie's hands trembled. She felt ashamed. How could she forget, even in the midst of her concern for Jack, the panic, the terrible vulnerability and confusion of being a runner, of trying to save the life of your child?

Marie took both of the woman's hands in her own and placed them around the wineglass.

"Drink, now. I'm a nervous old woman. Jack'll have a plan."

Silently, the two women sipped their wine and listened to Jack.

"Look, I don't think there's much danger. We were only together in the gallery for a minute or so. We could've just been admiring the same artist for a brief moment, and we didn't leave at the same time. But we can take a simple precaution with the crossing and separate you and Suzy."

"Tell me," the young woman lifted her chin. "I don't want to put you in danger. I won't make any more mistakes."

Early the next morning, while mist still hovered over the Niagara River, Jack and the young woman went down to the dock and climbed into the Forrest motorboat. They carried fishing gear, and the woman wore hiking boots and carried a small backpack.

Jack was a regular among those who lived along the riverside. Everyone knew he went fishing at dawn two or three times a week during the summer, though he never caught a thing. Jack, though, didn't care about the catch. He only wanted to establish the pattern.

Anyone up so early who heard his boat or saw his silhouette through the thin river fog would take for granted his familiar presence. In routine, in comfortable repetition, there was security.

The river was narrow along this stretch, less than a half mile between the American and Canadian sides. In some places the high banks were sheer and sandy; in others they sloped more gently to the water's edge and were thick with wild shrubs and chokecherry bushes. Now and again, a patrol boat made a perfunctory run down the river.

Jack cut the speed of the motor, dropped his fishing line, and trawled slowly, angling ever closer to the overgrown riverbanks that lined the parkways along the Canadian shore. The morning was warm and still. The mist would burn off quickly as the sun grew stronger.

"Climb straight up the bank when I drop you," Jack whispered. "Watch out for any early joggers or cyclists. Cross the parkway at the top of the bank and wait at the first of the picnic tables. My son, Marc, will collect you. He'll ask you if you've been to the Albright-Knox Gallery."

The woman nodded silently. Then she reached into her shirt pocket and brought out a photograph. She handed it to Jack.

"Here. It's him. Just in case he tries to find me. He ... he's not Suzy's father. You and Marie should know that. You should know what he looks like."

Jack took the photo and studied it carefully. A man in his mid-thirties smiled back. He was fair, with regular, angular features and dark eyes. He was good-looking and seemed tall, even leaning against the black car at the edge of the photo. He was dressed casually, his arms akimbo, his hair parted on the right side and falling slightly across his forehead. The boy — or rather, the man — next door. He could be anyone. Jack shrugged and crumpled the photograph in his fist, tossing it overboard.

The woman's eyes widened in alarm. "Please, Jack. You don't understand. He's obsessed."

Jack nodded. "We'll be careful. Now, get ready."

The soft purr of the motor stopped abruptly. Within a few seconds she felt the boat scrape gently across the rocky bottom of the shore. Grabbing the backpack, she slipped over the side, the cold water slopping over the tops of her boots. It seemed to brace her.

She pushed the boat away, gave Jack a thumbs-up sign, and began to climb.

Marie was waiting again, part of her listening to Suzy's chatter and part of her straining to hear the sound of Jack's boat. The paying guests had had their breakfast already and now Suzy was trailing bite-sized pieces of French toast around a pool of maple syrup. Her bright hair tumbled across her shoulders.

"Tell me again about the hide-and-seek game," the little girl said.

Marie made her voice light and cheerful.

"Your mama has gone to hide with some friends. When Jack comes back, we'll all take a boat ride together and find her. You have to spot her before she spots you to win the game."

Suzy pushed away her plate and put her chin in her hands. She frowned.

"But Mom always finds me first."

"We could surprise her."

"How?"

"We could dress you up, put on a disguise."

Suzy giggled.

"You mean like Halloween?"

"Sure, sort of."

"Okay. I want to be a fairy princess!"

"Well, to win the game you'll have to be inconspicuous. Otherwise your mama will notice you right away."

"What's in — incon ... ?"

"It means you have to blend in, look like all the other children."

"There'll be other kids playing the game?"

"Yes, *cherie*, lots. Maybe we could disguise you as a little boy."

Suzy crinkled her nose.

"I don't like boys."

"You would have liked my little boy. He's all grown up now, but I still have some of his clothes. You want to win the game, don't you?"

"Y-yes."

"Well, c'mon. I'll show you some of Marc's toys I've saved."

A few minutes later, Marie and Suzy were rummaging around in a trunk in Marc's old bedroom. They found battered dump trucks and teddy bears, a pair of jean shorts, a dinosaur T-shirt, and a New

Just MURDER

York Yankees baseball cap. Marie coaxed Suzy to try on the clothes. Suzy looked at herself in the mirror and shook her head.

"I don't look like a boy at all."

"Not yet," agreed Marie. "But I have an idea. Let's hide your hair."

"My hair?"

"But, of course!" Marie clapped her hands. "I'll put it in French braids and then we'll pin them up and hide them under your hat. I used to braid my daughter's hair all the time when she was young so it wouldn't get tangled when she played."

"You have a little girl, too?"

"Yes, *cherie*. But she's a woman now."

"Where is she?"

"She lives in France. My, you ask a lot of questions. Bring that teddy bear along if you like, and we'll get started on your hair."

Just then, Marie heard the boat returning to the dock.

At noon, when traffic on the river was at its peak, Marie, Jack, and a small child holding a scruffy teddy bear and wearing a baseball cap pulled low over her forehead, went for a boat ride. A bit of shiny red hair peeked out the back of the cap, but Marie had done her best to make Suzy more ordinary. They docked the boat at a busy marina on the Canadian side of the river, and wandered into a playground built at the edge of The Riverside Restaurant.

Suzy looked all around. "Is my Mom here?"

"Not yet, *cherie*, but you can play with the other children. Remember your name is Sam. And don't lose your hat."

Marie winked, and Suzy winked back.

An hour later, Jack came to fetch her from the swings. They bought hot dogs and ice cream, and joined Marie at one of the picnic tables. Suzy kept an eye out for her mother, but couldn't see her anywhere. Just as she was thinking how hot she felt with the cap on, a tall, dark man joined them.

"Hey, Sam," he said. "I'd know that T-shirt anywhere. I'm Marc and I know where your Mom is. Let's go into that little gift shop over there and we'll buy her a present. Then we'll sneak up on her and you'll win the game."

Suzy looked at Marie and Jack and they both smiled their reassurance. She gave them a little wave and took Marc's outstretched hand.

The man and the child strolled along the path and disappeared into the interior of the large, crowded tourist shop, while Jack and Marie ambled arm-in-arm back to the dock. They were a respectable elderly couple, out for a leisurely stroll along the river.

Tuesday, July 13, New York

When the call came in, Paul Abbott took it on his private line.

"Mr. Abbott? We've found the car. It's ... "

"Not over the phone. Meet me in twenty minutes, same place."

"It's gonna take me at least an hour, maybe more."

"An hour. No more, unless you're prepared to have my time deducted from your fee."

Abbott slammed down the receiver. *Damn Sloane.* The man was incompetent. Kathleen had been gone now for almost three and a half days. Anything could happen in that time. She could be anywhere. Sloane had better have a bloody good explanation.

Still fuming, Abbott left his penthouse on Madison Avenue and walked the few blocks to Central Park. Everything he saw reminded him of Kathleen, feeding his rage. How dare she try to leave him now. Nobody left Paul Abbott, not once he'd chosen her, taught her how to dress, how to behave. He had to find her and bring her back. Knock some sense into her for good. Her and that child.

Abbott couldn't bear Suzy, much less her banal name. He'd tried to charm her with the usual gifts, but she remained silent and aloof, clinging to her mother. Every time he saw her, Abbott felt a stab of pain and resentment. She was a permanent reminder of Kathleen's life before him.

Central Park was glorious in the sun. Having suffered the brunt of terrorism, Manhattan seemed determined to re-embrace its green heart, reclaiming the park's open, free space as a symbol of its defiance. Nannies strolled along the pathways with their clamouring charges. A group of young men played impromptu soccer on one of the grassy fields. Two lovers sought privacy and each other under the shade of a chestnut tree.

Abbott scarcely saw them. He moved as if he were in a desert, a sere, heartless landscape without the succour of Kathleen. Her clean fragrance, the roseate curve of her lips, the luxurious abandon of her nakedness — these memories tormented Abbott, hovering like cruel mirages on some invisible horizon. The children, laughing in their games, were surely mocking him. As he approached two teenage girls, one swung her head around to watch him pass. It took all of Abbott's self-control not to smash his fist into her pouty lips. How dare they taunt him.

He'd given Kathleen too much freedom, that's all. She was confused by her past, by the strain of having to deal with an unruly child. Once he found her, proving his devotion to her, she would be grateful. He would have to punish her for her disobedience, of course, but after she had been cleansed, they would make love and she would learn what a perfect life he could give her. *Damn it, where was Sloane?*

From the roof garden of the Metropolitan Museum, Sloane placidly watched Abbott stride along the pathway and sit on one of the park benches just at the edge of the Met's back lawn. He knew he could have made the rendezvous in twenty minutes. Hell, he could have made it in ten, but since Abbott was such an arrogant son-of-a-bitch, he figured it wouldn't hurt to make him cool his heels. The guy must have looked at his Rolex at least three times in the last minute.

Sloane took another drag on his cigarette. *May as well finish it,* he thought, *Abbott will be all worked up anyway.*

He took out his photo of Kathleen and pondered her face again. The last time he'd seen her, just before she'd given him the slip, she hadn't looked like this: open and trusting, with a smile that could light up a room. In fact, Sloane conceded, she hadn't looked like this for about six months, not since the court order against Abbott to stay away from her and the kid.

Not for the first time, Sloane wondered why Abbott was trailing her. At first, he'd persuaded himself that it was a lover's spat, but it had gone on too long for that. Abbott had paid a small fortune for surveillance, including having her phones tapped. If you were rich, Sloane figured, you could make an ass of yourself on a pretty grand scale. Still, if his Ruby had moved apartments, changed her job, and unlisted her phone, he was pretty sure even a schmuck like him would get the message, and Abbott was anything but stupid. Sloane butted out his cigarette. He was glad she had gotten away. He hoped she was blackmailing Abbott. All he knew for sure was that Abbott was steaming mad.

As he made his way to the park bench, Sloane was pretty sure that this would be his last payoff. Abbott was getting a little too spooky for him anyway, expecting him to come like a trained dog. As soon as he could see Abbott, he picked up his pace, huffing and puffing as he sat down.

"Whew. Got here as soon as I could. Lovely day, isn't it?"

"Cut the chatter, Sloane. What have you got?"

Sloane looked up abruptly, tempted to tell Abbott to go fuck himself, but he changed his mind when he saw his eyes. They seemed almost opaque, he thought, like a shark's eyes.

"I found the rental car. She dumped it in the parking lot of the Albright-Knox Gallery in Buffalo."

"And?"

"And, nothing. No one saw her there. All the hotels in the area were a negative. I went up there personally and even talked to some of the border guards at the Queen Elizabeth Bridge, but no one remembers her or the kid. It's like she disappeared."

Abbott said nothing. His face was expressionless, but Sloane could see white on the knuckles of his left hand as it lay across the back of the bench.

"The thing is," he blundered on, "I've checked the apartment — bribed a security guard who has access to the keys — and there's no overt sign of her leaving. Suitcases are still there and her passport, too. There's even stuff in the fridge and her clothes look undisturbed. That receptionist at the architect firm says she's on vacation. So, maybe just spur of the moment like, she decided to go off. She might be back in a couple of days."

"Are you really that thick, Sloane?"

"Well, no. But I don't think you're gonna like the alternative."

"Which is?"

"That if she's decided to vanish, she had to have had help this time. Look, she has no documents with her except a driver's licence. If she's lucky, their birth certificates might be enough to get them into Canada. But she's left her passport behind. So my bet is that she's still in the States or she was smuggled across the border, likely someplace up river. She hasn't used her charge cards or withdrawn money from her bank account or even used an ATM machine. So somebody is feeding her cash, maybe even hiding her."

"And you have no idea who that is, do you Sloane, even after watching her for all this time?"

"Beats me. The tapes are clean. Not a word to anyone on the home or office phones. Mind you, she could have talked to someone face-to-face, but I don't know who. She doesn't go out. Doesn't seem to have friends. Ever since that first move — ridiculously easy to trace — she's been living like a nun. I could ask around."

"No, Sloane, that won't be necessary. You're fired."

"Yeah, well, I sort of figured we'd come to the end of the trail, so to speak. What's she got on you, anyway?"

"Got on me?" Abbott regarded Sloane with contempt. "Oh, please. She's simply a friend I'm trying to protect from herself."

Liar.

"Right. So, before I go there's the little matter of my recent expenses."

"Certainly, Sloane." Abbott drew out a thick plain envelope and handed it over without a quibble.

Relieved to be so easily quit of his disagreeable client, the detective rose to leave, but couldn't resist one final barb.

"Well, you've got to hand it to her, Mr. Abbott. She sure is a sly one, giving us the slip like that."

He winked and turned to walk away. The vicious kick in the small of his back sent him sprawling onto his hands and knees, his chin smashing down on the asphalt walkway. Pain flashed along his spine. He opened his mouth to protest and watched a thin stream of blood drip onto the envelope of money still clutched in one hand.

In an instant, Abbott was at his side. He hauled him to his feet and handed him a handkerchief. "Really, Sloane. That was quite a tumble you took. You must be more careful."

Numb with shock, Sloane looked up at Abbott. His eyes were a dead matte black, seeming to reflect no light.

Jan Rehner

His nights were increasingly disturbed by snatches of nightmares, flashes of glowering faces and wavering forms that evaporated almost as soon as he opened his eyes. Awake, he could push the shapes away as easily as cobwebs, but the lack of sleep threatened to drain him of resolve. Not knowing where Kathleen was gave him physical pain, a constant knot in his chest. It blighted everything. But what was finally unendurable, what fuelled his anger and stiffened his will, was not her desertion, but her calculated deceit.

He had been a fool to trust Sloane. He was a good enough track dog, good enough for spying and prying, but he hadn't the finesse for a woman like Kathleen. Even Abbott hadn't expected her capable of guile. No wonder she had outwitted Sloane. Now she had earned herself a more worthy adversary. Now she was a matter for his own personal attention.

Once he had made the decision to take direct action, he felt a burst of confidence. He could see now that this is what he should have done from the very beginning. Incompetence sickened him. He had no patience for the time wasted by disorderly thinking and polite fumbling. If she had gone to the Albright-Knox Gallery, then someone had surely seen her. Abbott would not be turned away without finding that information.

Sloane had sworn he'd talked to the guards, but who would tell anything about a lovely young woman to a bald guy in a wrinkled suit? Abbott looked just right: clean cut, expensively dressed in casual clothes, just a touch of strain around the contour of the lips. He'd shown around the picture of Kathleen with a small catch in his voice. More importantly, he'd shown the photo of Suzy. There was something visceral about a missing child: people try harder to remember. Abbott had looked disconsolate. "It's been five days," he worried aloud. "There's a reward." Money. It always worked.

And so the story stumbled out. One guard remembered that another guard had called in sick on the day in question, and that guard remembered that his place was filled by a casual worker. Wallets were opened and records were opened. Della Jordan. Four twenty-two Cherry Street, about fifteen minutes away.

Abbott sat in his car, gazing stonily at the neighbourhood and a lifestyle that was totally alien to him. The two-bedroom, post-war brick boxes with meager front stoops lined both sides of a treeless, cherryless street. Many of the cropped patches of grass were littered with lawn ornaments — bizarre cartoon animals with legs that spun like pinwheels in the wind. Neat strips of flower beds were bordered with miniature plastic American flags. Paint peeled and roof shingles curled. Abbott felt repulsed.

He could not imagine Kathleen here in this ordinary, common place. He needed to get out of his Jaguar, incongruous in Cherry Street, and walk up the front steps and knock on the door of Della Jordan's house. But his knees felt locked and, suddenly, looking at this tedious place, he understood how deep Kathleen's betrayal was. He would have given her everything, every luxury, every grace of living, and she had scorned him, traded down for Cherry Street. He had never felt so humiliated. And he understood in that moment that it was too much to forgive. Kathleen had become unworthy, polluted. She must be punished.

Lost in the maze of his own thoughts, Abbott did not see the woman approach him. She rapped on the car window and he looked up, startled. She was a large Black woman, with greying frizzled hair and a moon face, smooth and unwrinkled. Her mouth began moving and Abbott stabbed the button to lower the window.

"Are you the young man looking for his wife? Gus called. Told me you were draggin' around like you had the whole world piled on your shoulders. I'm Della."

Abbott got out of the car and extended a hand. "I hope you can help, ma'am, I'm at my wit's end." He held out the picture of Kathleen with a wistful sigh.

He watched impatiently while the woman scrutinized the photo, first from a distance of about two feet and then several inches from her own face.

"You know, she does look kinda familiar. Mind you, her hair wasn't like this and she wasn't wearing any of that makeup, either."

"You saw her!"

"Well, now, keep your shirt on. I think I saw her. I was in that room with the painting of that skinny gal with the long neck."

"The Modigliani?"

"Yeah, whatever. She's so skinny I get hungry just looking at that painting, but I remember thinking she had red hair, too. Just like the little girl."

"Suzy!" Abbott exclaimed, digging out her picture.

"Yes, sir. That's her all right. Pretty little thing, isn't she?"

"How were they? Did they seem okay? I've been worried sick."

"So you say, mister. But your wife seemed a little jumpy to me. How do I know she wants to be found?"

"It's nothing like that," Abbott protested. "I would never hurt her. It's a misunderstanding, that's all. I must find her."

"Well, now, you can't blame me for asking."

"No, of course not. It's just that I feel so lost without her. You know her car was found in the gallery parking lot. Anything might have happened."

"Might have, but didn't. I can set your mind to rest on that score. As far as I could tell, she and the little one went off with Jack."

"Jack?"

"Jack Forrest. He and his wife run a country B & B in Little Falls, not too far from here. Me and my hubby stayed there for a weekend a few years back, and that's probably where your wife and little girl are staying right now. Jack's a real nice man. He took my William fishing with him in those little streams up in the escarpment, and then his wife cooked up the catch for us. Best fish I ever tasted. I would have said hello, 'cept he was in and out of the gallery in a flash."

Abbott felt exultant. "Della, thank you. You don't know how much you've done."

"Well, that's okay. Me and my hubby had some rough patches, too, but it all worked out in the end. Hope you find them, a nice-looking man like you."

Oh, I will, thought Abbott, *I will.*

Marie Forrest settled down in her favourite easy chair with a brandy and a gardening book. She stretched her limbs contentedly, and listened to the chirping of crickets in the shadows of the fading light.

It was a tranquil night, her time alone all the more delicious for being stolen. She and Jack always closed The Lifeboat for a few days after a runner had come through, just to be on the safe side. Jack had tried to pack her off to visit Marc, but she had insisted on staying home to nurse her herbs and flower beds. Even now, the heady scent of climbing roses wafted through the open window. She closed her eyes, her grey head resting on the back of the chair, drinking in the perfumed air.

Much as she loved Jack and Marc, she relished her solitude. They fussed too much. And here she was, an old woman — *cantankerous*, Jack would say, just needing breathing time to herself. When friends had asked Jack to guide them on an overnight hiking trip, she'd practically pushed him out the door. In the meantime, Marc would call several times, on some pretense or another, to make sure she was all right.

Whenever she thought of her son, Marie thrilled with pride. He was a fine young actor, versatile and inventive. She never tired of watching him become different people under the floodlights — a gentleman suitor, a Cockney con-artist, a smooth-tongued politician. He'd played with repertory companies all over the States, but had settled down in Niagara-on-the-Lake with the Shaw Festival when she and Jack had started The Lifeboat. He'd wanted to help. He'd been so supportive of Jeanine. Her ordeal had changed them all, Marc most of all. He'd become more solicitous of family, less casual in his relationships with women.

The faint tapping on the screen door roused Marie from her thoughts. She entered the kitchen and turned on the porch light. She hadn't heard the approach of a car on the gravel lane. In the halo of light, she saw a fair-haired man with dark eyes. He had a somewhat boyish face despite the strong physique and he was wearing a black T-shirt, khaki shorts, and hiking boots. He flashed her a tentative smile.

"Mrs. Forrest? I was wondering if Jack was at home."

Marie spoke to him through the screen, not unlatching the door. "You know Jack?"

"I'm hoping to, ma'am. Della Jordan used to work for me, and she and her husband, William, visited here a few years ago. They told me no one could fish like Jack Forrest. I'm a novice myself, looking for an experienced guide. My gear's in the car. Della and William said to say hello, by the way."

"Thank you, that's very kind of them. But, I'm sorry, Jack's not here. He won't be back until tomorrow sometime."

"Oh, I see." The man looked down for a moment, disappointed, then raised his eyes. "I wonder, in that case, if I might book into the guest cabin tonight and wait for him?"

"I'm sorry. We're closed until tomorrow. I hope you haven't driven a long way."

"All the way from New York, ma'am." He smiled, and shrugged one shoulder. "What's another day? I'm sorry to have disturbed you. Do you happen to know of another place in the area where I could spend the night?"

Marie hesitated. She remembered Della and William. They were kind-hearted people.

"Well, it is late and you've come a long way. I guess I can let you have the suite tonight. Hang on a moment and I'll just get the keys."

Marie vanished from the doorway while Abbott leaned confidently against the frame and waited. He felt smug. His plan was working flawlessly. He'd been surreptitiously watching the house for several hours and knew perfectly well that Jack Forrest wasn't home.

In a few minutes, Marie returned and Abbott's polite mask was firmly in place. She led him to the guest suite, built over a cedar-shingled garage about a hundred yards from the main house. He feigned interest while she told him about its amenities, but his attention was riveted on the cabin's situation. It was set well back from the country road, at the edge of a small pine woods. The second-storey windows faced toward the river and gave a wide vantage over the back of the property and the house. Perfect. He would see Jack coming long before Jack saw him. He opened a window and leaned out, smelling the fresh river breezes and the spicy pines. A phone rang in the distance.

"Oh, that will be my son, Marc. I'd better answer. Breakfast at eight-thirty. Is that okay?"

"Please don't trouble yourself, Mrs. Forrest. I'll go hiking at sunrise. I've food in my pack and I can make coffee here. Thank you for your hospitality, though. Good night."

"Good night, Mr. — "

"My name's John. John Abbott Jones." He took her hand. It was dry and warm, light as a leaf. Abbott felt he could crush the bones. She hurried away to the insistent phone and he listened at the window until the ringing stopped. Later tonight he would have to do something about the phone lines.

Marie swept back her hair into a tidy bun and smoothed down the skirt of her summer shift. She was still slim, even after many years of her own fine cooking. Her arthritis wasn't too bad today. She flexed her fingers, thinking she might whip up an herb soufflé for Jack's lunch, one of his favourite dishes. There'd be enough for their guest to join them, if he was back from his morning hike. The gesture would make up for not giving him breakfast.

Marie glanced at her watch — 10:30. She wondered why Marc hadn't called as he usually did for their morning chat, but she mustn't wait any longer. She decided to slip up to the suite and change the linens while John was still out. It was quite a long hike, she thought, if he'd really left at sunrise. She thought it odd, too, that his car was gone from the drive. Usually hikers just struck off on their own, but if he didn't know the area, perhaps he'd felt more secure driving to the State Park and following the marked trails.

She climbed the stairs up to the suite and checked the bathroom first. The shower had been used, and a few towels were rumpled on the floor. Humming to herself, she began to clean, polishing the marble tub and sink.

When she was finished in the bathroom, she surveyed the bedroom. It was a pleasant space, she thought, with the sun streaming through the windows. Funny that John had closed them during such a warm night. The three casement windows opened like shutters. Marie unfastened the latches, letting fresh air into the room. She turned back to the burnished mahogany bed and began stripping the sheets. She was just tugging at the corner of a fitted sheet when she glanced up at the dresser.

My God. It can't be.

Slowly, her heart pounding, Marie dropped the sheet and walked to the dresser, reaching for the framed photograph. She held it in trembling hands.

Suzy. Suzy.

Marie felt cold. The low voice, when she heard it, was so close she screamed, the frame slipping from her fingers, the glass shattering.

"So you do know her, don't you?" Abbott whispered.

Marie gaped at him. He was standing so close she couldn't turn around. She stared at him in the dresser mirror. His face was so pleasant, but the raspy whisper cut through her consciousness like a blade. The contrast was horrible. She couldn't move. She couldn't stop staring at him.

He grabbed her around the throat, propelling her backward into an armchair at the side of the dresser. He hovered over her.

"Where is she?" he shouted.

Marie flinched as if he had struck her.

"I — I don't know."

Abbott smiled. He walked methodically to the door, picked up his backpack and removed the gun. Sitting on the bed across from her he aimed the pistol at her forehead.

"Where is she, Mrs. Forrest?"

Marie was transfixed by the gun. It was blunt-nosed and ugly, like some small lethal animal.

"I don't know. I don't know what you mean."

In one fluid motion, Abbott leapt toward her, hitting the side of her head hard with the gun barrel.

"Stop lying to me. You know where she is. You helped her, didn't you, you and Jack? He picked her up at the gallery and brought her here. Jack's hiding her."

"No — no. She's just a little girl." Marie could feel blood from her ear trickling down her cheek. Her head throbbed.

"Oh, I don't care if the little girl stays lost, Mrs. Forrest. I want the mother."

The mask slipped. For an instant, Marie saw the contortion, the glaze of obsessive hatred in his eyes. It braced her.

"She isn't here any longer. She stayed for a few hours and she left with the child."

"I don't believe you."

"She isn't here."

Abbott rose from the bed and turned his back on her. Then he swung around, the full weight of his body behind the punch to her stomach. Marie lost consciousness.

When she roused herself, she had no idea how much time had passed. She felt nauseous, and began to gag. She tried to move her hands to her stomach, but they were tied. She leaned forward. Her feet were also bound. The voice came to her from across the room. He was standing by the door, watching her.

"Feeling a little better, Mrs. Forrest? Would you like a glass of water, Mrs. Forrest?"

Marie nodded. Abbott disappeared into the bathroom and carried the glass toward her, bringing the water to her lips. She drank thirstily, but some of the water trickled over her chin and onto her dress.

She felt a surge of anger. She thought of Jeanine, her brave Jeanine. She'd ached with compassion when her daughter had been attacked, but never knew until now the depth of the agony, the spiralling panic.

Where was Jack? She must save Jack.

"What are you going to do with me?" she asked.

"Well, that's up to Jack, isn't it? I'm willing to make a trade. You for Kathleen. We'll just have to wait and see."

Marie slumped forward in the chair, gritting her teeth against a spasm of pain. She knew there would be no trade. She could identify the hunter. He would not let her live. She struggled not to pass out again, willing herself to stay alert. She had to find a way to warn Jack.

Thursday, July 15, New York State

Ben's article on Jeanine Forrest had deeply moved Lily. He had managed to convey through his lean prose something of Jeanine's courage and dignity. Since their lunch together, Lily had slogged through the newspaper accounts of the attack, taking in the sordid details with growing horror. She wished she could find Amanda. Jeanine's words would have comforted her.

She began to understand why the police would not care much about finding Roger Mahoney's body, alone on a deserted street on a cold December night. Perhaps it was Nemesis. But somehow, Lily thought, Jeanine would care. Not for the sake of revenge, but for the peace of knowing the ending of the story, knowing how the threads of lives were gathered up and woven together. After months of silence, months of being afraid to write anything, Lily wanted to write that ending, to find out how Mahoney had come to die with a bullet in his brain. If she couldn't get to Amanda, she would follow the next best lead.

Lily crossed the border at the Peace Bridge about noon. She'd found the name of Jeanine's parents and her hometown in Ben's notes. Skirting the edge of the American side of Niagara Falls in her old blue Toyota, she'd driven along highway lined with evergreens, poplars and clumps of birch, broken only by the occasional expanse of farmland. Soon little towns began, stringing themselves along the edge of the Niagara River.

When Lily reached Little Falls, she pulled into a gas station and asked directions to The Lifeboat. Thirsty, she bought a Coke and drank it while chatting with the attendant, a young high school student proud of his local knowledge of the area. It was a pretty town, and she took the time to take a few shots of the narrow main street with its nineteenth-century facade and old-fashioned lampposts. There was a dusty-looking general store, a bait and tackle shop, an ice-cream parlour with a few children scattered around its takeout window and, at the far end of the street, a cosy looking pub covered in vines.

A few minutes later, Lily pulled into the driveway of The Lifeboat, her tires crunching the gravel. She got out and looked around. The place looked deserted, but a door at the side of what must be the guest cabin was ajar. Lily began to walk toward it.

Upstairs, Abbott strained to hear every sound. The old woman's head was leaning back on the chair, sagging to one side. Her body was limp. He positioned himself beside her, the gun to her head. *Welcome home, Jack.* He heard the car door open and shut. He listened to the footsteps on the gravel, coming closer. There it was. The first tentative step on the stairs.

Marie suddenly lunged forward, with a fierce, warning cry.

"Run, Jack! Run!"

The gun jumped in Abbott's hand as he gawked at her, the explosion deafening him.

Lily whirled and raced for the car. The keys were in the ignition. She hit the gas and the car shot forward, swerving on the gravel. She slammed it into reverse, her eyes trained on the gaping doorway. At the end of the drive, she saw the man emerge from the cabin about twenty-five yards away. His eyes widened when he saw her. He raised the gun. Lily straightened the car and shot away on the road back into town. She didn't think, her mind as blank as a ruined negative. She flung herself out of the car and raced into the pub. Every face turned toward her.

"Please help," she gasped. "Something terrible's happened. I saw a man with a gun. I heard a shot. At the Forrest place."

A tall elderly man stood up, knocking over his chair behind him as he lunged for the door.

A friend rushed after him, trying to restrain him. "Jack, don't be stupid. Wait for the state troopers. They'll soon be on the way."

Jack pulled free and drove off. When he reached home, there was no one in sight. He climbed the stairs to the guest suite. Gently, he touched Marie's face. Hands shaking, he untied the ropes holding her upright in the chair and eased her to the floor. There was nothing more he could do for her. The bullet had struck her in the chest. Kneeling beside her, he gathered her into his arms. He rocked her like a child and wept.

Monday, July 19, New York State

Lily stood slightly apart from the circle of mourners around Marie Forrest's graveside. An old cemetery, its headstones dated back more than a century, was set off from the sloping lawns by a low cedar hedge. Towering evergreens and chestnuts threw tall shadows across the coffin on its little platform and the gaping hole beside it. Lily looked away, tears blurring her vision.

She had stayed in Little Falls for the funeral and to answer what questions she could from the state police. She'd described again and again what she had seen and heard. And at night, when sleep finally came, her mind replayed the scene in slow motion over and over: Marie's cry, the man emerging from the cabin, raising the gun toward her. In her nightmares, Marie began to call her name, not Jack's. *Run, Lily, run!* Sometimes she didn't cry out at all and Lily would climb further and further up the stairs, swinging open the door at the top, stumbling across the threshold into the grasping arms of her own death. Awake again, she would taste the salt water in her stomach from swallowing her tears, and think again of the woman she had never known who had saved her life.

The priest sprinkled holy water on the coffin. Slowly it was lowered into the grave. Lily watched Jack. He raised his head, scanned the tight grouping of family and friends, and caught her gaze as she stood alone at the edge of the circle. He nodded, almost imperceptibly. A thin strand of his white hair lifted in the breeze. His face was weathered, tanned by years of sun and the outdoors. But his eyes were sunken, and despite his erect posture, he looked frail.

The young man beside him took his arm and together they stepped forward to say their final goodbyes. A rain of flowers drifted across the casket. The mourners began to shift position, breaking the circle and pacing soberly toward their cars.

Lily lingered in the cemetery until only Jack and the young man remained. She had dreaded this moment. She couldn't help but feel that her unannounced arrival at The Lifeboat had somehow precipitated the tragedy, that her blundering had been the catalyst of a shattering violence. She approached them tentatively.

"Mr. Forrest?" she said, touching his arm. "I'm Lily Ross. I'm — I'm so very sorry."

The face that turned toward her was filled with a kindness she didn't expect.

"Of course. I know you've tried to help the police. This is my son, Marc."

Lily reached forward to shake his hand. She had known this must be the Forrest son. He looked enough like the pictures of Jeanine she'd seen to be her twin. His black hair was slightly wavy, slightly too long, combed straight back from his forehead. He had the same high cheekbones and Gallic features as Jeanine, the same straight nose and faintly olive skin. But where his sister's dark eyes emphasized her classic features, his were more like Jack's. Light hazel, and oddly incongruous, given the dark complexion.

"Hello, Ms. Ross. It was kind of you to stay on for the funeral." His words were merely polite, but spoken with a gentleness that disarmed her.

"I — yes — well, I'm so sorry."

Lily turned away. She had expected anger, questions, dismay, anything but warmth. She blushed and felt the sting of tears. She knew in an instant that she had come here for her own comfort as much as for theirs.

"It's just that I feel so responsible," she blurted out. "If only I hadn't come perhaps she'd still — "

Jack shushed her.

"You mustn't think that, Lily. You couldn't have stopped him. I couldn't have stopped him. Marie saved both of us. Let that be a part of her legacy."

Lily didn't think she could stand such forgiveness. She didn't deserve it. This family had already suffered too much. In trying to bring them news of an old story, she had brought them only more suffering, and worse. She wanted only to get away from them now and pretend she'd never come. She mustered a smile, said goodbye, and forced herself to walk rather than run back to her car.

She had almost reached it when Marc Forrest caught up with her.

"Ms. Ross — Lily — wait. Why did you come to Little Falls?"

Ah, this was more like it. Now the questions would begin. Perhaps the Forrests were not all-forgiving, after all. Lily looked up at Marc and squared her shoulders.

"I came to tell your parents something that I thought Jeanine should know, that's all."

"You know Jeanine?"

"No, not exactly. I mean I feel I know her but we've never met. It's just that — well — I — " Suddenly she felt she couldn't speak Roger Mahoney's name in this sacred place, not in the shadow of Marie's grave. "It doesn't really matter, now. I'm sorry. I shouldn't have come."

Marc regarded her silently for a moment, seeming to make up his mind.

"Look, the police have told us you live in Toronto. Are you going back there now?"

Lily nodded.

"Well, I'm driving my father to the Toronto airport tomorrow. He's going to France to be with Jeanine. Will you have dinner with me tomorrow night? Dad and I both feel we owe you an explanation."

"*You* owe *me*?"

"Believe me, it's a long story. Can we meet somewhere quiet? I'll be in Toronto in any case."

Lily rummaged around in her shoulder purse until she found one of her business cards and wrote her address on the back.

"I can't cook," she said. "But I'll feed you something, and I can guarantee quiet. I don't think I'm up to a restaurant."

Marc was still staring at the card she'd handed him.

"You're a journalist?"

"A photographer, mostly. I do — I did — a little freelance writing. Is there something wrong? You look surprised."

"Oh, no. Not at all. I'll see you at seven, if that's okay, Lily Ross."

"That's okay."

She watched him striding across the grass in his dark suit until he reached his father, putting his arm around him. She granted them their privacy and drove away.

When her car had disappeared, Marc handed her card to his father. "She's a photographer, and a writer of sorts. Do you still think we should trust her?"

Jack stared at the grave. "I don't know, son. It's up to you now."

Tuesday, July 20, Toronto

Home had never seemed such a haven. Lily had almost kissed the hardwood floors when she'd finally closed her front door behind her. Her living space had looked so normal — a slanting pile of unopened mail that had been dropped through the slot, the red light blinking on her answering machine, the sun streaming through the French windows that opened onto the back garden. She'd spent the next day banishing memories in the sanity of routine, returning her calls, scheduling some photo shoots — a Toronto travel brochure, a wedding in August. She decided not to return Ben's call, not yet.

Methodically, she began sorting through her mail, the wastepaper basket slowly filling with advertising flyers. Near the bottom of the pile, she found one surprise. A postcard from Mexico City, a picture of a mural painted by Diego Rivera on the front. She flipped it over:

> *Dear Lily —*
> *Great news. I've been offered a terrific assignment here and will be away for two or three weeks. The weather is almost as hot as the food. There are several other models with the group, and two excellent photographers, but I miss you behind the lens. There's promise of more work, maybe in Spain, when we wind up here. Wish me luck, and thanks for listening.*
> *Love, Amanda*

There was no return address.

Lily stuck the postcard up on her crowded bulletin board and contemplated it, her chin resting on her hands. She was pleased that

Just MURDER

Amanda sounded so happy, but her brief allusion to confidences shared — *thanks for listening* — meant that she hadn't entirely forgotten what had passed between them.

Lily sighed. She wished she could forget it. She was still convinced that Amanda had seen or heard something that could lead to the killer, but perhaps it was better for everyone if Roger Mahoney remained buried. She was beginning to feel that every life he'd touched was poisoned. And every story she wanted to write was cursed. She'd tell Marc what she had wanted to tell the Forrests and then she would just move on. She had no choice anyway. Amanda had been whisked away. Lily laughed aloud at herself. Did she really think a simple modelling job was part of some sinister conspiracy? No, it was too ridiculous.

She wandered around her study, tidying up all the papers she'd been reading about Jeanine Forrest: the articles Ben had written with such compassion, newspaper clippings on Mahoney's trial and, later, a terse paragraph on his murder, her own notes attached with a clip to a photo of Amanda. She knew she should throw them away. She even wanted to throw them away before they brought more misery. But ... didn't she owe it to herself to see the story through? She wished she had a modicum of Jeanine's courage. She reached for a file folder, stuffed the papers inside, and slipped them into a desk drawer.

By ten to seven, Lily's bravado had begun to wane. She wished she hadn't asked Marc to her house, after all. The shadows she had been trying to push into corners all day would loom like ghosts the moment he walked through the door.

She checked the table and the food for the sixth time in the past hour. The neighbourhood restaurant at the end of the street had rescued her again, sending over cold poached salmon in a tangy orange sauce, a beet and endive salad, an assortment of rolls. At first, Lily had thought the choice was perfect; now she thought the food was too fancy or too planned. She should have just torn open a bag of potato chips and slapped down some dip.

She went into the kitchen and opened a bottle of Bordeaux. *At least something's breathing*, she thought. *Get a grip, Lily. You owe him this.*

The doorbell rang as if on cue.

She ran her fingers through her hair, and opened the door.

Marc looked at Lily's wide-eyed expression and knew instantly that she was as nervous as he was. Her eyes were a disturbing colour of grey flecked with green. Her dark lashes and eyebrows didn't quite match the sun-streaked light brown hair. One unruly curl stuck out above her ear.

"Hi, Lily. Thanks for letting me come." He didn't move, or offer his hand.

"I don't mind telling you I'm not sure *why* you've come."

"Me neither."

"Oh God. How rude of me. Come in."

Marc smiled and crossed the threshold as if he were stepping onto a stage. He had the same butterflies, but this time he had no script. How much should he tell her? How much should he trust her?

The room he entered was long and narrow, open from the front of the house all the way to the back windows, still streaming light from the late sun across the polished wood floor. Colourful rugs were scattered here and there, and the walls were filled with framed posters and photographs. He stopped in front of a travel poster, a row of narrow Venetian facades mirrored in the surface of a canal, their pastels dissolving into abstract swirls in the gently lapping water.

"This is beautiful," he said. "It captures what I always felt in Venice — that I was moving through a hallucinatory city. Have you been there?"

"Oh yes, I know what you mean. I took this shot."

Marc surveyed the room more closely.

"Is this all your work?"

"Only a few shots are mine. I collect from friends, mostly." Lily offered Marc a glass of wine. "Are you hungry?"

Marc hesitated. He had to do something to help him make up his mind. He needed to try to read her character.

"Lily, would you mind if we went for a walk first? I need to get to know you a little before I tell my story and I'm as nervous as a cat."

Lily took back his wineglass.

"Thank goodness," she grinned. "I thought it was only me."

Several hours later, Marc polished off the last bite of salmon and leaned back in his chair.

"Delicious ... I thought we'd never eat. I was starving."

Lily laughed and went to fix coffee. She felt easier now in his company. The walk had cured their awkwardness, helped them to set aside for a moment the mutual explanations both were dreading. Marc had asked about the house and Lily had talked about her own mother, the courage she had shown in the last months of her illness, the happier days they had shared when it had been just the two of them on their own. She'd skipped over the early days of scrimping and saving, the shabby apartments and second-hand clothes, emphasizing instead the way her mother had rebuilt her life. Like a magician pulling happiness from thin air, she had transformed the potentially lonely days of an only, fatherless child into a treasury of memories. Long walks in the park, hours spent reading aloud to each other, winter afternoons watching old movies in revue theatres, eating smuggled-in popcorn from home because they couldn't afford the refreshment counter. To this day, Lily stashed treats in her purse whenever she went to a film.

Her musings allowed Marc to open up a little about Marie. He and Jeanine had always called her Maman, in the French manner, and she would scold him in rapid French whenever he was naughty. He admitted he was fluent in French swear words, but he shied away from more intimate memories.

"How's your father doing, Marc? I should have asked earlier."

She carried the tray to the living room and the two settled themselves into facing armchairs.

"He's okay. Dad has a lot of strength. And seeing Jeanine will make all the difference. She's having a baby, you know. That's why she didn't come to the funeral. There'll be a memorial service over there, for old friends. And then Dad will stay on for the birth. There'll be a new life to celebrate."

"What about you? Could you not get away from the theatre to join them?"

"Oh, I'll take some time off, maybe join them later. There are some — some loose ends."

Lily nodded. She assumed he was talking about the dreary task of wills and probates, settling the unfinished affairs of a life snatched away too soon for those left behind. She'd done the same for her own mother, the odd letter arriving months after her death, sending her into a fresh spasm of grief.

"I know this sounds trite, Marc, but if there's anything I can do to help. I still feel so terrible, responsible somehow. I keep thinking about what your father said to me at the cemetery — that saving my life is part of your mother's legacy. I hope I can earn that, somehow."

Marc was silent for a moment. "Lily, what did you want to tell my parents?"

"I — I met a model on an assignment. Her name's Amanda. She told me that she had been sexually assaulted, and I'm certain it was Roger Mahoney."

"Mahoney?" Marc was alert, his jaw line tight.

"The fact is that Mahoney was out on parole. He'd been drifting around the city, supposedly looking for work. The same night he attacked Amanda, he was killed. Shot."

"But how? Did this girl shoot him?"

"Oh, no. I don't think so. But I do think she knows more about what happened than she told me. Anyway, when I searched around trying to find out more about Mahoney I read about the old case and, well, about Jeanine and all she'd tried to do to help other women. I thought she would want to know that he was dead, that he couldn't hurt anyone else again. To close the chapter, so to speak."

"Is that all? Is that the only reason you came?"

Lily glanced up, surprised to find Marc studying her. Had he detected the subtext beneath her carefully rehearsed words?

"I know it doesn't seem like much. But I wanted to do something for Amanda. I wanted to write a story that might help someone rather than ... Look, it doesn't seem to matter now. Instead of help-ing, I triggered an even worse act of random violence. If only I'd honked the car horn or called out, your mother would have known I wasn't Jack. She wouldn't have tried to warn him. And perhaps — perhaps she'd still be alive."

"Is that what you think?"

Lily nodded, avoiding eye contact.

"Well, you couldn't be more wrong. I'm glad I've come now, Lily. First of all, I'd be willing to bet my own life that Maman would still have shouted a warning, even if she knew it wasn't my father on those stairs. More to the point, it wasn't a random act of violence."

"What do you mean? Are you saying that she knew her killer?"

"Not exactly. But she knew what he was after. She'd found the photograph."

"Marc, you're talking in code. I don't understand. What are you saying?"

He looked away from her for a moment and Lily could see he was struggling with the decision of what and how much to tell her. When his eyes met hers, she had the oddest feeling she had passed some sort of test.

"In a way, it is the end of a chapter, or at least a story come full circle," he began. "When Jeanine was attacked, tortured really, by that animal Mahoney, my parents were devastated. They thought their love could protect us from anything, especially from cruelty. It's not that they were naive — far from it. Maman grew up in occupied France during the war. She was only eight when her father was killed by the Germans in reprisal for resistance activity in their village. After that, her mother became part of the Comet line, one of the most successful of the resistance networks, with contacts all over the south of France. She carried messages, scrounged for food and clothing for downed airmen. Several times, Maman's home was used as a safe house where airmen and Jews were hidden before Comet could move them down the line and across the Pyrenees.

"It was a terrifying time for Maman. Klaus Barbi was stationed in Lyon then and many people disappeared in the prisons of the Gestapo after 'The Butcher' interrogated them. She missed her father; she knew her mother lived in constant danger. She would fall asleep at nights listening to the urgent whispers of adults, waiting for the thumping of German boots on the stairs. So when she left her childhood behind, met and married my father, it's hardly surprising that she wanted to give her own children a feeling of safety, above all."

Marc paused in his story, as if in its telling he had discovered anew the poignant futility of Marie's search for security. Lily abandoned the coffee, pouring brandy instead. For awhile, the two sat in silence, swirling the liquid in their glasses, as if in its amber depths they could fathom either the past or the future or the precise moment when safety nets stretched carefully over the gaping abyss would be torn away. Lily had no idea what Marie's childhood had to do with her death, but she felt Marie's son had a right to tell his story in his own way. His voice, when it reached her again, seemed to come from far away.

"The assault on Jeanine touched all of us in different ways. I'm three years older than her, but she had always been more serious, more focused. I was the rebel, the carefree spirit seeking the spotlight, the performer. I guess you could say that I grew up during that terrible time. I began to realize there was more to life than self-indulgence. My parents, too, felt they had made an error in judgement. They came to believe that by shunning the possibility of violence entering their lives, they had done nothing meaningful to stop it. Strangely enough, it was Jeanine who was the strongest. She had been tested. She had endured the terror and she rose above it, reaching out to help others. So when my parents got the call, they answered it."

"The call?"

"A woman came to see them. Much like yourself, she had read about Jeanine. My parents had never seen her before and they never saw her again after that day. She told them about an underground network of sorts, one that helped women and sometimes their children escape from men from whom they were in danger. The women were never criminals or kidnappers, but they were helpless before the laws which failed to protect them. Often they were the victims of stalkers and abusers, harassed beyond endurance. The network gave them new lives and, when it was necessary, new identities. The woman asked my parents to help. They agreed."

"But what did helping mean?"

"You've seen where my parents live. Helping meant meeting the runners — the women who were fleeing for their lives or, at the very least, their sanity — and smuggling them across the border into Canada. I presume the network also smuggled Canadians into the United States, but my parents were never asked to do that. Despite stringent security, it's much easier to get people *out* of the States than in. My parents simply avoided the official border altogether. There's miles of unguarded river between the two countries."

"Still, it's a terrible risk."

"Not so terrible. The two countries have a long history of illegal crossings — Loyalists fled here during the American Revolution, slaves sought freedom on the Underground Railroad, and draft dodgers had an escape network during the Vietnam War. It didn't seem so fantastic when the woman explained it this way, especially after what had happened to Jeanine, especially to Maman, whose own mother was part of the Resistance. The women hadn't broken any laws; they weren't fugitives or criminals. They posed no threats, and were only fleeing for their own protection. No, the only real danger was from the hunters — the men who were so obsessed that they couldn't give up — who would try to track down their victims."

"And this man, the one who shot Marie, he is a hunter?"

"Almost certainly. When my father found Maman, before the state police arrived, he also found a photograph of a little girl named Suzy. We helped her and her mother cross only days before. He must have brought the photograph with him, perhaps to test Maman. We also know he cut the phone lines. I tried to call Maman that morning, but couldn't get through. So you see, Lily, you are blameless. It was my father and I who underestimated the danger. We left her alone. We failed her."

Lily could think of nothing to say. Outside, the garden was dark and quiet. She had not turned on any lights yet, and her living room was deep in shadow.

"Why did you come here?" she whispered.

"At first, we — Dad and I — thought you might have been sent by the network to warn us, just as that first woman came from nowhere to ask my parents to help. Then, later — "

"Later you thought I might know this hunter, might even be helping him."

"No. We just weren't sure how much we could trust you. How much we should tell you about the network."

"Why? Surely you've told the police."

"We can't do that, Lily. If I tell this story, I will put the network, and perhaps many lives, in jeopardy. These women and children are hiding under new identities for a reason. I can't expose them. Maman died to protect them. Besides, I can't even reach the network. I don't know how. They communicated with my parents by mail, just a postcard with a date and time whenever they were to collect a runner. The cards were usually mailed from Toronto; that's all I have. I doubt the network even knows about Maman's death. If it is headquartered in Toronto, none of the papers here would have covered a murder in Little Falls."

"But that man's still out there. He's still looking for that mother and child."

"Oh, I think it's much worse than that, Lily. That's why I've come. He's seen your face. I think he's looking for you."

Saturday, July 17, Boston

Eva Renault sat in a corner booth near the ladies' room at the end of the bar. The jazz club was beginning to fill up with well-to-do thirty-something customers. Some of the men smiled at her and Eva smiled back, but not invitingly. She glanced at her watch frequently to give the impression she was waiting for a date. She didn't want company.

Her view across the room to the diagonal corner was frequently obscured by customers coming to the bar to order drinks, but she could still see him. He was of medium height, slightly built, with a high forehead made higher by a receding hair line. He wore round, wire-rimmed glasses, a navy blazer and tan dockers. He looked inconspicuous and innocuous. Periodically, he studied his watch, but he didn't fool Eva. They were playing the same game. Whichever young woman he was observing didn't matter. Eva would make her move soon. His table was near the entrance and the pay phone. She could take advantage of that.

She signalled a waiter and ordered another drink, a long cool gin and tonic in a tall thin glass. It would be better if her glass were full. She swung her long red hair with its corkscrew curls over her shoulder and tapped the edge of the glass with her nails.

Dr. Butler, Bruce Butler, was a psychiatrist. He liked redheads. He'd started practising in Texas, then moved to Florida, then California, and now here he was in Boston, starting over again with a new state medical board. As usual, none of the complaints against him had been upheld. Patients were easily discredited, rebuked more often than validated, regarded with pity for having sexual fantasies about their therapist. But the pattern was there, if any ethics board had tried hard enough to find it.

And the abuse was escalating. The young woman in California had committed suicide. The good doctor had only narrowly escaped charges.

Eva looked across the room again. He had taken out a book and was pretending to read. She picked up her glass and purse and negotiated a path to the pay phone. She put the requisite change in the slot and dialed a twenty-four hour weather station. She didn't want the change coming back, jangling noisily down the return slot. She had a lively conversation with the recording on the other end of the line. Anyone bored enough to eavesdrop would assume she was calling her recalcitrant date. She hung up the receiver.

Just as she was passing the man's table, Eva tripped. The gin and tonic splashed across the shoulder of the pristine navy blazer. The man leaped to his feet while Eva grabbed a table napkin and began sopping up the spilled drink.

"Oh my goodness! Oh, I'm so sorry. Here, let me help you."

The man pushed her hands away.

"It's all right. Don't bother." He removed his jacket. "I'll just sponge it off in the men's room. If you'll excuse me ... "

Eva was standing squarely in his path. She moved to the side to let him pass.

"Oh, but you must let me pay for the cleaning. I'm so clumsy. I really am sorry."

She fumbled in her purse, its contents suddenly spilling to the floor in a clattering shower of loose coins, pens, keys, lipstick and mascara tubes. Several people looked around at the disturbance.

"Damn!" Eva knelt quickly to the floor and began scrabbling for any rolling objects, the straight skirt of her pale green dress riding up well above her knees.

Butler knelt down to help her.

Eva smiled at him appealingly. "You must think I'm hopeless, dangerous even."

"Not at all," he replied gallantly. He extended his arm and the two rose together.

"I'd still like to pay to have your jacket cleaned."

"No, really, it's not a problem. But I would like to get to the men's room."

"Of course."

Eva watched him disappear and then entered the adjacent ladies' room. She would have to work quickly. She locked herself in one of the cubicles and began taking impressions of his keys. It had been simple to slip them out of his jacket pocket when he was gathering up the contents of her purse. When she was finished, she carefully wiped the keys and re-entered the bar. He was already back at his table, scanning the area under his chair.

Eva approached him from behind: "I believe you must be looking for these." She dangled his keys from her fingertips. "They must have gotten mixed up with mine."

For a moment, Butler's eyes narrowed. But then he took the keys with good grace, thanking her.

"Well, I'll be off then. Enjoy the music. Good night."

Butler nodded. He was already scanning the room for another woman.

Two hours later, Eva paid the taxi driver who had taken her to Carlisle. It was an expensive trip from Boston to the small village community almost an hour away and, no doubt, the driver would be able to describe her long red hair and green dress perfectly. There was only one motel in the village, but it was dark by now and no one saw her enter her room at the end of the wing to the right of the reception entrance.

Eva changed. She was herself again, the cornsilk hair tied in a ponytail, a dark sweatshirt and bicycle shorts, sports gloves and sneakers. She slipped outside and walked to the edge of the woods skirting the back of the motel. In a few moments, she found the bike she had hidden there two days previously, and stashed her gear in the carrier. She was about four miles from Butler's house. She pedaled hard, praying that the jazz band back in the club was as good as its billing.

Butler's keys were on a leather thong tied around her neck, cool against her skin. The person who helped her cut them wouldn't talk, probably wouldn't even care about why she wanted them. She'd told the tale of the ex-wife without access to the matrimonial home, complete with tears and appropriate outrage.

When she turned into Butler's lane, she dismounted, hiding the bike in a tangle of bushes, and approaching the house on foot. Like most in the area, it was cedar shingled, set well back from the road in a wooded lot. There were no lights on. She checked the garage first, but it was vacant. Then she walked a full circle around the house, slowly. It was large, but oddly shaped, its classic lines spoiled from the back by an upper extension supported by pillars that jutted out over part of the pool area. From ground level, Eva couldn't see whether the extension had windows. Perhaps it was a screened upper deck with shutters that could be removed.

Eva took the thong from around her neck and crept up to the front door. The first key she tried slipped into the lock as smoothly as a knife through butter. She opened the door. The blinking alarm was to the right of the entrance hallway. She had approximately one minute. She held her breath and pushed seven, three, sixty-five. The blinking stopped. She waited, but there were no sirens, only the rhythmic bass chorus of frogs from the marshy pools and bogs of the woods. She breathed a sigh of relief. People too frequently picked numbers they wouldn't forget themselves and she'd re-searched Butler's birthdate.

She took out her flashlight and surveyed the first floor of the house. The decor was neutral and masculine, with tan leather furniture and oatmeal rugs. The stone fireplace took up most of the end wall, and the other walls were empty, giving the impression of a cool, even chilly, space. She would find nothing here.

She skipped the kitchen and began climbing up the wooden spiral staircase. She would have a better chance of finding evidence against Butler upstairs, perhaps in an office or a bedroom.

The first room to her left was a combination guest and storage room. It looked habitable if anyone should come to visit, but hasti-ly put together. Cardboard boxes were lined up against one wall. Eva checked them. They were all empty. Butler hadn't tossed them out yet, even though he'd bought the house five months ago. She moved on.

His bedroom was as sterile as the rest of the house. Eva wouldn't have believed that any personality could be so blank. No pictures. Nothing out of place. The furniture was expensive, but bland. The king-size bed was neatly made, the dark-brown velvet drapes closed.

She found the office next. Here, at least, was evidence of activity. She emptied several boxes of computer disks into the bag she'd brought with her. They could be checked later just in case he'd put anything on electronic files. She hit the button on his answering machine. There were a few messages from his service about re-scheduled appointments, and then a woman's voice, pleading. "Please leave me alone, Butler. If I see you following me again, believe me, I'll go to the authorities." Eva punched the rewind button, and listened to the message again. It surprised her. Usually Butler's victims came to him willingly, eager for his help until it was too late. The message suggested a shift in his pattern, a warning that his aggression was escalating, that he was losing control. She hesitated, but then removed the tape, tossing it into the bag along with the disks.

She moved to the floor-to-ceiling shelves and began rifling through the books. She was hoping to find letters, mementos, perhaps even a diary or journal. Nothing. There were no drawers or filing cabinets. She would have to try to get access to his Boston office somehow, but that would be risky once he realized someone had infiltrated his house.

She was halfway down the stairs when she remembered the extension. Where was the door to the upper deck? Surely she couldn't have missed it. She retraced her steps. There was no doorway from the hall. She closed her eyes, remembering the layout of the house from outside, and then re-entered Butler's bedroom. The entrance to the extension had to come from in here. She walked to the north end of the room, to the closet door. It was a spacious closet, but not large enough, she thought, to explain what she'd seen. She pushed aside a row of tailored suits hanging along the back wall like disembodied soldiers standing guard, and found the door. It was locked, and she fumbled with the keys until she found the right fit.

Darkness shrouded the interior and the air was still and fetid. The beam from Eva's flashlight swung in a smooth arc around the room, then jumped and stuttered as her hands began to shake. She swallowed bile, biting down sharply on her lower lip. The cramped room, roughly ten feet by seven feet, was a torture chamber. There were no windows, only a narrow band of glass bricks positioned about a foot below the ceiling. There was a Spartan toilet and sink, and a bizarre-looking bathtub, fully padded in some kind of cushioned, obscenely pink material. Breathing rapidly now, Eva forced herself to steady the light on the mock bed. She had seen others like it many times before, but never in this context. Here, the black padded examination table, complete with stirrups, and fitted with restraining straps, was repulsive. Nestled at its head was a small, ruffled, heart-shaped pillow. Eva moved closer to it, a wave of nausea pushing up from her stomach. Pinned to the centre of the pillow was the head-and-shoulders photo of a young woman, the sharp tack driven through one open eye. Like a mutilated butterfly, Eva thought, its moment of beauty arrested.

She flicked off the flashlight and stood trembling in the darkness. She breathed deeply, slowly, fending off the shards of her own cruel memories, fighting for calm. The very walls of the room seemed to contract. The floor began to tilt. She had to get out.

And then she heard him, pounding up the stairs.

Instinctively, she darted to the wall beside the door and flattened herself against it, her muscles tensed. Blindly, she ran the palm of her hand up and down and in small circles across the wall's surface, searching frantically for a light switch. She couldn't remember any light fixtures in the room, but there had to be light. If he got to the switch first, the glare would momentarily blind her. If she found it first, she might be able to startle him.

She heard the scrape of a suit hanger, just outside the open door. Where was the light switch?

Tentatively, she moved her hand, and in that instant, touched his. He gasped.

Eva aimed her sideways kick at the sound, her eyes squeezed shut against the explosion of light. Her foot caught his throat, propelling him backward into the closet. She heard him grunt as he hit the floor, but she knew he wasn't unconscious. She dove for her bag and swung around to face him.

Butler fired his own gun blindly. Too late, he saw her silhouetted in the door frame, her pale hair gleaming in the light. It was the last thing he saw before the bullet from her 9mm pistol entered his brain.

Eva cycled back slowly to the motel, careful to leave the country road whenever she heard a car approach. It was after midnight.

Methodically, as if watching from a distance the movements of another woman entirely, she had done what needed to be done. She had dragged Butler's body into the hideous room, locking the door and rearranging the closet behind her. She had placed her gun beside him, returning the computer disks to where she had found them. She'd kept the tape, though, and the photograph, to protect the owner of the pleading voice on the answering machine. She'd reset the alarm and locked the house, using the keys one last time to put Butler's car in the garage. The keys would be easy to lose, and her gun couldn't be traced.

Back at the motel, she ditched the bike in the woods, and then took a steaming shower, scrubbing at her skin as if to scrub away her revulsion. She was weary and angry. She was beginning to make mistakes. She tried to tell herself it was only the horror of the room that had paralyzed her judgement, but she knew it was more than that.

She had been too quick to kill.

She was beginning to frighten herself.

The next morning, still feeling drained, she took a taxi to the airport. She was dressed casually in black jeans and a white shirt, her hair hanging loose on her shoulders, swept back from her forehead by a single black barrette. She lost the red wig and the green dress in the washroom and then picked up her ticket from the SwissAir counter.

Despite her fatigue, her senses were fully alert, assessing the tone of every voice and the scrutiny of every airport official. She yearned to board the flight, to be far away from and far above the dead body she had hidden in an evil room. It would not be long now. She would be able to sleep on the flight. Hours and hours of obliterating sleep.

Her body jerked to attention. Straining, she picked out the garbled syllables of her name over the public broadcast system.

"Would Miss Renault, Miss Eva Renault, please pick up the nearest courtesy phone? Miss Eva Renault to the courtesy phone, please."

Her heart skipped a beat. Something was wrong.

But she had been Eva Renault for a long time now. Her documents had been checked many times. She told herself that she had no reason to panic.

Coolly, she approached the counter and turned over her passport. The official glanced at it briefly, then smiled and nodded toward the white phone a few feet away. She picked it up, her palms slick with sweat.

"Yes, this is Eva Renault."

"Hello, Eva. Are you all right?"

She recognized the voice instantly.

"Yes."

"We need you to come home. There's a ticket waiting for you at the Air Canada counter. Cancel the flight to Switzerland first. Amanda will not be able to meet you at the airport. She's gone to Mexico. But we'll send a car."

Eva hung up and walked away. She was going home. She was, temporarily, safe.

Friday, July 23, New York

Paul Abbott had had a hellish week. He hadn't meant to kill the old woman, not then. His hand had simply convulsed when she had screamed out. It was an accident. He'd been immobile with shock for just a few seconds before tearing down the stairs after Jack. But instead, another nasty surprise. He didn't know who she was, but she had seen him clearly. She'd seen the gun, too, the compact Colt 45 that had been a present from his grandfather.

Abbott was grateful for the clarity of his mind, the numbing of emotions that had helped him stave off panic. He'd had the fore-sight to hide the Jaguar earlier in the morning and his gear was still packed. No one knew about the car except the old woman and she wouldn't be talking. He'd doubled back through the woods to the State Park and simply driven away, due east. The humming of the Jag's tires as it ate up mile after mile of open highway soothed him. Slowly, the sour taste of his ruined plans abated. He was methodi-cal, disciplined. He would start again, reassessing the shift in cir-cumstances, forging a new plan. The reflection that Kathleen had duped him flicked in and out of his consciousness like the quick tongue of a snake, but he pushed it aside. First things first. He needed patience, money, a plausible cover.

From his grandfather, Abbott had learned to despise any show of weakness. He was a proud, towering figure to the small boy, with his thick grey hair, fierce eyes, and strong profile. Abbott had followed everywhere in his wake, imitating his actions, memorizing his phi-losophy as if it were his catechism. His grandfather had taught him to live by old-fashioned phrases — to brook no fools, give no ground, turn adversity to advantage. He had amassed his fortune during the Depression and had chosen Abbott to be his successor. His son, he said, was a coward, his daughter-in-law, a tramp. But Abbott was chosen.

He had learned to despise his parents, to see them through his grandfather's eyes. When he was very young, his mother would come to kiss him good night, smelling of fresh air and lavender. Later, after his father had abandoned her, driven away by his grandfather's ceaseless ridicule, Abbott would remember only her hot breath against his cheek and the stink of gin. The first time he had recoiled from her embrace, she had slapped him, hard. She never touched him again, but would often gaze at him from across a room, pretending not to notice his stony indifference. His father was invisible — a voice on the phone, a postcard in the mail, a present on his birthday. Never mind, his grandfather had said. He was a weakling. He had lost his chance to be a man. Abbott never knew what had caused the rift between them, but since his father didn't care to defend himself, Abbott had accepted his grandfather's word. After a time, Abbott even forgot to raise the question. It was enough that his father had abdicated his responsibilities. He would take his place, instead.

At first, the lessons were harsh. Abbott had to excel. Be the best swimmer, the best golfer, the head of his class. His grandfather had picked his clothes, his hobbies, his friends. When he failed to meet these expectations, or showed even a spark of resentment, his grandfather would shun him or, worse, ridicule him openly. But when he performed well, his grandfather would reward him. They would sit in his study in leather chairs, and he would tell Abbott about business, about women, about money, unravelling the myriad ways to outwit the faint of heart.

When Abbott was fourteen he finally proved his mettle. It was surprisingly easy, an impulse he acted upon without thinking. His mother had dragged a ladder from the gardener's shed and propped it against a sugar maple to rescue one of her cats. She was always doing embarrassing things like that. *Let the stupid animal starve,* Abbott had thought. But no, she had to make a display of herself.

He had followed her out to the back garden, as much to witness the spectacle as anything else.

"Here, puss. Here, puss," she'd whined. He could hear her plaintive voice even now.

He'd watched her climb, stretching upwards to reach the frightened cat, but he had refused to help her. When she was close, about to gather the cat into her arms, it had raked her cheek with its claws.

Instinctively, she had recoiled. The ladder swayed and swung away from the tree.

"Paul!" she yelled. Just his name, just that single syllable, hanging in the air like her body suspended in space.

For a moment, he had wavered, part of him wanting to rush forward. Instead, he had turned his back, and walked away. He heard her scream and the thud of her body as it hit the ground. He remembered turning on the television inside the house, but he couldn't recall now which program he had watched. When it was over, he had gone outside again to look at her. Her neck was at a peculiar angle. The cat had long since vanished. Could he have reached the ladder in time? Could he have broken her fall?

He had called his grandfather at his office and then the police. He explained what must have happened. The officers had felt sorry for him, but his grandfather had said nothing, just fixing him once with his fierce eyes. They never discussed the incident, but when the funeral was over, his grandfather had clapped him on the shoulder: "I'm proud of you, boy," he'd said. It could have meant anything, that he was proud of him in a general way, or proud of him for not shedding any tears, but Abbott was sure he knew that Abbott had seen everything, and done nothing to save his mother.

Eventually, he had inherited everything: the estate, all the money, the status. And he had learned how to keep it, how to win. He was the embodiment of his grandfather, his legacy. He would turn the unexpected blunder of the old woman's death to his advantage, and he knew how.

Before reaching the city, Abbott pulled off the highway at a rest station and parked his car among dozens of others close to the service complex. The smell of gasoline and hamburger grease sickened him. He would never contemplate eating such disgusting food. He found himself staring at a tired-looking mother leaning against her car, feeding French fries to a cranky child, chewing relentlessly at her own burger. She reminded him of a cow with her vacant eyes and placid, pasty face. Soon she drove away and he dumped the fishing gear in a black barrel trash can. Then, quite deliberately, he reversed the car into the brick corner of the service building, smashing one tail light and tearing a jagged strip of paint from the rear left side. A few people looked around at the sound of the collision, but Abbott ignored them, hitting the accelerator and swinging back onto the highway.

He reached home an hour or so later and told the parking attendant that he'd been in a small accident. The Jag would need fixing, would he please see to it? He could tell the garage that he wouldn't be needing the car for some time. Upstairs in the penthouse, Abbott ran a hot bath and then called his lawyer. Abbott paid him well, and he followed instructions discreetly. Abbott told him he'd inadvertently backed into a parked car during his holiday, Ontario plates, number 238 HZC. Would he please track down the driver? He would like to pay for the damage.

After that, it had simply been a matter of waiting and preparing. The New York papers carried no reports of the unfortunate incident in Little Falls. Why would they? They had their own cesspools of muggings and murders to wade in. He'd had a few bad moments when he'd unpacked, realizing with a chill that he no longer had the framed photograph of Suzy. It must have fallen to the floor when he'd crept up behind the old woman and he hadn't thought of it again. Well, no matter. Only Della Jordan could connect him to both it and the Forrests and he was reasonably certain the police wouldn't look for her. Only Jack and Kathleen would realize its full significance, but, if they wanted him, they would have to come out of hiding. He liked his chances.

It took his lawyer three days to track down the licence plate and the owner's name. Abbott pressed for the address. He wanted to make amends, he said, in person.

During the days, he kept to his routine, checking in with his broker, visiting the museums, working out at the gym. He bought maps and studied them for hours. He felt calm, rooted in a steady resolve. He dropped by his bank and put the gun that had killed the old woman in his safe deposit box, along with a large amount of cash. He didn't suppose he would need either, but planning against any exigency was only logical. It was the kind of orderly thinking his grandfather had ingrained in him, and he found the idea of the secret cache comforting, a testimony to his clear-headedness.

The nights were more difficult, the forced inactivity preying on him. He cleansed the apartment of every vestige of Kathleen. She hadn't been there for months, but he had kept everything waiting for her. Her perfume, her favourite music, a bottle of her favourite wine.

One night he dreamed of his mother, only the familiar scenario melted into a surreal horror: he saw it was him on the ladder, reaching up for Kathleen who was crouched on a tree branch, hissing, her back arched like a wild cat's, spitting at him. When he woke up, disoriented and clammy with sweat, he took out all the clothes he had bought to surprise her, the elegant velvets, the shiny satins, the coloured silks, and shredded them with a sharp knife. They were merely rags now. They meant nothing to him.

Finally the second call from his lawyer came. Abbott contacted the travel agent, arranged for a furnished apartment in Toronto, and packed the maps and the clothing he thought he would need. His entry into Canada would be perfectly legal and there would be nothing in his luggage to raise suspicion. Except for a large amount of cash in his wallet, which customs would be very unlikely to query, he was clean. He could buy whatever else was needed once he had crossed the border. He wouldn't use his cards. Cash was untraceable.

And now the week was over. He smiled. He was dressed in a black jogging suit, sitting in a small park. There were swings and slides painted in bright primary colours in one corner, and a large open space where people let their dogs romp and chase sticks. A row of statuesque maples sheltered it from the street. But best of all, it was not two hundred yards from Lily Ross' front door.

Part Two

THE NETWORK

" ... ninety-eight, ninety-nine, one hundred! Ready or not, you must be caught!"

Kathleen opened her eyes and scanned the bedroom. First, she crept to the closet and flung the door open. Suzy's few clothes hung in a short row, and she bit her lip, trying not to remember all that had been left behind: the party smocks, the hand knit sweaters from her grandmother, the overalls and matching T-shirts. Suzy didn't seem to miss them, but Kathleen ached for the normalcy they once represented, the simple childhood routines of school, birthday parties, piano lessons, and scraped knees.

She turned away and crouched down, peering under the narrow twin bed. Nothing, not even dust. She hadn't been here long enough to worry yet about housecleaning. She sat up and studied the bed itself with its scrunched up pillows and ragged teddy bear, smiling when she saw the tiny pink toes peeking out from beneath a heap of blankets. She pounced and Suzy squealed with laughter.

"Gotcha! I win!"

Suzy wriggled up from beneath the blankets, her cheeks flushed and her green eyes dancing. Her ebullient spirit was contagious and once more Kathleen felt buoyed. She had a new life to begin, and if Suzy could still laugh, so could she.

"Breakfast in five minutes, and then we'll plan our day. What do you say? Oh, and gather up your sheets for the laundry, okay?"

Kathleen gave Suzy a hug and then went to the kitchen to fix cereal with sliced strawberries. The upstairs flat was small but comfortable, one of four in a remodelled, 1940s brick house on Orchardview Boulevard. Kathleen had feared something more sterile, perhaps a barely furnished apartment in a high rise, or even the cramped and anonymous quarters of a halfway house or a hostel. But she would have gone anywhere that was safe.

After Marc Forrest had dropped them at Union Station, Kathleen had located a bank of public phones and dialled a number to await her instructions. She was surprised when the directions given had led her to a quiet, residential street in midtown. The houses were close together, set near the street, with cement steps leading to wooden verandas with low railings. Sloped roofs extended over the verandas, and above the front doors were pointed dormers, each with a casement window. No doubt the houses had all been built by the same contractor, probably in the 1930s Kathleen guessed, but the owners had painted the verandas in a range of colours — blue, green, even purple — to insist upon their individuality. People carried on lives here, she thought, safe, neighbourly lives.

Their duplex was an oddity on the street, larger than the other houses, close to where the road tailed off into the parking lot of the North Toronto Arena. And to Suzy's delight, there was a huge park stretching off to the right, its wide green lawns following the contours of a valley bed. Their refuge had been carefully chosen.

Inside, the network had even tried to make her safe house welcoming, with fresh flowers in her bedroom, well-stocked cupboards and refrigerator, and a small stack of story books and art supplies for Suzy. There were two bedrooms and a bath, a galley kitchen, a bright living room with a bay window, and a tiny balcony overlooking a maze of backyards and gardens. The furniture was a bit scuffed and worn, but everything was clean and fresh. Kathleen couldn't help wondering how many other young women had been hidden here before her, and if each of them had succeeded in rebuilding a life without a past.

The apartment was hers for six months, or until the network was certain that Abbott was making no effort to trail her. Kathleen still felt shame and anger when she thought of him. Shame because she had trusted him, even thought once that she could love him a little. Anger because he had grown obsessive, hounding her, usurping her life. She had taken all the sensible and rational measures — obtaining the restraining order, changing apartments, unlisting her phone — but still he kept coming. The legal documents were scraps of paper in the face of his terrifying insistence. She knew she was being watched. Her privacy was violated. She felt unbearably exposed.

And then the photographs had arrived, slipped under her door in an eight-by-ten manila envelope. They were shots of her, walking across a street, entering her office, sitting in a restaurant with her friends, all taken without her knowledge, with a telescopic lens. And there were shots of Suzy, the last one of Suzy alone, playing in a sandbox, unprotected, so vulnerable.

Kathleen had felt crippled with fear. Every moment that Suzy was out of her sight was agony. Kathleen became a prisoner in her own home, only going out to work or to run necessary errands. Worse, she began to make Suzy a captive, too, forbidding her from playing with friends, smothering her. Her own few friends were worried at first, but eventually stopped calling altogether. Her erratic behaviour must have seemed like pure paranoia to them. Abbott's threats were so subtle, a poisonous mind game of hints and insinuation. There was never anything explicit, never enough to prove the danger she felt. Alone, she couldn't match either his pathology or his bank account. She knew it had to end, somehow.

The network was like an invisible lifeline, thrown to her unexpectedly. Kathleen was not entirely certain how it had found her, but she thought it must have been the librarian. She had started to do research in the law library, looking up case after case of women who had fled with their children from abusive husbands or male guardians. And she had read about stalking laws, or the lack of them. She knew that many women went underground in similar circumstances, but who could she contact, how could she reach the right people?

After several months of sleepless nights, she'd picked up one of the library books she'd checked out, and a handwritten note had fluttered onto her lap: *If you need help, call us. Do not use your own phone.* That, and the number, was all the note had said. Would it have been enough a month earlier, or even a week earlier, for Kathleen to act upon? She couldn't be sure, but she was now. She kept seeing in her mind's eye the kind face of the librarian, with her white hair and thick glasses. They had never spoken for more than a minute, but somehow Kathleen knew she had understood.

The next morning, Kathleen had taken Suzy to school and had asked to use the office telephone. It was the first, tentative step in the journey toward her new identity, her new start.

The network was only a woman's voice to her then, a voice that over the next few weeks, at appointed times over borrowed phones, had told her where to go, what to pack, who to trust. She had believed in that voice because she must. She had followed its instructions to a Barnes & Noble bookstore in Manhattan. She had asked at the counter for a copy of the *Oxford Companion to English*

Literature, on special order, and been handed a package by an anonymous clerk. But when she reached home and opened it, there had been no book. There was money instead, in both American and Canadian funds, just as the voice had promised, and a set of directions: when to go, where to leave the rental car, a description of a man named Jack, and a phone number in Toronto that had led her to Orchardview Boulevard. She was here now. It had all been real.

Suzy bounded into the kitchen, dragging sheets behind her. Her hair was a tangle of red silk which Kathleen managed to gather into a ponytail. Over breakfast, she watched her little girl. She was so good, she never complained. But she must be lonely without her friends, her grandmother, her own familiar places and childhood treasures. The network had advised Kathleen that she could not seek employment until her new identity was fully documented, and Suzy would not be enrolled in school until the fall. Otherwise, their movement was unrestricted. It was Kathleen who had chosen not to venture more than a few blocks from the apartment. Her own wariness had curtailed their freedom. But it was time to re-enter the flow of life. She had a new phone number to call now, if she needed anything. Somewhere, the network was watching.

"So, Suzy, let's have an adventure today."

"Okay, Mom. What?"

"Well, I've been looking at these transit maps and I think I can figure out how to get to the zoo."

Suzy beamed. "Do you think they have 'raffes there?"

"I'm sure they have giraffes. Let's do the laundry first, and then we'll pack a picnic to take with us."

By mid-morning, Kathleen was folding sheets in the basement laundry room and Suzy was colouring on the floor beside her. Suddenly, they heard someone clattering down the stairs. Kathleen's stomach muscles clenched. She had not lost the habits of running, the suspicion that made every encounter with a stranger a potential danger. She held her breath.

An attractive woman in her late twenties loaded down with a heaped laundry basket, entered the room. She was slight, but athletic-looking, with long dark brown hair, brown eyes, and an easy, open smile.

"Oh, hi," she said. "I didn't know anyone was down here. My

name's Teresa Mordelli. I'm in 1A."

She knelt down in front of Suzy and extended a hand.

"And who are you?"

Suzy, tongue-tied, took the hand, but leaned perceptibly in the direction of her mother. The sudden shyness hurt Kathleen even as she recognized its source. Suzy had always been so trusting; now she was learning caution, withdrawal.

With an effort she hoped sounded sincere, Kathleen smiled and offered her own hand.

"Hi. I'm Kathleen and this is my daughter, Suzy. We're in 2B. We haven't met anyone else in the building yet."

"Call me Terri. I'm not surprised you haven't met the other tenants. Just below you, there's a couple of retired academics. They're old-world polite and a bit shy, so you'll rarely see them. Above me lives a dentist. Works all the time, and spends weekends with his girlfriend. What do you do, Kathleen?"

"I'm — I'm a designer. But I'm taking the summer off to be with Suzy. I'll look for something in the fall, I guess."

"Great — I'm a law student. I should be using the summer to prep for the fall term, but I'm not very disciplined. My family has a cottage north of the city, and I'd rather swim than study. Hey, Suzy, do you like to swim?"

Suzy looked up from colouring a purple sky.

"I earned a badge at the pool before we moved. Are there places to swim here?"

"Oh, lots of places. But at my cottage, you can swim in a lake. Would you like that?"

Suzy nodded, and looked up at her mother, her eyes seeking permission.

"Well, maybe someday soon," Kathleen smiled. "We're new to the city, just learning our way around."

"Oh, I can help you, there," Terri offered. "I've lived my whole life here. Toronto's a wonderful place to be in the summer — there's the Royal Ontario Museum, the planetarium, the zoo ... "

"The zoo!" Suzy echoed. "Mom's taking me to the zoo today."

Teresa looked away from Suzy's eager expression toward Kathleen, as if aware for the first time of her edginess.

"Look, I don't mean to be pushy. But you haven't got a car, have you? I mean, I haven't noticed one in your parking space. If you really want to go to the zoo, why don't you let me drive you? We could all go together. It would be good company."

Kathleen hesitated. *Company.* The word felt strange to her ears. Her own loneliness welled up inside her. She hated herself for thinking, if only for an instant, that a threesome would be good cover. Teresa's brown eyes regarded her calmly, steadily.

"Thanks, Terri," she sighed. "We'd love company."

Thursday, July 22, Toronto

Lily was doing her best to keep her balance in a tilted universe. The ground seemed to slope and the sky slid whenever she allowed herself to imagine a lone man roaming the streets, looking for her. His figure emerged from the doorway — the stony face, the eyes dark and startled, the hand with the gun slowly swinging up, taking aim — and burned on her retinas like the afterimage of an explosion.

She attacked her work with an almost frenetic energy, accepting assignments she might otherwise have passed by and using her newspaper contacts to solicit new ones. Whenever she had a lull in her schedule, she filled it with freelance photography, combing the city's markets and ethnic neighbourhoods, finding solace and safety in the streets crowded with shoppers, hawkers, tourists, and buskers. She silently blessed the sheer size of the city, forgiving its traffic snarls, grateful for the noisy vibrancy of its downtown core which seldom emptied, even at night. If she were a target, she would be a moving one, slipping in and out of very public space.

At home, she took whatever reasonable precautions she could, keeping her doors and windows locked. The only space that truly spooked her was her darkroom. Once content to spend hours there watching ghostly images emerge into sharp-edged shapes, Lily suddenly found the confined space claustrophobic and the infrared light eerie. She'd seen too many movies of women absorbed in tasks in rooms without exits, oblivious to shadowy figures creeping up behind them. Her imagination was in overdrive and only her exhaustion ensured that she slept regularly.

After warning her about the gunman, Marc had returned to Niagara-on-the-Lake only long enough to arrange for a leave of absence from the theatre and to help prepare the understudies who would assume his roles. He was determined to stick close to her, he said, to offer what protection he could. But Lily thought there were other motives: a chance to appease his guilt for leaving his mother alone when the hunter came calling, even a chance to pick up the gunman's trail with Lily as the bait. But she kept her suspicions to herself. She didn't relish being alone right now.

In the meantime, they tried to puzzle out a strategy for alerting the network or for finding Kathleen and Suzy, but if Lily could hide in a city of almost three million, so could they. The network had taken good care to protect itself and the women it sheltered — Marc had been given only the bare information he needed to transport Kathleen and Suzy to Toronto. Of the network's inner workings, he knew nothing. They were stumped, shifting around the pieces of a jigsaw with no cover picture to guide them. One of those pieces was the gunman's face and, despite herself, Lily's hand kept straying toward it. They needed help, and tonight they would meet with Ben Kelter to find it.

The bar on King Street was on two levels, buzzing with the after-theatre crowd. Ben was late, as usual, and Lily and Marc settled into a booth on the lower level to wait for him. A middle-aged couple, sitting with friends at a table across the aisle, had recognized Marc and were trying unsuccessfully not to stare at him.

"You're famous," Lily grinned. "If we were in New York, those two would ask for your autograph."

Marc shrugged. "Maybe I just remind them of a relative. It's dangerous to make assumptions. A couple of months ago, an elderly woman approached me at the theatre after a performance. I signed her playbill with a flourish, and she looked at me like I was crazy and told me she was just looking for directions to the ladies' room. You can't be too careful."

"No, I suppose not." Lily scanned the room slowly, looking for the face.

"Sorry, Lily. I didn't mean to remind you."

"Oh, I know. I'm just skittish. I've been looking over my shoulder too much. Let's change the subject, at least until Ben gets here."

"How long have you known Ben?"

"I guess about six years, now. He was my mentor when I worked at the paper, and we kept in touch after I left. We dated for a while and then, afterward, managed to remain friends. We can trust him. I told you that he was very impressed by Jeanine?"

"Jeanine has that effect on people. You two should meet."

"I'd like that, someday."

"No, really. It's an option, Lily. We could always jump on an airplane and disappear. Go biking around France, leave all of this behind us. What do you say?"

Lily lowered her head for a moment. Part of her was already halfway to the airport, but she knew Marc would never leave his mother's death unresolved, or the people she had died for unprotected.

"I'd say you were losing your judgement in a gallant effort to distract me. Running away isn't your style."

"Style? Good Lord, Lily, I don't have a style for coping with this. I'm floundering. You should hear some of the crack-brained ideas I've been coming up with this past week. I even thought I should place an ad in the personal columns of the Toronto dailies, some sort of coded message asking Kathleen to get in touch with me. My guess is that the last thing she's looking for is a single white male seeking-to-outwit-psychopath. All I'm left with is a vague notion of loitering around children's playgrounds hoping to spot Suzy. The idea doesn't appeal. I'd probably be arrested."

"You know, that's not such a bad idea."

"Gee, thanks."

"No, listen. We could send out some kind of message. Hope that the network finds us, rather than the other way around. I'm in danger, aren't I?"

"Indeed. Speaking of which, I have a proposition. Another idea I've been hatching in the midnight hours ... "

But Lily wasn't listening to him. She was looking over his shoulder and laughing.

"So soon?" Ben waved at Lily, and approached Marc from behind. "I thought you two had just met. Hi, I'm Ben Kelter. Sorry to ambush you. I can't resist a straight line."

Ben gave Lily a quick kiss and slipped into the booth beside her. He shook hands with Marc. "Let me make amends," he offered. "What are we drinking tonight, Lily?"

They ordered an earthy Chianti, evading the point of the meeting until the wine was poured. Then Marc, his voice lowered and grave, recounted the story that he had told Lily less than a week ago in her darkened living room. Ben listened soberly, his eyes scarcely leaving Marc's face, his arm hugging Lily close when he learned about the hunter.

Marc finished talking and the three sat in silence. Gradually, the bar sounds of clinking glasses, chatter, and laughter re-invaded their consciousness and surrounded them with a sense of normalcy.

Lily looked up at Ben. "So, can you help us? Have you ever heard any rumours about such a network based in Toronto?"

Ben shook his head. "Nothing. Not even a whisper. I imagine journalists would be anathemas. Oh, I know such organizations exist, sometimes quite openly, in the States. But I've never heard about one here, or about moving people across the border. The best I can do is probe a little here and there. I have contacts who work at women's shelters. If the network is effective, surely they have some way of identifying women in danger. Marc, how many women did your parents help? What were they like?"

"I was involved in about a dozen crossings, though sometimes my parents may have worked alone. They didn't always tell me, though often I could guess. The women were young, in their late twenties or thirties, usually with children, though two or three were alone. What were they like? I'm not sure what you mean, but they were all scared."

"Were they all educated, all from the same class, all the same colour?"

"All colours, certainly. Judging from their accents, they seem to have come from the Northeastern States. It's hard to tell about class. Most seemed well educated, but they came with nothing. Only the clothes on their backs and maybe a knapsack or small bag."

"And where did you take them?"

"I always drove them here, to Toronto. I dropped Kathleen and Suzy at Union Station. My parents were told where I should go each time. The sites varied, but were usually subway stops in the down-town area. I never took anyone to a shelter, or to a building of any kind, for that matter."

"So from Union Station, they could have gone anywhere, even taken a train to another part of the country."

Lily leaned forward. "Yes, but Ben, Marc and I are pretty sure they're still here. If you were going to hide, wouldn't you choose a huge city? And I've been thinking, if they're here illegally, they can't work. So how do they live? How long could you live on your savings before running out of funds? Besides, if you cleaned out your bank accounts before running, you'd risk tipping off your escape. And if you kept drawing cash on the run from ATM machines, couldn't that be easily traced?"

Marc picked up her logic. "Lily and I think that the network must be funding the runners, at least finding them places to stay, maybe even creating new identities with passports and social insurance numbers. Believe me, these women do not want to be found. My guess is that they want to stay in the country permanently or at least for a very long time. That means being able to work, being able to pass as Canadian. If the network is involved to that extent, it would have to be well funded and well hidden. Tighter security in both countries makes forging identity papers a serious crime."

"Okay, I'll widen the net, talk to some people in Immigration about false identification papers. But if the network is as organized as you suppose, it's much more likely to avoid the risk of forging documents in favour of identity theft."

"What's the difference?" asked Lily.

"The difference is that identity theft is much harder to detect than forgery, but it takes time and careful planning. It's not just a matter of assuming the identity of a person by stealing her credit cards or identification papers. That happens, of course. But if you steal an identity that already exists, you'll inevitably be caught because the victim will report the crime. Much more clever is the kind of identity theft which steals from someone already dead. So you find a child who died at the right age — that is, one who would be about your age had he, or in this case she, lived — and you create a whole new identity for yourself in that name."

"But how?"

"It wouldn't be that difficult. Marc's already said that the women were all approximately the same age. All the network would need to do is comb the obituaries in old newspaper files. You'd be surprised at the information they contain — the child's birthdate, birthplace, father's name, sometimes even the mother's maiden name. With that background, and the right fee, of course, someone acting for the network could write the provincial vital statistics office and request a birth certificate. If you said the certificate was required for a passport or a driver's licence, and if the mailing address was in Canada, there'd likely be very little hassle."

"That's it? It's that easy?"

"Not quite, but close. Despite renewed vigilance, the birth certificate is still the first link in the document chain. I'll follow up with my sources for more details. Photo ID is trickier. In the meantime, what about this man you call a hunter? Why are we not asking the police for protection for Lily?"

"Good question," Marc shifted his attention to Lily. "Look, that's what I was trying to suggest when Ben here interrupted me. You're a material witness in a murder case. You can describe him. It wouldn't be at all surprising if you asked for protection. We don't need to tell them more than that. You thought it was a random attack. So will they."

"Exactly. So I'll have short-term protection, but the police won't have enough information to actually catch this guy? Lousy idea. I have a better one."

Ben groaned. "I'm going to hate this, Lily. This is not smart."

"Would you two mind telling me what you're talking about?" Marc asked.

Before Lily could answer, Ben explained. "This is a stubborn woman, Marc. I know her. If we can't find the network, she'll let the network find her. She'll put it about that she's in trouble and wait to see what happens. If the police are in the vicinity, the network will back off. Am I right, Lily?"

"Well, do you have another suggestion?"

"I do," said Marc. His tone was almost belligerent. "You can forget about the network. That's my problem. Let Ben and me try to warn Kathleen and Suzy. If you won't go to the police, you can stay out of it."

Lily's grey eyes widened and she regarded Marc with a look of utter dismissal.

"I'm already in," she snapped. "*You* told *me* about the network, remember? Did you think I'd hide if you scared me enough?"

"C'mon, Lily. That's not what I mean. You don't have to prove anything."

"Oh, but I do," she whispered. "I owe your mother. I have a legacy to earn. Running away is not my style, either."

Ben watched the moment stretch between them, the air charged with all that was not being said aloud. Finally, he cleared his throat to remind them that he was still there.

"Round one to Lily, I think. Trust me, Marc, it's best to give in gracefully. Now, would you two consider a suggestion from a third party? If not the police, why not a bodyguard of sorts? Marc's going to be in town anyway, hotel rates are exorbitant, and I happen to know that Lily's guest bed is serviceable. What do you say? It's one or the other, Lily. You can't have your cake and eat it, too."

Marc grinned at Ben. Lily shrugged.

"I can't have you trailing after me while I'm working," she insisted.

"Deal."

"And I have a lot of film to process in the darkroom. I'll be locked up for hours."

"Even better."

Lily cocked an eyebrow. "The guest bed's in my study. You'll be cramped."

"Sounds cosy."

"Good, that's settled," Ben announced, cutting off any further objections from Lily. "Now, let's show Marc the sights."

The trio paid their bill and crossed the crowded floor to the exit, Lily leading the way. Ben stopped briefly to chat with an old crony who hailed him from an upstairs table, and caught up with Lily and Marc on the sidewalk outside a few minutes later. He didn't tell them about the fair-haired man regarding him so intently as he left, because he had no idea what Abbott looked like.

Friday, July 23, New York

Harry Sloane was catnapping in his office on West 35th Street at 4:00 in the afternoon. He had no particular reason to be there — business these days was run from his home in Brooklyn by phone, fax, and e-mail — but he liked to indulge his fantasies. He liked the deep-roasted aroma that percolated up from the coffee shop downstairs. He liked his name, H. Sloane, spelled out in slightly chipped gold lettering on the half-glass door, the battered filing cabinet, the grain in the fake veneer of his ramshackle desk, and the whir of the old-fashioned rotary fan. Best of all, he liked the fact that people seldom came here, and seldom stayed long if they did. He had time to think, to thumb through his collection of old Dashiell Hammett paperbacks, to study the dust motes dispersed in shafts of sunlight whenever he snapped the venetian blinds.

The sharp rap on the glass first alarmed, then annoyed him. He yawned, deliberately slouching further down in his cracked leather chair. Then, lethargically, he called out an invitation to enter.

Her perfume, an exotic mix of spices and jasmine, stirred him before he saw her and jerked to attention. Her straight blonde hair fell to her shoulders in a silky pageboy, framing a delicate oval face, a sensual mouth, startling violet eyes. She wore a straight cut, sleeveless linen dress, icy blue, with a vee neck and pearl buttons marching down the front. He stared at her wordlessly, thinking incongruously of cool lakes and birdsong, while her eyes swept the shabby room.

"Mr. Sloane?" Her voice had a deep, resonant timbre.

"Ma'am."

"My name's Eva Renault. May I?" She sat down in the vacant straight-backed chair, crossing her long legs. "I must say, this is a most unusual office. I feel like I've wandered onto the set of *The Maltese Falcon.*"

To his dismay, Sloane blushed.

"Most people don't guess. It's just a fancy of mine."

"Don't worry. It's one of my favourite movies. Warner Bros., 1941. Tell me, does the "H" stand for Humphrey?"

"No ma'am. Just Harry. Though some of my friends think I have a passing resemblance to Peter Lorre."

Eva laughed. It was a spontaneous, contagious laugh and Sloane felt gladdened.

"They are imperceptive, Mr. Sloane. You look more like a kindly priest in a supporting role. *Going My Way*, perhaps. Paramount, 1944."

"Ah, well. I've never been too good as the hard-boiled gumshoe. Watch out, though. I can be shifty, despite the innocent mug."

"Why, Harry, how perfectly delightful. So can I."

There was a moment's silence as they sized each other up over the desk. Slowly, they smiled at one another.

"Harry, I have a lot of money in this handbag which I'm happy to give you. But I think you're going to want to help me mostly for the sheer fun of it."

"Let the good times roll, I always say. Just what do you want me to do?"

"Sing, Harry. Tell me everything you know about Paul Abbott."

Sloane raised his eyebrows and leaned back in his chair, making a steeple of his pudgy fingers.

"He's bad news, that guy. Got a screw loose and a shitload of money — excuse my language, ma'am — to hide behind. I'm no match for the Abbotts of this world."

"Oh, but Harry, I am. And with your help, I think I can nail him for a murder in Little Falls. Have you ever heard of that town, Harry? It's not far from Buffalo, about half an hour's drive from the Albright-Knox Art Gallery, as a matter of fact. What do you say? Two against one?"

Sloane stared at her. Sweat broke out in little beads across his forehead and he closed his eyes. But he could still see the wan, strained face of the woman Abbott had hired him to tail. It had felt wrong from the first. He should have listened to his gut.

"It wasn't Kathleen, was it?" he asked quietly.

"Not yet."

"Is she safe, then?"

"Temporarily."

"Well, good for her. I hope she stays that way, but I'm out. Abbott fired me before I could quit. I figure I'm well rid of the bastard."

"So that's it? You disappoint me, Harry. When I saw your, ah — office decor — I was sure you had a streak of gallantry."

"Just who are you, anyway? Are you one of the people who whisked her away? I knew it, damn it. I knew she had to have help to give me the slip."

"You were easy, Harry. But, as you say, Abbott's a different story. Help me stop him." She leaned forward across the desk, her tone suddenly conspiratorial. "I think you owe him at least that much, don't you? C'mon Harry. Let's get even."

Sloane blinked. It wasn't sex she was selling, but pure mischief. He found the invitation irresistible.

"Oh, lady," he said. "You can keep your money. C'mon, let's go for a drive. I want you to see my real office in Brooklyn and if we're lucky, and you're hungry, my Ruby will throw some burgers on the grill. That's Ruby Zaplacinski — she insisted on keeping her maiden name though not a soul can spell it. I'm suddenly ravenous."

Eva was feeling a little giddy, a result of both the Sloane house drink
— a boozy concoction with a lemonade base — and Ruby's whirl-
wind hospitality. She'd been taken to the home office first, a suitably
high-tech attic conversion outfitted with shiny chrome and the
requisite computers, modems, printers, and telephones. Harry, it
seemed, was the legs of the operation, but Ruby was the brains. She
ran the business with a military efficiency and dabbled in what she
called a little creative research on the side. With the push of a
button and the snap of a highly organized drawer, she retrieved the
Abbott file, filled with both commissioned and uncommissioned
information.

While the three compared notes, Ruby fixed supper without
seeming to lift a finger or miss a word of the conversation. She was
a heavy woman, close to two hundred pounds, with perfect skin,
expressive brown eyes, and nut brown hair. Eva was quite out of
breath watching her.

"Ruby, please sit down. You're spoiling me."

"Back in a minute, hon. I'll just fetch dessert."

Sloane winked at Eva: "It's a pie. Raspberry. Ruby makes champion pies."

"Oh, I couldn't. I'm stuffed."

The pie seemed to materialize in front of her and the Sloanes
coaxed her to take a taste. In deeply appreciative silence, Eva ate two
slices before mustering the will to push her plate away.

"Ruby, you'll be the ruin of me."

"Better to ruin Abbott, my dear. What's your plan?"

"Well, first, we have to find him. We'll need to get access to his
apartment. Do you think his lawyer will talk to us, Harry?"

"Not a chance. Not even to a stunner like you. We can also
scratch his broker, his accountant, his bank manager. He may be a
lone wolf, but a rich man always has allies. They may not like him,
but they'd be fools to cut the purse strings."

"We need to find the little people," Ruby suggested. "Ones he
thinks he can flick off like fleas, like my Harry. Or like Dora."

"Who's Dora?" Eva asked.

"Oh, every Abbott has a Dora. This Dora works for a high-class
cleaning company. I always do a little research on Harry's clients,
just to be on the safe side, and I found Dora months ago. I do
believe she has keys to that penthouse, and she'll know the security

code, too. But, mind you, she's bonded. You won't take anything, will you? I wouldn't want Dora to lose her job."

"You're a wonder, Ruby. I promise we won't take a thing. But we need to act quickly. Any chance we can get in there tonight?"

Ruby sprang into action. "Now why don't I just phone Dora? Might be she'd like a little pie for her dessert tonight. And a few bills from that fat envelope you flashed at Harry probably wouldn't go amiss."

Eva reached for her purse. "Spend it as you see fit. But keep some for yourselves, please."

"No thanks, dear. Harry's not too proud of what he's done. Oh, at first, we thought Kathleen was a bit crooked, maybe a blackmailer or something, but she's not, is she?"

"No, Ruby. Nothing like that, I promise."

"What's going on?" asked Harry. "Why's Abbott so keen to find her?"

"Now, Harry. You know she can't tell us a thing. Don't pester her."

"I can tell you that we know he used your information to find the gallery. He told people Kathleen was his wife and someone must have given him enough information to get to Little Falls, but the trail ends there. I'm trying to pick it up from here. I'm hoping to find a lead in his penthouse. That's all I can say, except that he's every bit as dangerous as you feared, Harry. He killed a woman there, a woman in her sixties. She was helping Kathleen, too."

Ruby clicked her tongue and left the room, shaking her head.

Harry looked hangdog. "I'm sorry, Eva. I should have known. It never felt right, you know? She was a pretty little thing, but over the months I followed her she faded like a cut flower. But Ruby didn't turn up any worms when she dug over Abbott's past. Best schools, big estate in Connecticut, no shady dealings. I'd like to make amends. And I sure am sorry about that poor old lady. Mighty sorry. Wish I'd never given the bastard a head start."

"It's okay, Harry. If not you, Abbott would have found someone else. And at least you have a conscience. Do you think you can get me by the doorman?"

"Oh, sure. I do an obnoxious drunk. I'll have a little chat with the parking guard while I'm at it, too. You'll be okay up there on your own?"

"Just fine. If you don't mind though, I think I should change into my working clothes, just in case Ruby can get the keys tonight."

Harry smiled. "You might have noticed already, ma'am. Whatever Ruby wants, she usually gets."

When Eva came downstairs ten minutes later, she wore an off-the-shoulder black mini-dress in a soft, clinging material and black stiletto heels. Her hair was upswept, with just a few tendrils curling about her face and neck.

"Very classy," Ruby pronounced, while Harry whistled.

"Well, just in case the doorman isn't convinced by Harry's drunkenness, I'm an old school chum of Abbott's from the hallowed Ivy League. And I've left something rather personal in his bedroom. How's Dora? Are we on?"

"We'll just swing by her place. It's on the way. And raspberry's her favourite. She and I will have a little visit while you two are busy elsewhere."

Manhattan glowed a delicate rose in the sunrise, and its myriad buildings, rising from the mist and the grime far below, scraped a cloudless sky. Eva and Harry were on their way to the airport.

"Now, you sure you got those muffins Ruby baked? You didn't eat much breakfast."

"Harry, I wouldn't call eggs Benedict not much. You and Ruby have been wonderful. We can't thank you enough."

"Who's we?"

"Sorry, Harry."

"Okay, okay. You'll let us know if there's anything else we can do."

"You've done plenty. If you hadn't found out about Abbott's car repairs from the parking attendant, I would probably have missed the significance of the licence plate number he'd written down."

"I'm surprised he left it lying around."

"He didn't exactly. I lifted the imprint from a pad of paper."

Harry chuckled. "You're full of surprises, aren't you? What are you? Some kind of spy?"

"Harry — "

"Okay, okay. Are you sure Abbott's in Toronto?"

"Oh, I think so. And after what Dora told Ruby — you know, finding the shredded clothing in the penthouse — he's already killing Kathleen in his mind. There's luggage missing, and toiletries. I suppose he may have skipped to the Cayman Islands, but I don't think we'll be that lucky."

"Well, here we are." Harry pulled into the curb. "Good luck; I hope you find her in time to warn her."

"Find *her*? Oh, Harry," Eva leaned over to kiss him goodbye. "I know exactly where she is. I always have."

Monday, July 26, Toronto

Kathleen and Suzy were returning home from the corner store, their steps quickened by the freshness of the day, when they saw Teresa waving to them from her front window. They hadn't seen her since the trip to the zoo, a glad day for Suzy, who had warmed quickly to her new neighbour. They had craned their necks at the giraffes, shuddered at the pythons, and ridden the camels. Kathleen had almost forgotten days without care. Almost.

Terri came down the steps to meet them in her bare feet, inviting them for coffee and juice. But Kathleen demurred. She was still feeling cautious, hesitant about planting new friendships in case these, too, had to be uprooted. She was putting away groceries when Suzy began pouting.

"It's boring here."

"I know you miss your friends, Suzy. I know it's been hard. But you understand why, don't you?"

"No. Why can't we have breakfast with Terri?"

"We mustn't impose. We just met her."

"But she asked us. Don't you like her?"

"Oh, Suzy, stop it. Of course I like her. We just don't know her very well, that's all."

"We don't know anyone anymore, do we?"

Kathleen's heart sank. Children could be brutally insightful.

"I'm sorry, Suzy. But it's only for a little while longer. In the fall, you'll be able to go to school. You'll have a new name, remember? Suzy McLaren. And you'll meet lots of new friends, I promise. Why don't you get your crayons and show me how you can spell your new name, okay?"

"No. I want to play with Terri. It's a stupid name."

Kathleen didn't have an answer. It wasn't a name she'd chosen. But she and Suzy had to have papers, all the documents of identification to become persons in a new country. The network had assigned her the new name. It came in the mail with a Canadian birth certificate. Suddenly she had a new birthday and a new place of birth. But how could she tell Suzy that? Soon she was to apply for a provincial health card, her first piece of photo ID as Kathleen McLaren. The thought made her mouth go dry.

"Listen, Suzy. Can you keep a secret?"

"Yes, please."

"You promise?"

The little girl shook her head, solemnly.

"Well, you and I are still the same underneath. We're still Kathleen and Suzy Landers. But, here, in this new place, we need a new last name."

"Why, Mommy?"

"I'm in a bit of trouble. That's why we came here. If we have a new name, no one can find us."

"Did you do something bad?"

"No, Suzy, but sometimes other people are bad. I met a bad man once, back in New York, and he doesn't understand that I don't want to be friends with him anymore. He can't find me now; he's miles and miles away."

"Are you scared, Mommy? Is that why you cry at night?"

Kathleen was stunned. She thought she'd stifled the noise by burying her face in the sheets. She took a long breath.

"Oh, no, there's nothing to be scared about. I just cry because I'm lonely, too, sometimes. I'm sorry you heard me. I won't cry anymore, I promise. And there are lots of people helping me, sort of like imaginary friends. You can't always see them, but they're there. Now, I think we need some new clothes to go with our new name. Would you like to go shopping? Yes? Then, run downstairs and ask Terri if she'd like to come with us."

Terri had driven to a sprawling mall on the northern edge of the city. Normally, she explained, she would have preferred to poke about the neighbourhood, where walking in fresh air between shops tended to counteract the spending frenzy, but the mall had the allure of a play area for Suzy. Kathleen entered willingly into the spirit of the day, buying bathing suits, cotton shorts and tops and, at Terri's urging, a cream-coloured sundress for herself. She twirled in its full skirt, laughing at Suzy's applause. Finally, Terri marched them into the play corner where children somersaulted and scrambled over gym pads and giant bean bags in geometric shapes. The two women sat at an adjacent table and sipped coffee, watching Suzy frolic like a suddenly unleashed puppy.

"Your little girl looks a lot like you," Terri commented. "Same eyes. Was your hair that shade when you were younger?"

"No, Suzy gets that unruly mop from her father."

Terri didn't press. Kathleen appreciated the gift of silence, and changed the subject.

"Terri, I want to thank you for taking such an interest in Suzy. She's not had much fun lately."

"Sure, no problem. It's hard, starting over."

"Suzy makes friends easily. She'll be okay."

"And you?"

Kathleen shrugged. "I'm a harder case. I have reason to be wary of my judgement. But I like you, Terri. I'm trying."

"I know. Look Kathleen, there's something I should tell you. Kathleen? What's wrong?"

"Oh, damn, I've spilled my coffee." She grabbed Terri's hand. "Look after Suzy, will you?"

She turned away and fled to the public washroom. Terri began mopping up, giving Suzy a wave. She scanned the mall. Something had frightened Kathleen. She had seen the flash of terror in her eyes, the convulsive jerk of the hand holding the glass of iced coffee. Something was wrong, but what?

The washroom was empty, the doors of the cubicles yawning open. Kathleen ran to the end of the row, slamming the door behind her, turning the knob. Still standing, she leaned her head against the cold tile wall and breathed. The panic was back, the dry mouth, the pounding heart, every muscle tensed. *It can't be him. It can't. The tall, fair man at the coffee bar.* She forced herself to breathe. She'd only seen him from behind. She was paranoid. She was seeing things.

She had to go back out there. Slowly, the numbness receded and she realized she felt wet. Coffee stained her shirt and shorts. She turned to open the cubicle door. She would wash herself, splash cold water on her face. She would go back out. Her hand froze. Someone else was in the room.

"Who's there? Terri?"

She waited, straining for every sound. She thought she heard some shuffling, a low snicker. Instinctively, she climbed on top of the toilet seat, balancing on the rim, cowering down so her head could not be seen above the partition. *Oh, God, Terri. Help Suzy, get Suzy away.*

From the far end of the room, she heard the footsteps approaching slowly. She couldn't see anything. The footsteps sounded heavy. They stopped for a moment and she heard water gush from one of the sinks. Then more footsteps, coming closer. Another faucet. The water made it impossible for her to hear. She strained forward and gasped. She could see the feet now. Sneakers and the bottoms of blue jeans. Slowly, a hand slid over the top of the partition.

"Hey, what the hell's going on in here?"

The feet turned and ran. Kathleen heard the thud of bodies colliding, and then Terri's voice, breathless, "Kathleen, are you all right?"

She opened the cubicle. Terri was on the floor by the exit, legs sprawled in front of her.

"What happened? Who was it?"

"Some gang of teenage girls. I saw four of them swarm at the entrance just after you came in. They sent one in alone, probably to nab your purse. She had all the grace of a truck. I think my tailbone's broken."

"Suzy!"

"She's fine. I left her guarding our parcels with one of the play supervisors. Hey, c'mon, Kathleen, the least you can do is help me up."

Kathleen extended her hand. It was shaking badly. Terri felt its coldness and dropped her bantering tone immediately.

"Hey, it's okay. You're okay. C'mon. I'll take you home."

She led Kathleen back to the table.

"Hey, Suz. We have to go now. Your Mom's had a bit of a scare."

Kathleen shook her head at Terri, but it was too late.

The little girl ran to her mother and hugged her knees.

"Are you okay, Mommy? Was it the bad man?"

"No, Suzy. But look, I've spilled coffee all over me and I have to change. What a klutz I am."

She looked over her daughter's head directly into Terri's wide brown eyes. "Later," she mouthed, in silence.

During the drive home, Terri looked straight ahead. She turned the radio on and sang along to the music at the top of her lungs, while Suzy groaned and giggled at her off-key voice. When they pulled into the driveway, she turned to Kathleen.

"Look, why don't you take a long hot bath? I'll take Suzy into the park at the end of the street and we'll pick up some dinner on the way home. See you about seven?"

Kathleen nodded mutely. Her head was in a vise, part of the aftermath of her panic. She felt calm but drained. She gathered up the shopping bags and turned at the front door to see Terri and Suzy already skipping down the street, hand-in-hand.

At precisely 7:00, she opened her door to Terri's knock. She carried a bag of deli sandwiches and two bottles of white wine.

"Hi. You look a little better. Suzy is sound asleep on my couch. She said to tell you she likes pistachio ice cream, only it didn't quite come out as 'pistachio.' We're practising saying it, so she can order it herself next time."

"You're amazing, Terri."

"No, I'm just — I'm just trying to be a friend. And before you start worrying, let me show you this little gadget." She walked into the kitchen, put down the sandwiches and wine, and placed what looked like a phone receiver on the table.

"See this red flashing light? Well, there's one just like it beside Suzy. We can hear her if she wakes up. Oh, and I locked the door. She's perfectly safe. You, however, are not," she paused, but Kathleen didn't flinch from her gaze. "The wine, Kathleen. This wine is powerful stuff, homemade by my Italian grandfather. Vintage Guido Mordelli, absolutely authentic. You'd better eat something with it, or you'll pass out."

Kathleen smiled. "Okay, I'll eat. But I made a decision when my head cleared. I'd like to tell you my story, if you'll listen."

"Of course I'll listen, but you don't have to — "

"No, I do. I've been running too long. I've been trying to bury the past, but that's wrong. I need to learn how to take strength from it instead of just a vague dread. You put yourself in danger for me, this afternoon."

"That girl? No way, she just caught me off balance."

The two burst out laughing.

"It's funny now, Terri. But it mightn't have been. I saw my life flash before me in that washroom."

"The bad man?"

"Yes."

"You saw him?"

"No, but I imagine I see him, and that's somehow worse. As long as I can't free myself, push away the sickness and apprehension, I can't claim to be fully safe."

There was recognition and compassion in Terri's face, but Kathleen seemed not to notice. She was staring into her wineglass. She started, and then stopped several sentences, as if the words felt clumsy in her mouth. Finally, she took a long draught of the wine and squared her shoulders.

"Well, here goes. I don't know where to start, but I think you need to know a bit about me to understand. I grew up in Virginia; my parents were both teachers. They always wanted more children, but it never happened, so we were very close. A quiet, happy family. When I was fifteen, my father died quite suddenly of a heart attack and my mother, well, she sort of gave up wanting to live. She sent me to Chicago to stay with her sister. At first, I was angry and hurt, but my aunt's family was so kind and so, well, exuberant — she had three children of her own — that pretty soon I didn't want to go home anymore. I lived with them until I started college and, in my last year at Columbia, I met David. David Landers. We were both studying architecture. I soon switched to design, but David, he had a grand talent. He would have been a master. We fell in love and were married after fifteen months. David took a job with a firm in New York, and Suzy was born a year later. She was only three when David was killed — another victim of a drunk driver. I'm not sure she remembers him very clearly, but she has his gift, I hope. She draws beautifully, and she's always building bridges and castles and …"

"Kathleen, you don't have to do this."

"No, let me finish. I was lost when David died — he was torn from our lives so needlessly. But I was determined to live a life to honour his memory. And determined that Suzy wouldn't be abandoned. David's firm offered me a job as a designer and slowly, with Suzy and my friends, the pain abated. For three years, I didn't see anyone, any men I mean, and then, one day, I met Paul Abbott. I was hired to redecorate his apartment, a penthouse on Madison. I was dazzled. He was handsome, rich, very charming at first. He had a reputation as a bit of a playboy and I was flattered that he noticed me. I'd like to think the money didn't matter — I hope it didn't — but I was lulled by the lifestyle. We started dating. He took me to operas and ballets and museums. We ate in all the best places. It was a world I had only glimpsed from the periphery. And Paul was always very correct, very self-assured and attentive.

"Then, about four months into the relationship, he asked me to spend the weekend with him at his estate in Connecticut. We hadn't yet had sex together and I was nervous, but I thought it was time, perhaps, to move our relationship forward. So I agreed. I began to have second thoughts during the drive, and disliked the house right away. It was forbidding and isolated on the outside, a mausoleum on the inside. But I didn't want to hurt his feelings, he was so proud of it. So I stayed.

"We — we made love for the first and only time. I can't really describe it, Terri, but it felt wrong. It was like he wasn't really with me, but only watching me. Like he was, I don't know, almost gloating. Then he did the most bizarre thing. He led me by the hand — we were still naked — down to the front hall and stood me in front of a portrait of his grandfather. 'This is Kathleen,' he said, as if the man in the picture were still alive, 'I have chosen her.' It was disgusting. He made me turn full-circle in front of the portrait. He paraded me. I felt suddenly terrified, spinning out of control. I knew I'd made a terrible mistake.

"We left the next day, and I tried to pretend that everything was still okay until I was safe at home again. He didn't seem to notice my mood. He was crazy. He called me his Pygmalion maiden — he'd bought clothes for me to wear. He said we would be born again together. He talked about marriage and a boarding school for Suzy. I was stunned. I couldn't wait to get away from him.

"It didn't turn out to be easy. At first, I just refused all his invitations. I was busy, I didn't feel well, I was too tired. I used every excuse, but he just kept coming. Flowers. Telephone messages. Then he started showing up unannounced at the office or at Suzy's school. Finally, I just told him I never wanted to see him again. He was enraged. He grabbed my arm and shook me like I was a petulant child. He told me I was only confused, that I was testing him like some kind of grotesque coquette. It was as if I wasn't a separate person with a will of my own at all. And the stalking continued. If anything, it got worse. I would see him in the grocery store. He would wave at me when I was in the park with Suzy. I would go to the dentist and he would be one of the people in the waiting room.

"I began to feel desperate. I got a court order. My friends in the firm got me a new job with another company. Suzy and I moved and she changed schools. I unlisted my phone. For a while, I'd hoped it worked. But in my heart, I knew it hadn't. I stopped seeing him, but I still felt watched, like an animal paralyzed in the headlights of an approaching car. He must have hired someone. Then, one day I found a bunch of photographs *inside* my apartment, pictures of me I never knew had been taken and one of Suzy, all alone. He wanted me to *know* he was still there. It was a form of torture, to know that he could act at any time of the day or night.

"Have you ever known such fear, Terri? To feel that every step you take is on quicksand, that around every corner is the face you dread?"

"Yes, I have," Terri whispered, but Kathleen was so caught up in her own story she didn't hear her.

"Perhaps I should have stood my ground, but his tactics worked too well. I even thought about sending Suzy to my aunt — my mother all over again — but, in the end, I couldn't bear to be separated from her. And I was terrified that if I tried to disappear alone, he would find her and use her as bait. Eventually, don't ask me how, some unknown friends, an underground network of sorts, contacted me and brought me here. I left everything behind, my name, my belongings, everything I own. I brought a few clothes, photographs of David, my wedding ring, that's it. But I have Suzy, and I have a chance to be whole again. And unafraid. It's like learning to walk and talk again. Learning to trust again. I'm not going to run anymore. This afternoon, cowering in that bathroom — no more. Not ever."

Terri poured more wine and smiled. "You don't have to do this alone, Kathleen. You can trust me. I'm a friend."

"I know. What you did for me today meant a lot. Maybe now you understand how much."

"I always knew. That's what I've been trying to tell you."

Kathleen looked again into the dark brown eyes of her companion, as if she were seeing her for the first time.

"That's right," Terri smiled. "Let's start again. My name's Teresa Mordelli and I know who you are because the network told me."

Monday, July 26, Toronto

Marc had been staying with her for three days, long enough for Lily to yearn for the privacy of her darkroom. As long as there was someone else in the house, it didn't seem spooky anymore. In fact, it seemed a haven. Methodically, she dipped her negatives into chemical baths, watching luminescent faces and figures slowly crystallize into discernible lines and planes. Her familiarity with the developing process never blunted her sense of anticipation: a minute more here, a minute less there, and she could soften light, alter the density of shadows, call forth a spectrum of colour from the tips of her fingers.

Her mother had surprised her with her first camera on her tenth birthday, a present that had immediately enchanted her. From that moment on, she had thirsted to learn all she could about photography, ever mindful of its rapidly evolving technology that challenged even the most gifted of students. Sometimes, her nose twitching from chemicals, she dreamed of state-of-the-art darkrooms, or of digital cameras and dazzling computer programs. But, in the end, she preferred the simplicity of old-fashioned processing, wherein patience and a delicacy of timing could tip the balance between a flawed composition and a startling one. Inside her darkroom, the tangible world outside receded and was born anew in a kaleidoscope of tones, angles, and depths of field that sharpened and reshaped perspective. Lily lost herself in this world, her cares as muted as light reflected through a diffusing filter.

When she finally heard the tapping at the door, she had no idea when it had begun or how long it had continued.

"Come out, Lily."

"Go away, Marc."

"But it's been four hours. Ben's here. We've made lunch."

Lily grimaced. Ben had a flair for exotic and decidedly peculiar combinations like pineapple in tomato sauce, and Marc, she had discovered, had inherited none of his mother's highly reputed culinary skills. A weekend with him in her kitchen had taught her to be wary. She could only imagine with a shudder what the two of them might have concocted between them.

Another knock, this time louder.

"Okay, okay. Give me five minutes to finish up."

Stepping across the threshold from one world to another was always slightly disorienting to Lily. She paused on the landing at the top of the stairs and peered across the living room to the open French doors, blinking her eyes to adjust to the flood of light. She could see Marc and Ben seated at the small picnic table in the back garden, already munching on sandwiches.

She sighed. At night, alone in the darkness, knowing that a man with a gun might be tracking her, she was glad of Marc's presence in her study-cum-guest room. But during the day, she sometimes felt unaccountably, ungratefully, cross and impatient with him. He fidgeted. He took up quite a lot of space. Most of all, he threw Lily off balance. Even though the violence of Marie's death and the invisible threads of the network bound them together, they were strangers still. She didn't know how to react to him, nor whether to trust him completely. Was he there, as he insisted, to protect her, or merely to use her as a convenient means of finding his mother's killer?

Puzzling over Marc's motivations, Lily crossed the hall to her bedroom. The clothes she had been working in all morning were pungent with the chemical smell of developing fluid and she needed to change. But as she moved about her room, discarding clothing and reaching for jeans and a fresh T-shirt, she felt a sense of disquiet, an uncanny feeling that the order of her things had been disturbed, however slightly. She stopped moving and looked all around her. The closet door was ajar. Surely she had closed it behind her earlier in the day? Was it her imagination, or had her favourite photograph of her mother been turned an inch or so from its customary spot? Had someone picked up and looked through the slanting pile of mail on her dresser?

Lily shivered. She must be wrong. Marc would have no reason to enter her room. Locked in the darkroom, she would have heard nothing. But why would he do such a thing?

His voice, coming from the bottom of the staircase and cutting through her thoughts, startled her.

"Lily, what are you doing?"

She jumped involuntarily and suddenly felt very silly. She was losing all sense of proportion and judgement. She just felt crowded, that's all, forced by circumstances to share her privacy. Surely, there had been no one in her room. Quickly, she ran her fingers through her hair and dressed.

"So, what's this?" she asked a minute later, reaching for a sandwich and giving Ben a quick kiss on the cheek. "Sardines and peanut butter again?"

Ben feigned a hurt expression. "Unfair. You're hardly in a position to be a food snob. It's plain ham and cheese."

"Great." Lily bit into her roll and looked across the picnic table at Marc, who was staring at her curiously.

He smiled. "What have you done to your hair, Lily Ross?"

Lily resisted the temptation to smooth the short curls back into place. She smiled back, but said nothing.

"Ben has news," he announced.

"Well, nothing really startling. But maybe a lead. I visited a contact at the Ministry of Human Resources this morning and it seems my earlier hunch was right. If someone needed to disappear with a new name, generating a set of documents by using the birth certificate of a deceased child would be more difficult to trace than a set of forgeries. And I also discovered that there's not much cross-referencing done between provinces, so the best protection against detection would be to find a child born in one province who died in another."

"There's not some centralized agency?" Marc asked.

"Nope. Vital statistics—birth and death records—health cards and driver's licences are all under provincial jurisdiction. If, and when, cross-referencing becomes more systematic, it will start with recent records, simply because it's too expensive to go back very far. So the network could be providing deep cover as long as it planned ahead and was reasonably cautious. If it varied the Canadian address that birth certificates were to be mailed to and, frankly, if the names were as ordinary as, say, Lily Ross, the risk would be worth taking."

"But what about photo ID?" Lily objected. "The network couldn't generate that without some kind of forgery."

"Simple," Ben shrugged. "Suppose the network only did the groundwork. Then, once the women were safe in the country, they could complete the process themselves. They could smile for the camera themselves. First a health card, then a driver's licence. After that, a social insurance card and a passport would easily follow. There's just one problem."

"Which is," Marc sighed, "that knowing how the network might be operating still doesn't help us make contact. That's the issue, isn't it? How does the network *know* when a woman is in trouble? It must have some way of verifying stories."

He glanced across the table at Ben and Lily, expecting some response, but neither seemed to have heard him. Indeed, they were looking at each other so intently, it was as if he were no longer there.

"Have I missed something?"

It was Lily who finally answered. "It's the timeline, Marc. The network plans carefully, plans in advance. I can't expect a quick response to the news that I'm in danger. Even if the story found its way to the right ears, the network would move slowly and we haven't the time to wait. We have to find the network some other way."

"But how? We've been through this. I don't know who these people are."

"But they know you," Ben interjected. "How did they know you and your parents would be sympathetic? How did they know you wouldn't just dismiss them, or worse, report them?"

"My parents swore they had never seen the woman who approached them before."

"Marc," Lily whispered. "Don't you see? Someone sent her. Someone who knew your parents. Someone who knew about what happened ... to Jeanine."

"A lot of people knew," Marc snapped. "There was a trial, remember? The reporters had a field day — " He broke off, turning away from Ben. "I'm sorry. She respected you. But she was stripped of her privacy. She lost a lot of things to Mahoney."

The three fell silent. Lily felt a sickening inevitability at hearing Mahoney's name. It was as if she were trapped in a devious maze, with every forking path twisting back to the monster at its heart. What had begun two weeks ago as a puzzling mystery had been transformed into the sobering reality of lives torn asunder, a terrifying reminder of the perverse and the unpredictable. Perhaps Amanda Martin had been right, after all, to turn and run.

She stole a glance at Marc. He was still brooding, his expression closed, his eyes lowered. She hardly dared speak, but she knew she must.

"You're right. I found out about Jeanine from Ben's articles. It's how I found Marie. I'm still sorry. But there were other women hurt by Mahoney, weren't there, Marc? Women whose names Ben and the other reporters never knew. Only Jeanine knew them, and your parents knew them."

Marc refused to look at her and she saw the stubborn flex of his jaw. The minutes stretched between them, agonizingly slow.

Then, finally, he spoke: "Hayley Quinn. And her best friend's name was Bonnie. That's why they couldn't testify. They hadn't come forward immediately, and by the time they did, the Crown Attorney's Office worried that the closeness of their relationship — they were childhood friends — would taint their testimony. There were fears that they could be said to have collaborated on their stories and that the defense attorney would use that to weaken the whole case against Mahoney. So Jeanine went ahead on her own. I remember Agatha Quinn, Hayley's mother, being furious at the law, but it was hardest in some ways on Bonnie. You see, she was the first to be assaulted, at least the first we knew about. And she didn't tell anyone. She blamed herself for what happened later to Hayley and Jeanine."

"Where are they now, Marc?"

"I don't know. We lost touch. I know that sounds callous, but after the initial shock and the trial, there came a time when it was easier to mend lives apart from each other rather than together. The mutual support was a kind of double-edged sword because seeing Hayley and Bonnie was also a reminder of the pain. When Jeanine had felt she had done all she could, she moved on. She went to Paris to complete her studies. The Quinns live here, in Toronto. I would visit them occasionally, but though we were friends, I was a poor substitute for Jeanine. I didn't want to press. I haven't seen either woman for a few years now. I promised never to reveal their identities."

Abruptly, Ben stood up and walked toward the house, beckoning to Lily to follow him. She picked up the platter of half-eaten sandwiches and joined him, a bit reluctantly.

"Leave him be for a while," Ben urged. "He has to arrive at the only solution by himself."

Lily looked back over her shoulder toward Marc. He seemed dejected and vulnerable. "It feels mean. He didn't want to tell us who those women were."

"No."

"Isn't there another way?"

"I can't think of one, can you?"

Lily went into the kitchen, opened her fridge and found a bottle of wine.

"Here. Open this, will you?" She waited until Ben poured, then stated flatly, "He's going to resent us."

"A little. But he needs to find the network as much as we do. Our mutual dependence is undeniable for the time being. My contact at the Ministry's going to do some digging, look for patterns, but she may not uncover much. This is our best chance. Do you mind so much — about the resentment, I mean?"

"Yes. I think I do."

"Hmmm."

"What's that supposed to mean?"

"I simply cleared my throat."

"Suggestively. Let's hear it."

"Okay. Look, Lily, go slowly. He seems a great guy, but, well, where was he this morning when you were in your darkroom? I called, you know, to invite myself to lunch, but no one answered the phone. He should have been here looking out for you. That was the deal."

Lily felt a frisson of alarm.

Maybe he was busy searching my room, she thought, but she didn't say so.

"Jeez, Ben. Maybe he was taking a shower. Maybe he went out-side to read a book. He's not a bodyguard."

"Sorry. I'm just worried about you."

Lily smiled. She tried to look braver than she felt.

"It'll be okay, Ben."

"Sure."

They both looked up as Marc entered the room.

"Fine," he said. "I'll call the Quinns and ask them about the network. But Lily comes with me."

"Why? They don't know me. Won't I only make them feel uncomfortable?"

"If they know anything at all, I want them to realize that I'm not just being curious. There are people in danger. You're in danger."

Lily and Marc left the house around 7:00 to meet with Agatha Quinn. She had invited them for coffee and dessert, expressing a polite enthusiasm for seeing Marc again, but, he reported, not without a hesitation that was a few seconds too long. He did not doubt her sincerity, but accepted that his sudden reappearance in her life would cast a shadow harkening back to more sombre times. She had spoken not a word about either Hayley or Bonnie.

As Lily had feared, the Rosedale address was not easy to find, the streets curving at odd angles to one another as they traced the edges of the city's network of ravines. The white noise of city traffic did not penetrate these graceful boulevards and gently winding cul-de-sacs. In fact, though the main streets of Bloor and Mount Pleasant were only blocks away, it was possible to imagine oneself in the countryside, more likely to hear the hoot of a night owl or the bark of a red fox than the intruding blare of a horn.

The old stately homes were monuments to wealth and individuality, a far cry from the cookie-cutter, so-called "monster" homes of brasher, newer builders. Styles ranged from the black wrought-iron balconies and pale stucco of French country houses to turrets and Tudor facades, but all seemed deeply rooted, solid, ready to weather another century or so. Lily thought it a contradiction that, despite their grand size, the houses seemed unextravagant, modest, tucked back almost shyly from the roadsides, sometimes further sheltered by climbing or flowering vines, sprays of clematis or wisteria, curving drives or low brick walls with sturdy gates. In general, Rosedale suggested retreat and privacy, a mild rebuff to the curious who might drive by with either envy or amusement in their hearts.

"Here, Lily. This is it. The gate's open."

Lily followed the drive as it twisted between several willows and evergreens, parking her car in the cobblestoned courtyard. Close up, the grey stuccoed house was imposing, sedately trimmed in black, with two trellises of flame-orange roses climbing up either side of the black double doors. With a quick look at Marc that she hoped was more reassuring than she felt, Lily lifted the ornate bronze door knocker and let it fall once. It felt just as she knew it would in her hand — smooth with time, heavy, and slightly warmed by the evening sun.

They stood silently, side by side, listening for footsteps which, when they finally heard them, seemed to come from a great distance. Lily had expected a maid, perhaps, even more romantically, a butler, but she knew instinctively that it was Agatha Quinn who opened the door.

Lily tried not to stare. Hazel eyes under still-dark brows, high cheekbones, and a strong chin. The prominent cords and looser skin of her neck most betrayed her age, though a closer scrutiny of the oval face showed a soft feathering of wrinkles across the forehead and around the eyes and mouth. Lily thought she was lovely.

Surprisingly, it was Lily whom Agatha looked at first; a long, appraising look that was not unkind. Then she turned to Marc and extended her hand. The fingers were gnarled, the skin discoloured by age spots, but the gesture was regal.

"Marc, how kind of you to come."

Somehow, Lily didn't believe her.

"It's been a long time. Do come in. And this is — ?"

"Lily Ross, Agatha. She's a friend of mine."

She nodded politely and lead them through the marble foyer and down a long hallway to a spacious sun room that stretched across the full width of the house. It was a glorious room in watery shades of green and blue, facing west so that it drank in the lowering sun and opened onto a breathtaking view of sloping lawns, bursts of gladioli, and finally the wild tangle of the ravine woods. The room was uncluttered and the cathedral windows so huge that there seemed to be only the whisper of a barrier between inside and outside space. The furniture was gay and comfortable-looking, but Lily noticed that the rugs were silk. Marc had positioned himself in front of an oil portrait hung over a grand piano in one corner of the room.

"This is Hayley, isn't it? She looks marvellous."

Lily joined him, but said nothing. The painting transfixed her. The woman was certainly beautiful, with blue eyes, Botticelli hair, and skin like porcelain tinged a pale peach, but Lily saw more than she wanted to. The mouth was petulant, the eyes restless. To her, the face seemed intense and strained. It was a haunted face, the expression one of deep self-absorption. Finding Hayley's gaze too painful to bear, she turned her head away and immediately met Agatha's eyes. She was staring at her from across the room. Lily blushed, as if she had blurted aloud her misgivings about Hayley's image.

The moment passed quickly as Marc asked questions about the artist, and Agatha poured out coffee, offering fruit and biscotti. They chatted in the polite way of acquaintances about Marc's acting career and Lily's photography, avoiding more serious topics and not sure how to turn the agenda to their real concerns. Gradually, inevitably, the questions became more pointed.

"Tell me, Lily," Agatha demanded. "What do you think of Hayley's portrait?"

The question was so direct Lily felt there was no way to duck it, no way to disguise the impression she had of a distressed, even neurotic personality. She tried to be as tactful as she could, even as she sensed Marc's surprise.

"She's very beautiful, but she seems restless to me, troubled. Forgive me, but, at the moment when the painting was done, I would say she was deeply unsatisfied with her life."

She heard Marc's indrawn breath, but Agatha was silent, regarding her closely. "And would you say, Lily, from seeing this portrait, that my daughter was spoiled?"

"I'm sorry, Mrs. Quinn. But I didn't know her, I couldn't say. A person is many things at once. It's one of the secrets I've learned through photography. If you take thirty pictures of one face, even on the same day, you will capture many different personalities, many shades of feeling, glimpses of deeper emotions that alter the face slightly. Sometimes you capture an image in a split second that even the person herself wouldn't recognize."

"No need to apologize, Lily. She was spoiled. Beautiful, outrageous, irresistible, and, at the end, careening out of control. She died shortly after this portrait was completed in a car accident in Antigua. I've never been sure whether it was carelessness or something more deliberate. But, as you say so wisely, a person has myriad personalities. I don't suppose I'll ever know. She died, I am told, instantly and without suffering. She had had her share."

Flushed with surprise and anger on his behalf, Lily glanced appre-
hensively at Marc. Agatha had revealed the news about Hayley in a
particularly brutal way. She felt as if she could read his pain in the
tightening of his hands.

But Agatha seemed oblivious.

"Perhaps I should have tried harder to reach you, Marc, you and
your family. But it was too great a weight for me to bear at the time.
To be honest, I wanted to block out the Mahoney case, forget everyone connected with it. Not Bonnie, of course. She stayed here with
me for a while. But we both agreed. What good could it do Jeanine,
or you, to know that Hayley had died? The ties between the families were broken long ago. And now Mahoney's dead, too. Did you
know? A shooting sometime this past winter. The police came to see
me."

"I did know, Agatha. The name is not one I'd ever forget. I am so
sorry about Hayley. Jeanine will be, too."

Lily felt the tension like a dull vibration in the room. There was a
moment of thick silence and then Agatha's cool, pale profile turned
toward him.

"Yes. Of course. I see that now," she relented. "Perhaps it's time to
move forward, for all our sakes. Jeanine is well?"

"Expecting a child. Lily and I hope to visit her in France soon."

The mood of the conversation had somehow shifted. Marc was
improvising a scene different from the one she'd imagined, but she
decided to play along as best she could. She crunched a biscotti,
hoping that she might avoid any direct questions if her mouth was
full.

"And Bonnie. Is she still living in Toronto?" Marc asked.

"Oh no. She lives in British Columbia now. A little town on the
Sunshine Coast. I still get letters and cards from her. I think it's
difficult for her to come here, to this house. She and Hayley were
always underfoot when they were growing up. Too many memories
now. Some days I feel her spirit fills the rooms to overflowing. Other
days, the house is desolate. I think poor Bonnie feels only the deso-
lation."

Agatha's voice, when she talked about Hayley, was deceptively
calm, but she addressed Lily in gentler tones and with an apparently genuine interest.

"Tell me, dear, how did you meet Jeanine?"

Lily's cup rattled on her saucer.

Marc saved her. "Actually, I found Lily on my own. Lucky for me. Jeanine is looking forward to meeting her."

Lily tried not to stare at Marc, and smiled wanly.

"Tell me, did you grow up in Toronto?"

"Yes. I'm an only child. There was just my mother and me. She died several years ago."

There. She had given Marc his opening to talk about Marie and the network and she would wait to see what he did with it. But it was Agatha who continued.

"And what of your father? You must forgive an old woman, my dear. I find I'm curious about people's lives these days."

"I don't mind. My father left before I was born."

"I see. Perhaps that explains your insights about Hayley. That, and your photographer's eye, of course. Her father and I divorced when she was just an infant. So she, too, was an only child with a single parent. I think she always felt the gap."

"Oh, but it isn't always a hardship to have only one parent. I adored my mother. And Hayley had Bonnie, too. She sounds like a sister."

"Yes. There was always Bonnie. Her parents struggled financially and I tried to help. She was like one of the family. I miss her."

Lily thought Marc must have nodded off for the last few minutes, but finally he spoke.

"Agatha, thank you for seeing us. I wonder, before we go, if I might ask you something rather, well, unusual. I hope it isn't too painful."

"Of course. What is it?"

"Around the time of the Mahoney case, perhaps a few months afterward, did anyone ever approach you about a network for helping women in danger?"

"You mean a women's shelter? I'm on several boards."

"No, not exactly a shelter. This would be more of an underground network of the sort you sometimes hear about operating in the States. Hiding women and children. That sort of network. Someone did approach my parents and I wondered if anything like that had ever happened to you. Or Hayley or Bonnie."

"No. Nothing. But then, as you might well remember, Hayley and Bonnie's identities were kept from the public. They were prevented from testifying. If anyone had asked, I don't mind telling you I would have said yes."

Marc smiled. "I believe you would have, Agatha. Might I ask you, since you are involved with women's shelters, to let me know if you hear anything? I'll leave you Lily's phone number."

Agatha raised an eyebrow. "Lily's?"

"Yes. I'm visiting for awhile."

"I see. And this network, it's important to you?"

"I'd like to contact them, yes. I — we — would be very discreet."

He rose to leave, effectively cutting off any more questions, and Lily, in a daze, rose with him.

"Please," Agatha said. "Before you go, I'd just like to show Lily the garden. And Marc, I've a book of poems here that was one of Hayley's favourites. She'd have wanted you to have it."

She went first to the bookshelf, taking down a slim edition of poetry by Pablo Neruda. As she handed it to Marc, Lily couldn't help but notice that their hands touched. The look that passed between the two was so intimate, she suddenly felt an intruder.

Lily turned away and stepped into the garden, still lit in splashes by the last rays of the dying sun. In a moment, Agatha joined her and the two women looked back at Marc sitting in the shadowed room, the book held tenderly in his hands while he slowly turned the pages.

Agatha reached out, placing a hand on Lily's arm. Her skin was dry and warm, her touch as soft as the flowers that surrounded them.

"Marc's a good man, Lily. Kind. You should go to France."

"Yes, well, someday perhaps."

"I've enjoyed meeting you. You remind me of Hayley, you know, before the trauma. Though I dare say you're much smarter. She was a sweet girl once, but not very clever. What you saw in her, the struggle, the selfishness — that only possessed her at the end. She just couldn't find the courage to reinvent her life. Thank you for being honest with me about the portrait."

A few minutes later, during the drive back to Birch Avenue, Lily turned to Marc.

"What was that all about? Why didn't you tell her about Marie?"

"I just couldn't. Not after hearing about Hayley. More violence, more death. I just couldn't. She seemed so frail."

"She looked strong as an ox to me. And why did you hint that we had a personal relationship? I thought I was coming along to play the part of the damsel in distress."

"I changed my mind. Don't you think Agatha has had enough distress in her life?"

Suddenly it all made sense to Lily: Agatha's initial coolness to Marc, the odd feeling she'd had that there was a subtext to their words that she couldn't read. The shocking way Agatha had imparted the circumstances of Hayley's death.

"Oh, Marc. I should have realized. You had an affair with Hayley, didn't you?"

"Yes."

Lily felt a surprising flicker of jealousy and pushed it aside quickly. "And Agatha Quinn wanted to punish you a little."

"It's okay. The relationship ended badly. My fault. At least I know Agatha has forgiven me."

"She has?"

"Sure. She gave me the Neruda book. Hayley was bored by poetry, but Agatha always loved it."

"Well, I can't help but wish she'd given us more," Lily complained. "I don't mean to be selfish, but we've come to another dead end with the network. It seemed such a promising lead."

"Don't give up yet. If she asks her contacts, she may turn up something after all. An elderly woman asking questions has to be less threatening than Ben and I poking around. We're the wrong gender."

Unamused, Lily kept her eyes on the road, but she could feel Marc studying her.

"Hey, are you okay? Nothing's happened, has it? You haven't seen him?"

"Nothing's happened. Everything's changed. Sorry. It's just that I don't know how I feel about your living in my house. Not you — I mean the reason why you're here. And I can't help thinking that we're running out of time. Don't you feel it too?"

Marc reached over and gently touched the back of Lily's neck.

"I do, Lily Ross. I do."

Jan Rehner

Tuesday, July 27, Toronto

Eva had trained herself to be a light sleeper. She answered the phone on the first ring, instantly alert.

"Yes?"

"We need a meeting. Safe house number one. In an hour?"

"I'll be there."

"Best to jog, I think. No cars, please."

She waited for the click and the dial tone, then stepped into the shower. Her skin tingled, and she shivered in the cold spray. Meetings were rare, safe house number one a code not only for place but for caution. There must be danger, but for whom? For her? For Kathleen?

She twisted her wet hair into a knot and pulled on her jogging clothes, then listened at her door before opening it. The building was still, no one else stirring yet.

Once outside, she began to run smoothly. Then, glancing at her watch, she adjusted her stride. She shouldn't arrive too early. She would walk the last few blocks to cool down, regulate her breathing. Occasionally, she swung her head around in a careful surveillance, but the streets were unnervingly quiet.

Eventually, she slowed down, easing into a steady walk. A few blocks from the house she found a tree to lean her forearms against, stretching out her calf muscles and checking behind her. No one was following her, but she wouldn't feel easy until she knew where Abbott was.

Without knocking, she slipped into the house through a side entrance that lead into the kitchen, then up the stairs to the right, to the study that served as the meeting room. The door was already partially open.

There were two women in the room, both strangers to Eva. She nodded and settled into an armchair by the fireplace. There would be no introductions. The members of the network were, for the most part, content to remain unknown to one another, their efforts coordinated by a central organizer. Still, Eva sensed that the women in the room must be close to the heart of operations. She could guess little about their lives or occupations from their neat, tailored clothes, though clearly neither had jogged here, and, having seen no cars or bicycles in the drive, she speculated that they must have come from close by, or perhaps were even staying in the safe house. For the first time, she wondered with alarm if the network itself might be in danger.

She shifted her position in the chair to relieve some of the tension she was feeling and, by so doing, drew the other women's eyes to her. They smiled, and she took some solace from the fact that they seemed relaxed.

From somewhere below the study, from deep in the house, she heard a clock strike 6:30, and the woman who had called her entered the room. Her handsome face, Eva thought, bore the stamp of fatigue, but her voice, when she spoke, was clear and resolute.

"Good morning. I've asked you here because I trust you most. We, this small circle, must trust each other as never before."

Eva bowed her head while the woman recounted the news of Marie Forrest's murder at the hands of Paul Abbott.

"There's more," the woman continued. "We don't know where Abbott is, but we do know that, at least temporarily, his target is not Kathleen. A young woman named Lily Ross can identify Abbott as the gunman she saw at the scene of the murder in Little Falls."

Eva was deeply shocked, but her face remained expressionless.

"Lily Ross knows she's possibly in great danger, but so far she hasn't gone to the police. Since she's been observed in the company of Marc Forrest, the son of the murdered woman, there's only one explanation for this behaviour. They are trying to contact the network. They, and a second man, Ben Kelter, have been asking questions that are potentially ruinous, especially to our efforts to provide runners with documentation of their new identities. Those of us in this room are especially vulnerable if the network is uncovered and the ... the full range of our activities is investigated."

"But why should they want to expose the network?" Eva demanded.

"We must assume, I think, that that isn't their intent, even though it may be the consequence. I believe that they're trying to contact us in order to warn Kathleen. They have no way of guessing how much we already know."

One of the other women spoke up: "Then there's nothing for it but to tell them. Let them know by some message that we are already alerted and looking after the Landers. No phones — hers might be tapped — and nothing by mail either, until we know where the Ross woman stands."

"Yes. I think that's our only recourse for the time being, despite the risk. We can be certain that Abbott is watching her, so the message will have to be delivered carefully. Our best way of finding him is to shadow Lily. In the meantime, his photograph will be distributed to each of you through the normal channels. Watch out for him. He knows that someone has been helping Kathleen. We mustn't underestimate him again. If you see him, contact me immediately."

She rose, signalling the end of the meeting. The two women unknown to Eva left quickly, but she lingered, knowing that the meeting was not over for her. When the house was silent again, her companion spoke softly.

"You understand who Lily Ross is?"

"I think so. That night in the Beaches ... she's the woman Amanda Martin spoke to, isn't she? It makes sense. The Mahoney connection is what lead her to the Forrests?"

"We can't be certain, but it's very likely. I do know that Amanda did not tell her everything."

"Still, she saw me, if only for a moment. She might recognize me, if she saw me again."

"Yes."

"And Marc Forrest. Can he protect her on his own? Does he even know what Abbott looks like?"

"He only has Lily's description of him."

Eva sighed. "They're amateurs. You need me to pick up Abbott's trail. There's no one else."

"Then we must find someone else. It's too dangerous for you otherwise, even in disguise. No one, least of all Lily Ross, must even suspect that you are connected with the network. You see that, don't you? And there is still Kathleen and the child to consider. Abbott will not have forgotten them. No, we can't abandon them, or Teresa, just yet."

"But who else can deliver the network's message? Who else can protect Lily Ross?"

The woman smiled. Eva's eyes widened in sudden comprehension.

"Yes. I thought you would see the inevitable, my dear. We must trust Marc. And, in the meantime, you must leave Lily to me."

Just MURDER

Reporters in the copy room were humming to the tune of yet another political scandal. They shouted to each other across cubicles, confirming details, pressing for new leads. Ben Kelter enjoyed the rush of a new scent as much as anyone, but was glad to be on the periphery this time. He was engaged in an investigation of his own, a little private research into the background of Agatha Quinn.

Marc's revelation about Hayley's connection to Mahoney had surprised him. The Quinn name was prominent in Toronto, yet he had heard not a whisper linking it to the earlier sexual assaults. Usually, wealth attracted gossip like a magnet, but not this time. The Quinns had once run a communications consortium with majority stocks in two newspapers, a radio station, local television cable, and several national magazines. Agatha Quinn's divorce had been rocky enough, and her ex-husband's business acumen slight enough, to shake consumer confidence. While she still controlled two magazines, *Designer's Edge* and *Children's Corner*, the rest had gone, and the Quinn name was now featured more often on the lists of charity foundations than on company mastheads. Still, choosing privacy and achieving it were quite different. The obituary of Hayley Quinn was a terse twelve lines, and not even Marc had seemed to know she had died. Ben could understand Marc's desire to protect the Quinn's past. He just hoped Marc cared as much about Lily's future.

Between the flurry around him and his own speculations, he almost didn't notice the persistent ringing of his phone.

"Ben Kelter here."

There was a long pause.

"Are you taping this?" A young man's voice.

"No."

"I saw you in the office on Monday. I heard you asking about tracking birth certificates, maybe creating new identities with them."

Ben sat up straight. "Who are you?"

"Someone who might be able to help. If I do, what's in it for me?"

"How about a sense of civic responsibility?"

"Fuck that."

"Okay, sorry. It's just that you've been watching too many American movies. I don't pay for information. But I'd really appreciate your help and I can protect your identity."

Ben held his breath. Like most reporters, he'd taken many calls like this over the course of his career. This was always the crucial moment. Either the caller would discover his conscience or the line would go dead. Or maybe he had some ulterior motive or personal grudge that would keep him talking.

"Okay, what the hell. Will you buy me a beer?"

"Sure."

"Meet me at the Madison. Early, around four-thirty this afternoon. Just ask for Frank. They know me there."

Ben drove west along Bloor Street, which formed one border of the part of the city dubbed the Annex, well known for its multicultural chic. Just north of the eclecticism of Bloor, Madison Avenue was a haven of architectural, ivy-covered harmony. Most of the red-brick, three-storey houses, with their graceful arches, had been built in the early 1900s and converted into boarding houses, fraternities, or residences for university students. One of these grand houses was now the Madison, a neighbourhood pub which blended perfectly with its surroundings, and whose dark red interior with multiple rooms still conveyed a sense of an old-fashioned home.

Ben parked his car near the one oddity on the street, a Tibetan Buddhist temple painted bright yellow with an even brighter red door. He stopped to study the golden circular carving on the temple's facade — a tree with two exotic animals on either side. He hoped it was symbolic of good fortune.

Four-thirty on a summer's afternoon guaranteed that the pub, frequented mostly by students, would be virtually deserted. It was. Ben glanced around the ground floor and spied a waitress wearing black lipstick and reading *Elle* slouched against the bar. He asked for Frank and she waved her hand laconically in the direction of the roof deck without once looking at him.

The temperature on the roof was searing. The lone man who had to be Frank had already removed his jacket and tie and was struggling with a sun umbrella. Wide cheekbones and a snub nose made his face look flat. His thinning, stringy hair looked like it had only a passing acquaintance with a bottle of shampoo.

Ben reached up to snap the umbrella into place and offered his hand.

"We could go inside," he coaxed. "It's air-conditioned."
Frank's handshake was predictably wet.
"No way. I spend most of my days in an office without windows. It's bad for you, you know, all that cold air blasting away. And think what it's doing to the ozone."

Ben wondered if maybe Frank didn't also think that shampoo was full of chemicals damaging to the environment, but he sat down cheerfully enough and ordered two Upper Canada lagers.

"So, Frank, you work in the Ministry of Human Resources?"

"Yeah. For seven years, issuing social insurance numbers. First, though, you gotta tell me what story you're working on. I've a family to think of."

Ben weighed his answer carefully. He could smell that Frank was bursting to tell him something. Would a hint of danger appeal to his sense of melodrama or send him scurrying to the nearest burrow?

"Leaks in security, Frank. Everybody knows the system is complex, unwieldy. So if too many cards are issued, the discrepancy in the numbers is put down to human error. Occasionally some fraud is uncovered, usually around health cards. I'm looking for specifics. Names. Maybe somebody on the inside who isn't making mistakes, but is issuing social insurance numbers deliberately, maybe even systematically."

Ben could tell he'd hit his target. Frank crouched forward and lowered his voice. "This could be dangerous, man. There could be some bogus company paying big wages to a whole series of fake social insurance numbers. You know, laundering money, that kind of scheme."

Ben maintained a poker expression and leaned in toward Frank. "Um, I think Revenue Canada might catch on to that fairly quickly. I'm thinking about something smaller scale than that. Maybe an illegal immigrant who needs a shortcut? I'm not talking terrorists or criminals here, Frank. They'd be scrutinized. Just ordinary folk who want to cut through the red tape. Could that be done?"

Frank smiled, a smug little stretch of the mouth across his teeth.
"You bet. Easy as pie, if you know how."

"And you know, Frank?"

"Sure. The trick is not to try to make up a bogus number. You need a real one. The first digit indicates the part of the country the number is issued in. The next seven digits are random, and the last digit is called a check digit. If you have a false number, the central computers in New Brunswick will spit it out, triggering an inquiry into citizenship status. Most illegals are caught this way. But if you have a Canadian birth certificate and one other piece of ID, you fill out a form, show up to answer a few questions, and you're done."

"Show up?"

"Yeah, in Toronto you show up. There's an interview, except in poky little towns."

"How tough is it?"

"Pretty simple, if you have the right accent and know a bit about your so-called hometown. Remember, the person's supposed to have been born here."

"And you've found some suspicious interviewees?"

"Not me. My supervisor. The bitch. Got some kind of grudge against men. You know the type?"

Ben shrugged and took out his pen and notebook. Frank would feel better if he looked like he was writing something down. He sketched one circle inside a larger one: that was Frank, a little cog in a big bureaucratic wheel. Then he drew a caveman with a club. That was Frank's gender politics. When he was finished doodling, he gave Frank a conspiratorial glance. "So, who's your boss?"

"Hang on, I'm gettin' there. Like I said, I've been suspicious, so I've been eavesdropping occasionally on some of her sessions. Normally, she wouldn't stoop to interviews, but there've been three women over the last six months. I traced their backgrounds. All three women had the same trail. Birth certificates issued to them in Ontario. All left Canada as young teenagers with their families. All went to different colleges in the States, which is why they never needed a number before. Some coincidence, eh?"

"It still seems pretty thin to me. There must be a few thousand people who'd fit that profile."

"Who all had their birth certificates mailed to the same address in Toronto?"

Ben was listening intently now. He knew enough to realize that if someone were working *inside* a social insurance office, handling the women's forms, the document deception would be virtually undetectable. Only someone with a personal vendetta, like Frank, would bother cross-checking birth certificates against mailing addresses.

"How do I find these women, then?"

"That's the best part," Frank gloated. "I have the mailing address." He reached under the table and opened up a somewhat battered briefcase, handing Ben a computer printout. "I figure, if I give you these three names, you can find out if these women are legit. If they're not — we blow the whistle on my boss."

Ben scanned the list, then folded the paper and slipped it into his notebook. "Thanks, Frank. I'll follow this up. Why don't you phone me again in a week or so?"

"That long?"

"Hey, we don't want to spook anybody."

"Yeah, okay. Thanks for the beer."

Ben suddenly felt generous and a bit mischievous. He flipped a twenty out of his wallet and placed it under his glass. "Have another." He raised a finger to his lips. "And remember, not a word to anyone." The hint of secrecy, he figured, would keep Frank happy for at least a week.

Ben strode away, feeling exultant. Three names, one address on Orchardview Boulevard. There were no Kathleens, but actual names would hardly matter if Frank had stumbled across the network. Downstairs, the pub was beginning to fill up with students hungry enough to take advantage of the Madison's free appetizers. Ben ignored them, making straight for his car and his cellphone. He needed to find Marc, right away.

He slid into the front seat and punched out the number. *C'mon, Marc, c'mon.* The answering machine clicked on. Ben swore and shifted into gear. Manoeuvring a quick U-turn, he headed off in the direction of Birch Avenue. He could drive there in ten minutes with any luck.

As Ben turned onto Dupont Street, his heart sank. Cars were backed up for two blocks waiting to make the left onto Avenue Road. He glanced at his watch — peak traffic time and the main downtown arteries were choked. He called Lily's number again. No answer. He drummed his fingers on the steering wheel and twisted around in his seat, but he was trapped. There was too much traffic even to think about another U-turn.

Thirty minutes later, sweaty and impatient, Ben pulled up in front of Lily's. He knocked and walked around to the back garden, but it was clear no one was home. He checked his own service, but Lily and Marc had left him no messages. What should he do now?

Wait? Go back to his office?

He made his decision quickly. He'd been a reporter too long to let go of a lead. He'd just drive by the address, check out the street. Then he'd return later with Marc to see if Kathleen was staying there. She would trust Marc. He tore a page from his notebook and scribbled a message: *Call me. Urgent.* He slipped the single page through the mail slot and returned to his car.

As he pulled out onto Yonge Street, a dark blue Oldsmobile slid into place behind him.

The traffic thinned out immediately once he turned off Yonge Street onto Orchardview. He wasn't sure what he'd been expecting, but the street surprised him nonetheless. It looked like a well-established neighbourhood, the kind where parents looked out for each other's kids and where strangers would be conspicuous. The street even had speed bumps to discourage drivers looking for short-cuts to Avenue Road. A couple of youngsters were skateboarding, a little red-headed girl was skipping rope, all under the eye of adults watering their tiny lawns or chatting on doorsteps. He parked the car several houses down from the address Frank had given him, but there wasn't much to see. The house was large, probably converted into condos or apartments. It wasn't exactly toney, but neither did it stand out from the single-dwelling homes as a rental. If Kathleen were indeed here, the network had chosen well. He waited a few minutes, watching while another car negotiated the speed bumps only to discover that the street ended in the parking lot of the North Toronto Arena. Slowly, the Oldsmobile turned around, retracing its route, and Ben followed it reluctantly. There was nothing more he could do without Marc.

He thought for a moment of returning to Lily's, but then decided on the office. It could be hours before she and Marc got his message, and, knowing his work habits, she would try reaching him there first. He'd grab a takeout supper and eat at his desk. He tried her number one last time, but his luck for the day had run out.

By 10:00, Ben had become philosophical. Lily must be on a shoot, and perhaps she had consented to let Marc trail along. Willful Lily, he thought. Maybe now, if they found Kathleen, she would consider her own safety. He tossed out the empty cartons of Chinese takeout and made his way to the parking lot.

He entered the half-light of a city night, never dark enough to reveal the stars. A few tattered clouds drifted across a pale moon. The lot was mostly empty, though a few of his colleagues, still hot on the trail of erring politicians, had not yet given up the chase for the comforts of home. He'd known some of them to work until dawn. On the edge of his awareness, he heard a car start up, but didn't turn around. Too late, his mind registered the surging sound of acceleration. He felt an explosion of shock and pain as the car hit him, tossing him into the air. For a moment, he floated in slow motion above the pavement, like a Chagall angel. Then, he lost consciousness, and neither felt nor heard his skull smashing as he hit the ground.

Thursday, July 29, Toronto

It was just past seven in the morning. Lily had promised to wake Marc in time for him to accompany her to a magazine shoot for a perfume ad. But she had changed her mind. One of the models working on the shoot was from Amanda Martin's agency. This might be Lily's only chance to ask about Amanda's sudden trip to Mexico without arousing suspicion. The Mahoney murder was a touchy subject around Marc. She decided an extra half-hour of sleep would do him good.

She tiptoed down the stairs. But when she entered the kitchen in search of coffee, she jumped involuntarily.

Marc was already there, leaning his weight nonchalantly against the counter, smiling at her over the rim of a coffee cup.

It was the smile that disarmed her. "Damn it, Marc. I thought you were still asleep."

"Good morning to you, too, Lily. Coffee?"

"Please."

"Where are we off to today?"

"We?"

Marc didn't bother to respond, choosing instead the implicit disapproval of silence.

His strategy worked. Her excuses spilled out less gracefully and less convincingly than she had planned. "It's a tough shoot. Lots of technical stuff around the lighting ... I sort of need, I mean, it's important to concentrate. There'll be lots of other people around.

You'll be in the way."

Sometimes, when he frowned, Lily thought, his dark eyebrows nearly met over the paler hazel eyes, giving him the wild look of a corsair. In fact, his face seemed to her an endless source of disguise, with expressions that shifted without warning from concern to restlessness to steady calm. She expected objections, but once again he baffled her, executing the perfect Gallic shrug.

"Well, if you're sure."

At once, Lily felt treacherous for lying. She also felt disappointed. In order not to meet his eyes, she finished her coffee in a gulp and began rinsing her cup in the sink.

"Well, I'd better get going," she said lamely.

"Do me a favour?"

"Sure."

"Be careful, okay?"

When Lily looked up, Marc put his hands on her shoulders and leaned forward to kiss her cheek. Then he was gone. Lily felt immeasurably cheered.

As she entered the Summerhill station and descended the long, steep flight of stairs to the platform, the air felt clammy on her skin and her nose twitched. A waft of mold emanated from the underground tunnels. Despite the glare of artificial lighting, the platform was gloomy. A dozen or so people slouched against the walls, while others leaned into the darkness as if their earnest expressions would pull the train faster along the tracks.

Standing with her back against the platform wall, Lily scrutinized their faces. Despite the impression of bravado she tried to give Marc and Ben, she was always looking now for the one face that wished to do her harm. In transit, she was vulnerable. She was careful not to let anyone stand behind her. One quick shove, with the train screaming into the station ... she checked her imagination, pushed away her fear. These were just ordinary commuters.

As she watched, a street woman shuffled slowly along the line of people, peddling a newspaper printed by the city's homeless community. Predictably, most people averted their eyes, embarrassed by her layers of ill-fitting clothes and floppy sneakers.

Lily smiled as the woman approached her, but she was too surprised or perhaps too tired to smile back. She looked old, her face

stained and creased by unkind weather, but Lily knew it was point-
less to guess at age. Some of the street people she'd asked to photograph in the past had looked old enough to be her grandparents and
had turned out to be her contemporaries. She held up the newspaper, and Lily nodded, handing her a few dollars in exchange.

"Thank you." Her voice was hoarse, either from too many ciga-
rettes or infrequent use. "This will give you somethin' to read on the
train. There's good stuff in there."

Lily was about to respond, but was momentarily distracted by the
rattling of the train as it raced into the station. She looked back to
wave as the doors opened, but the woman had already moved on,
oblivious to whatever scrap of human kindness Lily might have
offered her.

The brief exchange mildly depressed her, and she stuffed the
newspaper into the outer pocket of her tote bag. She would be
shooting an ad for perfume today, while the homeless scrounged for
a bar of soap. It was absurd to feel guilt, but the injustice bothered
her nonetheless. Once again, she recited to herself the litany of
practicality — she had bills to pay, and her independence to
preserve — but deep inside, she was increasingly convinced of the
aimlessness of her work and her failure to find a use for her creativ-
ity that would make a difference to people's lives.

Twenty minutes later, she was set up in a studio on Church Street,
ready to be professional, if not enthusiastic. But her mood seemed
to be contagious and the morning went badly. She had no chance to
speak to any of the models. One of the portable light stands fizzled
and popped its way into a stubborn dimness; the models were stiff
and cranky; the odour of perfume was so thick that she began to
sneeze, ruining a dozen shots with the involuntary jerking of her
body. She was not surprised when the representative from the perfume company called an early lunch.

She wandered outside in search of fresh air and the comfort of a
hot-dog vendor. Ben, she recalled with a smile, referred to hot dogs
as missiles of death, loaded with fat and additives of mysterious
origin. But she loved them anyway. After munching her way
through a foot of sausage and sauerkraut, her spirits were somewhat
restored. She was ready to put her own agenda into play. She looked
around for the woman from Model Fashion, Amanda's agency, and
finally found her drinking coffee at a sidewalk table.

"Hi. It's Julia, isn't it? Mind if I join you?"

"Sure, have a seat. No one else is likely to join us." Julia waved her hand back and forth in front of her face in response to Lily's quizzical expression. "God, can't you smell it?"

Lily tugged at the front of her T-shirt, sniffing, and then laughed. "Bloody awful, isn't it? If only I could convince the rep that we don't actually have to wear the perfume to take pictures of the bottle."

"Fat chance."

"Hmm ... I have an idea. Will you help?" Without waiting for an answer, Lily paid for Julia's caffeine lunch and hustled her back to the studio. As she expected, the representative was nowhere in sight. She scooped up the various bottles of Chanson d'Amour, hurrying Julia into the washroom.

"Here," she ordered. "Dump this stuff down the sink and help me fill up the bottles with water. The rep will never know, and we'll be able to breathe this afternoon."

Julia giggled like a schoolgirl — the first time, Lily thought, that she'd shown any spontaneous emotion since the shoot began. Her hopes for the afternoon began to rally. If she could gain Julia's trust, she might be more willing to talk about Amanda.

Lily decided to take the plunge. "It's always fun working with Model Fashion. I did a shoot not long ago with Amanda Martin. Do you know her?"

"Yeah, sure. We used to be pretty good friends."

"Used to be?"

Julia shrugged. "Amanda's been withdrawn, even cold, for a long time now. She changed, you know? Didn't want to go out anymore or hang out with us. We've all been a bit worried about her."

"Really? She seemed fine when I met her," Lily lied. "But maybe that explains why she never returned my calls. And then the agency told me she'd gone to Mexico. I thought it strange that she never told me she was leaving town. It was so sudden."

"No kidding. I was in the running for that job, and the next thing I knew Amanda was sending postcards. The whole set-up was crooked, if you ask me."

"Why crooked?"

"Oh, c'mon, Lily. You've been around agencies long enough to know how they work. First, the magazine says it's looking for a blonde, and goes through the whole process of screening portfolios, then suddenly it hires the raven-haired Amanda? Give me a break. Executives don't change their minds like that at the last second, especially for a location shoot. Not unless someone else is picking up the tab."

"Are you saying that someone *paid* some magazine to hire Amanda? What magazine? Couldn't someone just have seen her picture somewhere and decided her image was perfect for the layout? I know that's rare, but it happens."

Julia pouted, as if offended by Lily's naïveté. "That's what we're supposed to think, but the timing was way off. Look, when I submitted my portfolio to *Designer's Edge*, I was told by the agency that the shoot was scheduled for August. Then, boom. Amanda flies to a private villa? Sounds fishy to me."

It sounded odd to Lily, too. It was one thing to replace a model at the last minute, quite another to reschedule an entire crew. She remembered her first thought that Amanda had been whisked away because of her connection to Roger Mahoney, a thought she'd dismissed as being too far-fetched. Now she wasn't so sure.

The door handle to the washroom rattled loudly, and Julia jumped. "Uh-oh. Everyone's back. How are we going to explain this?" She held out the doctored bottles of perfume, looking exactly like a teenager who'd just been caught smoking in school.

"Leave it to me," Lily whispered, as she began stuffing her pockets with bottles. "You distract the rep."

"Right. And I'll tell Amanda to call you, shall I?"

"What?"

"Do you want her to call you? She got back two nights ago."

"She did? I mean, yes, of course, ask her to call." Lily hadn't expected this news at all. It made her clumsy.

"C'mon, hurry up," urged Julia. "I can hear them getting restless out there."

A few minutes later, while Lily fiddled needlessly with her cameras, she heard Julia swear.

"Damn! I've caught my stocking. It's ruined."

She tried not to laugh when Julia hiked up one side of her skirt to hip level and began peeling off the offending article. No one, much less the rep, was likely to notice the photographer in floppy khaki pants as she slipped the ornate little bottles back onto their velvet drop cloth.

"Okay, let's go," Lily called. "I'm ready."

The models took up their positions. The sales representative held up his hands and reached for the atomizer, spraying the room generously in their direction. Lily squeezed the shutter just as Julia tilted her head back in a burst of genuine laughter.

It was just past ten in the evening, when Lily, bone-weary, dragged herself to the subway. As she entered the train, finally able to relax, she allowed herself to speculate on Julia's insinuations about the Mexican shoot. They confirmed her own suspicions, stoking her curiosity. But now, if Amanda was home, she was sure she could lay that curiosity to rest. She wished she could talk to Marc again about the Mahoney murder, but she knew the subject would be taboo to him. Ben would listen, though. She could always turn to Ben.

The train jarred her from her thoughts as it clamoured into the next station, picking up a few more passengers. A middle-aged businessman sat down opposite her, avoiding eye contact by immediately opening up his newspaper. The action was contagious. Lily reached into the pocket of her tote bag and pulled out the thin paper she had bought that morning from the homeless woman. What had she said? *It will give you somethin' to read on the train.* Lily scanned the articles: an appeal from a community food bank; a close-up feature on a grandfather who volunteered at one of the soup kitchens; an editorial on an outspoken politician who consistently underplayed the problem of poverty in the city in order to gloss over his own mean-spirited record. "Gilding The Lily," it was called.

Her eyes widened. She blinked and looked again. She was right. The word *Lily* was underlined in yellow highlighter pen. She sat up straight and began flipping quickly through the remaining pages. The marked words and phrases leapt out at her. *Advise, danger, network, we know, safe, leave town.* Their order was jumbled, but she was sure they spelled out a message. She scrambled for a pen in her bag, and, after a few tries, she managed three short sentences that made sense to her: *Lily, we know the danger. Advise leave town for your own protection. K. is safe with the network.*

They'd done it. They'd contacted the network. She felt exultant, and also blind. The homeless woman. Lily had looked right into her face, but even with her keen visual memory, she couldn't have described her now. She'd seen what everyone sees in the homeless: weariness, blank hopelessness, a face mapped with the lines of despair. With chagrin, she knew she had looked and seen not a person with identifiable features, but a phenomenon, a social problem. She couldn't even be sure of her age or her weight. Who could say where the layers of clothes ended and a human form began? Who she was and how she had found Lily were still mysteries, but, for now, she only felt enormous relief.

The spectre of the gunman had lurked at the edge of her consciousness always, sometimes only a wavering shadow, sometimes looming and ominous. She felt a rush of freedom. She *could* leave town now, outdistance the shadow. She needn't stay if Kathleen had been warned, if she were already being sheltered by the network. Maybe Marc would still want her to go with him to France. She could meet Jeanine and take some personal time to assess what she wanted to do with her own career. And what she might want to do with Marc.

At Summerhill, her weariness forgotten, she jumped from the train, and took the platform stairs two at a time. Her cameras thumped uncomfortably against her side, but she felt nothing as she sprinted onto her street. She didn't slow down until she saw Marc sitting on her front stoop. Then she stopped dead.

His head was buried in his hands, his elbows resting on his knees. He looked more despondent than she had ever seen him, even after the death of Marie. He glanced up at the sound of her approach, and the grimness of his expression frightened her. She dropped her gear where she stood.

"What is it? What's wrong?" she murmured.

Marc looked at Lily for a long minute, silently rehearsing the words, which, once spoken, would burn forever. She was dusty and crumpled looking, her cheeks flushed from running, her hair in disarray. She stood, still as a statue, as he gathered her into his arms and whispered the words into her ear.

"No," she cried aloud. "Not Ben. My Ben."

Turning away, she stumbled forward a few steps. She heard a rushing sound like ocean waves. Then silence, and a darkness she could not begin to fathom.

The night was achingly long. Lily held Ben's note in her hand and waited for dawn. Despite the blanket Marc had wrapped around her, her fingers were icy. Her head, leaning against Marc's shoulder, throbbed. She felt the traces of tears on her cheeks, but she did not want to wipe them away. They were all she had left. Tears, and the crumpled note in her hand. She would not let Ben go until she knew what he had wanted to tell her.

She watched Marc's chest rise and fall, and thought only of Ben, still and cold. Sometime in the endless night, she and Marc had made love slowly and tenderly. She had luxuriated in his touch, memorized his skin and his breathing, sought oblivion in the rush of pleasure. Now, his dark hair against the pillow, his mouth parted, exhaling slowly, Marc looked at peace. She felt only bereft. Without speaking, she left the bed and turned on the shower. She couldn't cope with Marc right now. She thought she would scream if he said anything kind to her.

The water, hot and pulsing, could not wash away her fatigue. Her reflexes had slowed. She felt a great heaviness as if gravity were pulling her down with increased intensity. By the time she returned to the bedroom to dress, Marc was gone.

She sat on the bed's edge, surveying the abandoned clothes of the night before, the empty glasses, the smell of alcohol. Marc, she remembered, had found Ben's note too late, arriving at the downtown office amid the wailing of sirens and the drama of a hit and run. He never saw Ben. The police had cordoned off the parking lot. But the handful of people who had gathered knew the worst and, like people everywhere shaken by tragedy, had shared it. Numb with shock, she had managed to tell him all about the homeless woman and the coded newspaper, but with none of the joy she had anticipated. The words had tasted like ashes in her mouth. She was sick of danger, sick of death. She cursed the network. She cursed the blind cruelty that had taken Ben away.

Twenty minutes later, she entered the kitchen, managing to throw a weak smile in Marc's direction. "Sorry," she said, pretending to look for a coffee mug so as to avoid his eyes, "I don't mean to be rude."

"It's okay, Lily. Here, the paper came."

She took the *Toronto Press* and looked for the story she knew would be there:

Just MURDER

TORONTO PRESS REPORTER KILLED

Ben Kelter, a city reporter for twelve years, was struck last night by a hit-and-run driver while walking to his car in the Toronto Press parking lot on Front Street. Kelter left his office at approximately 10:00 p.m. and was killed minutes later. Several co-workers claim to have seen a black or dark blue sedan, possibly a mid-90s Oldsmobile, speeding away from the scene. Police say Kelter died on impact. They are treating the case as a homicide.

Lily clenched the paper in her hands. She opened her mouth to speak, but no words came.

"It's not necessarily what you think," Marc warned. "It could be a drunk driver, a weirdo, an old enemy with a grudge."

Lily stared at him mutinously, her grey eyes dark with anger.

"I'm going down to Ben's office. Now. Are you coming or not?"

"Of course I'm coming. But slow down. You'll do no good running off half-cocked."

She pushed past him on the way to the door, her expression stony.

All around her, the relentless business of putting out a daily newspaper flowed on. Ben's death was copy. She was grateful, at least, that the atmosphere was sombre, voices hushed and pensive. She nodded at the few faces she knew, a silent exchange of mutual sympathy, and turned away from the curious. Listlessly, she confronted the city editor and handed him Ben's note.

"This is Marc Forrest. As you can see, Ben was trying to reach us yesterday. I'd like permission to go through his files. Whatever he was trying to tell us, well, it might have a bearing on what happened."

The editor, a balding, normally amiable man named Crosby, eyed her suspiciously: "Were you working on something with Ben?"

"No," Marc interrupted. "Nothing like that. But we were friends, we'd like to know why he was trying to contact us."

The editor hesitated, unconvinced by Marc, but moved by Lily's disconsolate expression. "Look, Lily, I know you and Ben were tight. But, even if I wanted to, I couldn't give permission. The cops have already been here — we were up all night going through Ben's files, looking for some kind of lead. All his stuff's potential evidence now. Untouchable."

Lily sighed. If she'd stopped to think, she could have predicted this, but thinking right now seemed unbearable. She needed to stave off the inevitable with actions, even purposeless ones.

"I understand. I should have realized." She turned to leave, and then asked, her voice breaking slightly, "If the police are finished, would you mind if I just visited his desk? I'd like to say goodbye."

"Sure. Go ahead." The editor watched Lily and Marc begin to walk away, all of his well-trained instincts aroused. After a brief struggle with himself, he called out. "Hey, Lily, if you knew something, you'd tell me, right?"

She met his gaze without the slightest hesitation: "I promise. Ben was my mentor, remember?"

Marc took her elbow and guided her gently away. The short distance to Ben's desk was a gauntlet of eyes quickly lowered, hands reaching out to comfort, condolences murmured. There was nothing here as far as Marc could see, except for a lack of presence, a space drained of the life and intelligence that had once animated it. The files were gone, drawers gaping open, computer disks conspicuously absent. There were a few postcards taped to the wall, a scattering of pens, an uneven stack of paper beside the printer.

Lily touched the chair, picked up a pen with a chewed end, straightened the stack of paper, automatically riffling through its edges. She noticed one sheet had been folded and would not lie smooth. She flipped it over.

"Marc," she whispered urgently.

He looked up, surprised at the tenor of her voice.

"Hold me," she ordered. Under Crosby's nose, and under the cover of Marc's embrace, she deftly removed the single page and stuffed it down the front of her sundress.

Saturday, July 31, Toronto

Teresa's assignment was clear: warn Kathleen and get her and Suzy away from the Orchardview safe house. For the short term, her cottage was the perfect place. Remote, approachable only by water at the eastern edge of a small jewel of a lake, it offered sanctuary and plenty of room for Suzy to run. Running — that was the sticking point. Ever since Kathleen had vowed to confront her fears, especially those in the shape of Abbott, Teresa had noted incremental changes: her smile was wider, her eyes brighter, even her posture had altered, her spine straightening as if she had suddenly emerged from a room whose walls and ceiling had been pressing in upon her. Teresa dreaded seeing the dimming of those eyes. She hadn't yet found the courage to tell Kathleen that she had an ulterior agenda, that the trip to the cottage promised to Suzy was more than a simple weekend excursion.

Already the lies had multiplied. She'd had to tell Kathleen that the Jeep she'd borrowed was better suited to navigating dirt roads than her own car, that she should pack more clothes for the weekend than a person was ever likely to use in the Haliburton Highlands. Worse, Kathleen and Suzy trusted her completely, and Teresa felt keenly the falseness of her position. She was a solitary person, as unused to confidences as Kathleen had been, for reasons that were not dissimilar. Her growing affection for the people entrusted to her confused and unsettled her.

She hefted a duffle bag into the back of the Jeep and surveyed the street yet again. She saw nothing untoward, but she was jittery, anxious to be on the road. She would tell Kathleen en route, she decided, when there was no choice but to continue the journey. She glanced at her watch: 7:20 a.m. If they left now, they would miss the worst of the cottage traffic. She didn't want traffic. She needed empty roads where she could speed if necessary, where she could more easily spot anyone following them.

She opened the front door and hollered up the stairs. "Hey, c'mon, you two. The taxi's leaving." Her voice echoed in the stillness of the morning. She hoped it would wake the other tenants. They should know that the rest of the house was empty if anyone should come asking.

A huge beach ball with legs appeared at the top of the stairs, followed by Kathleen.

"Be careful, Suzy. Throw that down to Terri, and help me with these bags. Are you sure we need all this stuff?"

"You never know. It can get chilly at night." Teresa caught the ball and bundled her charges into the Jeep. "Buckle up, Suzy. It gets bouncy in the back seat. Right, we're off."

She headed for the 401 highway that skirted the top edge of the city, and turned east. From there, she would cut north on the 115 to Peterborough, and then straight up 28 to the old mining town of Bancroft where a series of county roads, some little more than gravelled paths, would lead them to the lake. It was not the most direct route, but it was one she knew, imprinted on her from childhood. She gave the maps she wouldn't need to Kathleen, hoping she would trace the route automatically, as tourists often do.

There were more cars on the road than Teresa had expected, part of the weekend migration from Toronto that is a hallmark of summer, but she made good time, cheered by Suzy's excitement. Just outside of Peterborough, where the Otonabee River curved under a wooden bridge, Teresa pulled the Jeep into a parking spot across from a small park. The air smelled of cut grass, trees, and water, fresher and sweeter than any city's.

"This is one of my favourite places," she confessed. "The town's called Lakefield — a mystery since it's built on a river — and it's famous for its ice-cream parlour." She pointed to a low, long white-frame building that stretched along the street at the foot of the bridge. Some of its paint was peeling, and a few roof shingles curled in the beating of the sun.

"It doesn't look famous," Kathleen laughed.

"Oh, it is. Trust me." The words were out of her mouth before Teresa knew what she was saying, and she lowered her eyes briefly, ashamed. If she really wanted Kathleen to trust her, she must tell her, tell her now that they were running again.

"Ice cream in the morning?" Suzy's eyes were round with delight.

"You bet. It's part of the tradition of going to the cottage. The Jeep just stops here of its own accord. I couldn't drive by, even if I wanted to. There are thirty kinds, all homemade. Cherry vanilla, chocolate and peanut butter, rum and raisin, butterscotch pecan — "

"Stop, already," Kathleen interrupted. "Let's go."

While mother and daughter ogled the selection, Teresa stood at the windows and watched the cars coming over the bridge. The spot was a renowned bottleneck for traffic and she studied the drivers as they slowed down for the single lane. Muscles tensed, her eyes followed the navy car with the fair-haired man. She saw his head turn away from the road for an instant when he passed the parked Jeep. A block further, he pulled to the side.

"Terri, Terri, guess what kind I'm having?" Suzy tugged at Teresa's shirt and she looked away from the road, startled. The little girl's eyes danced. "I can say it now. Pis – tash – i – o."

"Great, Suzy. That's great." Her eyes snapped back to the car. He was getting out. With relief, she started to laugh. He was too short, too heavy. It wasn't him.

The three sat in the park with their cones, Teresa trying to screw up her courage. But Suzy, normally only too eager to run to the swings or dangle from the monkey bars, was too excited about getting to the cottage to leave her mother's side. There was no opportunity. It would have to wait.

Back in the Jeep, Teresa talked about her childhood at the lake, and tried not to make her frequent checks in the rear-view mirror too obvious. She told them about bonfires on the beach, all her special hiding places — *that silver Honda, had she seen that before?* — the summer she had found an abandoned baby rabbit and nursed it back to health. There it was again, the sun just glinting off its windshield as it topped the hill behind her.

Just south of Bancroft, she turned onto a county road, a narrow stripe of asphalt which had buckled badly in places with the winter thaw. The woodlands were thick here, pressing close to the steep ditches that sheltered clumps of black-eyed Susans and Queen Anne's lace. The road twisted around huge outcroppings of stubborn rock, their edges softened by pale green lichen and patches of orange fireweed. She wouldn't be able to see very far behind her. But the woods were quiet. Her ears were her best defence now. They were almost there, but she wanted to be certain that the silver Honda wasn't following.

She found a small verge and squeezed the Jeep off the road.

"Sorry, I have to use the cover of the woods for a minute. Nature calls. I'll be right back."

She got out of the driver's seat quickly, leaving Kathleen to explain what all that meant to a puzzled Suzy. Teresa disappeared into the forest's edge and ran back along the road for about a hundred yards. Then she dropped to the ground and lay on her stomach, her head raised. She listened to the chirping of birds, the shrill vibrations of cicadas, but there was no car. She would have heard its motor, the whine of its wheels. Satisfied, she doubled back to the Jeep.

Twenty minutes later, her spirits soared when they reached the landing site and the safe barrier of the lake. There was no road into the cottage. If, by some fluke chance, Abbott managed to tail them, he could rent a boat as easily as she could. But the lake was small, with few visitors. He would be remembered. He'd never take the risk. She would tell Kathleen tonight, when she'd had a chance to fall in love with the place, while Suzy slept.

They loaded their clothes and supplies into the boat, Teresa steering into open water toward the calm bay on the eastern shore. From here, the cottage was still hidden from view by a long point of land, but soon they would round it, and it would shimmer on the horizon like a northern oasis.

By eight in the evening, Kathleen and Suzy began to yawn. It was the purity of the air, Teresa explained. Swallowing it in great gulps, along with a bucket or two of lake water during an afternoon's swimming, always made one sleepy. They ate a leisurely supper of cold chicken and fruit, Teresa promising Suzy a fire on the beach the next night. Teresa had watched for boats while they were playing in the water, but had seen only a few fishermen. Still, once or twice, she'd caught the glint of sun off glass in the distance. A birdwatcher's binoculars? Probably, but a bonfire would be a beacon, and for the first night at least, she wanted the velvety blackness of a forest. By 10:00, Suzy's head was definitely nodding, and she reluctantly agreed to bedtime stories and a bunk bed. While Kathleen went to settle her down, Teresa stepped quietly into the soft night.

The quality of darkness was always a surprise. High overhead, stars crowded the sky, and a heavy orange moon, a hunter's moon. Teresa mused, was reflected in the smooth mirror of the lake's surface. The cottage itself, set back amid a circle of towering pines, was deep in shadow, the pale light from its windows penetrating only a few feet.

Teresa leaned against the grey shingle of the western wall and listened. She heard the distinctive call of a whippoorwill and, far off in the distance, the eerie laughter of loons. Whoever had said the countryside is quiet at night had always lived in the city. Twigs snapped. Small animals skittered through dry leaves. The trees whispered. The forest was alive.

She walked around to the back of the cottage and peered in briefly at Kathleen, curled up in a chair with a blanket and a book. It was time. She completed her circle of the building and reached out for the door, then froze. *What was that?* Instinctively, she dropped into a crouch, out of the light, and crept back to the end wall of the cottage. She was certain she'd heard a splash, the sound magnified by the stillness of the water. It was too clumsy for a fish; too loud, too suddenly choked-off, for the slap of a beaver's tail. Motionless, she studied the southern shore, scarcely blinking. Whatever had caused the splash, she knew, would be further away than the sound had seemed. She tried to calculate distance, and held her breath. A shadow moved. Almost imperceptibly, it glided away from the water's edge and melted into the trees.

There was no time to think. He could only be a quarter of a mile or so away. She whirled back to the door, opened it noiselessly and approached Kathleen. Raising her finger to her lips, she removed the book from Kathleen's hands.

"Listen to me," she urged, her voice low and even. "He's found us, Abbott. You must get Suzy away. Do you understand?"

"Where?" Kathleen whispered, her body now fully alert.

"No more than a quarter of a mile away. We have to move quick-ly. Do as I say."

She nodded.

"Get into your jeans and hiking boots. Suzy, too. Follow the northern shore. Stay as close to the trees as you can. It's about five miles back to the landing. We can't risk the boat. Can you make it?"

"Yes. But I'll stay. I'll face him."

Teresa gripped Kathleen's arms, the strength in her hands causing her to wince.

"Don't be stupid. He'll kill you, all of us. This isn't the place. Get Suzy ready, fast. Tell her anything you like. Just keep her quiet."

Kathleen disappeared into the bedroom while Teresa extinguished the oil lamps and grabbed her duffle bag. She found the flashlight, pulled black tights and a black sweatshirt over her top and shorts, scribbled an address on a piece of paper, stuffed the Walther P99 automatic into her waistband. She looked up when Kathleen and Suzy entered the room, their eyes dark and serious against pale faces.

Teresa hugged Suzy, giving her her best smile. "You'll be fine. Just follow Mommy, okay? Quiet as a mouse?"

The little girl nodded.

"Go down to the little spring, the one at the edge of the lake that I showed you today, you remember? Good girl. Follow the beach, but don't let your feet slip into the water. You'll hear Mommy and me talking and laughing for a minute and then Mommy will join you. Off you go." She took Suzy's hand, giving it a final squeeze, and gently opened the door for her. Then she turned to Kathleen.

"Look, Abbott's sure to have disabled the Jeep. When you get to the landing, go to Tom's cottage, where we rented the boat. Tell him the outboard motor's dead. Tell him Suzy's sick and he'll drive you back to the city. Go to this address." She stuffed the piece of paper into Kathleen's hand. "Don't lose this. Are you ready?"

"You're not coming with us." A flat statement, not a question.

"I'm going to try to lead him away from the north shore. Don't worry. Even in the pitch dark, I know every hollow, every cave, every trail. With luck, I'll get him good and lost. But first, I need your help. Follow my lead. Don't sound scared, whatever you do."

The two women left the cottage, locking the door behind them. Teresa led the way onto the long skinny dock that jutted out into the lake. She picked up several flat stones and began skipping them noisily into the lake. Mercilessly, the moon silhouetted their figures and she prayed that Abbott didn't have a rifle. She had weighed the danger of being seen against what she knew of his obsession and cruelty. She was betting her life, and Kathleen's, that he wouldn't kill from a distance.

"Isn't it a beautiful night?" Her voice echoed in the still air, and she nodded encouragement to Kathleen.

"I — I've never seen so many stars." Apart from the initial stutter, her voice was strong, easily recognizable.

"That's a city girl for you." Teresa laughed. "Hey, I know a great place to see the stars from — there's a hill, just behind the cottage. C'mon. Follow me."

Behind the cottage, where the moon could not penetrate the interlocking pine boughs, they crashed around in the bush for a minute or two. Then Teresa pushed Kathleen away and waited until she vanished into the trees. She flicked on the flashlight, pointing an arc of light in the direction she wanted to go.

"This way, clumsy," she shouted.

She kept the beam steady, occasionally swinging it behind her, as if guiding a friend, hoping it would snare the enemy instead. She tried to listen for him between the deliberate noise of her own footsteps. Finally, she thought she heard him, to her right and coming closer. She doused the light, stooping quickly to bury it under a fall of needles at the foot of a tree. She didn't need it, and she wanted Abbott to have no advantage. She began slowly to change direction, slanting away from the footpath, allowing her feet to follow a slide of land that led to a deep, grassy hollow. She knew a place she could hide there, and wait.

Carefully, meticulously, she lifted a spray of brambles from the mouth of the low cave and crawled inside, crossing her fingers that no bush animal — a raccoon or a fox — had already claimed it for a lair. She feared their noise more than their bite. She flipped onto her stomach, fingering the gun in her right hand. Through the screen of brambles, she watched for him.

She wanted to kill him. She felt not the slightest compunction. It would be so easy. A single blast, ripping through the blackness. But she knew the sound would terrify Kathleen and Suzy, toll the death knell of the network. She couldn't be anonymous here, not in this place hallowed by her childhood.

She heard him before she saw him. He twisted his ankle at the foot of the slide and swore softly. She opened her mouth and breathed shallowly. She watched his feet pass the mouth of the cave. Several steps beyond her he stopped. They were not four yards apart, and she could hear him trying to catch his breath, his feet now circling as he strained to penetrate the gloom. Suddenly, close by, she heard the shriek of a field mouse and the flapping of an owl's wings. The sound spooked him and he crouched instinctively. Now, if he turned, they would be at eye level. He would see her. She could feel the gun in her hand, slick from her own sweat.

Slowly, he rose. She heard him begin to move away. He was making for the path again. She pressed her forehead against the ground and forced herself to wait. She had maybe ten minutes, no more. Then he would begin to circle back to the cottage, convinced that he had lost them. She stretched her muscles, willing the tension to leave them. She needed to be as supple and graceful as a cat now.

She removed her boots and edged her way out of the cave in her stockinged feet, following the soft grass to the end of the hollow. There, she took a full knee-bend and swung herself up to a low branch. Her hands gripping the bark, she swayed back and forth several times, then twisted her body up and onto the path above her. Speed was everything now. She ran as fast as she could.

At the lake's edge, she stripped down to her bare skin, folding the few clothes she would need into the black sweatshirt, making a tight roll she could tie around her waist. She hesitated, but the gun would be useless. She put her hand under the water and let go, watching the gun sink quickly to the bottom. She waded to the back of the boat and began unscrewing the motor. Her wet fingers slipped on the bolts. She tried again. She could hear him now, pounding along the trail.

Any moment he would see her. At last the bolts turned, and with a gulp of air, she heaved the motor free, dragging it along with her as she ducked underwater, her feet kicking furiously. A hundred yards from shore, deep enough she thought, she let the motor go and surfaced. The boat would be of little use to Abbott now. She heard him bellow as he rushed toward the dock.

She turned away and dove again. The landing site was only three miles distant across the lake, much faster than by shore. She was a strong swimmer. The water welcomed, invigorated her, cold and silky, caressing her naked skin. Still underwater, she lifted one hand to her head, pulling off the dark, long-haired wig, her own hair spilling free, floating in the currents of her movement like a spray of golden filaments. Her head broke the surface and she settled into a smooth, steady stoke. He couldn't catch her now. Rosa. Teresa. Eva. She smiled, abandoning herself to the pleasurable rhythm of a midnight swim.

Tuesday, August 3, Toronto

Lily sat on her front stoop with a cup of coffee, watching the neighbourhood children playing on the swings in the park opposite her. Their squeals of laughter comforted her after the pressing silence of Ben's funeral. She felt as if she had crossed a border in her own life, entering a foreign territory where different rules applied. It would be so easy to drift in this strange place, to swing, without care, back and forth like the children, letting someone else guide her motion. But drifting was no longer an option for Lily. Ben's murder had galvanized her. She was determined to make her own choices, determined to find her own answers to the questions surrounding the network and the gunman.

Behind her, from inside the house, she heard the phone ring, and Marc's voice screening her calls. Lily found herself thinking more and more about Marc, but her thoughts remained tangled and uncertain. Sometimes, the sight of him caught in her throat. She loved his strong arms, his smell, his sad hazel eyes. In those moments, she opened to him, longing for his salty taste, feeling her body melt and her blood quicken. However it had begun, what they shared was more than comfort now. Lily felt lit up around him, glowing as if dipped in some bright substance.

At other times, Marc seemed more restless than ever, gone from the house for long stretches of time and evasive about where he'd been if she asked. Perhaps he needed mending, too. Perhaps he had his own regrets. But Lily had overheard murmured conversations and urgent whispers. She worried whether she could trust him, and about how much or how little he knew.

It was time to find out.

He was inside, sitting on the sofa, pretending to read the morning paper. She settled herself beside him, and peered over the top of the newspaper.

"I think we should talk."

The paper slid to the floor as Marc turned to face her, his eyes betraying only a hint of frustration.

"What more is there to say, Lily? We know from the notes you found in Ben's office that he somehow found Kathleen. We've agreed that he probably saw her, or at least went to that address. If that was the reason for his death, there are only two possibilities: the network itself, or the gunman who was following him instead of us. I don't believe the network would do such a thing. They've assured you that Kathleen is safe, or at least *was* safe. They seem concerned for *your* safety. That's it, unless I've missed something. Have you decided what you want to do next?"

Lily bit her lower lip, and tried again.

"It's not just me anymore, it's us. Isn't it? Whatever we've gotten involved in affects both of us, doesn't it?"

"It does. But I don't see how to move forward. Do you have any suggestions?"

"Two. Go to see Agatha Quinn, and then go to the police."

"Agatha? Whatever for?"

"Because there's something else I learned from Ben's notes. Agatha

Quinn owns *Designer's Edge*. That's the magazine that hired Amanda Martin. Don't you see? She was directly involved in Amanda's arranged trip to Mexico. Maybe even in Mahoney's murder."

Marc stiffened. "Hold on. That's a huge leap to make."

"Is it? I think she lied to us. We go to see her, ask her about the network, and then, suddenly, they make contact with me? I don't believe in coincidences. She's had something to hide all along."

"But, Lily, suppose you're wrong? I don't want Agatha hurt. She's been through enough. And why go to the police now, after all this time?"

"It's a risk, but I don't think I'm wrong. And we can't handle this on our own any longer. We need the police. By not telling the story, we're protecting the gunman at least as much as we're protecting Kathleen and the network. If we go to Agatha first, if she is involved, she has time to warn the network."

Marc turned away from her. He stood up, paced, and sat down again.

"Lily, I'm not sure every story *should* be told."

Lily felt her throat constrict. She flinched as if he had slapped her. "So Ben told you about the last story I wrote. He told you about the woman who died after I revealed her identity?"

"He didn't describe it like that. And he only told me because I pressed him. I wanted to know why you wouldn't — or couldn't — write anymore. Why you were so defensive."

"Great. So now you know. But it's got nothing to do with this. What's wrong? Don't you want your mother's killer caught?"

"Of course. But I don't want her to have died in vain, either. What about the lifeline we might be putting in jeopardy? There could be exposed identities, even deportations. Women who are in the midst of rebuilding their lives could be in peril again."

"I'll admit that's a weak point. But what choice do we have? Two people are dead. And the gunman's still out there. What if — "

"You're right," he murmured. "I'm as scared as you are. I'll call Agatha. I'll tell her it's urgent."

Once again, Lily and Marc stood before the black double doors of Agatha Quinn's house in Rosedale. It was late, past ten in the evening, and the courtyard was plunged in shadow. Lily noticed that the outdoor lights had been switched off. The house looked more imposing than ever, and unwelcoming. *Probably*, she thought, *a sign of Agatha's pique at Marc's insistence over the phone.*

In an instant, the courtyard was flooded in light so blinding that Lily instinctively shut her eyes. When she opened them, Agatha Quinn was standing in the open doorway regarding them steadily. She greeted them with imperturbable calm and asked them to follow her. This time, she did not lead them to the gorgeous blue and green silk room that stretched along the back of the house, but to a small library just off the foyer. There were no windows, but the soft rose of the walls gave the room a warm glow, enhanced by a scattering of Tiffany table lamps in shades of ruby and gold.

A cosy grouping of velvety pink chairs and sofa was tucked into one corner. Agatha invited them to sit and abruptly left the room. Disconcerted, Lily raised an eyebrow at Marc. His response was a frown which spoke volumes. Lily began to fidget nervously. Unaccountably, she felt — what was that old expression her mother used to use? — a pricking of the thumbs? If Agatha were deliberately trying to throw them off balance, her tactics had certainly succeeded.

An edgy silence settled upon them, and then, suddenly, Lily thought she heard a muffled conversation in the hallway. She couldn't distinguish the voices, but thought immediately that Agatha must have other guests. Perhaps her cool demeanour was simply annoyance at having been interrupted in the midst of some social occasion.

A moment later, Agatha entered the library, carrying a tray with steaming mugs. She smiled at them for the first time, her manners impeccable. "Please join me," she invited, setting the tray down on an ormolu table. "Even in midsummer, I find a cup of hot milk quite soothing. There's some brandy, if you'd like to add some."

Lily and Marc both declined, while Agatha took up her own drink and curled up on the sofa. In a long brown dress and paisley shawl, she looked elegant, and completely relaxed. She wore her hair in a simple chignon, held in place with a tortoiseshell comb. The subdued lighting helped to smooth her face of wrinkles, giving her an aura of youthful vulnerability. Lily began to dread their mission.

Marc cleared his throat. Lily clenched her hands, expecting him to speak. But it was Agatha's voice she heard.

"Marc, dear, before you start, let me say how sorry I am, for both of you, for your loss. Mr. Kelter was a fine, decent man. I didn't know him personally, of course. But I had read his articles about Jeanine and the work she was doing. He had a rare empathy. I wanted to attend the memorial service, and thought to speak to you both then, but I didn't like to intrude on your privacy."

Lily's heart sank. In contrast to this kindness, she and Marc were ready to ride roughshod over Agatha's feelings. *Thank you so much, Ms. Quinn, and by the way, we think you lied to us.* She could think of nothing to say to help Marc. She felt, rather than saw, his distress. She tried not to squirm in her chair.

"Oh, dear. I can see I've made you uncomfortable. Tell me, Lily, is there any chance you might go to France? A holiday would be so good for both of you right now."

"I — we — no. Not just yet."

"You're sure? You won't reconsider?"

Agatha looked at Marc. Marc looked at Lily. Suddenly, she felt as if the alliances in the room had subtly shifted, leaving her all alone. She felt a flicker of anger and her resolve strengthened.

"No, I must stay here. For a while. I've come here to ask you — "

Her voice trailed off when Agatha raised her hand in a silencing gesture.

"There's no need to explain yourself, my dear. No need. You must be very insulted that I doubted you both, but you'll understand I had to be discreet. Now, there's someone here I'd like you to see. Do come in, Kathleen."

A slight woman with thick, shoulder-length auburn hair and green eyes materialized in the doorway. She looked forlorn and, at the same time, resolute, as if her rigid posture was an act of sheer will. When she saw Marc, she lowered her eyes.

"Oh, Marc ... your mother. I've only just learned ... "

He reached Kathleen in two strides and gathered her into his arms.

"Suzy?" he asked.

Lily watched from the sidelines and saw how Kathleen's smile transformed her face. It became luminous, as if lit up from somewhere deep inside. In that instant, she was beautiful, almost ethereal.

"She's upstairs, sound asleep." She turned to Lily, the smile vanishing as suddenly as it had appeared. The light in her eyes died, and her face became plainer, more intense. "You must be Lily Ross. Forgive me. I've put you in terrible danger."

"Nonsense." Agatha almost shouted the word from her perch on the sofa. "Come and sit down, all of you. The man's a murderer, Kathleen. You've done nothing to be ashamed of. Now, who would like some brandy?"

This time all three guests nodded their assent. Agatha rose and opened a cabinet, turning to face them with the bottle in her hand. "It's time we started working together," she announced. "Abbott must be stopped."

She poured the cognac into four large snifters, and they raised their glasses together, somewhat self-consciously.

Abbott. The gunman had a name. Lily felt slightly dizzy, but not from the brandy.

"I'm ready to go to the police," she offered, "now that Kathleen and Suzy are safe. I can testify. I can put Abbott at the scene of Marie's murder. I want him to pay for Ben's death."

She heard Kathleen gasp, saw her shoulders stiffen.

Marc studied the paintings on the wall behind her.

Only Agatha regarded Lily steadily. "That may not be wise, dear."

"Why ever not? You said yourself he must be stopped."

"Indeed. But do you think the police can stop him? Ask Kathleen. Do you think justice will be done? Ask Marc about Jeanine. Ask me. This murderer is powerful, Lily, and held in high social esteem. He has resources, lots of them, and people he pays well to be loyal. He can buy alibis. He can buy justice. Experience has taught me that the laws will work in his favour."

"I don't believe this. Just because you think he can't be convicted, you're all doing nothing to stop him?"

"Ah. I didn't say that. Listen. We're not without resources, either. I've an idea or two. They're unethical and certainly illegal. But if they work, they will help us keep the network safe, and the others like Kathleen and Suzy safe a little longer. Will you grant us that time, Lily? I'm counting on you to play your part."

Lily hesitated while everyone else in the room seemed to hold their breath. Perhaps she owed it to them to listen. She was hardly the only one who had suffered loss. Slowly, she nodded her head.

Agatha looked from one face to another. Seeing and hearing no dissent, she began to sketch out a plan.

Tuesday, August 3, Toronto

Abbott was a chess player. A very good chess player. Though winning was his sole reason for playing, he took some pleasure in the subtleties of the game, the unexpected move, the false retreat that was really a trap. He preferred the clever opponent who could do battle with him to the careless opponent who surrendered too quickly. The greater the challenge of the game, the deeper the satisfaction of the final move, the master stroke.

But the game had taken a twist.

No sooner had he eliminated one piece from the board than another was introduced. A woman. It had been a mistake to underestimate her. Having been clever enough to find her, he had thought that Kathleen was vulnerable, so far away from the city, so alone in that godforsaken wilderness with only the child and that woman to protect her. But it had been a trap, a ruse designed to humiliate him.

Check, but not checkmate.

They were clever, but they lacked mettle.

He would not make the same blunder. Given the opportunity, he would not hesitate to kill. Kathleen had made her choice and there was little they, or anybody else, could do to save her now.

Abbott settled back on a bench in an urban square ringed with tall buildings and appraised his situation. Marc Forrest was perhaps 100 metres away from him, unaware that he had been followed. It was a fine morning with lots of people about, lots of men and women in business attire, seated singly or in small groups chatting and people-watching. Beside the square was a large concert hall that reminded Abbott of an upside-down glass dish with curved sides. Tourists strolling across the square aimed their cameras at it, or stopped in front of the splashy noise of the fountain. Forrest glanced around, probably even looked straight at him, but Abbott wasn't worried. Forrest wouldn't recognize him in sunglasses and a baseball cap. He wouldn't recognize him because, just like the reporter, he didn't expect to see him. He supposed that Abbott's focus was on the Ross woman, and that his own movements would be of little interest, except insofar as his absence from Birch Avenue would seem to leave her unguarded.

But Abbott had learned a great deal from watching and waiting. His one bold move, so swift and daring, taken so early in the game that it had caught them completely unawares, had given him an enormous advantage. He had information they didn't know he had.

The dull mind was predictable. It took flair and risk to gain an advantage. Weeks ago, Abbott had simply waited for Marc to leave the house on an errand. He hadn't needed much time. He'd entered the house in broad daylight, not in the stealthy still of the night as they were expecting. He only wanted to know if Kathleen were hiding there. If she wasn't, he would take Lily. He would trade.

But there had been no sign of Kathleen. No sign of Lily except for the locked room.

In a split-second, he had reassessed his choices. He could try to force the door, but anyone might be behind a door. Anything might happen if you gave your opponent the noisy warning of smashing a lock. Instead, Abbott had quickly scouted through the bedrooms and in the second one, usually a kind of study he supposed, he had rifled through the desk drawers and found a folder bearing the Forrest name. He glanced at its contents, a slow grin transforming his features. Fools got the luck they deserved, either good or bad. The clever man made his own luck.

Not all of the information in the folder made sense to him, but Ross' notes made an intriguing link between the reporter named Kelter, a woman named Jeanine Forrest, and a dead man named Mahoney. Abbott figured Marc Forrest was Jeanine's brother. Was he also her avenger? He wasn't sure yet how the Ross woman was involved or who Amanda Martin was, but he would find out. In the mean time, he'd learned that Kelter was a serious player and his decision to follow him had paid off. Eventually, Kelter had led him straight to a dead-end street where little Suzy Landers was skipping rope.

Abbott had read the newspaper accounts of Kelter's death with little concern. Sometimes, he knew, the cops kept information back to mislead suspects, but he didn't think there was any bluffing going on here. They had nothing. He'd ditched the car within an hour of the incident and it couldn't be traced to him.

Across the square, Forrest was glancing at his watch again, a sure sign that he was waiting for someone. Someone who was late?

Who were these people? How many were there? Of course he knew now that Kathleen was a liar and a conniver, but she had never given him even a hint of any connection to the Forrests, or any connections in Canada. He didn't like Canadians. Smug bastards. And too cautious by half. This was the part of the game that Abbott couldn't puzzle out. Why had Kelter been visiting government offices that dealt with immigration matters? Why hadn't Ross and Forrest come after him openly? Why had they hidden Kathleen in a separate house?

His lips thinned in distaste. Kathleen. The night at the lake was already blurring into nightmare punctuated only by snatches of sound, flashes of images. The slap of a pine branch across his cheek. The rifle shot of a snapping twig. Her laughter drifting through the dark. Her long legs, shining wet in the moonlight. His blind, plunging race along the shoreline, his eyes stinging with sweat, the taste of salt and blood in his mouth as he tried to swallow his rage. Soon, he promised himself, she would cry aloud, flutter like a small bird trapped in the rough cage of his hands, pressing and squeezing —

His head snapped up. Forrest was sitting at a table now, leaning forward, his dark hair almost touching the dark hair of the woman leaning toward him. Abbott cursed. Their conversation looked urgent, yet he could hear nothing. He could not risk moving closer.

He studied the woman. Her long hair shone blue-black in the sun. The smooth skin of her bare arms was golden. She placed a hand on Forrest's forearm. He covered her hand with his own. She nodded, and her hair glistened again with the motion. How long had they been talking? From which direction had she come?

Forrest swung a small backpack from his shoulder and took out a package, handing it to her. It was long and narrow, some sort of thick envelope. She smiled and slipped it into her purse.

Forrest looked at his watch again. He was nervous. He had been too long away from Lily. His intentions could not have been clearer had he written them out and handed them to Abbott, who waited for him to leave the square, to leave his path clear to the dark-haired woman.

But she rose first instead, tall and graceful, a black sundress floating to her ankles, a gaily patterned scarf of orange and red twisted around her waist. She began to stride away, but Abbott couldn't move.

Forrest was keeping watch. If Abbott stood up, if he so much as shifted position to watch her retreating figure, Forrest would spot him instantly. Abbott forced himself to turn his head away, to look in the opposite direction of Forrest and the woman.

His eyes caught a splash of orange and red. His heart thudded.

He could see her, a slowly disappearing shape perfectly reflected in the mirrored sides of the concert hall.

As soon as Forrest left, Abbott would know which direction to follow to pick up her trail. He had not the slightest doubt that he would find her and find out who she was.

Part Three

THE PLAN

Monday, August 9, New York

It was raining heavily. The plane stuttered a few times in the uncertain, electric skies. Kathleen couldn't be sure whether she was more nervous about the plane crashing or arriving. It was, to say the least, an unorthodox journey.

The plan had seemed logical, even compelling, in Agatha's study on that long night. They had all agreed. They would take the initiative away from Abbott. To act was a kind of relief from the weeks of waiting and watching, never certain where to look, or when. But almost a week had passed since then, five seemingly endless days. Time enough to begin to put the plan into action, but also time enough for doubts to rise like a low ground mist.

Kathleen shivered. She turned to her companion, who was pretending to read, for the second time, the airline magazine. She ignored his feeble ruse to seem preoccupied.

"This is crazy," she blurted out.

Marc immediately closed the magazine and stuffed it back into the seat pocket. He studied Kathleen's profile. She looked healthier than when he had first met her. The sun had freckled her nose, and she'd managed to gain a little weight. But there were still bluish smudges under her eyes, like faint bruises from sleepless nights. Would she be strong enough, he wondered, for what lay ahead? The plan wouldn't work unless she was convincing.

"Not crazy. Just a bit outrageous. Are you worried about leaving Suzy with Agatha?"

"No. It's not that. She's safer away from me now. I just wish we could have seen Terri before we left. Suzy trusts her."

Marc was equally sorry he hadn't seen Terri. The woman who had decoyed Abbott away from Kathleen and Suzy in the forest would have been worth meeting.

"Who is Terri, anyway?"

"Teresa Mordelli. A friend. She said she was a law student, but she obviously works for Agatha. How extensive is this network of hers?"

Marc shrugged. "She's wise not to tell us much. Who knows how many women she's protecting? And children, too. You know, the network reminds me a little of Maman's stories about the French Resistance — people then never knew much about each other, or about the overall design of the escape lines. It made it harder for the enemy to dismantle them. Who was it who said that three people could keep a secret only if two of them were dead?"

"Two dead. Lily is sure that Abbott killed her friend?"

"She is. We both are. Look, Kathleen, we've rehearsed this again and again. Agatha's plan is our best chance to end this. Are you up to it? I'll be with you every step of the way."

"Yes."

Marc reached for her hand and squeezed it. "We're going to stop him. No more running, no more killing."

Kathleen squeezed back. "No more." She tried, but her bravado stopped short of a smile.

The plane plunged into the clouds and nosed its way toward La Guardia.

Sloane stretched up on his tiptoes, then rocked back onto his heels. He repeated the motion until he found a comfortable rhythm. Tiptoe and heels. Tiptoe and heels. On the way up, he scanned the crowd of arriving passengers, looking for her. On the way down, he thought about why he knew her face. He'd watched it. He'd followed it. He'd photographed it. The memory still made him squirm. Inadvertently he'd been Abbott's tool — *a hired bloody hand*, Ruby had said with a little shake of her head — paid to hound a young woman. Well, he could make up for his error in judgement now. This time, Abbott was the target, and Sloane and Ruby were on the side of the angels. Roguish angels. He looked forward to playing his part with a kind of perverse glee.

He saw the auburn hair first and waved frantically.

"Over here, Ms. Landers. I'll be right there for your luggage."

He straightened out his uniform and remembered to remove his cap. He was rather proud of the long black jacket and trousers which camouflaged some of his middle-aged bulges. He almost whistled as he elbowed his way toward her.

She looked good. No smile, but perhaps that was too much to hope for. He thrust out his hand.

"Sloane's the name, Ms. Landers. Your chauffeur."

For a moment she just stared at him, his hand dangling awkwardly in mid-air. She knew now that this was the man Abbott had hired to follow her. He'd been in her apartment, had touched her private things. Had he really changed sides? Under her cold gaze, Sloane flushed and his own smile wavered.

The awkward moment was broken by Marc's low voice — "Ms. Landers?" — prompting her to action.

Landers. At least she had her own name again. Sloane had entered her apartment one last time, found her passport and mailed it to her so she could cross the border legally. She was grateful, she supposed, for that.

"This is Marc Forrest, Mr. Sloane. My lawyer. Shall we go?"

Sloane looked up from his five-foot-three vantage point. Now here was a man who looked the part: elegant in an Armani summer suit, as Ivy League as Abbott. Only a telltale tan line suggested that his dark hair had recently been cut. Sloane couldn't be sure, but he thought — just maybe — he'd winked when they shook hands. Sloane busied himself with their luggage and then led them to the waiting limousine.

"Here we are, folks. Make yourselves comfortable. You'll be in the city in no time."

He stored the luggage and slid into the driver's seat. As he pulled into traffic, he pushed a button to lower the tinted glass panel that separated him from his passengers.

"Ms. Landers, I'd just like to get this off my chest. I'm real sorry for your trouble. I don't know how much you've been told, but I'm real sorry for my part in it, too. I want you to know that me and Ruby — that's my wife — we're on your side now. All the way. Okay?"

Her green eyes held his gaze in the rear-view mirror, and she nodded.

"We're going straight to Abbott's penthouse now. I'll slip you the key when I open the car door for you. You two just go right on up. I'll deal with the doorman. Ruby's already there. Any questions?"

"No questions," Marc replied.

"By the way," Sloane grinned. "How's Eva? She sure is a delight. Me and Ruby really took to her."

Marc frowned. "Eva?"

Oh, thought Sloane, *he's good. Really good.*

"Okay, I get it. 'Nuff said. 'Nuff said." He laid a finger to the side of his nose as the glass partition slowly rose behind him.

As soon as they were in private, Kathleen and Marc stared at the blank sheet of glass and then at each other.

"Well, at least one of us is having a good time," Kathleen remarked. "Do you think he can really get us by the doorman?"

"Absolutely. He's like an old character actor. No nerves at all. He really believes he's a chauffeur. He got the key from Abbott's cleaning lady, and apparently his wife has had no trouble getting in as her replacement."

"And who's Eva?"

Marc raised his eyebrows. "I've no idea, but my admiration for Agatha is growing." He paused, and then slid his arm around Kathleen's shoulders. "Are you ready for this, Kathleen? Entering the apartment, I mean. It's bound to stir up some bad memories."

"Not memories. Nightmares. But, yes, I'm ready. I feel a bit like a gladiator entering the coliseum, but if that little man can do it, so can I."

"Good. Now, if you don't mind my saying so, Ms. Landers, your costume is incomplete."

Kathleen looked down at her lavender suit, the soft tan Gucci shoes and bag. She disliked the clothes. They were the kind of tailored, impeccably designed clothes that Abbott would have dressed her in. She could hardly wait to change into cut-offs and an old shirt. But what was missing? Then she remembered. She opened the bag and found the jewellery box, slipping the two rings onto the third finger of her left hand.

If Kathleen was surprised by and a little wary of Sloane, she was flabbergasted by Ruby Zaplacinski. Shielded by Marc's acting aplomb and a disdainful arrogance she had never detected in the narrow face before, they had swept past the doorman, leaving Sloane and their luggage in their wake. As the elevator doors closed on the polished marble foyer, they caught a last glimpse of Sloane circling the doorman, fashioning some credible story out of thin air with an imaginative repertoire of hand gestures.

The elevator doors opened onto a wide, quiet hallway. Even Marc, who had been chattering to distract her, seemed subdued. Her hand trembled as she fit the key into Abbott's lock. This was *his* space. She sensed it would be permeated with his personality. His contempt, his obsessions, his very breath that would fill her lungs like poison gas, making her dizzy and nauseous. She held her breath in anticipation and opened the door.

And there, instead of the baleful miasma she dreaded, was Ruby. She had wreaked havoc on Abbott's penthouse. Scattered papers covered the silk carpets; a hand-crocheted afghan in a blaze of jarring orange and lime-green smothered the dark burgundy of the sofa; even the gilded lamps had been pushed aside in favour of practical spot lamps with snake joints extended over the walnut desk. A half-eaten Danish oozed raspberry filling over the pristine surface of a side table. Spanish guitar music with an irrepressibly joyful beat thumped away in stereo. Best of all, Ruby's energy and open smile slipped around Kathleen's shoulders like a warm shawl. Abbott's lingering presence was flattened against the walls by Ruby's invasion, left to curl mournfully into the shadows.

"Well, c'mon in you two. I've had a busy morning. Harry'll be up in a jiffy. I expect you'd like to change out of those stiff clothes. C'mon now. I've tried to make the place a bit more comfy." She grinned wickedly. "I expect it's a bit changed since you were last here. I don't mind telling you I took an instant dislike to the man's decor. Too stuffy, by half."

Kathleen looked all around her, wide-eyed. Even the counters of the large open kitchen, where she had never seen even a single dirty coffee cup, were heaped with overflowing grocery bags and a trail of coffee grinds. "He'd hate this," she murmured.

"Too bad. I'm just getting started. Now, let's have a look at you." Ruby held her at arm's-length, then leaned over and kissed her on the cheek. "Why, you're thin as a rake and pale as a ghost, girl. We'll have to fix that." She shook her head and clucked her tongue. "I owe you, Kathleen Landers, and Harry and I always pay our bills. First off, you need a good lunch."

"No, really, we ate on the plane."

"That isn't food, darlin', that's advertising. I expect the suit you came in with could use a bite." When she turned her 100-watt smile on Marc, he felt like laughing aloud. Harry was no fool, he thought.

A thumping at the door roused him from his reverie, and he helped Harry in with the bags. There were only two. If all went well, they would only need to stay for a few days.

"Any trouble, Harry?" he asked.

"Piece of cake. I've got a note, here. Permission to use the apartment, signed by Abbott himself."

"But how — "

"Oh, I've some buddies from the old neighbourhood who've dabbled a bit in forgery. You'll see."

Marc didn't press for details from the past. Instead he picked up the bags and ushered Kathleen to the spare bedroom. He would use Abbott's himself.

When the door closed behind him, Marc leaned against it, finally alone, bracing himself for a rush of emotion. Abbott's essence leaped forward as he knew it would. Ruby hadn't worked any miracles here. He stood silently for a minute or two, then walked to the bureau and picked up a photograph of Abbott and an older man. As he finally looked upon the bronzed, chiseled face — the face that had filled his mother's dying moments, the face that gave shape to Lily's fears, and that had ruthlessly tracked a gentle man across an empty parking lot — he felt a pulse of hatred surge through his entire body as if he had touched a wet finger to a light socket. He was gripped by a savage anger, an atavistic instinct to kill. The glass in the frame snapped in two under the pressure of his hands.

He hadn't Lily's talent for reading images, but he thought the lips looked cruel, marring the harmony of the prep boy's features. Was he merely projecting his own disgust? Certainly, the old man looked like a caricature, a modern version of Dorian Gray.

He tossed the photo back onto the bureau and stripped down to shower. He was shaking. Tears streamed down his cheeks. For a moment, he wanted only what Lily had wanted. Blind vengeance. Violent confrontation. He wanted to smash his fist into the face of the brutal murderer, again and again, until he felt blood and bits of jagged bone. He saw again — would he see it forever? — his mother's chest exploding and Ben lying crushed against cold pavement. He cried aloud. He sank to his knees.

He was still a long time. This was their chance to break the chain of deaths. Agatha knew that. Knew it was the only way for Lily and for him. He tried to think of Lily clearly — her quirky smile, the wide grey eyes with their dark serious brows, the sunny unruly wisps of hair around her ears. He was surprised to find himself missing her. He thought it important not to disappoint her. Yet he knew she would believe he had betrayed her.

Under the guise of shielding her privacy, Marc had intercepted her calls after Ben died. And when Amanda Martin had called, it was Marc who had gone to meet her. He had said nothing to Lily. He had done what he must to keep Lily from connecting the network to Mahoney's murder.

He rose and went into the shower, making the water as hot as he could bear, trying to melt the hatred and scour Abbott from his skin.

When he emerged, dressed in black jeans and a T-shirt, three faces swung around expectantly to meet him.

"I'm okay," he said simply.

Harry lifted a bulging pita high in the air.

"Chicken salad. If you're a health nut, you can add some bean sprouts. Ruby's just about to catch us up on her research."

"C'mon," Kathleen invited. "Sit here." She was curled up on the floor beside Ruby, whose fingers were flexing over the keyboard of a computer in Abbott's office space.

"Hacking's a bit of a hobby for me, but I'm not as talented as some. We've had to hire some help. An on-line detective."

"Really?" Kathleen said. "I've never heard of such a thing."

"Oh, sure. You can buy all kinds of information. On-line detectives work for legitimate companies. They track a person's Internet activity — Web sites visited, products bought — that sort of thing. What most people are just beginning to realize is that they can also track banking transactions, credit-card numbers, and passwords. Some of these companies sell computer worms that enable you to access someone else's e-mails and private files. You send the worm in an e-mail and as soon as it's opened, you're in. Abbott clears his e-mail dutifully."

"Surely that's illegal," Kathleen protested.

"Shady, but surprisingly not illegal. I just had to sign a statement assuring the company that I would not use the information for any criminal purposes."

"But, you will — "

Ruby looked at Kathleen fiercely. "Criminal's a bit harsh, isn't it? We're just going to use the information temporarily. To our advantage. Besides, Harry and I had already done some research on Abbott's background, names, dates, and so on. The man hides behind logic, that's his little safety net. Once you know that, you can punch a big hole in his security with or without on-line detectives. Passwords are often obvious. He calls that estate in Connecticut Oakwood Manor. Once you know that — oh, and the old man's name was Arnold — "

She interrupted herself to beam down at Kathleen, "What do you think, darlin'? Think anybody ever called him Arnie?"

Kathleen laughed, actually laughed, and Marc could feel the tension beginning to drain from his body.

"Anyway," Ruby rolled on like a truck going down a steep gradient, "Harry and I've been busy ever since Eva called. We've found investment portfolios and bank accounts. I'm pretty sure there's a little side action in the Cayman Islands that the IRS would love to take a gander at, but that's proving tricky. Me and Harry might need to take a quick vacation down there, but I suspect that's a job for Eva. She's more Cayman material than we are. Now, Harry, don't you even ask. They're not gonna tell you a thing about that gal, so just put your curiosity back in your pocket — "

Kathleen and Marc both looked at Harry, who raised a quick finger to his lips.

" — and I've sent off a cleverly worded fax or two, so we might not even need to pester her if we're lucky. Kathleen, jump up here and look over my shoulder. Look at this string of numbers I've got here and see if you can make sense of them. Think dates, girl. We've got to break this code and cut off his escape routes. All except the one we're counting on."

Monday, August 9, Toronto

The plan was risky, a mix of larceny and luck, at best a leap of faith. Lily fell asleep at nights counting all the ways it could unravel. In New York, the Sloanes had searched Abbott's apartment looking for the gun he had used to kill Marie. Finding no weapon, they had instead followed a paper trail to a safe deposit box in Abbott's bank. They were betting that Abbott had kept the gun, that he would retrieve it if he felt sufficiently squeezed. If they could trick him into leading them to it, perhaps the network could be saved. *If. If. If.*

The network seemed less abstract, less fanciful to Lily now that she'd met Kathleen and Suzy. Their faces had brought it an urgency and a name, a specificity she hadn't fully understood before. But it was Agatha who really gave it shape. She was its inventor. She was the creator of the labyrinth whose twisted paths protected the innocent and confused their hunters. She kept its secrets.

Lily had been startled to learn that it was Agatha who had shuffled up to her on the subway platform, thrusting the coded newspaper into her hands. She had been well and thoroughly duped. She would never have recognized Agatha out of the dignified context of her Rosedale home, never have connected her with one of the invisible homeless. Yes, Lily was willing to give Agatha some time to protect the network. But neither would she forget her promise to Ben.

Lily sighed and bit her lower lip. She and Marc and Ben had been like blundering children, never imagining that Abbott would isolate and follow Ben. He must have unwittingly led Abbott to Orchardview Boulevard, thereby ensuring his own undeserved fate. It was an unfairness beyond fathoming, as old as the world, and it would last forever. If only Ben had never found that address. *How* had Ben found the address? She'd probably never know now.

She finished dressing and heard Agatha calling her from downstairs. She was wearing Hayley's clothes, a pale blue shift. She felt like an interloper into another life, but she had no choice. She couldn't go back to Birch Avenue until the timing was right, until she had told her story.

They had done their best to minimize the danger. She and Marc, and Kathleen and Suzy had stayed in Agatha's house rehearsing the plan. Agatha told them that Terri had not returned to Orchardview Boulevard. She would go into hiding. But, having lost Kathleen's trail, Abbott would be watching again. He would never dream that Kathleen was in New York. His only lead was Lily. She felt exposed, but surely the police would help this time. And Agatha had promised that others would be watching, too. Lily wondered who. Did she have an army of watchers?

Lily paused on the threshold and took a last glance at Hayley's room. Her own presence had not altered its unbearable sense of emptiness. A dead girl's room. It had once held her dreams, her spirit, her promise, even her pain. A grouping of photographs on one wall documented a privileged childhood: Hayley on vacation,

Hayley peeking out from behind a young Agatha's skirts, Hayley holding hands and grinning cheek-to-cheek with her best playmate. Little Bonnie had a sweet expression, her shiny brown hair in pigtails. But Hayley eclipsed her. She was all light, her blonde hair loose, glittering in the sun.

Now the room was simply forlorn. Drained. Lily didn't entirely approve of Agatha's contempt for the law, but she empathized. It had failed her dismally when Hayley and Bonnie were in need. The network, she argued, was damage control, a lifeline when the law turned its back. But Agatha was willing to risk it all to protect Lily. If the plan didn't work, Agatha would trade the network for Lily, and let the law have its fickle way. All Lily had to do in the meantime was tell the truth, or most of it. That, and flush Abbott into the open.

She reached the bottom of the staircase where Agatha was waiting for her.

"It's time, Lily. Are you ready?"

Lily nodded and turned to go, but then reached for Agatha's hand. In that moment, their eyes met and Lily suddenly saw how old Agatha seemed, her face a map of all the sorrows in her life.

"Why? If the plan fails, the network must end. Why are you willing to gamble that for me?"

Agatha took no time to reflect. She looked at the young woman dressed in her lost daughter's clothes and her voice was both firm and caressing. "Because you are alive," she said.

Lily took a taxi to the head office of the *Toronto Press* and socialized her way to the city editor's desk.

"Hi, Billy. Do you have a moment?"

William Crosby looked up from the copy he was editing, and raised a skinny white eyebrow.

"Lily. I didn't expect to see you here again. How are you? The service for Ben was — well, a hell of a thing. We miss him around here."

"Me, too."

"Can I get you a coffee? Some water?"

"No. Nothing. Billy, you asked me once if I was working with Ben on something, and I told you the truth. There was nothing,

nothing for the paper, I mean. But, privately, I think I may know what happened to Ben, why he was killed. I need your help."

"My God, Lily. What are you saying?"

"I'm saying I'd like you to come with me to the police. As a friend. If they'll allow it, you'll get your story first-hand. Do you have a contact there? Someone sympathetic, willing to listen?"

Crosby stared and scratched his balding head. Then he went into action, his hand reaching for the phone.

"Give me two minutes to set it up. My car's parked out back."

The police interview room didn't look at all like the sterile cells on television — no hot lights dangled from the ceiling. There was a window, with curtains even, and comfortable chairs pulled up to a round table. But there was a tape recorder. There was a palpable seriousness in the room.

She had reached a watershed of sorts, a moment when the action she would embark on would change everything afterward. Most often, she recognized these defining moments in her life only in retrospect, but she accepted fully that she was creating this one deliberately. She felt a flutter of panic like a bird's wings beating inside her chest. The mechanical click of the tape machine being turned on sounded like a gong in her head.

"This is Detective Sergeant Meyers. I'm here with Mr. William Crosby and Ms. Lily Ross. Ms. Ross wishes to make a statement concerning the death of Mr. Ben Kelter. It's Monday, August 9, and the time is ten-fifteen a.m. Whenever you're ready, Ms. Ross."

Lily looked at Meyers. He was ridiculously young. He had red hair and blue eyes and freckles. He reminded her of Opie from old *Mayberry* reruns. She would have preferred an older, wiser Andy Taylor. But Meyers must have something. He was Crosby's contact. She took a deep breath.

"I'm ... I'm not sure where to begin. July, I guess. I went to visit friends in New York state. A place called Little Falls. When I arrived, I heard a gunshot. I saw a man. He'd killed the woman I was going to visit."

Lily paused and tried to hold her hands still in her lap. She read the shocked facial expressions around her. She noticed the shifts in body language: full eye contact, a slight leaning forward, a cessation of hand movement as if to amplify the sense of hearing.

"When in July?" Meyers' voice was low-pitched, softer now.

"July 15th. The woman's name was Marie Forrest. I'd known her and her family for years. The gunman came running out of the guest cabin ... The Forrests run ... ran a bed and breakfast on the property. The man aimed the gun at me, but I drove away. I went to the village pub. Someone called the state police, and Jack, that's Marie's husband, found Marie in the cabin. She'd been shot in the chest —"

"Forrest," interrupted Crosby. "I know that name. Ben did a piece on Jeanine Forrest, two or three years ago. Is that the connection, Lily?"

"Please," Meyers held up a hand. "I'd like this to be a one-way conversation for the time being, if you don't mind. Continue please, Ms. Ross. Did you report all of this to the police in Little Falls?"

"Of course. I'm a photographer. I saw the man's face clearly, and I described him accurately. But I'd never seen him before. None of the family knew who he was or why he would have murdered Marie. Perhaps she, and then I, disturbed him in the process of a robbery, but there was very little to take. There was no other car in the drive, but he must have had one hidden somewhere. The state troopers found no trace of him."

"Okay, Ms. Ross. We'll send off a fax and get a full report from Little Falls. What happened next?"

"Marc Forrest came back here after the funeral to stay with me. His father went to France to be with Jeanine," she turned to acknowledge Crosby briefly. "We were worried, that is, Marc and Ben were worried, that maybe, maybe the man might be able to track me somehow. That I shouldn't be alone for awhile."

"Why didn't you come to us in July, Ms. Ross, if you felt you were in danger?"

Lily swallowed. Perhaps Meyers wasn't so inexperienced, after all.

"Because nothing happened. We watched, but I never saw anyone following me. A week went by, then another. I didn't want to be alarmist. But then ... then a few days before Ben died, the three of us went to a bar. I thought I'd glimpsed him, the gunman, among the crowd, just for a second or two. I told Marc and Ben I wasn't sure, it could just have been someone who resembled him, but Marc took me outside and Ben stayed there on his own, studying the faces. I'm just guessing now, but maybe the gunman saw that Ben was looking. Maybe he thought he'd seen him and recognized him from my description. The point is that Ben left a message for Marc and me on the day he died." She reached for her bag and pulled out a crumpled piece of notepaper, "It says, *Call me. Urgent.* I've tried, but I can't think of anything else that Ben would have thought urgent."

Meyers leaned back in his chair. She could see him coolly dissecting her story, thinking about each sentence as if he were holding an object up to a light for a better view.

"Why didn't you give us this information immediately, Ms. Ross?"

"I'm sorry. I was very close to Ben, as Billy here can tell you. I've been ... well, I can only describe it as trying to surface from a very deep point underwater."

Meyers regarded her in silence for a split second too long.

"I see. And have there been any sightings since of the man you saw in Little Falls?"

"No. But I haven't been at home. Marc and I have been staying with a friend since the funeral."

Lily hesitated. She had reached the moment in her story when it would be natural to name her friend and give Agatha's name, but she felt reluctant to do so, almost protective. The impulse to shield her came as a surprise, but Lily honoured it. She had spent many hours talking with Agatha, living in her home, touching the objects imbued with her memories. She felt the pull of the old woman's personality, her intelligence, her vulnerability. Yet, for their plan to work, she must be ready to return to Agatha's house on short notice to mind Suzy while events unfolded in New York. Logic dictated that once the police knew of the gunman, she would be watched and expected to keep them informed of her whereabouts. This would bring Meyers dangerously close to the network, but they had all agreed she had no choice. Perhaps, as Agatha believed, he would find nothing even if he chose to look.

"My friend's name is Agatha Quinn. I think that the gunman might have discovered where I live and maybe that's what Ben was trying to warn me about."

Meyers leaned back in his chair, but the relaxed posture belied the intensity of his gaze. "What I don't understand, Ms. Ross, is why the gunman would go after Mr. Kelter instead of you. Especially if, as you suggest, he had somehow discovered where to find you."

"I've thought about that, too. Perhaps it was because Ben was alone. I had Marc with me, you see. And when I was working, I had people around me all the time. Ben was vulnerable. Perhaps Marc and I are meant to be next."

"Perhaps. But I frankly find it hard to believe that an unknown gunman — unknown to you, that is — would go to the trouble. Why bother? You've said the state police could find no trace of him. A witness who saw his face, but can't name him, who doesn't know why he might have been in Little Falls in the first place, doesn't seem very threatening. Unless, of course, you do know something that would connect him with the Forrests."

"Now, just a minute — "

Lily put a restraining hand on Crosby's shoulder. "It's okay, Billy. It's a reasonable question. I'm not stupid, Detective Meyers. If I do know something, or if Marc does, we don't know what it is. We've considered the possibility of the gunman believing we know more than we do. We're at a loss right now as to what that could be. But we'll keep trying. In the meantime, I'd like to return to my home. And I'd feel safer doing that if I could give you a description of the man I saw. And if Billy is willing to run a sketch of him in the paper, perhaps someone else might have seen him on the night Ben was killed. You don't have any other leads, do you?"

"No. We found the car, but it's a dead end. Probably bought privately from a 'For Sale' ad for enough cash to bury the registration and change of ownership. If we have that sketch we can take it around to the former owner of the car and see if we get lucky. In the meantime, Ms. Ross, is Mr. Forrest still staying with you?"

"No."

"No?"

"He left this morning. He had business in New York."

"I see." Meyers said it as if he clearly didn't see. "In that case, it seems far more sensible for you to stay with Mrs. Quinn, doesn't it?"

"I have work to do, Detective Meyers. I'm self-employed, I run my business from my home. I need to return, if only for a few days, to get my life in order again."

"Is there someone else who could stay with you, if only for a few days?"

Lily didn't think the repetition of her words was sarcastic, but she couldn't be sure. Being willing to go home alone was a sticking point in her story, but whatever Meyers' interpretation was, she knew the danger to be real and she couldn't invite anyone she knew to enter it. Nor could she tell him that Agatha would have the house watched. She decided to plunge on with her thin tale, for better or worse.

"If I am right, Detective, and this man is out there looking for me, then inviting someone into my home strikes me as outrageously selfish. I've already lost Ben. If I am wrong, I am safe to be alone. Either way, alone is the only way to go. I would feel safer if Billy were allowed to print my story. It might scare the man away."

"That's exactly the point, Ms. Ross. If your speculations are correct, a newspaper story might well scare him away from us, as well."

Stalemate.

Lily held Meyers' gaze while Crosby fidgeted.

Then Meyers shifted his gaze to Crosby. "You said earlier that Mr. Kelter wrote something about the Forrests. They would seem to be the link, here. What did Mr. Kelter write?"

Lily held her breath and didn't dare look at Billy.

"It was a social justice piece of sorts. Jeanine Forrest was sexually assaulted. She spoke at a number of public forums to women's groups. Ben admired her courage, wrote about the flaws in the legal system, the lack of adequate counselling, that sort of thing."

"And when did this sexual assault occur?"

"I can't remember exactly. I'd have to check the archives. A few years back, I'd guess."

"But surely, Ms. Ross, you know. Being a close friend of the family."

Shit, thought Lily, *where's he going with this?*

"Yes, it was three years ago." Once again, Lily felt cornered into revealing more information than she wanted to, but anyone would find the same facts should they look. It would be better for her credibility if the name came from her. "It was the Roger Mahoney case."

"Really? Now that's interesting. Not my case, but there was a lot of talk around here when he was shot in December. Did you know that, too, Ms. Ross?"

"Yes. December 12th. And before you ask, I was in Calgary, in Banff to be exact, on a photo shoot."

Meyers held up both hands, palms outward.

"Don't leap to conclusions. I'm just speculating. The case is unsolved. Maybe your gunman is somehow connected to Mahoney. Isn't that possible? Maybe his murder caused someone to snap. Maybe he's harbouring some kind of vendetta against the Forrests. That strikes me as no less ludicrous a motive than a fumbled robbery attempt. I'm assuming that Jeanine Forrest's testimony put Mahoney in jail, didn't it?"

Lily felt as if she were being sucked under by quicksand. She hadn't rehearsed this. No one had mentioned Mahoney in their carefully laid plans. She was stranded, forced to improvise. If Meyers followed this treacherous path, and she was sure now that he would, he wouldn't find Abbott, but he would find Agatha's connection to the old case. Surely it was better to lead him there, wasn't it? She decided to make one last attempt to fling herself, and Agatha, to firm ground.

"In my opinion, Detective, Mahoney put himself in jail. Jeanine was the victim, remember? The only connection here is that we all rallied around her. That's how Ben and Marc met, and that's how I met Agatha Quinn. Her daughter, also a victim, was prevented from testifying. You'll find it all in the police records. We were drawn together by a tragedy. It's as simple and as sad as that. I read the paper's account of the Mahoney shooting. There was no mention of the Forrests. Naturally, Ben and I talked about what little he knew of the investigation. Your colleagues made no connection to the Forrests, and neither did we. It stretches credulity to suppose that someone else did. But since I don't know why Marie Forrest was killed, your guess is as good as mine, I suppose. In the meantime, what about Billy's permission to run the story?"

Meyers looked slightly deflated, but not daunted, by Lily's speech. She hadn't put him off the trail, but she hoped she'd slowed him down. She'd done her best. Except for the timelines and several crucial omissions, she had told the truth.

"Okay, Ms. Ross. I'll buy your story for the time being. Give me two days, Crosby, before you print it. I'll set up a meeting with the computer people now. They can produce a sketch. And, if you still insist on going back to your home, Ms. Ross, I'll have an officer accompany you and have a look around. I don't need to remind you to be careful, and, of course, you'll call if you think of anything that might link the man you saw to the Forrests."

"Of course." Lily had hoped for three days, but two days should be enough. She felt a brief flush of victory, but she feared in her heart it was a pyrrhic one.

Monday, August 9, Toronto

It was after 6:00 when Eva saw the police cruiser pull up in front of Birch Avenue. She watched until the two women, one in uniform, one in a blue shift, opened the front door and vanished inside.

She waited. She'd kept her own vigil for two days and two nights, off and on. But she'd seen no sign of Abbott. His absence puzzled her. Where was he? She had expected him to be waiting for Lily, waiting and watching, just as she was. The icy thought that he had somehow entered the house while she was sleeping and was waiting for Lily *inside* unnerved her.

But nothing happened. The house remained quiet. A half-dozen children played on the swings in the park, a couple of parents looking on. People began straggling home from work, and the dog-walkers emerged. A half-hour later, Eva saw the officer return to the cruiser and drive away.

If anything, the street was too quiet, too neighbourly. People knew each other, often stopping to chat. Strangers were noticeable. On the first day, Eva had disguised herself as a student, spreading a blanket beneath a tree and pretending to read or to sleep. On the second day, she'd carried a clipboard and hidden herself behind a pair of black-rimmed glasses. She'd gone from door to door, including Lily's, armed with an inane survey. A few people had actually talked to her. Now she sat on a bench, abstractedly compiling a set of phony survey notes and eating a sandwich supper.

She couldn't linger much longer. She twisted a strand of her shorn, now coppery-brown hair, and punched a number into her cellphone. Agatha answered.

"It's me. Lily's home. No Abbott."

"Did the police accompany her?"

"Yes. One officer. She checked the house. I'm just waiting to see if the police return, if they're going to swing by the street periodically. But I can't stay much longer. Have you got coverage for tomorrow?"

"Yes."

"A couple might be best. It's difficult for a single person to fill the hours inconspicuously. Residents on the street are watchful. And I'm suspicious that Abbott hasn't shown yet. Perhaps he's spotted me. Since the episode at the lake, he may be looking for any single woman of the same age."

"I'll see to the couple. I've another idea as well, just in case. Do you need help tonight?"

"No. I've been sleeping. Now that Lily's here, I've enough adrenaline to stay awake. But I can't risk more days here. I'll sleep in the mornings and be on standby. Did you find an apartment?"

"Yes, furnished apartments on Glen Elm. Do you know them? They're further away than I'd hoped, but they expect transients. You're in number eight. Buzz the supervisor and ask for the key."

"I know them. Less than a mile from here, just above St. Clair. I'll pick up my bike. It'll be faster if there's traffic ... Here's the police car again." Eva checked her watch. "Looks like they believed her story if they're going to swing by every hour. It's more than we could have hoped for."

"It won't last. Where will you be tonight?"

"There are some houses being constructed on a little side street that runs into Birch about a third of the way down. I'll slip inside the one closest to the railway embankment. From there, I'll be able to see Lily's house, the park, and the bottom of the street. But not the top. Phone Lily. Tell her to stay inside tonight, no matter what."

"She has her instructions."

"Yes. But will she follow them?"

Eva didn't wait for an answer. She gathered up her half-eaten sandwich, stuffed her clipboard and her cellphone into her bag, and drifted away into the early evening light.

Gradually, as the hours ticked by, the street seemed to close in upon itself, settling deeper into the shadows. The children and the dogs were gone, leaving the park still. The flickering blue light of an occasional television set spilled out from behind partially drawn curtains. The leaves of the maples, dusty from the August sun, rustled softly. Eva greeted the darkness like an old friend and looked up through streaky clouds at the city sky. She lay on her back in the wild green tangle of the embankment, listening to the night sounds and waiting for the train.

She didn't waste her energy fretting about the plan. She simply gave herself up to the moment. To Eva, doubt was treacherous. Doubt, and anything could happen next. *Ask one question, and a dozen others will flood your mind. Better to move instinctively, let the muscles of the body do the thinking.*

Eva had two rules: never make jobs personal, and identify with the vulnerable, the women and children in jeopardy. Once she would have called them victims, but she'd soon dismissed that label. Victims were passive, boxed in. They learned helplessness. Even those who felt pity for them despised them a little for their failure of courage. She had learned to use her wits instead, to hone her strengths, to fight back, to struggle, to insist on being. She and Agatha, the other women in the network, and the women hidden in its lifeline, would not stay still, would not be passive. Being vulnerable was only being human. Being a victim was giving up some part of your spirit by giving in to the inhumane. Eva had forgotten her rules only once. Had forgotten for a moment, and stumbled badly.

She propped herself up on her elbows and looked across the street at Lily's house. It was dark, without lights in any of the windows. But she knew the woman inside would not be asleep. She would be restless, she might even be pacing. She would be listening to the murmurs of the night and the beating of her own heart. Eva felt strangely connected to her, as if their wills were merging in the hunt for Abbott. The irony of the situation was not lost on her. She knew that Lily could be her undoing. Lily might still recognize the face beneath the copper-brown hair that had once been blonde, and had once talked in a restaurant to Amanda Martin. It didn't matter. Eva wished her only safety.

She heard the train from a long way off in the still air, and slowly, quietly, shifted into a crouching position. She watched the end of the track. As soon as she saw the globe of blinding light, she used the metallic thundering of the churning wheels to cover the noise of her descent from the embankment and scaled the temporary fence of the construction site. As the thunder began to fade, she vaulted herself through a ground-floor hole designated for a window in the partially built house. Not trusting the still flimsy plywood floorboards, she balanced on beams and climbed to the upper storey and a cut-out window space from which she could see Lily's house.

Her view of the top part of the street was now completely

blocked. She had to hope that Abbott would not come that way, it being too close to the streetlights and the cars on Yonge. Surely the most logical approach was the park side of Birch where the embankment melted into solid black, where there were fewer houses, fewer eyes, and where a myriad of one-way and dead-end streets would make travel on foot faster than a police car, if Abbott had timed their checks.

Eva squatted on a beam and leaned her shoulder against an outer wall. An hour went by, and another. The darkness deepened as, one by one, the lights in upstairs windows were extinguished. In the hush that followed, Eva waited. She stood and stretched every fifteen minutes or so.

Her sharpened senses jumped at the sound of rustling, close by, in the underbrush of the embankment. But it was only a stray calico cat, tugging at the corner of a discarded plastic bag caught up in the weeds. She looked back at the street in time to see a police car nosing its way past Lily's. It crawled along, did a U-turn six houses down, and swept away. Agatha was right. Their checks were lagging. And casual.

Eva studied the embankment again. She heard nothing, but for a moment, she thought she saw — *there.* She blinked, and peered into the blackness. Yes. For just a second, she saw a thin shadow separate itself from the larger pool of darkness beneath the trees and then vanish again.

The sudden blaze of light from Lily's windows caught her off guard. She whirled away from the shadows, almost slipping off the beam. Three times, fast, Lily turned an upstairs light off and on. Eva grabbed her cellphone from the waistband of her jeans. She was already on the move when Lily picked up on the first ring.

"Where is he?" she demanded. Noise didn't matter now, only speed.

"At the back. He's come through the back gardens."

Eva tossed the cellphone aside, lowered herself from the upstairs window, and dropped the last seven feet to the ground. The piles of soft earth around the site broke her fall, but she was still momentarily winded. She pushed herself up and raced across the street, but the cedar fence slowed her pace. By the time she bolted into the garden, it was too late. She could hear his footsteps receding into the distance.

She looked up at the three windows overlooking the garden, any one of which Lily could be watching from, and slowly shook her head.

Wednesday, August 11, New York

Kathleen and Ruby had been barricaded in one of the bathrooms for over an hour. Marc glowered at Harry, since he was the only person available to blame.

"What, I ask you, can they possibly be doing?"

Occasional peals of laughter emanating from the bathroom had ruffled him even more.

"Now, you oughtta know better, Marc. You're the actor. Kathleen's gonna look great, and she won't be so spooked if she's made up to play her part."

"Okay, okay. I just wish they'd get on with it. We can't be late meeting Marley."

"If I didn't know better, I'd say you had a touch of stage fright yourself. We won't be late, but it'd be worse to be early. You sure you got all the documents you need?"

"I've got them. I just hope we haven't overlooked any accounts."

"Put your money on Ruby, if you'll pardon the pun. That's my philosophy. She and Kathleen have spent hours poring over that computer. Maybe they haven't found everything, but they've found enough to give any lawyer, especially Abbott's, a fright. I'll bet there's plenty Marley doesn't know. He'll get more than one shock at this meeting. Well, would you look at this — "

Marc turned as Kathleen and Ruby entered the living room. Kathleen, discreetly made up, with colour in her cheeks and long lashes, was a different woman. She looked sophisticated enough in the lavender suit to be convincing, and modest enough to be disarming.

"Perfect," Marc exclaimed. "I'd believe anything you say, Kathleen, and I know you'll be lying."

Kathleen smiled, one of her luminous smiles that brightened her eyes.

"Ruby, I don't know how to thank you for all you've done. Marc and I won't come back here afterward. We'll stay at a hotel close to

La Guardia. But I'll call you and let you know what happened. Goodbye."

"Now don't be giving me goodbyes. We'll see each other plenty when this is all straightened out. I'm looking forward to meeting your Suzy. You be steady, Kathleen. Marc's gonna blow Marley's socks off. He won't be saying much back."

She kissed Kathleen, and Marc and Harry too, for good luck.

"Show time," quipped Harry. "Let's go."

Twenty minutes later, Kathleen and Marc were ushered into the inner sanctum of Jonah Marley's law office on Madison Avenue by a stiff, but openly curious, secretary. The office was spacious, but not ostentatious. One wall was lined from floor to ceiling with shelves, each filled with the thick, sombre-looking books, perfectly aligned, that seemed to be the hallmark of the profession. Indeed, Marc mused, there must be a course in law school in decorating for success. As if ticked off on a checklist, every item of the law office template was here. The wall of books, the framed degrees and memberships in various professional associations, the gleaming oak desk fringed by cushy chairs for clients, the appropriately jammed appointments calendar, the discreet intercom phone set, and, yes, the photo of the happy family: one wife, one boy, one girl. Colours were the predictable cream and grey. The single, large painting was an original — an expensive, unprovocative Mark Rothko.

Marley dismissed his secretary with a wave of his hand and rose to greet them. He looked like Marc's stereotype of a rich man's valet, sharp-featured and fastidiously dressed, with a bow tie. Who still wore bow ties? He was tall, but spidery, with protruding dark eyes and bushy brows. Marc half expected him to rub his long-fingered hands together in the fashion of Uriah Heep, but instead his voice when he spoke was low and clipped, with not a trace of insinuating humility.

"Mr. Forrest, do have a seat. And this is ... ?"

"The reason for our meeting, Mr. Marley. It's a matter of some urgency that we talk, and we appreciate your squeezing us into your schedule. May I introduce Kathleen Abbott. Mrs. Kathleen Abbott."

Kathleen did not offer to shake hands. She took a chair, crossing her legs and placing her left hand over her right on top of them, the wedding band and diamond plainly in sight. Marc watched Marley closely. He fairly sank into his seat, but somehow managed to nod civilly.

"Pleased to meet you, but I'm afraid I don't understand."

"It's quite simple, Mr. Marley. I'm Mrs. Abbott's lawyer. She and your client, Mr. Paul Abbott, were married on Thursday, July 15 in Niagara Falls of this year. I have the papers here." Marc handed over the marriage certificate and turned solicitously to Kathleen. He allowed the silence that befell his announcement to stretch uncomfortably and prayed that Harry's cronies were champion forgers. Marley broke first.

"Well, I suppose congratulations are in order, Mrs. Abbott. Mr. Abbott told me nothing of his plans, but there is no reason to suppose he should if you had no prenuptial agreement. I'm afraid I still don't see why it was urgent to meet."

It was Marc who responded.

"Your client, Mr. Marley, has behaved abominably. He deserted Mrs. Abbott the day after the wedding and returned here to New York without her. They had several painful telephone conversations during that week, but we do not know where Mr. Abbott is at present. Mrs. Abbott has not heard from him since the twentieth of July."

Kathleen lowered her head briefly and then appealed to Marley, her voice catching.

"I — I can't understand why Paul would do such a thing. We had a stormy courtship and a terrible argument on our wedding night about my daughter, Suzy, but it's not like Paul to disappear. I thought, perhaps, he needed time to think things through, but I've heard nothing. Please, Mr. Marley, can you help me find him?"

Marley stared at them, caught off balance and clearly rocked by the news. But he clung to a vestige of composure.

"I'm truly sorry, Mrs. Abbott. However, I've no idea where Paul is. Surely this is purely a personal matter between you and your — er — husband."

"I'm afraid not, Mr. Marley," Marc interrupted. "On my advice, Mrs. Abbott wishes to begin divorce proceedings. Perhaps legal action will get Mr. Abbott's attention where common decency has failed. I have here a complete listing of Mr. Abbott's various bank accounts and stock portfolios." Another sheaf of papers landed on

Marley's desk. "Perhaps you'd like to look them over. You will notice that everything — everything, Mr. Marley — is jointly registered under Mrs. Abbott's name. We have taken the precaution of transferring all funds and assets. Temporarily, of course, Mr. Abbott will shortly have a cash-flow problem.

Marley gripped the papers, torn between reading them and venting his outrage.

"But this is preposterous. We're talking about huge sums of money, here. You can't do this."

"On the contrary, we already have. It's perfectly legal. Mr. Abbott signed the necessary papers on the twelfth of July."

Marley ignored him and turned his attention to Kathleen.

"Mrs. Abbott, no court will uphold this outrage. Starting divorce proceedings is one thing, but this systematic transferring of funds will not be tolerated. It smacks of mean-spirited vengeance, not to mention skirting robbery. You will only cripple your case. I assure you that Mr. Forrest has given you very poor advice, indeed, and I urge you, for your own sake, to reconsider. I am sure some equitable settlement can be reached without these draconian measures."

Kathleen twisted the rings on her finger and sighed.

"Mr. Marley, please understand. I do not want Paul's money. I have not touched a penny of these funds. Find him. Get him here, and every cent will be returned."

"Even if that were possible, and I promise you I will certainly do my best to locate Mr. Abbott now, I feel obliged on behalf of my client to begin immediate proceedings against you. You must return the funds first."

Kathleen looked at Marc, and nodded slightly.

"Very well, Mr. Marley. I understand your position. But I will not return the funds until Paul is found. And, I warn you, if you begin proceedings against me, Mr. Forrest and I will go to the IRS. With this."

Marc leaned over and placed a final set of papers in front of Marley, listing several offshore accounts from the Caymans. Marley sputtered.

"But, I assure you, I knew nothing of this. Much of Mr. Abbott's financial affairs are private, even from me. This ... this is blackmail."

"Call it what you will, Mr. Marley, but I trust you will act in your client's best interests. Paul has humiliated me with this sham marriage, and I will not let him brush me aside. I want his attention."

Marc rose and took Kathleen's arm, while Marley remained slumped in his chair. "I think we're finished here. Thank you for your time, Mr. Marley. We'll be in touch."

The first part of the plan was complete. Abbott had every reason to return to New York.

Thursday, August 12, Toronto

From where he sat, the second booth back from the window of the quirky little restaurant at the top of Lily's street, Abbott was certain he couldn't be spotted by casual passersby. The restaurant, painted a vivid red, was set above street level on a banked verge and could only be reached by climbing several steps. Yet he could still see a slice of the sidewalk clearly, as if from behind one of those trick two-way mirrors that functioned as windows from one side. The early afternoon sun reflecting off the glass only enhanced the effect, and Abbott settled back to wait.

He sipped his coffee, studied the old black-and-white photographs, album covers, and posters that made up the retro decor, and dawdled with the menu. He had all the time in the world. Sooner or later, Lily would pass by. She would come alone, he thought, but he wouldn't be fooled this time. He knew that someone else, somewhere, would be following her. She was cheese in a mouse trap, but he wouldn't nibble again.

Wednesday night had been close. He'd been wary of the nosy Birch community, avoiding the street during the days. During the nights, the house had looked deserted. Lily and Forrest had apparently vanished. He'd hoped to find some easy way in again, and some evidence of where they were hiding Kathleen. He'd had no idea Lily was inside until she'd flashed the lights. That had been a shock, but it was a stupid, impetuous act. He would have waited until the intruder was inside. Then they might have had him.

A lesser man, he thought, would see only the bleakness of his situation. Kathleen had disappeared again. He was back at square one.

But Abbott had pushed ahead. Acted, as his grandfather had taught him, rather than simply reacted. With variations, he had held to his plan to discover as much as he could about his enemies. And his newly gleaned information about Forrest changed everything. He had leverage. It all made sense. Forrest. Mahoney. Amanda Martin, the beautiful dark-haired woman in the urban square. She'd been coy, evading his questions, but Abbott had seen the visceral leap of shock in her eyes when he had pressed her about Marc Forrest. And he himself had seen the envelope change hands. The payoff.

He would bide his time. Perhaps, after all, he had found something he could trade for Kathleen. The thought gave him a delicious shiver of pleasure that he felt in his groin. He imagined his rendezvous with her, the leisurely way he would kill her.

But first, Lily was the key. They'd clearly assumed, for example, that he would try to eliminate her, but they were wrong. For the time being. For now, she was more use to him alive, wandering around on a long rope. During the days when they'd thought to stymie him, when no one had returned to either Birch Avenue or Orchardview Boulevard, he'd had time to construct his own safety net. He simply hired someone to trail Lily, as he had once hired Sloane. Now he would use her, just as they were using her, to see where she might lead him.

A young couple entered the restaurant and took the window booth, partially obscuring his view of the street. He glowered at them, but they didn't move. The woman, he noticed, was heavily pregnant. The couple held hands.

Abruptly, he signalled the waiter and ordered a salad plate, shifting down in the booth so as to regain some window view beyond the thickened body of the woman. But the waiter waltzed over to his new customers, beginning one of those syrupy conversations that pregnant women seemed to invite. *Oh, you look wonderful. When is the baby due?* Blah, blah, blah.

Abbott fidgeted. Finally, the waiter moved away from the window and turned back to the kitchen. The husband reached for his newspaper, and the restaurant was blissfully quiet again except for the murmured conversation of the expecting couple. They had the good sense to lower their voices. During his time in Toronto, Abbott had learned this was the Canadian way.

His salad arrived and Abbott had been eating for about five minutes when he had the prickly feeling of being watched. He glanced up in time to catch the husband openly staring at him, embarrassed enough to look away as soon as Abbott caught his eye. It was only a slight betrayal, but Abbott was disconcerted. Canadians, he'd also learned, looked discreetly, but seldom stared. He kept his head lowered as if he found his plate of spinach and mushrooms rivetting, but his senses had been alerted. He heard the couple begin to whisper, but could make out nothing of what was being said. A moment later, the woman rose with a falsely loud announcement that she needed the ladies' room. It was enough for Abbott. Their play acting was too clumsy. It was time to leave.

He threw enough money to cover his bill on the table, and strode to the door. It opened onto a small porch, with steps leading down to street level, and there, just passing, was Lily walking toward Yonge Street. She didn't see him. Abbott almost laughed aloud. Perfect timing. He felt luck was on his side. He watched her for a few minutes until she reached the corner, then turned away and set off in the opposite direction. He wished he could see the baffled expression of whoever was watching.

He cut slowly across the park. If the young couple chose to tail him, he would make it easy. He knew what to look for now. When he reached the far side of Cottingham School, he looked back, but could not see them. So, they'd chosen to follow Lily instead. Let them waste their time offering unneeded protection. It made no difference to him.

Still, he would not let down his guard. There may be others sent to trail him. There were people, as always, in the park, a gaggle of teenagers playing a pick-up game of basketball. He moved on, reaching Avenue Road and looping up to St. Clair, turning west toward Spadina Avenue. At the corner of St. Clair and Spadina, he could see the tall white tower of the building overlooking the ravine where he had rented a furnished apartment, but he turned north and walked to Forest Hill Village instead. There were several trendy coffee shops there where he could settle in with a newspaper and ensure that no one had followed.

At The Second Cup, he chose an outside table, and, behind sunglasses, surveyed the sidewalk crowd seeking caffeine and the shade of the café awning. No one seemed particularly interested in him, and no new customers entered behind him. He flipped open the newspaper. For a moment, he couldn't believe his eyes. His heart stuttered. He took a gulp of coffee so hot it scalded his throat.

He was looking at his own face.

It was on page three, a computer sketch, with the graininess of black-and-white portraiture, but the likeness was close enough. With a chill, he remembered the husband opening his newspaper in the restaurant, and staring at him. Quickly, he scanned the paragraph of text.

POLICE TRACK MYSTERY GUNMAN
IN KELTER HIT AND RUN

Toronto police are seeking help in identifying this man, thought to be involved in the fatal shooting of Marie Forrest, age 67, in New York state on July 15 of this year. Sources close to Ben Kelter, the reporter killed by a hit-and-run driver on the evening of July 29, say he may have recognized the gunman from the description of an eye witness who was visiting the New York area from Toronto. To date, state troopers have been unable to locate the suspect, but he is now thought to be in the Toronto area. Anyone recognizing this man is asked to contact local police immediately. He is considered to be armed and dangerous.

Abbott could feel a sharp cry pushing up from inside him like vomit. The bitch had gone to the cops. But why now, after all this time? He felt the frontal attack as keenly as if struck across the cheek with an iron glove. They were coming after him. They wanted their pound of flesh. And for what? An old woman? A careless newspaper reporter? The story was cagey, but surely they knew his name.

He chanced a look around him at the other customers, and beyond them to the casual shoppers and strollers ducking in and out of the Village stores. A moment ago, they had paid him no attention. Now, as if in a swirling nightmare, their faces seemed to waver, their expressions turning stony, their eyes glaring at him. A crowd of faces, swarming in and out of view, mocked him. He began to sweat. His hands were shaking. He had to breathe, quell the panic.

He closed his eyes, blotting out the prying eyes, and thought of his grandfather. His presence seemed almost tangible — the proud bearing, the same dark eyes as his own, the safe circle made with protective arms, the voice that would crash like thunder over the heads of his enemies. But even Abbott couldn't deceive himself with this image for long. It faltered, then shrivelled altogether. No, he couldn't expect an embrace there. Soon, his grandfather's disapproval would be directed against him. *Stand up. Stop snivelling. Do you want to be a coward like your father, or a drunk like your mother? Where's your backbone? Fight your own battles or get out of my sight.*

A high-pitched noise filled his ears. Yes, that was the way. Fight back. Giving up was never an option. It brought terrible punishments, much worse than adversity alone could devise. He would find a way. All he needed was a clear head.

He stood abruptly, the iron legs of his chair scraping across the cement. Several people turned at the noise and sudden movement, but it didn't matter now. They were all looking at him. He expected them to rise, as if one, and point their fingers at him. They were all dangerous.

He stumbled away. Back to the corner of St. Clair and Spadina. A motorist shouted obscenities at him as he crossed St. Clair against the light. He reached the bridge over the ravine, looking back, looking for police cars, already hearing their sirens shrilling inside his head. Finally, sweaty and ragged, he closed the door of his apartment behind him, leaning against it. His chest heaved.

The shrilling continued. He clenched his fists to stop it, but it went on and on. He had to relax. He forced himself to take in several long, slow breaths, expanding his lungs, exhaling through his mouth. The room began to focus. He listened to the shrills. Not a siren. The phone.

He picked it up.

"Paul? Is that you, Paul?"

"Who is this?"

"It's Jonah, Paul, Jonah Marley. What the hell are you up to?"

Silence. Abbott sank into the nearest chair.

"Look, your personal life is none of my business, but you've got to get back here. Your wife came to visit me ... with her lawyer. It's serious."

The room began to spin. Abbott gripped the arm of his chair and fought to keep control.

"What are you talking about, Marley?"

"I'm talking about Kathleen Abbott and a marriage licence dated July 15 in Niagara Falls. She and her lawyer, Marc Forrest, showed up here today. She's cleaned out your accounts, Abbott. And they've got a list of offshore accounts in the Caymans. You should have consulted me before doing anything so rash. As your lawyer, I advise you to get back here as soon as possible."

Kathleen. Abbott didn't hear anything but the name and the date. Kathleen. His wife? July 15. The day he killed that old woman. Forrest.

Marley again: "Look, are you listening to me? They've got documents —"

"I'll call you back." Abbott hung up.

He sat in the chair for a long time, trying to fit the pieces of the jigsaw together. It all came back to Forrest. He must be blackmailing Kathleen. Holding her hostage for money. Hadn't Marley said something about his accounts? Would they sell Kathleen for money? She'd been a fool to trust them.

But the existence and the date of the marriage licence still made no sense. If he pretended the marriage was real, it gave him an alibi for the old woman's death. What was Forrest doing? He thought again of his talk with Amanda Martin. Had Forrest murdered Mahoney? Was he preparing to trade a murder for a murder?

Outside, the sun was streaking red into the horizon of a navy sky. He must have sat for hours. He took a shower to calm himself, dressed in fresh clothes, and packed what little he'd brought with him into the black leather bag. He made three quick calls, the first to the airport to reserve a seat, first class, on the last flight out to New York. The second call was to Marley.

"I'm coming in. Pick me up at the airport. Last flight in from Toronto, Air Canada. We can talk on the way to Connecticut."

Marley sputtered about his appointments, but Abbott knew he'd show up. Giving orders settled his nerves. When he reached his childhood home, Oakwood Manor, he'd be on his own territory.

The third call was answered quickly.

"Watch her," Abbott ordered, and hung up.

The airport limousine pulled up in front of the apartment building to collect its passenger. Abbott slouched on the back seat, refusing conversation and keeping his head lowered over a map. He wasn't terrified of being recognized any longer, but he didn't want to be held up. Once he got to the airport, the panache of first class would be his best disguise.

He never noticed the motorcyclist pulling into traffic three cars behind, just as he'd failed to notice the teenage boy who had followed him that morning from the park. When he reached the airport, the sliding glass doors closed behind him, shutting out the night.

The motorcyclist didn't stop, but turned back toward the city, toward the house of Agatha Quinn. The neighbourhood was mostly asleep, and the driver regretted the racket, glad to pull into the long lane and cut the motor. As she removed her helmet, her copper hair glinted in the soft glow of the courtyard lights, left on to welcome her home.

The second part of the plan was complete.

Friday, August 13, Toronto

Suzy thought Agatha's house was the best place she'd ever stayed. It was filled with rooms and passageways, but the best was the ballroom at the very top of the house with round windows, like portholes in a ship, and a slanted ceiling made by the shape of the roof. She wondered whether to tell the new lady about her secret place. She wriggled around on the sofa, sticking her legs up in the air and placing her hands on the floor. From upside down, she studied Lily standing across the room. The lady's toenails looked like little pink shells, and she followed the long legs up to the grinning face.

"Suzy, all your blood is rushing to your head. What are you doing?"

"Your nose is big."

"Only from upside down."

"Can I colour my toes?"

Lily glanced down at her own feet. "If you sit up, we'll go and buy some nail polish. Then you can colour your toes."

Suzy straightened up and Lily's face swung back into proportion. "Can I have different colours?"

"We'd have to buy lots of nail polish for that."

"We can use Hayley's. There's a whole bunch of little bottles in a drawer in her bathroom. Like a paintbox."

"Suzy, you haven't been snooping, have you?"

"Aunt Agatha showed me." A frown puckered her forehead.

"Where's she gone, Lily?"

Lily looked into the heart-shaped face, the large, trusting eyes. *Poor Suzy*, she thought. *Everyone leaves her.* Lily wondered how she was coping with a mixed-up life. Lily had gotten her call late last night, and with Abbott gone, it was safe for her to return to Agatha's. She'd arrived at six in the morning, with Suzy still fast asleep. The little girl knew nothing of their audacious plans. She'd simply woken to another new face and another disappearance. But she was smart and observant. She'd followed her mother through a dark forest on the edge of a lake. She must have felt urgency and danger.

"Suzy, do you know what's happening?"

"Mommy is cross with the bad man. She's gone to tell him so. Is that where Aunt Agatha is?"

"Well, sort of. She's gone to New York, too. And in a few days your Mom will come back. And Agatha and Marc, as well."

"I'd like to go for a ride in a plane. Mommy and Marc took a plane."

"But you will, soon. If all goes well, you and your Mom can take a plane to New York, to your very own home."

"Will the bad man be gone?"

"We hope so, Suzy."

"Where will Terri be?"

"I don't know. I don't know Terri. Tell me about her."

"She's brave. She fooled the bad man and Mommy and I got away. But I think she's mad at me."

"Oh no, Suzy. I'm sure she's not. Why do you think that?"

"She never — " The green eyes brimmed with tears. "She didn't say goodbye. I heard her talking to Aunt Agatha last night, and she didn't come up to see me."

Lily was surprised. She'd thought Teresa, whoever she was, had melted back into the network and was no longer part of the plan.

"I'm sure she didn't mean to hurt your feelings, Suzy. She just thought you were asleep. You were supposed to be sleeping, weren't you?"

"Can we do my toes now?"

Lily sensed the change in mood. A distraction seemed the best remedy. "Sure. You lead me to the paintbox."

Holding Suzy by the hand, Lily entered Hayley's room. It was just as she had left it, except Lily thought for a moment she caught a whisper of perfume in the air and then it was gone. Suzy dragged her by the arm and led her to the treasure trove of nail polish. Carefully, they chose an array of colours, some frosted, some glittering like jewels. Suzy tugged off her shoes and socks and Lily lifted her onto the top of the dresser.

"Now, don't wiggle. Spread your toes apart."

She opened each bottle, one by one, applying each coat of polish to the small moons of nail with the precision of an artist. Suzy was delighted.

"There, miss; you're done. What do you think? Your toes are a peacock's tail."

"What's a peacock?"

While Lily explained, she tried to camouflage a growing sense of misgiving. First there had been that faint whiff of perfume. Then she'd noticed that each bottle of polish had been fresh, not thick or crusted as she would have expected if the bottles had really belonged to Hayley more than two years ago.

"Suzy, did Terri stay here last night? Did you hear her leave before you fell asleep?"

"Uh-huh. There was a big roar."

"A roar, you mean like a car pulling away?"

"Louder. Lily, can we play dress-up now? Aunt Agatha lets me."

Lily's eyes widened. Dress up? In Hayley's clothes? She opened the double doors of the built-in wall closet. She looked at the row of dresses and pants and shirts and tried to remember if anything had changed since she'd last been there. Everything seemed the same, but she couldn't be sure. She hadn't paid attention.

"Not here, Lily. In the ballroom."

"Where? Suzy, there isn't a ballroom."

"Yes there is. It's my secret place. Aunt Agatha says she's too old to get up there anymore, but she opened the door in the ceiling and said I could play there. C'mon. I'll take you."

Together they climbed a steep, narrow staircase at the back of the house. Suzy halted on the top step and pointed up. Following the direction of her finger, Lily could discern the outline of a trap door flush with the ceiling. An attic?

Suzy stretched up her arms and pushed with all her six-year-old might. The door swung up and then thudded backward onto the floorboards of the room above them.

"You have to climb the rest of the way. I put my elbows through first and then sort of crawl forward. Sometimes Aunt Agatha gives me a boost."

Lily boosted Suzy, and then levered herself into the attic behind her. Still on her knees, she gasped while Suzy laughed. It was a marvellous, magical place, as exotic a playground as any child could wish for or imagine. The room was huge, stretching across the whole of the house, and flooded with light from four round, deep-set windows edged with stained glass. They refracted spots of coloured light which danced in the air like a swirl of butterfly wings. The room was scattered with cast-off furniture draped in white sheets, but one corner, with two wooden rocking horses and a heap of stuffed animals, had obviously once been used as a playroom.

Lily recognized immediately the feature that most captivated Suzy — a simple clothes rack hung with a line of prom dresses like a row of flowers in velvet, satin, and chiffon. She could almost smell corsages of pink carnations. A jumble of shoes and fanciful hats with ribbons and saucy feathers circled a free-standing, floor-length oval mirror.

It had been a long time since Lily had had an afternoon of old-fashioned dress-up.

Together they swirled about in glamorous skirts, delved into open trunks and made faces at each other from under the floppy brims of outrageous hats. Finally, they lay on their backs on the bare floor and watched the shadows in the corners stretch long fingers into the centre of the room.

"Lily?"

"Mmm."

"There are shadows in my room. Spooky ones. They move."

"Is that why you can't sleep?"

Suzy nodded solemnly.

"Okay, show me. But first, let's eat. I'm famished."

They sat together in the kitchen, munching hot dogs and choco-late cookies. Then Lily persuaded Suzy to take a bath and put on pajamas. She tucked her into the four-poster bed and lay beside her, reading the chapter of Toad's "Wild Ride" from *The Wind in the Willows*. But even Toad's reckless adventures couldn't dispel the shadows. Suzy's eyes were wide open.

"You know what, Suzy? The shadows come from the furniture. That big bureau over there and the posts on the bed. They move when the moon drifts across the sky." Suzy's expression didn't change, but Lily knew she'd just said a stupid adult thing. She tried again. "Okay, I have an idea. Can you wait here for me? I'm going back up to the ballroom. I think I saw something there that will make you feel snug as a bug in a rug."

"I don't like bugs."

"It's just as expression. You'll feel cosy. Wait here."

Lily went down to the kitchen and rummaged for a flashlight, then climbed the attic stairs and threw back the trap door. She aimed the beam of light at the place she thought she remembered, and there it was. A sleeping bag.

As she crossed the room and tucked the sleeping bag under her arm, her glance fell on a group of stuffed animals arranged on the top of a trunk. They were all too cutesy. She set them aside and opened the lid. She dug around, shining the flashlight into the recesses of the trunk, finally spying a suitably barbarous gorilla with tufts of springy fur. She reached for it and her fingers froze.

There, in the pool of light, lay a bound leather journal with black velvet ribbon ties. It had been well hidden, pushed to the bottom of the trunk. Without thinking, she undid the ties and opened the cover. It was a diary.

She flipped to the first page, expecting to see a child's handwriting. But this was an elegant script, the writing of a young woman. Her eyes fastened on the date. If she remembered Ben's notes correctly, the diary entries began one month after the Mahoney rapes. She dropped the journal abruptly as if it were a live flame burning in her hands. It was private.

Lily picked it up to return it to its hiding place, but then hesitated. What if Suzy found it? She could read. Maybe not everything, but enough.

Lily tucked the diary into the waistband of her shorts, gathered up the sleeping bag with its jungle mate, and returned the flashlight to the kitchen. She laid the journal on the table. She stood looking at it silently for a minute, then raced back up the stairs to Suzy.

"Okay, out of that giant bed. You're going to sleep under the stars, like Toad. Well, almost under the stars. And I've brought a guard."

She tossed the gorilla through the air and unfurled the sleeping bag. Lily positioned the head of the makeshift bed directly opposite the window so any shadows cast on the wall would be behind Suzy. Suzy approached slowly, stretching out one toe as if testing the temperature of bath water.

"C'mon. Jump in. You'll see."

Suzy looked back at the bed once, then dove into the sleeping bag as if choosing the lesser of two evils.

Lily zipped her up snugly and fetched a pillow. "What do you think? Better?"

A small smile appeared above the top blanket. "Is there room for the gorilla?"

"You bet." Lily stuffed it alongside Suzy and sat back on her haunches to admire her solution. "You look as snug as — "

"I know, that bug thing."

Lily sat alone at the kitchen table with a bottle of Agatha's best brandy and stared at the diary. She knew she shouldn't read it. She knew as soon as she'd tucked it into her waistband that she would.

She wondered at the maze that had brought her to this betrayal in Rosedale, with a child sleeping above her, afraid of shadows. Lily was entangled in a strangeness beyond her experience, misleading the police and participating in a scheme to outwit a murderer. She felt she'd stepped over a threshold into a foreign world without the gravity of rules.

She picked up the journal and fingered the velvet ties.

She needed answers to her questions. She'd stood at too many gravesides lately.

Yet she was a thief, about to steal a woman's innermost thoughts, the most egregious of thefts.

She opened the journal and began to read soundlessly.

It was all there, vividly recorded as if the very loops and curls of the written word could act like cords to bind the pain, or as if the page could absorb the horror as it did the ink: Mahoney's initial approach in a bar, his sleek charm, the slow dancing, then the drive back to his house, more drinks.

Mahoney, Lily knew, had used Rohypnol, the date-rape drug. His victim had woken up to find herself naked and helpless, lashed to the bed and gagged. He raped her repeatedly. Then the threats began. *You came here of your own free will. No one will believe you now. If you tell, I will find you. I promise, I will find you.*

Finally, when her spirit was truly broken, he'd dressed her and driven her in his car, still bound and gagged, to another part of town. He'd removed the ropes and her own scarf that had gagged her, and dumped her with a final warning to keep silent.

But it wasn't over. Left tied were the invisible ropes of fear, and shame, and degradation. The diary, Lily thought, was Hayley's inferno. *I am mute. I am flesh made stone, my body alien. I am heartless. I am muscle, and bone, and hate.*

Lily took a slug of the brandy and read on. She searched the words for some miraculous grace, some signal, however faint, of healing. She saw flickers of it in the pages about Jeanine. She could almost hear the soothing voice of Marc's sister urging forgiveness. Not of Mahoney. No, not of that. But forgiveness of the self. The wisdom that no flaw of a woman's judgement deserved such consequences.

The struggle to regain joy was palpable, and Lily's heart ached. There was a long passage about Agatha, her kindness and her disappointment. Lily thought it an odd word to choose — disappointment — until she remembered that Hayley had not been allowed to testify. How Agatha had railed against that injustice. And there were passages, too, about Hayley's childhood friend who had also suffered the same ordeal. These passages were nostalgic, almost lyrical, as if trying to recapture the melody of childhood and vitality of adolescence. Lily remembered the photos of the two girls arm-in-arm, smiling into a camera lens, looking unknowingly into the same dark fate.

We shared every secret, every hope. I see her now, slim and supple. A shaft of light dancing in the dark. I close my eyes. I hear her laughter all around me. She is clear water flowing over bright stones.

But the poetry drifted away like summer smoke, and the anger returned: recurring images of death, a yearning for invisibility and silence.

Then, Lily read the final sentences. She rubbed her eyes, and read them again. *I'm going away, flying away, to fashion my own death. To reclaim my life. When Mahoney dies, only then will I be fully free. Retribution.*

The last word echoed in Lily's ears as if it had been uttered aloud by a ghost. Was this a suicide note, or a promise to return to balance the scales? Lily was sure Agatha had never seen this diary. She'd told

Suzy she couldn't get up to the attic any longer. How long?

Lily sat motionless at the kitchen table, nursing the brandy and her worst fears. She thought about the trace of perfume and the nail polish, the bedroom kept just as it was when Hayley was alive. She walked slowly down the hall to the blue and green silk room and stood before Hayley's portrait. She climbed the stairs to Hayley's bedroom and studied the photographs on the wall.

Maybe. Just maybe. The woman she'd glimpsed in the restaurant with Amanda Martin had also been blonde.

No matter how many twists she had encountered since, Lily realized that the moment her life had changed could be traced back to Amanda's bleak tale whispered in the twilight of a summer park. From that moment, her questions had triggered an unpredictable chain of events, more like shattering explosions. Marie. Ben.

She had allowed herself to be convinced by Agatha and Marc that there was no solid evidence to tie Abbott to Ben's murder and that, without it, there was nothing she could do, legally, to bring him to justice. So she had agreed to the plan, agreed to protect the network, agreed to take a gamble on neutralizing rather than convicting Abbott.

But she hadn't agreed to be duped.

She'd been floating for days, but she was ready to act now.

She remembered what she'd been told at her last photo shoot — before the shock of losing Ben had numbed her senses — that Amanda was back in town. Lily would find her. She intended to discover exactly how Mahoney had died and why Agatha, who owned *Designer's Edge,* had arranged to send her away.

Saturday, August 14, New York

Under a low cloud of exhaust fumes, the street was gritty and littered, but the polished doors of the bank shone like a beacon. From across the street, Ruby kept watch on Abbott's bank in upper Manhattan. Eva had arrived yesterday from Toronto, bringing the information that Abbott had driven into the city with Marley. The repaired Jag was once again in its allotted parking space. Ruby wished she could have seen Abbott's expression when he'd discovered the messiness of his penthouse, but such petty triumphs were a luxury reserved for her imagination. Timing was everything now. They'd come to the riskiest part of the plan, part guesswork, part luck.

With the help of the on-line detective, she had been able to transfer funds from Abbott's bank accounts and unravel some of the offshore dealings in the Caymans, but despite her thorough search of the penthouse, she'd found no key to the safe deposit box she knew was registered in this bank. Without the key, they were helpless. They had to hope that Abbott would open the box for them.

He would need cash, but Ruby knew that was almost beside the point. Soon after he'd boarded the plane in Toronto, Abbott's credit cards had been reported stolen by Harry. If Abbott tried to use them, there'd be a hassle. They'd left him only one escape route, the very one Ruby had been sent to watch.

Ruby had a lot of faith in Eva. She was smart and savvy. Just seeing her again raised her spirits, to say nothing of Harry's. But at this critical juncture the plan hinged on little more than a knowledge of human nature and the law of averages. It could easily go awry. Abbott might simply enter the bank and demand immediate replacement of his cards. Or he might get money from Marley. They knew there was a safe at the estate in Connecticut, and Abbott had surprised them by going there first. But they still clung to a thread of hope. If he felt that the network was closing in, he might panic enough to clean out his safe deposit box. Especially if he had kept the gun that had killed Marie Forrest. If it wasn't lying at the bottom of some river or sewer in upper New York state, the gun would be in that box. Not in Connecticut. They were betting it would be at arm's-length, but accessible. And Abbott was too smart to have tried to smuggle a weapon through airport security, so the gun wouldn't have been taken to Toronto. Ruby knew that the money squeeze was only short-term security. The cash transfers would buy them time and get Abbott's attention, but the gun was crucial. It was life insurance.

When the Jag pulled into the parking garage, Ruby crossed the street to enter the bank just before Abbott. She trailed away to one of the counters where she could innocently fill out forms but keep an eye on him. He approached a counter opposite her and spoke with a young woman. A few minutes later, he was escorted to a glassed-in office.

Ruby waited. She completed one form and began another while Abbott and another gentleman disappeared down a corridor. She noticed one of the security guards studying her. Quickly she gathered up the forms and entered the longest queue she could find. When she was almost at the front of the line, she saw Abbott re-emerge from the corridor with a black briefcase in hand. She ducked out of the line and stepped into the street in time to see him striding toward the parking garage. She reached for her cellphone.

Harry got the call in his illegally parked car and signalled the garage attendant in Abbott's building. They were almost bosom buddies by now, but the friendship was only as good as the next bribe. He turned to Kathleen and wagged a finger at her. "If anyone comes by to move the car, stall them. I'll be back in a jiffy. And stay low. If Marc finds out I let you come along, he'll skin me alive."

"I promise. Hurry. Don't worry about me."

Harry crossed the garage to the door that led into the interior of the building. Eva and Marc were waiting for him by the elevators.

"It's on. Ruby's just called and he's carrying a black case. The attendant will signal you, Marc, and you can duck out of sight behind the parked cars. Damn it, Eva, why don't you wait in the car and let Marc and me go for the gun?"

"He'll recognize both of you in an instant, Harry. The last time he saw me was by moonlight and I looked quite different. Surprise will give us an advantage."

Harry frowned, looking at Eva's short coppery curls. He supposed it was possible that Abbott wouldn't recognize her right away. Maybe.

Eva smiled as if she could read his thoughts. "Don't worry, Harry. He might leave the case in the car where Marc can retrieve it all on his own. Wait for us in the car by the front entrance. It'll be over in no time."

Harry nodded. It was a simple enough strategy. If, as they hoped, Abbott was just stopping at the penthouse again on his way out to Connecticut, he might well leave the case in his car for a short time. Marc would then pop the window, snatch the case, and ring Eva once on his cellphone. Two rings would mean she would have one last chance to grab the case before Abbott reached his apartment.

A shrill whistle from the attendant alerted them that the Jag was in sight. Harry headed for the hallway exit, Eva slipped onto the elevator; Marc entered the garage and squeezed himself between two parked cars, crouching as low to the ground as he could.

Marc couldn't see anything, but after a few moments he could hear the smooth purring of the Jag's engine. The ignition was switched off. There was a click as the car door was opened. Marc waited, every muscle tensed, while he listened to Abbott's footsteps cross the garage. Then silence.

He rushed to the car, but there was nothing on either the front or back seats. Quickly he slid a thin strip of metal between the car window and door, popping the lock. He reached into the car and pulled the lever that opened the trunk. But there was no case. Cursing, he reached for his phone.

Eva was waiting on the sixth floor for Marc's signal. On the second ring, she pushed the elevator button and slipped her phone into the bag fastened to her waist belt. Her fingers grazed her gun. She thought again how simple it would be to kill him. She was wearing a sun visor to shade her face, and jogging gear and sneakers in case she had to run. But it was too late now. Kathleen, Marc, Harry — they'd all know. And Agatha.

Eva could hear the bell of the elevator growing louder as it ascended. The building had only one elevator. She could be certain that when the door opened, Abbott would be there. Her plan was to keep her face averted and move quickly to the elevator's back wall. When Abbott stepped forward to exit to his apartment on the ninth floor, she would move in behind him.

The door slid open. Eva kept her head down, but she could see Abbott's feet and one hand gripping the handle of the case. She moved into position, slightly behind and to his right. She felt the lurch of the elevator as it began to move upward again. Her heart pounding, she counted the seconds until the elevator stopped. Her hand closed around her gun.

When Abbott stepped forward, she moved without hesitation, pushing the barrel of her gun into the small of his back.

"Drop the case. Now."

In a split second, Abbott swung around, using the case as both a shield and a weapon. Instinctively, she tried to protect herself, but the case smashed against the left side of her face and shoulder. She heard rather than felt the cracking of a bone and lashed out with her feet. The briefcase clattered onto the elevator floor and Abbott staggered backward just as the door began to slide shut. She saw him lunge forward, but he was too late.

As the elevator began its descent, Eva dropped to her knees. As her adrenaline abated, pain flooded her senses and she felt a wave of nausea. The swiftness of Abbott's attack told her that he hadn't been surprised. Perhaps he had recognized her after all, or perhaps he had been suspecting an ambush. Her forehead was bleeding, blurring her vision as she felt around for the briefcase. But it didn't matter. She'd seen enough to know there was no gun inside. Abbott had already removed it. He'd been reaching for it when the elevator door closed.

Kathleen sat in the back seat of the car watching Marc and Harry through the windshield and listening to them argue. Poor Harry. Marc was furious with him for bringing her along, but she'd insisted. She'd come too far to hide any longer. She'd promised to be no trouble.

Suddenly, she saw Marc shove Harry aside.

"Get out of the way," he barked. "Look, she's hurt."

Kathleen leaned forward. The woman was standing at the front of the building, blood from a gash in her forehead trickling down her face. As Kathleen watched, she took a step forward and swayed sideways. Marc reached her before she fell, and Harry rushed to help. They half dragged her toward the car, and Kathleen manoeuvred her onto the back seat trying as best she could to cradle the injured head. She reached for a pack of tissues in her purse and began wiping away the blood.

Her hand froze.

Terri? The hair was different, but this was Terri.

Bewildered, she turned toward Marc, but in that instant he spoke urgently.

"Get down. Stay down. It's Abbott."

Kathleen ducked. She could hear Harry breathing heavily in the front seat. "Where is he?" he hissed.

As she crouched over Terri, she heard her faint whisper.

"Kathleen?"

She looked warily into Terri's eyes. She was still shocked. Terri and

Eva were the same person. The person, Kathleen remembered, who had saved her life. She squeezed the woman's hand.

"Kathleen," she murmured. "Listen. He's carrying the gun. Tell them."

As Eva slipped into unconsciousness, Kathleen sat up straight and prodded Harry.

"You have to get her to a hospital, Harry. Go." Then she reached for the door handle and stepped out of the car. So many others had put themselves in danger to protect her. No more.

The sight of Abbott across the street chilled her. Slowly he swung his head from side to side, like a dog trying to pick up a scent. In a few seconds he would see her. She heard Marc shout "No," but it was too late. She was already running.

She ran until she thought her lungs would burst. But she knew he was behind her somewhere. She paused in the summer crowd of tourists outside the Guggenheim, just long enough to catch her breath. Where could she go from here? Where could she hide? She thought about entering the gallery, but she couldn't do it. Its spiralling interior suddenly seemed sinister, like a set from Hitchcock's *Vertigo*. She felt sick.

Marc would come after her. If only she could find him before Abbott found her. She looked across the street at Central Park.

She tried to think of what Terri would do. If she ran now, the sudden movement would be like sending up a flare. But she had to get into the park. She could hide there.

She edged toward the back of the crowd. She knelt down as if to tie the laces on her dockers and inched closer to the curb. When the traffic stopped, she waited for people to surge forward and forced herself to walk slowly, to match her pace to theirs.

Abbott watched her approaching him from inside the park. She looked behind her often enough, but never looked for him in front of her. He almost admired her stealth. Central Park was the logical place to go. He and Kathleen had made the same choice.

As she turned into one of several pathways branching off from the entrance, he stepped forward from beneath the shadows of a spreading maple and slipped his arm through hers, pinning her close to his side.

"Hello, Kathleen. It's been too long."

She gasped but said nothing. Abbott allowed the silence to settle, remembering with a kind of physical shock how soft her skin was beneath his hand.

"I have a gun, by the way. So no screaming. Let's go for a stroll, shall we?"

She managed to walk, his grip on her arm pressing her forward. There were other people around them. Kathleen scanned their faces, looking for Marc, pleading with her eyes for help. A few people met her stare, then looked quickly away.

They walked and walked. For now, Abbott was keeping to the paths, but Kathleen knew he was leading her deeper and deeper into the park. With every step, her chances waned. She couldn't speak. Her mind was numb.

"I hear from Marley that you're a rich woman, Kathleen. But your lawyer's not very smart. I saw him buy a ticket for the Guggenheim just before you entered the park. Too bad."

Kathleen felt herself go rigid. So this was it. After all she'd been through, after all she'd done to shelter Suzy, she was alone with Abbott.

The long ordeal — the months of being stalked, the flight to Canada, the midnight hike with a frightened child along the edge of a black lake — had changed her. The people who'd died trying to save her had changed her. Terri and Agatha and Marc had changed her. Abbott didn't know her anymore. He thought she was weak. That assumption was her only weapon.

He began to walk more quickly, agitated by her lack of response. It had been a while now since they had passed other people, though she could still hear music occasionally and, in the distance, the hum of traffic.

Suddenly, he stopped and spun her around to face him.

"You bitch. You could have had it all. I'm going to make you sorrier than you've ever dreamed."

For a moment, she stared at him, completely without expression. Then she lowered her eyes and pressed her hands over her face. She began to sob.

"Oh, please, Paul. Please. I never wanted the money. They forced me." Her voice was a thin wail.

"It's too late, Kathleen. You've betrayed me."

Jan Rehner

"No, never that. I was overwhelmed, confused." Her words were rushed, muffled by her hands.

As he leaned in toward her face, she kicked out with all her strength, hitting him squarely in the groin. He doubled over, screaming in agony, and she brought her knee up under his chin. As he jerked backward, the gun he had been reaching for inside his jacket swung out of his hands. Kathleen followed its arcing trajectory and scooped it up seconds after it hit the ground.

It was heavy and slightly warm from his body heat. She was repelled. She almost dropped it.

She ran in the direction of the music. She didn't know where to put the gun. She thought briefly of hiding it, but she was too afraid to stop. She ran and ran.

When she could hear people again, she stuffed the gun down the front of her T-shirt and covered the bulge by hugging herself with her arms. Near the crowd that had gathered to watch the skateboarders do their tricks, she found a washroom.

She stayed there for a very long time, coaxing herself to move again. An hour went by, maybe two. She couldn't tell. She wandered back outside and tried to find an exit or a phone.

It was close to six in the evening when Ruby found her sitting on a bench, staring blankly into the distance, her arms still folded around her.

"Well, look at you. Just taking in the sights, are you? Marc and I are running all over this place like a couple of chickens with their heads caught off."

"Hello, Ruby. Is Terri okay?"

"She's got a lump on her forehead the size of an egg, four stitches and a broken collar bone, but she'll mend as pretty as ever."

"Abbott?"

"Last we heard, he was limping back to the Jag. Chances are he's hightailed it to Connecticut. Harry's trailing him. How are you?"

"There was no one else, Ruby. Finally, I had to save myself."

Tears came, but she smiled and unfolded her arms.

"I did it, Ruby. I got the gun."

Just MURDER

Harry's muscles were stiff and his old joints felt locked. He was accustomed to more comfortable surveillance in parked cars with a hamper of Ruby's cooking and a thermos of steaming coffee beside him. But there'd been no time. With Eva hurt and lying in a hospital bed with a mild concussion, it had been Harry to the rescue or nobody. He'd had to ditch the car in a nearby leafy lane, and he'd been lucky to find a protected vantage point on the hillside.

Stifling a groan, he crawled forward to the edge of the hollow and flopped onto his belly. Propped up on his elbows, he peered down at Oakwood Manor and lifted his binoculars.

The huge flagstone two-storey structure seemed to leap toward him. He could trace the lush vines climbing up and across the southern wall, swaddling it in dark green velvet.

Old money, thought Harry, *the place is like a fucking postcard.* The lawns, slanting down to pockets of wood, were not cut so much as groomed. The hedges were pruned, the flower beds ornate and geometric. He imagined Abbott tucked up in a warm gigantic bed between silk sheets. Harry's elbows ached and his stomach rumbled mercilessly.

The Jag was still parked in the circular drive lined with a graceful arc of towering oaks. There was no sign of activity.

Harry slid back down into the dip of the hollow and pondered the possibility of a few more hours sleep. But now that he was awake, he was too hungry and the ground was too hard.

He sat on his backside with his legs stretched out in front of him and listened to the morning come alive. The birds were making a racket now. Soon people would be waking up, taking hot showers, maybe sitting down to bacon and eggs, crisp buttered toast, and orange juice so cold it beaded the glass. He thought about slinking back to his car and driving into one of the small towns he'd passed while tailing Abbott, one of those little diners on one of those quaint main streets; they probably served blueberry pancakes smothered in maple syrup.

Feeling giddy from the siren call of temptation, he reached for his phone. Ruby's voice was like a glass of fresh water.

"How's Eva?" he asked.

"*I'm* fine, thank you, Harry, and Eva is sound asleep. The doctors sedated her, but only after she fussed. Seems she wanted to spell you on your vigil, but I assured her you'd be fine. You are fine, aren't you, Harry?"

"Oh, you betcha."

"Where are you exactly?"

"I had to hide the car. I'm in the middle of a hollow, on the side of a hill, somewhere in God's country overlooking Abbott's spread. He's tucked up somewhere inside, quiet as a field mouse."

"Poor Harry. Are you hungry?"

"A mite, Ruby."

"Do you still have the binocular case with you?"

Harry looked around and spied it underneath the ledge of rock. He remembered he'd used it as a pillow during the long, uncomfortable night.

"Yeah, I've got it."

"Look in the zippered pouch. And hang on, Harry. Marc and Agatha are already on their way."

"Who's Agatha?"

But the line was dead. He staggered over to the case and opened it. Two slightly mashed roast beef sandwiches. Manna from heaven. The smartest thing he'd ever done was marry Ruby Zaplacinski. Life was good.

They pulled into Abbott's circular driveway at precisely 8:30. Marc was behind the wheel and he parked the rented Mercedes in front of Abbott's Jaguar. It seemed a sensible precaution. They didn't know what to expect. They didn't know much, except that Abbott was in there, and he was alone.

Kathleen had told them what she could remember of the layout and interior of the house. A front and back entrance, and a side door off the kitchen leading to a flower and herb garden. No live-in help. Wood-panelled walls, swagged curtains, oriental rugs, antique furniture. The manor remained unchanged since Abbott's grandfather had ruled it. Kathleen had talked a lot about the portrait, the scornful face glowering over the living room from its place of prominence. Agatha hoped she might use it to her advantage. There would be only one meeting, one chance.

Marc moved first, the car door thudding behind him. He gripped the gun rigidly by his side. He opened the passenger door for

Agatha, leaning forward to help her out, then swinging the door shut. From the security of his hollow up on the hillside, Harry heard the car doors slam like two gunshots ringing clear in the still morning. He scrambled into position, visible now from the house, standing upright with his old hunting rifle braced against his right shoulder.

From inside, Abbott jumped at the same sounds. He slopped some coffee over the edge of his cup, but he rose steadily enough. So they were here. Finally. He listened to the door chime. He'd known they would come. Kathleen would come to gloat, and Forrest would want money. Abbott would play along, bide his time. But he wasn't finished yet, not by a long shot. He clenched his jaw.

Slowly, he tidied up his breakfast dishes. He ran water into the kitchen sink and added soap. Let them wait. He dried his hands on a towel. Order soothed him.

When the kitchen was pristine, he nodded his approval at the room and crossed the hall to the front door. For a moment, he practised a pleasant smile in the side mirror. Nothing too wide or welcoming, just a relaxed curving of the lips. No surprise.

He opened the door and the smile collapsed.

Forrest's gun was raised. No Kathleen. An old woman. His eyes widened. The morning light caught him squarely in the face and he turned his head slightly, catching sight of the silhouette on the hillside behind them. The man standing there was armed.

The greeting he had planned died on his lips. He fumbled his words, took a step backward.

The movement was his undoing. Marc immediately thrust forward, prodding him with the gun. Abbott retreated, walking backward, his face draining of colour, emphasizing the purple bruise beneath his chin. The woman followed, her voice strangely calm in the circumstances, every word enunciated.

"Good morning, Abbott. We need a quiet place to talk. The living room, I think."

He turned and led them there, his mind working furiously. For the first time, he felt the icy touch of fear trace the length of his spine. They would kill him. Kill him, and loot the house.

He entered the room and walked to the windows, drawing the curtains, hiding the unsteadiness of his hands in the habitual movements of a lifetime in this house. This was his home. He would defend it. With a burst of adrenaline and the steeliness of sheer will, he forced himself to speak.

"Your arrival, I must say, is ruder than I had expected. I'm unarmed. Whatever it is you want, let's get on with it."

Agatha walked to the middle of the room, glancing up at the portrait of Abbott's grandfather. She deliberately positioned herself with her back toward it so that Abbott, facing her, could not avoid seeing it over her shoulder.

"We've brought your weapon with us. The gun Mr. Forrest is holding is a Colt 45, the one you used to murder his mother. Don't you recognize it? Sit down, Abbott."

He was about to speak, but Agatha held up a hand, silencing him and pointing to a chair. Marc took a step forward, his aim never wavering. Abbott sat. He had expected that Forrest would take the lead, but the man stood mutely over him, his face cold and stony. He forced his gaze away from him and back to the woman. She was studying him contemptuously.

"Who are you?" he snarled, "If you want money, I'm willing to negotiate for Kathleen."

Marc lunged toward him and Abbott winced, ducking his head and raising his arms against the impending blow. But nothing happened. He opened his eyes. He felt the cold steel of the Colt at the back of his head. Agatha stepped forward, looming over him.

"Did you really believe we would sell Kathleen?" She stared at him for a long moment and he squirmed under her scrutiny. Then she shook her head and sighed. "I have no need of your money. It can't buy you anything here."

Abbott's mind reeled. He was certain they had come to make some kind of trade. If not Kathleen, what? He tried to remain still, to keep his eyes and expression blank, even though his palms were slick with sweat. First he needed to discover what they wanted. Then he would know how to react. He cleared his throat, keeping his voice low and steady.

"Have you come to kill me then? I didn't mean to hurt her, that woman. It was an accident. She screamed. The gun just went off. I only wanted to find Kathleen."

"And what of Mr. Kelter? Was that an accident too? And Lily Ross? You've been following her."

"I don't know anyone named Kelter. I don't know Lily Ross."

"Oh, please, Abbott. This is childish. Sit up straight and listen to me. We know everything about you and what you've done. You're a stalker and a murderer. You deserve to die, but we haven't come to kill you. Stop lying."

The words galvanized Abbott. The woman's lips moved as he looked into her face, and then behind her, into the face of his grandfather. For a moment, the features of each seemed to dissolve, the two faces merging into one. She spoke to him as his grandfather might have spoken, in anger and bitter rejection.

"Are you ready to listen now?"

Abbott nodded, his eyes sliding against his will from her face to his grandfather's and back again.

"We are here to trade your freedom for Lily's and Kathleen's. We have given you an alibi for the murder of Marie Forrest, a forged marriage licence. That's your insurance policy. Admit to the marriage, and begin divorce proceedings immediately. Your money is flooding back into your accounts even as I speak. We never wanted it, only you. Of course, Marley now knows about your tax evasions through the Cayman accounts, but that's your problem. If he loves money as much as you do, it should be easy to buy him off. Now, here's the crucial point. Are you still listening?"

Marc prodded the back of his head with the gun.

"I'm listening."

"If you ever go near Kathleen again, or Suzy, we will expose the sham. We have your gun. It's registered in your grandfather's name. A simple ballistics test will prove you are a killer. That's our insurance policy. The consequences of exposure will be inconvenient for us, disastrous for you. Do you understand? Leave them alone. No phone calls, no private detectives, no photos, no surveillance. If she ever sees you or hears from you again, or even suspects your influence, we will go straight to the police with the gun and a witness.

"Oh, yes, Abbott. We have a witness. Lily Ross has already told her story to the police. But you know that, don't you? That's why you left Toronto so suddenly. She's told them everything but your name. Do you think they'll find you, Abbott? Will someone who knows you recognize your picture in the paper? Well, never mind. You have an alibi. You are safe as long as Lily is. If anything should happen to her, anything at all, I promise you the police will have enough to link you to Ben Kelter's death."

Abbott's face was a death mask, rigid and chalk-white. So long as they had his grandfather's gun and their eye witness, they had the upper hand. He listened to every word like a condemned man listens to a judge intoning his sentence, but he saw the weakness in their scheme at once. Probing it was his only chance. It was time to challenge them with the knowledge they didn't know he had.

"If you are so certain of your facts, why not go to the police immediately?" He tried but failed to keep the sarcasm from his voice. "I think it might be a little more than *inconvenient* for you to do so."

Agatha stared him down.

"You're wrong. There are people I must protect about whom you know nothing, but no matter the cost, I won't hesitate to destroy you if you push me. I won't be bullied. You've met your match, Abbott."

"As you have met yours. Or should I say as Forrest has met his?"

Abbott heard rather than saw the man behind him move to the side, the gun steady in his hand. He took a deep breath, but didn't have the courage to look at him directly. He heard the metallic click of the gun's hammer being cocked. His bowels felt loose while he struggled for control.

"Marc! Stop." It was the old woman interceding. "What are you talking about, Abbott?"

"Oh, I think Forrest knows. Ask him about a man named Mahoney who raped his sister. Ask him about Amanda Martin."

The woman stepped back as if slapped. Marc moved quickly to her side and glared at Abbott.

"What do you know about Amanda, you sonofabitch? If you've hurt her, I'll shoot you right now."

"Not with that gun, surely. It's your insurance policy."

"We won't need one if you're dead."

"Fair point."

Marc raised the gun again. "Talk."

"Very well. I saw you meet her in Toronto. I saw you give her what looked very much like a payoff. So I followed her to her condo building and read her name on the occupants' list. Once I knew who she was, it was simple. She's a charming conversationalist."

"Nice try, Abbott. But she'd never talk to you willingly."

"Oh, she didn't know who I really was. That would have been foolish. I told her I was a reporter, a friend of Kelter's. I told her I thought his death was linked to an old sexual assault case and that I'd found his notes revealing that she'd been attacked by Mahoney on the night he died. She was very — distressed. Gradually, it all tumbled out. How you saved her, Forrest. Very gallant of you. She also told — "

Abbott interrupted himself. He could sense a shift in the woman's attention. Once rivetted by his story, she had suddenly turned away from him and was staring at the portrait of his grandfather. Her lack of attention disconcerted him.

Marc stepped forward and pressed the gun to his forehead. "Did you hurt her?"

"No."

"Are you sure?"

"No. I mean no, I didn't hurt her. She's much more valuable to me as a witness. You have your witness in Lily Ross. Now I have mine. On tape. I'll trade you a murder for a murder, Forrest. *Quid pro quo.*"

"No, Abbott." It was the woman again. "My deal is the only one on the table. Stay away from the Landers and Ms. Ross or I'll go to the police."

"You wouldn't dare," he sputtered. "Forrest is already scared." He hesitated, then took his biggest gamble. "Kelter was helping him create a new identity. I trailed him to government offices. Saw him meet with people who worked there."

She smiled. She spoke to him in glacial tones. "You're very clever, but you've made a fatal error. You've blurted out too much too soon. Ms. Martin has already left the country and I'll see to it that you'll not find her again. Your illegal tape will never see the inside of a courtroom. You know, your grandfather — this is your grandfather, isn't it? — has the look of a disappointed man. Was it you, I wonder, who so let him down?"

Abbott flinched. Still mindful of the gun, he controlled his impulse to lash out. He was engulfed by a rush of hate intermingled with shame. She was taunting him. He found her loathsome. He sat in his chair as if her cold stare had turned him to stone.

"Come away, Marc. Kill him later if you can't resist, but don't do it here."

He heard them walk away from him toward the door and his muscles began to relax, his joints unlock. But then they stopped. Once more, her supercilious voice addressed him as if he were a child.

"We'll give you three days to make up your mind, Abbott. We'll be watching."

He didn't turn around. He didn't move.

Marc and Agatha left quickly, without glancing back. They opened the door, the brilliant sunshine a shock after the gloominess of the house, and signalled to Harry, who melted back into the hillside. They had done what they could, but they felt no pleasure, no triumph.

As they began the long drive back to New York, Marc slammed his fist against the steering wheel.

"I should have killed the bastard."

"Probably. But we'd have gotten a lot of other people into trouble."

"Did we even stop him?"

"We won't know for sure until we see what he does next. He has no idea what he's stumbled across."

"No, he doesn't, does he? Bravo for Amanda. She must have been terrified, but she still managed to lead him down a blind alley. How the hell did he find out about her? Even if he saw me meet her in Toronto, how did he know she was connected to Mahoney?"

"Is it likely that Ben really did have notes?"

"Very unlikely, I'd say. And Lily will have told no one. Are you certain Amanda's left the country again?

"I've no idea. It was sheer bluffing. But she had the money and the plane ticket you gave her. More importantly, she steered Abbott in the wrong direction. I don't think there's anything to fear from her."

"But?"

"Even though Abbott jumped to some wrong conclusions, he still jumped uncomfortably close. He can jeopardize the safety of a number of people more than he realizes. I think we should put the network on alert. Go quiet for a while. Will you help?"

"Just say how."

"Despite my threats to Abbott, it would be very dangerous to go to the police right now, even with the evidence of the gun. No matter how shaky his arguments, they'd listen to what he had to say about Mahoney. I need a bit of time to take care of that side of things."

"Sure. But I'm not about to go to the police. Who — " Marc groaned. "Why don't you trust Lily?"

"I do. It's she who doesn't trust us."

"She will in time."

"Do we have that time? She's just lost a dear friend, Marc. What we've done is enough for Kathleen and Suzy. Enough even to quiet the ghost of Marie. But Lily feels confused, guilty. A stalemate with Abbott, even if it works, might not be enough for her."

"I don't know what you expect me to do. She has a very deter-mined mind of her own."

"That's just my point, dear. She's every bit as smart as Abbott, and far less blinded by ego. That's what makes the little knowledge she has about Mahoney so dangerous. Talk to her, Marc. Make her let go. For her own sake, and yours."

Monday, August 16, Toronto

Lily lifted Suzy onto her shoulders and together they scanned the line of arriving passengers. Each time the automatic doors of the baggage area slid open, a few more people would emerge, and Lily could feel Suzy's anticipation mount. It was contagious. But Lily's anticipation was far from joyful. Bursting with doubts and ques-tions, she was steeled for battle. And Marc was no longer an ally. About Agatha she wasn't entirely sure either.

Kathleen emerged first, with Marc and Agatha close behind. Lily swung the breathless child over the barrier and watched her propel herself into her mother's open arms. The pair melded into one, in a blur of tangled hair, touching hands, kisses and laughter. *Uncomplicated love,* Lily thought ruefully, and felt a prick of envy.

She raised her eyes and found Marc smiling at her. She ducked away. She wasn't ready yet. This wasn't the time or the place.

When she turned, she noticed that Agatha was watching her, her face drawn and lined, her smile enigmatic. Lily flushed, remember-ing her stealthy reading of the hidden diary in Agatha's home. For a moment, Hayley seemed an unquiet ghost hovering between the two women. Lily stepped forward, reaching out her free hand as if to bridge the wavering divide, but Suzy intervened, hugging Agatha's knees, and Lily's hand dropped to her side.

People began to jostle around them and they were reminded of being in public space. Lily began to gather up luggage and kept her head down. *Later,* she thought, *I'll confront him on my own terms.*

The drive from the airport to Agatha's house was uneventful, though once or twice Lily caught Marc scrutinizing her in the rearview mirror. She calmly glanced away. When they reached the house, she made a point of putting her arm around Agatha and walking with her.

"You look tired," she murmured. "Was it very terrible?"

"Yes, my dear. It was. But Marc will tell you more, if you want to know. And you? You look unsettled. Has the waiting been heavy?"

Lily didn't respond, hoping that Agatha would misread her silence.

"Have you heard from Detective Meyers?"

Lily shrugged. "Only to say that the boy who sold the car to Abbott either refused to, or genuinely couldn't, recognize his picture. So you were right. Chances are they'll never find enough evidence to connect him to Ben."

"And that still troubles you? Even though we may have stopped him?"

Kathleen came around the side of the house and waved to them, holding up a bouquet of snapdragons and gladioli Suzy had picked that morning.

"It's wonderful to see them together, Agatha. But are they really rid of him?"

"I hope so. Will you stay to lunch?" She smiled at Lily's hesitation. "No, of course not. You'll want to go home. Marc will take you."

Lily was about to protest, but stopped herself. Best to get it over, she thought.

"All right. Just let me say goodbye to Suzy. She's had enough of not being told what's really going on and enough of people disappearing." If Agatha detected the irony of Lily's words, she gave no sign.

Birch Avenue seemed an oasis. Lily turned the key and entered her living room as if she were reclaiming her space. Marc's suitcase stood pointedly at the bottom of the stairs. She felt it made a suitably blunt statement.

"I don't think *I've* left anything out," she smiled.

He caught the double entendre.

"Okay, Lily. I know you're angry. Will you give me a chance?"

"I gave you too many chances, and you took advantage of them all. You must have searched my room, you went through my files. Tell me, did you ever mean to help Ben and me, or were you just sent by the network to spy?"

"Not guilty."

"Sure, Marc. Whatever you say. Will you tell me, before you go, who you were protecting? I know it wasn't me or Ben."

"I didn't betray you, Lily. Despite how it looks. I didn't go through your stuff, though I know now who did. That's how he knew about Amanda."

Lily stared. "What? Are you saying Abbott was in this house? In my bedroom?" She shivered as if she had just brushed against a cobweb in the dark.

"Did you have notes on Amanda and her connection to Mahoney's death? Notes on the earlier assaults and Ben's articles on Jeanine?"

Lily nodded. "But how? When?" She frowned, trying to concentrate. "I remember when you first came to stay, I felt someone had been in my room. I put it down to the strangeness of sharing my house. If only I had trusted my instincts and told Ben. I might have warned him."

"It wouldn't have mattered. It wouldn't have saved him."

She felt the sting of tears in her eyes and she pushed away her regrets about Ben. "Maybe not. But you could have trusted me. Did you know about Agatha and the network all along? Did you know that Agatha arranged for Amanda to go to Mexico? It must have been amusing to watch me fumble around in the dark."

"It wasn't like that at all."

"Wasn't it? Why did you intercept Amanda's call to me? Oh, yes. I found out from a mutual acquaintance that Amanda tried to reach me when she first returned to Toronto. What were you afraid she might tell me?"

Marc looked shaken but he held his ground.

"Okay, I should have told you. But the reason isn't sinister. You weren't well."

"Oh, please."

"And Agatha asked me to meet Amanda."

"Why?"

"Lily, drop this. Whatever you're imagining, what happened the night Mahoney died has nothing to do with Abbott or with Ben's death. It has nothing to do with the network."

"I'm sorry, but I don't believe you. And I've much more to go on than my imagination."

Suddenly Marc's calm abandoned him. Exasperated, he grabbed her by the shoulders. "What are you talking about? Why should you give a damn who killed Mahoney? Believe me, he deserved to die. Do you have any idea what he did to those women?"

"I do. I found Hayley's diary."

Marc dropped his hands from her shoulders immediately. Lily could see he was deeply shocked, and a flood of compassion softened her anger against him. His own sister had been brutalized by Mahoney. Hayley, she remembered, had been his lover for a time. She led him into the living room and pushed him into a chair.

"Are you all right?" she asked.

He nodded.

"Then listen to me, Marc. I care because I owe it to Ben to be certain the network is not involved in Mahoney's death. I've agreed to let Agatha deal with Abbott in her own way, outside of the courts, for the sake of Kathleen and Suzy and all the other women hidden by the network, even though my silence means that Ben's killer remains free. I can't keep silent if the network is also protecting a murderer."

"Something in the diary makes you think the network is involved?"

"Yes."

"Tell me."

"I found the diary in Agatha's house while I was minding Suzy. And ... I read it. It was written in the first person, of course, but it describes the assault and a terrifying descent into rage and self-hatred. And Marc, it ends so ambiguously. I've memorized the words. Listen: *I'm going away, flying away, to fashion my own death. To reclaim my life. When Mahoney dies, only then, will I be fully free. Retribution.* It's dated just before Hayley flew to Antigua. Do you know what really happened there, Marc? That first night we went to see Agatha ... I know the news of Hayley's death shocked you. Isn't it possible she's still alive?"

"That's a huge assumption. She might have written those words intending vengeance and still died in a car crash. People say things, even write things in diaries, that reflect the pain of the moment. You can't read those words as a statement of fact."

"But what does *fashioning my own death* mean then? It doesn't sound like a suicide message to me. Doesn't it suggest staging her own death, even faking her own death?"

"I don't know, Lily. But Hayley can't be alive. Agatha would know, and I refuse to believe she would live that lie. Do you really think she's capable of that?"

Lily felt miserable. "What are the rules, Marc? Go to any lengths to protect women and children you don't even know and not protect your own daughter? I don't want to believe it either, but what if Hayley is the woman Amanda Martin saw that night? What if she killed Mahoney?"

Throughout her explanation, Lily had been kneeling in front of Marc, looking directly into his eyes. She saw them cloud with emotion, and when he finally spoke again, he sounded weary, as if every word uttered was an act of will.

"Kathleen and Suzy are flying out of the country tomorrow. Until we know what Abbott's going to do we thought it best to get them away. There's no chance of hiding them here any longer or of fixing new identities. I'm going with them as far as Paris and then staying on to visit Jeanine. Will you come with me, Lily?"

Without warning, he reached out and touched her face, stroking it with his fingertips from her forehead and across her cheek to her chin. His touch stirred memories: the gentleness of his hands when they'd made love, the slow, steady rise and fall of his chest as she'd lain across him, feeling the heat of his body under hers.

Abruptly, she stood up and turned her back to him. It wasn't possible. It couldn't be.

"Will you come?" he asked again.

"I can't," she whispered.

"Lily, look at me." He didn't wait for her to respond, but came and stood before her. "Hayley didn't kill Mahoney. It isn't true."

"You can't know for certain."

"I can. I do. I talked to Amanda. She saw a woman with a gun in the dark when she was half mad with fear. She ran away. She never saw who pulled the trigger. It could have been anyone. It could have been me."

"Why would you say that? Why are you doing this?"

"Because I want you to stop, to move on. Lily, listen. A few months ago, you wrote a story that hurt others. Mostly, it hurt you. Don't make the same mistake again. Come with me."

Lily wavered. She felt a longing to start fresh, to clear her mind of doubt and questions. But she couldn't do it. Not yet. She shook her head.

They stood motionless together for a long time and then Marc walked to the door and picked up his suitcase.

"Tread carefully. Agatha is many things, but wherever the truth lies, she's still a mother who's lost her child. Goodbye, Lily Ross," he said, and then he was gone.

Lily covered her face with her hands.

The weather had cooled overnight, the first faint whiffs of autumn drifting in the air. Once more, Lily found herself knocking on Agatha's door, this time alone. She had half-hoped and half-feared that Marc would call her before he left, that she might hear his voice once more, but when she had dived for the phone it had been Agatha, inviting her to afternoon tea.

Agatha led Lily to the blue and green sun room and settled comfortably on the sofa beside her. "At last," Agatha said, smiling. "Quiet. I've forgotten how taxing a six-year-old can be. And Kathleen is almost as excited. She must have looked at her passport a dozen times. I'm not sure what delights her more — not having to look over her shoulder, or having a passport in her own name."

"I've wondered about that," Lily confessed. "The network would have given her a new identity?"

"Yes, with time. I suspect your friend Ben discovered quite a bit about that side of the network. The penalties, should we be detected, are serious, but not nearly so serious as the circumstances of the women we've hidden."

"How many women?"

"It's really best for you not to know. I'm sure you understand. Still, I wanted to see you in part to assure you that the activities of the network have been temporarily suspended."

"You're not convinced that Abbott has been stopped?"

"I'm convinced we must be cautious, that's all. Though I must admit, Lily, you sometimes sound as if you'd like the plan to fail."

She flushed. "It's not that. Only, I wanted to see him pay publicly, in court, for what he did to Ben."

"And you still believe the law would have punished him?"

"I understand the risks, the price we would have had to pay, but, yes, I believe that. Or I want to. It angers me that Abbott walks the earth, while Ben lies beneath it."

"Ah, Lily. You want someone to blame for the cruel things that happen to us."

"I'm not a child. I've known loss before. But I've never known violence or fear and I find that all my guidelines are shifting. Ben was like a brother. I can't settle for doing less than my best for him."

"Forgive me, but I don't think this is about Ben. It's about you. You want catharsis and closure. But the law will not give you that. You would find little comfort there, much less safety. Abbott could well walk away from any formal charges with less restraint on him than we've provided."

"But I am guilty, Agatha. If only I hadn't involved Ben."

"We're all involved. But Ben made choices, too. He chose to place you in his life and to try to help you. You must honour that choice. He would not welcome your self-punishment as a substitute for punishing Abbott."

"Then help me, Agatha. Help me understand how to live with the injustice. How did you learn to cope with what Mahoney did? A paltry few years in prison can hardly have been adequate. Didn't you rejoice when you heard of his death?"

Agatha regarded her with unruffled calm.

"I did not. Oh, once I suppose I yearned for it. But his death came too late for my personal gratification. I'd already learned that it could not reverse events or restore all that had been lost. Like all men of violence, he eventually courted his own death."

"Not quite. He was murdered."

"Murder. What does that mean, really? What makes a killing a murder? When it is planned? When it is malevolent? Or self-serving? I think evil is the crux of murder, as Abbott is evil. He enjoys inflicting suffering on others. But what of killing without evil intent? Mercy killing, or self-defence? What would you do, Lily, if you had the choice and the means to save a life by taking a life? Would you ponder moral absolutes and let events take their course while young women, some barely adults, suffer and die? Or would you act and risk everything?"

Lily stared. "What are you trying to say, Agatha? That killing is justified?"

"No. Only that context is not irrelevant. That you cannot find the peace you are seeking in moral certainties. We are sometimes called upon to make decisions in extreme circumstances. Suppose you had a cherished friend whose seventeen-year-old daughter was corrupted by an older man, for profit and his own amusement. He promised her a dazzling career of the sort that turns a young girl's head, and then hooked her on drugs and used her to make pornographic videos. She was beaten when she resisted, and finally died a miserable death at the end of a dirty needle. There were others like her.

"The man finally was investigated by legal authorities, but the law he'd learned to skirt could not touch him. Those young women he had broken were too frightened or too damaged to testify. Then the man was deliberately set up by illegal means, and information leaked to the police about his partners in drug dealing. One of those partners killed him in reprisal. Would you call that an arm's-length murder, or a just execution?"

Lily opened her mouth to speak, but Agatha ignored her.

"Or suppose you knew of a psychiatrist who systematically betrayed the trust of his female patients. A serial rapist, really, protected by a title and a degree. Then a young woman commits suicide, driven to that lonely darkness by his assault. He is reported to the medical board, but they look the other way, embarrassed by their dirty laundry. After all, his patients are by definition unstable. He relocates to another state. And it all begins to happen again. You break into his home, looking for evidence to convict him, and he bursts in upon you. You had no right to be there, but you shoot him. Is that murder, Lily, or self-defence?"

Lily was now frightened and confused. "I — I don't know. Are you telling me these things really happened, that these scenarios are true?"

"Of course they're true. Things like this happen every day. The statistics on violence against women are staggering, but the individual stories seldom end so aptly. All I'm saying, Lily, is that it isn't always easy to judge. I might have planned Mahoney's death, but I didn't. The network is not guilty of this."

"I never thought — "

"You suspected."

"I worried. I have a right to know the full story. I'd like a chance to make my own choices without being manipulated. I'm inclined to protect you, Agatha, as you have protected me. But if Detective Meyers pushes, will he find anything, anything at all, that he mustn't know?"

Agatha regarded her with surprise. "I'm glad you care, Lily. More than I can say. But he will find only an old woman, turned philosophical."

Lily felt soothed but still cautious.

Agatha reached out and took her hand. "Take your time. Think carefully. I'm sure you'll find your way."

Wednesday, August 18, Connecticut

Abbott had bet everything on Kathleen, and everything was ruined. She was meant to belong to him, and she did not. She was meant to be grateful to him, and she had defied him. She was meant to be sorry, and she had evaded his punishment. He'd spent hours, days and nights, living with his failure. His mind crashed against it again and again like stormy waves against a cruel, immovable rock.

For several days, he wandered like a stranger through his own home. Everything he saw, everything he touched, was worthless now. Dust in his hands, gritty and irritating. He'd achieved nothing. He'd won nothing. The old woman's taunts had made him feel weak and useless.

Reeking of his own sweat, as his mother used to reek of gin, he tried crawling at night into the memories of his childhood. He was chosen. He was the heir. He was to be his grandfather incarnate. He prayed that the fragmented images of his youth would blur in memory, softening the sharper edges. But they never did for long. He kept cutting himself on the jagged bits whenever he leaned back too far into the past. He looked into his grandfather's eyes, the eyes that stared down pitilessly from the portrait, and winced. He could feel his scowl from across the room.

Who was the old crone? What was she to Kathleen? He saw the old woman's face, at times indistinguishable from his grandfather's face, puckered with lines around the mouth, spilling over with contempt. He remembered her voice, paper-thin and high-pitched, like a mosquito buzzing in his head. *We'll be watching. We'll be watching.* They thought they'd outsmarted him, left him beaten like a mangy dog flinching from a raised fist. But nobody had the right to humiliate him.

On the third day, he rallied. He began circling the study, slowly. Here, in this room, his grandfather's lessons had always begun and ended: reward when he excelled, hard won measures of affection and praise; punishment when he faltered, the stiffness of disgust, the slashing words. Methodically, coldly, Abbott began to break things. An exquisite vase of paper-thin Venetian glass shattered at his feet. He opened the china cabinet with its collection of antique snuff boxes and, one by one, smashed them against the walls. He ripped open books and tore out fistfuls of pages. The tearing and shattering power of his hands was good. He began to feel stronger.

He picked up a penknife, almost by accident, and stabbed a leather chair. He stabbed it again. He grabbed the chair by the legs and toppled it over. His breath came in rapid pants and a thin smile stretched his lips. He ransacked the room.

Later, exhausted but calm, he walked upstairs, humming, feeling the polished slide of the banister beneath his throbbing hands. He showered, shaved, and parted his hair neatly. He dressed in black slacks and shirt. *Almost ready,* he thought, *almost there.* He began to say the words aloud in a kind of chant, in a soft, sing-song voice. Then he reached for his phone, made the necessary arrangements, and sat down to wait.

Wednesday, August 18, Toronto

Lily dragged the last box down the stairs and tipped out its disordered contents onto the living room floor. Sitting down amid the clutter of files and print negatives, she began to sort ruthlessly. She felt lighter. Unencumbered. The morning's sorting was a creative act, forcing her to make decisions about her future and judgements about her past.

Yet the haphazard collage of images scattered across the floor refused to suggest a pattern. They captured shifts of light, the tracery of shadows, the subtle mutations of colour — all fleeting and insubstantial moments, sometimes delicately beautiful, but without the grounding of purpose. Lily sat among the memories of a thousand frozen moments, and listened to what the images told her.

She had looked keenly and deeply, but had lived less so.

She had focused through a viewfinder, beyond surfaces, searching out shades of emotion and mood, with the click of the shutter as if an audible signal to move on and away.

She had published a story that hadn't honoured those emotions. Perhaps one day she could make amends. In the meantime, she yearned to start anew.

She picked up a trash bag and began stuffing it with the distractions and burdens she no longer needed. Within the clear space she was creating, she would invent a purpose and a direction for her life. Perhaps because they both suffered regrets, she had spent hours over the last few days talking with Agatha, finding comfort and reassurance there. Marc was right. It was time to move forward. Her hand fell upon a photograph she'd taken two years before. Studying it, she remembered climbing out of bed at dawn, with the moon setting. She'd tried to film that evasive wafer of moon, but the developed print had yielded nothing more than a flat, white sky. She stopped. She thought she could do better.

The ringing of the doorbell surprised her, but she jumped up to answer it without hesitation.

She was no less startled to see Detective Meyers than he apparently was to see her. Gradually Lily realized that sometime during the morning it had begun to rain. The detective looked wet and cross. She stepped away from the open door.

"Oh, sorry. Please come in. I wasn't expecting anyone."

Detective Meyers nodded, but said nothing until he'd removed his damp overcoat. His quick, observant glance took in the chaos of her living room and her tousled appearance.

"I thought I'd drop by, Ms. Ross. See how you were coping. I must say, you opened the door quickly. From a policeman's point of view, even carelessly."

There was an undeniable reproach in his words, and Lily remembered somewhat belatedly that for Meyers nothing had changed. She was supposed to be cowering in her house, ever mindful of the lurking presence of an unknown gunman. Instead, she had flung open the door as if to a trusted friend, which, she reminded herself, Meyers wasn't.

"I looked through the peephole," she lied smoothly. "And, besides, it's hardly likely that he'd ring the bell."

Meyers raised a doubting eyebrow, but didn't answer. Embarrassed, Lily quickly changed the subject, falling back on the safe civilities of social interaction.

"I'll just make some coffee, if you don't mind. Perhaps you'll join me? I've been clearing out files all morning, but you're welcome to find a path to the sofa. I won't be long."

Another lie. Lily fled to the kitchen and took as long as she possibly could fixing the coffee without inviting undue notice. She fetched cream and sugar, and fiddled with cups on a tray, all the while calming herself with the story she'd memorized, and a dozen innocent reasons why a conscientious officer of the law might visit her after she'd told it.

Somewhat recovered, she served the coffee, found a chair opposite Meyers and smiled, she hoped, encouragingly.

"I'm grateful for your concern. I've seen the cruisers drive by. Several neighbours have even commented on the increased police presence on Birch Avenue. Perhaps you were right, and all the attention has frightened him away."

"Perhaps. You've not seen anything unusual, then? Or sensed yourself being watched or followed?"

"No. Nothing."

"And you and Mr. Forrest, Marc, you've not remembered anything which might connect the man you saw to the family or to Little Falls?"

Lily shook her head. "Sorry."

"Is Mr. Forrest staying here with you?"

"No. He left yesterday for France to visit his family."

"Really? Will he be staying long?"

"I think so. Perhaps as long as several months. There's no problem, is there?"

Just MURDER

Meyers sighed. "No, of course not. It's just — look, you seem remarkably unconcerned about staying alone. I find that odd."

"Would you feel the same, I wonder, if I were a man?" Lily asked mutinously.

"*You* came to see *me*, Ms. Ross."

The two glared at each other. Then Meyers moved on:

"I came to tell you we've reached a dead end on the Kelter case. Oh, we had a number of calls from the public after running the sketch of the gunman in the paper. *He's my dentist, or my mechanic, or my child's teacher. I've seen him following me ...* that sort of nutty thing. But nothing substantial. As a matter of fact, that lends credence to your theory. If he'd had a history or a life in Toronto, someone should have recognized him and come forward. I just can't figure out why he would give up on you — the only witness to the scene in Little Falls — and follow Mr. Kelter instead."

Lily shrugged. "I can't help you, I'm afraid."

Meyers regarded her closely, but she held his gaze. He rose to leave.

"Well, thanks. Sorry to bother you." Then he seemed to change his mind, and slowly sank down onto the sofa again. "Just one more query, Ms. Ross."

"Yes?"

"How well do you know Agatha Quinn?"

"Agatha? I think I mentioned, didn't I? We all met around the time of the Mahoney assaults. Jeanine introduced us."

"So you met Hayley Quinn and her friend, Bonnie Morgan?"

Lily hesitated. Should she have known them? What would make the most sense? What had Marc told her about them? The rule was, tell the truth as much as you can.

"Yes, I knew them. But we drifted apart after Jeanine left to study in Paris. Then, after Hayley's car accident, Bonnie moved to the West Coast. I've come to know Agatha better since then. She's alone now."

"Ah, yes, the car accident. Peculiar thing, that."

Lily's heart lurched. "Peculiar? Why?"

Meyers leaned forward. "Mrs. Quinn never discussed the details with you?"

"No. I mean, it was very painful. I think she wondered if the accident were deliberate, a suicide, but all that matters in the end is that Hayley died instantly."

"Now, that's interesting. I talked to the police in Antigua, and they faxed me the accident report. They wondered, too, if it was deliberate. There were some definite oddities, and some inconsistencies in the witnesses' accounts."

Lily furrowed her dark brows, but was afraid to raise her eyes. "Such as?" she asked gently.

"Hayley and Bonnie — "

"Bonnie?" Lily interrupted.

"Yes, Bonnie was with her, didn't you know?"

"No. Agatha didn't say."

"Well, the two of them were staying at the St. James Club between English Harbour and Willoughby Bay. That's on the southwest side of the island. It's a very posh place with a private yacht club and a casino. Very self-contained, as such resorts usually are. But on the night of the accident, Hayley and Bonnie drove clear across the island to St. John's. The roads in Antigua are notoriously poor — rough and coarse, many still unmarked. Most tourists take taxis at night, and leave the driving to the locals. The manager of the St. James tried to dissuade them, but it seems Hayley was determined. They went to a casino in St. John's, but witnesses say they didn't play the tables much. Seems they were engaged in a serious discussion, some said an argument. Anyway, Bonnie left and took a taxi back to St. James.

"After that, the picture becomes less clear. Witnesses say that Hayley struck up a conversation with another young woman and that they left together after drinking a good deal. Others say they think Hayley left the casino alone. In any case, the car crashed on All Saints Road, on a sharp turn near Sea View Farm. No skid marks. It rolled several times and burst into flame. Identification of the body was made by Ms. Morgan based on several pieces of jewellery her friend was wearing at the time."

Lily sighed. "Poor Bonnie."

"Yes; apparently she was quite shocked. She told the police that Hayley would not have been drinking as she was taking antidepressants. She said their discussion — she denied it was an argument — was about plans for their future, and that Hayley was feeling energized and optimistic on their vacation. She left because she had a headache, but Hayley had apparently promised her that she would leave the rental car in St. John's and not drive the roads alone. She had expected her to take a taxi also."

"She might have changed her mind. She was headstrong. What did the third woman say?"

Meyers leaned back on the sofa and spread his arms. "That's the problem. The police never found her. Tourists come and go all the time. They had no name and only a sketchy description, often a contradictory one, as witnesses' descriptions frequently are. Tell me, what does Bonnie look like?"

Lily stiffened. "Why would you want to know that?"

"I'm just thinking that the witnesses may have confused the time-lines. That there was no third woman at all, and they were really remembering Bonnie. The police in Antigua didn't think to ask that question. On the other hand, if there was a third woman, Ms. Ross, isn't it possible that she was in that car? An autopsy wasn't deemed necessary, scarcely possible in any case, and there were no dental checks run. If I were Agatha Quinn, I'd want to know for certain."

Lily was conscious of a dull pounding in her chest that was making it difficult for her to think or breathe. "I — I don't believe that what you are suggesting is possible. Agatha wouldn't ... I mean, she's been through so much. Hayley is buried in Mount Pleasant Cemetery. Marc went to visit the grave when he was staying here. He told me. The third woman must have been Bonnie."

"So help me," Meyers persisted. "What does she look like?"

Lily closed her eyes and tried to recall the photographs on Hayley's wall. "She's pretty and shy. About the same height as Hayley, fairly slight. She has sandy hair and blue eyes. I'm afraid I can't tell you much more. I only saw her a few times and, frankly, Hayley was so striking she overshadowed her. People have a tendency, I guess, to be struck by beauty and not to notice anyone else in as much detail."

Meyers nodded. "Well, that's pretty vague. But the description could fit."

Lily felt an intensity of emotion that she couldn't explain even to herself. She wanted to scream at Meyers, plead with him to squelch his curiosity. Only a few days ago, she had stood in this living room while Marc had made the same plea to her. She'd made her choice now. She'd moved forward, hadn't she? With every fibre of her will, she forced herself to speak.

"I fail to see how Hayley's death has anything to do with Ben, or anything to do with what I saw in Little Falls. Agatha was right, it was better for me not to know the details, and I'm sorry I asked. Now, if you don't mind, I'm very tired. I still have a great deal of sorting to do."

Meyers rose to his feet at her dismissal, but looked neither surprised nor insulted. "I'm sorry to have upset you. I'll see myself out."

He crossed the room without offering his hand, or Lily hers. When he reached the door, he turned around to look back at her, frozen in her chair.

"You know, Ms. Ross, it's funny that you didn't raise the obvious question."

"Which is?"

"If, by some miracle, Hayley *is* alive, why would she want people to believe she's dead?"

He closed the door behind him, and Lily closed her eyes, as if by doing so she could shut out her treacherous doubts.

Much later, in the early evening, Lily stared at her phone. She picked it up. Her hand was shaking slightly, and she felt very miserable. Her wariness of Meyers had hardened into animosity, but she was also alarmed that his thought processes so nearly matched her own. They had arrived, by different routes, at the same suspicion and, for Lily at least, the fear that Hayley was somehow, somewhere, alive. She was determined to make one last effort to prove the suspicion unfounded and settle her own mind.

The voice that answered was young and cheerful, though somewhat preoccupied by the chatter of a toddler in the background.

"Is this Bonnie Morgan?" Lily asked.

"Speaking."

"Bonnie, my name is Lily Ross. I'm sorry to track you down. The operator in Sechelt gave me your number. I'm a friend of Agatha Quinn's. Look, I know this is out of the blue, but I wonder if I might talk to you about Hayley, about what happened in Antigua."

"Is Agatha all right?"

"Yes, she's fine. For now. But there's been a policeman here asking questions. And — "

"A policeman?"

"Yes, it's difficult to explain. But he seems to think that ... I'm sorry, Bonnie, but he seems to think there's some chance that Hayley didn't die in that car crash."

Lily heard the sharp intake of breath on the other end of the line. She waited, the phone heavy in her hand. Finally, Bonnie spoke.

"I — I'm sorry. I can't help you. Please leave me alone."

Several seconds passed before Lily realized that the line had been disconnected. She put down the phone, staring at it transfixed.

Fear. There was no question that Bonnie's last sentence was spoken in fear.

Unsteady and confused, Lily walked upstairs and changed into jeans and a heavy sweater. It was all horribly clear to her. No matter what Amanda Martin had seen, or hadn't seen, as Marc had implied, no one had ever explained why Agatha had pulled strings to send her away to Mexico. There were the clothes and makeup in Agatha's house. The portrait and the photographs of Hayley. But, most of all, there was the diary. Lily hadn't sought out the missing pieces of the puzzle, the part of the story that happened in Antigua, but it had come to her nonetheless. And now she had to live with that knowledge.

Locking her door behind her, Lily stepped down into the dark blue dusk. The rain had softened into a misty fog and she welcomed its coolness on her exposed skin. She walked slowly, as if each step might bring her closer to a decision. What had Agatha said about choices? Her heart must make one now.

She paused at the Yonge Street entrance to Mount Pleasant cemetery, its tall, wrought-iron gates locked. She needn't go in. She could turn back now. But she felt compelled to go on. The cemetery was huge, a reminder of human fragility in the midst of the life of the city. She would have to circle the block, heading north and then east to enter the graveyard through the Mount Pleasant Road gates.

Her route took her downhill in the fading light. She felt again the oddity of cars passing her on one side, while on the other, rounded tombs and marble angels stood guard over the silent fields of the dead. Eventually, she reached Mount Pleasant and, as she had expected, her way was barred. But the gate was lower here, set into stone walls, and she scaled it easily.

For awhile, she kept to the broad paved paths. During the day, people walked and cycled here, for pleasure and quiet reflection.

Jan Rehner

The grounds were not uninviting. They were well treed, with a wide variety of oaks, poplars, maples, and firs. The air was drenched with the scent of pine boughs in the rain. Even at night, the darkness welcomed her.

She began to wander along the smaller paths, past the rows of gravestones marking remembered and, sometimes, sadly forgotten lives. She whispered the names aloud as she passed them, as if in utterance, even anonymous to her, they might live again on her lips. Many of the headstones were weathered by age, their chiseled letters blurred by fingers of moss-green lichen. Others were new, raw-looking, still sharply contoured.

Then she found it. *Hayley Quinn, Beloved Daughter and Friend.* The stone was simple and dignified, a smooth marbled rose, glistening with moisture. She knelt down and traced the carved letters with her fingertips. They seemed implacable, irrefutable.

"Who are you?" she murmured.

She listened to the rain dripping from the pines overhead, and in their silence recognized her choice. She raised a finger to her lips, making the gesture a promise.

Wednesday, August 18, Connecticut

In the hollow on the side of the hill, Harry saw and heard nothing. Occasionally, he would scoot over to the grassy ledge and peer down at Oakwood Manor, but its exterior was unchanging in the waning light. No one had seen or heard from Abbott in three days. At night, not even a trail of lit windows had marked his movements inside the house. All was darkness and silence.

Harry checked his watch. It was almost 10:00. The sharp outlines of the house and its surrounding trees were already melting into the thicker blackness of night. Clouds obscured the moon, and the wind was gusting. Harry didn't fancy getting wet if an August thunderstorm was building. He thought he might slip down the hill and peer through a window or two.

He crept toward the side door off the kitchen, expecting to find it locked. He jumped back, half in surprise and half in fright, to find it open. The air was stale and clammy, as if the windows had not been opened for some time, nor the air conditioner turned on.

Had Abbott slipped away?

The thought sobered Harry and gave him the courage to investigate further. The first few rooms yielded no traces of Abbott, and he gave them only a cursory glance. Silently he climbed the stairs, his legs shaky and his mind filled with images from the staircase murder of the private detective in *Psycho*.

He pressed on. In the bathroom off the master bedroom, the shower stall was still beaded with moisture. He found a damp towel, and a thin layer of stubble in the sink. He turned and saw that the bed had not been slept in.

Midway down the stairs, Harry's steps faltered. From this angle he could see clearly into the study. It was ravaged, the floor littered with paper and glass, the furniture toppled and marred with ugly gashes. Above the mahogany desk, its shiny surface clawed by a sharp blade, the door to the wall safe yawned open. He wove his way through the chaos and peered inside it. It was as empty as he feared it would be.

This was no burglary. This was an attack. The safe told him that Abbott had money and a passport. The ritual destruction of the room told him that Abbott had snapped. By why only this room? Why was the rest of the house untouched?

Harry crept into the living room. Everything was orderly and normal, the furniture undisturbed. And yet, he knew, this was the place where Agatha Quinn had delivered her ultimatums. Surely this room should have been the target of violence. He closed his eyes briefly and tried to imagine the scene. Here, he thought, is the chair where Abbott must have sat. He turned and took a few steps. And here, he thought, is where Agatha must have stood. His eyes lifted to the portrait and he felt his flesh crawl. Without thinking, he bolted from the room.

Eva's forehead still itched from its stitches and she rubbed it in the darkness. Her sleep had been disturbed by the sound she hadn't heard. It was just past 11:00, and the phone hadn't rung. Harry hadn't checked in.

She swung herself out of bed and wrapped herself in Ruby's terry cloth robe. It swam on her slender body, and she gathered up the excess folds and seemed to float down the stairs. Ruby didn't hear her coming. She was sitting in the pale halo of a single lamp, staring into mid-distance, one hand clamped on the receiver of the lifeless phone balanced on her lap.

"Something's wrong," Eva said.

Ruby turned to her and smiled sadly. "Yes, I think so. Harry's gotten himself in trouble, likely. He wouldn't miss a call. Not after he promised."

"He's only a half-hour late. Perhaps ... ?"

When the phone rang, both women jumped. Ruby snatched it up while Eva hovered, anxious to overhear. But Ruby said nothing. Her face slowly drained of colour.

"He's gone," she whispered. "Harry says he's disappeared."

Eva felt a surge of adrenaline and anger. They should never have let Harry stand watch alone. Despite her injuries, she should have gone with him. She grabbed the phone and shouted into it.

"Damn it, Harry. What's happened?"

His words shook Eva to the core, and she whirled away from the phone, taking the stairs two at a time. She focused her mind on Abbott while she pulled on her jeans. Not for a second did she suppose he had gone into hiding. She slipped off her sling, and forced her arm through the sleeve of a navy sweatshirt that Ruby had lent her. The pain was excruciating. She bit down on her lip, found her purse and took out her gun, her hands steady and sure, even if her heart wasn't. Then she lifted up the sweatshirt that fell to her knees and manoeuvred the gun into her waistband, the steel cold and hard against her flat stomach.

By the time she reached the front door, Ruby was backing her car out of the drive. Eva's spirits rose. It was a sleek-looking Porsche sports model.

"How fast can this thing go?" she gasped.

"Better hang on, honey. Get in. I'll drive."

Eva tried, but each time they swerved around a corner, jarring her shoulder, she winced and once or twice she cried out. Ruby wanted to stop, but Eva urged her on.

"Don't slow down," she urged. "Let's just get there."

"Where's there?" Ruby asked.

"The border. He's going after Lily. I know it."

She had no idea how much of a start he had, but Harry told her he'd abandoned the Jag. Would he risk flying? No, the border was more porous on the ground. That meant he'd have to steal, borrow, or rent a car. A car borrowed from someone — Marley? — would be far safer than stealing or renting one. It might take hours to trace. There was plenty of time to phone Lily and warn her. The simple, logical fact of distance between Connecticut and Toronto would save her.

It had to. Because Eva knew that Abbott was no longer contained by caution or the bounds of reason. He was no longer methodically, coldly, laying plans for his future, but thrashing about wildly in an irrational tangle of the present and the past. Harry had warned her. Abbott had broken before his grandfather's portrait and furiously gouged out its eyes.

Thursday, August 19, Toronto

Abbott lay hidden in the tall wet grass on the steep slope of the ravine and watched the sun rise, its tawny rose streaks vivid against a cobalt sky. The calm seemed preternatural after the turbulence of the summer storm that had shaken the city the previous night, uprooting trees and felling hydro poles.

Abbott had been slowed by the violence of the weather, but not stopped. The guards at the border had warned him about the storm while they checked his passport, and he assured them he'd stop at the first motel. Instead, he'd driven through rain so intense he'd felt he was underwater, his path lit only by jagged forks of lightning licking through solid black with a sharp suddenness. His car had rocked unsteadily in gale force winds, his tires barely finding purchase on highways-turned-rivers. Even now, in the eerie stillness of dawn, he could hear faint rumblings of thunder as the storm blew eastward. Much closer, much louder, the sirens of fire trucks and emergency vehicles wailed as the city began to repair itself from the night's havoc.

He should have been exhausted, but instead he felt rejuvenated. His mind was alert, his body vigorously alive. Once he'd left the car and entered the ravine, the rain had drenched him to the skin and he'd hunkered down amid the upended roots of trees, shivering in the wind. He'd scarcely noticed, discerning little difference between the shivers of cold and the tremors of excitement that shook his limbs and aroused his senses.

The sun, he knew, would be more treacherous than the storm. The higher it rose, the more he would be seduced by its drowsy warmth. He flipped onto his stomach and dug his fingers into the sodden earth, burrowing into the underbrush at the edge of the wide lawn. He watched the opaque blocks of shadow slowly begin to shrink into relentless light.

The garden lay in ruins, tall stems flattened, petals scattered like confetti, twigs and leaves and tree boughs littered across the grass. Abbott focused on the blond splinters of freshly snapped wood. How sharp they looked. How easily they would pierce through skin.

He was too smart to approach Lily's house. Now that the police had his description, the house would be a trap. He would wait for her here. Sooner or later she would come.

How stupid they were to think he wouldn't find her.

They'd sent people to trail him, like dogs pointing a scent. Well, he'd hired his own dog, long before they'd flushed him out of Toronto. The night he'd fled the city, he had made the call to have her watched and, oblivious, Lily had led him straight to this house.

He smiled. He turned his head and rested his cheek against the slippery ground. Most of his past was gone, a blank. He was molding a new shape, struggling upright like the first man on earth rising from the mud. His future flickered uneasily in the distance. They'd found his money in the Caymans but hadn't been able to touch it. There was plenty to hide him for a long time. Brazil, maybe, with its teeming streets and blithe disregard of strangers.

But beyond place, his mind refused to go. His far tomorrows had no texture, no detail. He imagined himself a ghost, disembodied, floating through walls and brushing against people who could neither see nor hear him. The image frightened him and he pushed into the ground, taking refuge in the solid and tangible.

Here and now. This house. Lily Ross. This sweet poison of hate that flowed through his veins.

Thursday, August 19, Toronto

Agatha opened her eyes from a restless sleep, her muscles too lethargic to lift her head from the pillow. She listened and wondered at the stillness of the dawn. Even the birds had been battered and subdued by the storm, but its rushing had neither frightened nor disturbed her. She rather enjoyed the spectacular effects of gothic weather, and had wandered the house in some awe before retiring. By 3:00 a.m., the hydro had been knocked out and the phone lines jammed. The lack of electricity was an annoyance, but she had survived worse. It was the loss of the phone that irked her, the feeling of being cut-off, even temporarily. She felt her age, and its vulnerability.

She slowly unfolded herself from the bed and felt her way to the bathroom. Meticulous about her appearance, she dressed in a dark paisley skirt and a navy long-sleeved blouse, fixing her hair in the pale light of early morning. Then she laid down her brush, folded her hands, and studied her reflection. She usually avoided mirrors. The image she saw in them frequently surprised her. Where had the years gone? She often felt not a day over forty, but the face that stared back at her did not agree. Even the once dark brown of her eyes had faded to a lighter hazel.

Never mind, she sighed, it scarcely mattered. It was the essential person beneath the skin that counted. Eva had taught her that. She could change the colour of her eyes, the colour of her hair, her way of walking, her way of talking at will. Some days, Agatha had trouble remembering which of all her names Eva might be using. Still, she was Eva, and Agatha loved her fiercely. She had always been a chameleon, mimicking voices and mannerisms so easily. But lately, Agatha had watched and worried. Some of the buoyancy was gone, she feared, some of the spirit drained by the weight of difficult choices and the too frequent, too real dangers. In the past few months, Eva had made impetuous mistakes. And now she was hurt. Perhaps by more than a few stitches and a broken bone.

Agatha felt a desperate need to protect her, to hear her voice. She picked up the receiver of the phone, and slammed it down again. She regretted her stubborn dismissal of modern cellphones. She would give anything to hear Eva's voice now, even through a cacophony of bleeps and blips.

She would have to wait. She would go to the garden in the meantime and survey the damage from the storm. Soon Lily was sure to come and check on her. Earnest Lily, who reminded her so much of herself. Who had guessed so much and had somehow managed to get so much of it wrong. Despite Marc's fears, Agatha did trust Lily, knew better even than she the core of her strength and loyalty. She had already planned to place her faith and the network's safety there.

She went to the front of the house first, disconnected the battery-run alarm and opened the door. She paused on the threshold a moment, appalled, then hurried forward. One of several willows along the drive had toppled, its trunk ripped open by lightning, its heavy crown effectively blocking the path from the gates. She picked up one of the thin, shattered branches, letting its feathery green fronds slip through her hands. She loved these trees. She always thought they'd outlive her. She was glad she hadn't seen it fall.

Once the phones were in order, she would have to call her gardening service to clean up the damage. She walked to the gates and opened them so that the service would be able to back the truck into the drive.

She turned and looked back at the house and saw that many of the vines and the trellises on either side of the open front door had been stripped by the wind. Then she walked around to the back garden and raised her hands to her face at the sight of the wreckage. She'd have plenty to keep her busy now.

She picked her way across the lawn and used her keys to open the French doors, slipping off her shoes before entering the sun room. In the kitchen, she dragged out a bucket, found her gardening gloves, and opened the drawer where she kept her clipping shears.

Her fingers closed on the handles convulsively. It was only the faintest of creaks, but she knew the house and all its whispers too well. She knew she was too slow to be able to reach a door in time to save herself. She stood still, only raising her eyes to the kitchen window before her. A vague outline, the barest of shadows behind her, was reflected in the glass.

Now that the moment was here, the moment she'd known would eventually come, she felt strangely calm. So many people she loved had been tested. She would not fail them.

She willed strength into her voice. "So, you're here, Abbott," she said, swinging around to face him.

His skin was deathly pale beneath the smears of mud. His blond hair was matted into darkened strands. She saw the blaze of triumph glitter for a moment in his cold eyes.

"My turn," he gloated. "Where's Lily?"

Agatha shook her head.

For a long time, ten, maybe fifteen seconds, they stood no more than three feet apart, staring at each other. Then he lifted the torn branch held in his right hand and swung it viciously into her face.

She crumpled to the floor in pain, but held onto the shears, only just concealing them in the pocket of her skirt before she felt her arm wrenched upward. He steered her clumsily to the kitchen island, sliding a knife smoothly from its wooden block, and then pushed her toward the stairs.

She couldn't keep her balance and she stumbled on the way up. Each time her steps faltered, he cursed and kicked her, hauling her up and thrusting her forward. She finally fell through the door to the study at the top of the stairs and he left her there for a while, struggling to gather herself.

Gradually, she raised her head and recognized where she was. In the room where the network was born, where she'd found new purpose, where she'd given other women, some she loved and some she never saw, a will and a new way to live.

He had gone to search the house, she supposed, but now she could hear him returning.

"Get up," he shouted.

She rose shakily, and moved to a chair by the fireplace. She smoothed her skirt and slipped her hands into her pockets, not daring to touch her face or wipe away the blood. She lifted her head, and struggled to keep the fear and disgust from her eyes.

"Lily's not here. But she will be. While we're waiting, you'll answer my questions. What are you to Kathleen?" he demanded. "A relative? Why would she turn to you?"

She shook her head and her voice seemed to come from a distance far away. "I'd never met Kathleen, never seen her until a few weeks ago."

"You're lying. You and the Forrests have been helping her for months. You'd never do that for some slut you didn't even know."

"She was a frightened young woman. She needed me. That was enough. I can quite see how you would fail to grasp that."

Abbott laughed and moved toward her. She braced herself for another blow, but he walked by her, behind the chair where she couldn't see him. One hand slipped gently under her chin, and he stretched up her throat until the skin was taut. She could feel the pressure of the blade against her windpipe.

"And what about you? Are *you* frightened? You'll tell me now where she is."

"Never." The word was strangled, barely audible, but Abbott heard her.

"Have it your own way, bitch."

She felt the pressure of the knife increase, the first razor slice of the blade. Had she been able to talk, she might have told him there were some things worth dying for. But there was no time. She gripped the shears and lashed out blindly behind her with every bit of her fading strength.

Thursday, August 19, Buffalo

Eva was frantic. Her journey had turned into a nightmare. She'd phoned Lily a dozen times. She'd phoned Agatha a dozen more. It was as if the whole world was not at home.

She felt nostalgic for the days when cellphones were novelties, when people carried them always and everywhere. By now, though, people had learned to guard their privacy more judiciously and often left their phones in their cars and turned them off in theatres and restaurants. And this, thought Eva ruefully, was supposed to be an age of instant communication. Where was everyone?

Cars sped by, dazzling her in their lights. The slanting rain, heavier now, streamed across her windshield, further blurring her vision. As she and Ruby neared the border, she saw a row of great trees flinching from the wind. The storm was intensifying. They pulled into the next motel. Eva calculated the time they were losing, a terrible arithmetic that added up to impending disaster. If they couldn't get across the border, all would be lost.

"Look, Eva," Ruby coaxed. "We can't go on. Neither, likely, could Abbott. We'll wait out the storm here."

When Ruby disappeared into the motel bathroom, Eva removed her arm from its sling and tied Ruby's scarf into a headband that hid the stitches in her forehead. There wasn't much she could do about the gun still tucked into the waistband of her jeans and hidden beneath the sweatshirt. She slid it around to the small of her back and hoped that she wouldn't be searched. She picked up the keys and headed for the car.

The border guard was a middle-aged, sour-faced man of considerable girth. So late, with the weather so foul, he looked as if he were alone, but Eva caught a glimpse of a pair of uniforms over by the customs building. She knew she must look desperate and since she couldn't disguise her nervousness, she decided to use it.

The guard was at the window, scrutinizing her face.

"It's a terrible time to be driving," he scolded. "Where are you going?"

Eva was not rattled by his brusqueness. Border guards were seldom friendly and seldom smiled. "I'm trying to get home to Toronto. My little girl's sick. She's been taken to the hospital."

"Identification, please."

Eva handed him her Ontario driver's licence and held her breath.

"This your car?"

"No. It belongs to a family friend, Ruby Zaplacinski. But I couldn't get a flight back from New York so I had to drive. Please, I'm in a hurry."

The guard hesitated, reading the concern on her face. For a moment, Eva thought he was going to wave her on. But a glance over at the uniforms changed his mind.

"Sorry. Rules are rules. Pull over. You'll have to fill out paperwork on the car. I assume you have the ownership?"

Did she? Eva had no idea. This was worse than she had expected.

She parked the Porsche by the customs building in the requisite space and got out, trying to hide the fact that her left arm was practically immobile by folding it across her waist. A man in a mechanic's jumpsuit began crawling around the car. He asked her to open the trunk. Eva shuddered to think what Ruby might have put in there. She turned the key and stepped back. It was neat as a pin, empty, except for, ironically, another useless cellphone.

"Pretty fancy car. Ownership?"

Pushing away her doubts, she walked confidently to the glove compartment and popped it open.

Empty.

"You don't have the ownership?" the man asked incredulously.

Her mind raced. *Think, Eva, think.*

She flicked down the visor on the passenger side and almost cried out in relief. Never before had she been so glad to see a piece of paper.

Inside, filling out forms, she'd learned the worst. The storm was battering southwestern Ontario, downing trees and telephone poles. Unless Lily responded to her cellphone, Eva might not reach her in time.

It took four more hours from the border, four miserable, lonely hours. Finally she shut off the engine in front of Lily's house, but could tell nothing from its mute facade. She staggered out of the car, rang the bell, and pounded on the front door. Perhaps Abbott had already been here. Perhaps she was too late. Perhaps he was waiting for her inside, but she didn't care. She just kept pounding.

A neighbour opened the door of the house to the right and glared at Eva.

She turned to him with a stricken face, her dark blue eyes bright and glassy with fever and pain. He immediately softened.

"You don't look so good, miss. Are you all right? Can I help you?"

"Lily. I have to find her. I've been driving all night — the storm." Her words came out in a rush, and she sank onto the top step of the tiny porch.

"Take it easy, it's okay. Lily's fine. I talked to her this morning. She's just gone shopping."

"Shopping?" Eva was incredulous. After the torment of the night, she couldn't believe in anything so mundane. She began to laugh, the high, looping giggles verging on hysteria.

The man regarded her more warily, then seemed to reach a decision. "You're hurt. Why don't you come inside and rest until Lily returns? My wife's inside. We can fix you a cup of tea."

The kindness brought tears to Eva's eyes, and the hysteria drained away. She smiled, for the first time in hours.

"No. Thank you. I'm okay now. I've someplace I can go, not far from here. Is your phone working?"

"Not yet. All we get is a busy signal. But I'll check again, if you like."

"That's okay," Eva didn't think she could bear even a second-hand report of the constant buzzing that had frustrated her every hundred miles or so from New York to the Canadian border. "May I ask a different favour? It's important."

"Sure."

"Will you watch for Lily? As soon as you see her, will you tell her to come straight to Agatha's? I'll wait for her there."

The man nodded, and Eva walked back to the car.

"Ah, just a minute, miss. Who are you? I mean, what name should I give Lily?"

What name, indeed? Eva tried to remember. "Terri," she said finally. "My name's Terri Mordelli." And for the first time, she spoke the name without conviction. Embarrassed, she drove away from the man's suspicion. She wanted to sleep. She wanted to wrap herself in Agatha's arms and wake up to who she really was.

When she approached the house, she saw the gates were open, but the drive blocked by a felled tree. She left the car on the street. She paused at the gates and looked toward the house.

Ahead of her, down the length of the obstructed drive, in the brilliant sunlight of midday, Eva could clearly see the front entry. A sob escaped her lips for she saw with horror that the door was slightly ajar.

A thousand innocent explanations aside, Eva knew instantly it was wrong. The tiny out of place detail sounded in her mind like a siren. She pulled up the baggy sweatshirt and fished the gun from her waistband. It fitted into her hand like an extension of her own body, and its weight sobered her. Her mind cleared. Her trained muscles responded automatically to danger. She felt weightless and moved across the lawn and through the door without a sound.

Inside, she cocked her head and listened. It was too quiet. She slipped off her sneakers and padded down the hall in her bare feet, checking rooms quickly as she went, letting the revolver lead her around corners. She entered the kitchen and read its terrible signs in a single glance. She moved nimbly up the stairs, skipping the third and the eighth steps, which she knew would betray her presence with their time-worn creaks.

At the top of the stairs, by the open study door, she crouched. One chair was out of position, angled to face the fireplace directly while its partner still graced its side. She nosed the gun across the threshold and rose quickly to her full height, scanning the room. But the arc of her circle was broken by the sight of Agatha's head resting on the back of the chair. She crept forward, and her foot landed in a wet puddle, invisible against the garnet carpet. Blood.

Her heart in a vise, her eyes burning, she dropped the gun and stretched out her hand. She was a little girl again reaching out for Agatha's embrace, Agatha's comfort that would make everything all right. She touched her shoulder.

Agatha slipped sideways, falling across the opposite arm of the chair, her head hanging over the edge, exposing the ugly slit in her neck.

Eva recoiled. Her knees buckled and her lungs gasped for air. Instinctively, she crawled toward Agatha, placing her hands gently on either side of the battered face. Carefully, slowly, she eased the body back into an upright position, as if Agatha were only resting in her favourite chair.

When she was finished ministering to the dead, she felt a flash of rage so hot she thought she must be burning alive. Her senses were on fire; she knew without looking that Abbott was here. In this room. She could smell him.

Suddenly the air around her seemed to thicken, and she felt the tiny hairs on the back of her neck stiffen. The branch struck her on the right temple, and she lifted not a finger to defend herself from the blow.

Thursday, August 19, Toronto

Lily was only twenty minutes away. She hadn't gone home after shopping, but had driven straight to Agatha's instead, anxious both to tell her that her choice was made and worried that she might need help after the storm. She hadn't been home to hear her neighbour's story of the frantic young woman banging at her door. She never heard the name, Terri Mordelli, which might have warned her.

When Lily reached the house, her actions duplicated Eva's: she saw the open gate and the fallen tree. She parked her car behind a sleek Porsche. It was as if their movements were synchronized, the same peril chaining the two women together.

But Lily hesitated when she saw the Porsche and its New York plates. She didn't believe in coincidences, and too much had happened in New York for her not to be wary. She stood at the end of the drive and saw the open door, but didn't find it alarming. She skirted the house, heading for the back garden, expecting to find Agatha repairing the damage from the storm. Agatha's shoes, left at the edge of the terrace, merely confirmed her guess and she moved through the French doors confidently, about to call out.

A muddy trail of footprints silenced her at the last second.

She wrinkled her brows, and thought about the New York plates.

She wasn't going to call out. She wasn't going to make any noise at all. She was going to go for the police. Now.

She began backing away, and then her steps faltered. She could hear voices. She strained her ears and tiptoed forward, down the hall, into the kitchen, to the foot of the stairs, until the words were distinct.

Eva's arms were tied behind her back with the scarf that had once been her sling and then her headband. The pain was so fierce, she had eventually gone numb, her body simply shutting down, except for her shallow breathing. She felt she was floating outside her body, surveying the room from a point somewhere on the ceiling. There she was, slumped against a bookshelf, her legs stretched out in front of her. Abbott sat across from her in the middle of the floor, fondling the gun.

"Why did you have to kill her?" Her words were thick and slurred.

Abbott shrugged. "She defied me. I'd never thought of knives before. They're so much quieter than guns."

He aimed the gun directly at her head and cocked the hammer.

She stared at him, refusing to close her eyes.

At the last instant, his aim swerved and the gun exploded. Eva screamed, the bullet slamming into the wall behind her. He tossed the gun aside, as if it no longer interested him.

On the stairs, Lily's bones turned to liquid. She'd heard enough to know that Abbott was in the study. But who was the woman who'd screamed? She wanted to run for the police, but it was too late now. She couldn't risk the delay. She couldn't turn away. Under cover of the deafening blast and the woman's screams, she forced herself to scramble up the last few stairs. She leaned so heavily against the wall outside the study that she imagined it would cave inwards and she would tumble into the room.

Abbott's voice again. "Where's Kathleen?" he asked softly.

Eva sighed and floated in the blessed numbness. She thought she should fight, and she smiled at the torn trousers and long gash in Abbott's leg, knowing that Agatha had not gone meekly. But Eva had lost something and couldn't seem to get it back. "I don't want to do this, anymore," she said, surprised she'd spoken the words aloud.

"Do what? All you have to do is tell me where she is. Simple, really. And it will save you so much pain."

Eva shook her head, and with that movement, saw the shadow. It was gone in a flicker of a second, but she'd seen it. Someone had come. Lily. Suddenly, passionately, the will to live surged through her. She looked for the gun, seeing it just inside the door where it had come to rest after skittering across the hardwood floor that edged the carpet. When she looked back at Abbott, he was smiling again, the same vapid, manic smile. Smiling, and holding a knife stained with Agatha's blood. She closed her eyes, lest they reveal the leap of hope she felt, and forced herself to speak laconically.

"All right. If it means so much to you. Kathleen's in France."

Abbott narrowed his eyes at Eva. "I don't believe you. Look at me!"

One last time, Eva reached deep down inside herself and found the hate that had almost shrivelled away, a dying leaf, its edges curled and brittle in the last days of an endless summer. She called it up into her eyes and focused it on Abbott.

"Suit yourself. But she's gone to France whether you like it or not. With her lover. Marc Forrest." She tried to find the words that would wound him the most, anything that would keep him from seeing the doorway in his peripheral vision.

In the hallway, Lily heard the lie and knew what the woman was doing. She had to act now. She had to do something. But nothing was real. She tried to grasp onto something solid — the wall, or the floor, or the gun just inside the door — but everything kept dissolving and swaying.

She dropped soundlessly to her knees.

The gun just inside the door.

She flattened herself and inched forward on her stomach.

If only she could get the gun, hold the gun, lift the gun.

She needed to pretend this wasn't happening. It was all a terrible game of dare, and risk, and subtle movement. *Simon says, get the gun.*

She began to snake her hand across the floor, first her palm, then her wrist, then her lower arm, her skin gliding across the polished boards. Closer, closer.

"No!" Abbott screamed.

Lily's hand froze.

Then she saw him rush at the woman, his fists rising and falling. Pounding into her.

She grabbed the gun. She looked at the woman, their eyes meeting for a fraction of a second, the blue eyes pleading, her own wide with terror.

She shifted her weight, trying to balance evenly on both legs and lifted the revolver, bracing it in both hands. She opened her mouth, opened the mouth of this dangerous stranger she had become, but the voice — loud, urgent, commanding — was undeniably her own.

"Let her go, Abbott."

She saw the shock leap into his expression as he turned to her.

"You!" He let go of Eva, and stepped toward her.

"Stop there."

He looked at her hands. They were trembling. He took another step.

She fired. The bullet whizzed past his ear and hit the ceiling.

She staggered back from the recoil. He was almost on top of her when she fired again. The force of the shot spun him around. Amazed, he clutched his hand to his side. When he pulled it away, it was bright red. He cried out, wailed, and lunged at her.

Terrified, she squeezed the trigger again. And again.

One of his hands grasped the front of her shirt. His face was so close to hers, she felt his exhaling breath. A spray of warm blood splashed across her cheek, and his hand suddenly went limp, sliding down the length of her body as he sagged to the ground and collapsed motionless at her feet.

She screamed in horror, dropped the gun, and lost consciousness.

Her sense of touch was the first to flood back, and Lily felt herself cradled in the woman's arms, a cool, soothing cloth wiping blood from her face. Her eyelashes fluttered and she saw that the woman had dragged her away from Abbott's body. For the first time, across the room, by the fireplace, she saw Agatha's body and cried out. The woman held her tightly. Lily looked up into the bruised and swollen face.

"Hayley?" she whispered.

Eva's eyes widened with shock. "My God, is that what you thought? No, Lily. Not Hayley. Hayley's dead."

"But she can't be. If she's really dead, then who *are* you?"

"I'm Eva. And Rosa and Terri and, a long, long time ago, I used to be Bonnie. Bonnie Morgan."

Lily and Eva sat together in the drawing room where they couldn't see the trail of footprints and the terrible story they told. But the images would always be with them, inerasable.

Lily had done her best to make Eva comfortable. She'd helped her bathe and change into fresh clothes. She'd found painkillers and made her swallow the tablets with a mixture of brandy and water. She'd even fashioned a sturdier sling with one of Agatha's shawls, redolent with her scent.

Eva buried her face in it briefly, drinking in what solace she could, and sighed. "I think she knew."

"That he was here?"

"That he would come. Maybe not so soon, but eventually."

"How did he find her?"

"We should have guessed. He had you tailed. We were all so intent on getting the gun and setting Kathleen free, we didn't see the obvious. I'm sure Agatha did."

"But why? Why confront him alone?"

"Because the law held no hope for her. Because she wanted to set us free. Because she had never been tested."

Lily nodded and raked a hand through her hair. It was rash, fool-hardy even, but it made sense. She was well beyond judging Agatha, who had been pushed to a place where there were no clear lines, no absolutes. In the room at the top of the stairs, Lily had joined her in that uncertain, ambiguous space. She'd squeezed the trigger in self-defence and in defence of Eva, but she'd also seen Ben's face in her mind's eye. It wasn't only fear, but hate that had propelled her actions. She was glad that Abbott was dead. She wasn't pure. And in the end, she thought she could live with that.

"What will we tell Detective Meyers?" she asked.

"The truth?"

"I don't think so, Eva. Not all of it." She smiled and reached for her hand. "If he finds you here, he'll have questions about Antigua, and about Mahoney."

"You know?"

Lily laughed. "Not as much as I thought. I found your diary and assumed it was Hayley's. I'm sorry, but everything I knew about her was so dramatic, I didn't consider the shy playmate, even when you were staring out at me from the photographs on the wall."

"That was how it always was. Hayley was the leader. If I'd had more of her fire, more of her courage after Mahoney raped me, I might have warned her in time. Maybe saved Jeanine, too."

"So you saved Amanda instead?"

"Yes. But I didn't know who she was. I was merely following Mahoney, fearful of what he might do. I thought the hate had gone. But it all happened so fast. He attacked her. I killed him. It wasn't an accident.

"I confessed to Agatha, and to protect me she asked Amanda to take the job in Mexico after you'd seen us talking together. We were afraid you'd unravel the truth."

"And Marc?"

"He tried to protect me, too. Agatha told him what I'd done soon after the night you first came here. She passed him a note in a book of poetry asking him to call. She felt he had a right to know about Mahoney. Later, he met with Amanda, told her the whole story, but not my name."

"And did he also know about the network from the first?"

"Oh, no. Not at all. He told you the truth about that, Lily. Not even his parents knew about Agatha. There was never a direct link between the network and Mahoney. There was only me. It was my responsibility alone."

"But the police claimed they talked to a Bonnie Morgan in British Columbia. *I* talked to Bonnie. If not you, then who?"

"She was the woman in Antigua that the police never found, the first woman through the network. Agatha knew her family and knew that she was in danger from an abusive husband. She also knew that I didn't want to live as Bonnie Morgan anymore. So she gave her the money to fly to Antigua and Hayley and I went down to meet her a few days later. We traded identities. She became Bonnie, and I became Eva. We both started new lives. But Hayley didn't come back."

"Was it an accident, or suicide?"

"I'm not sure. She seemed happier, pleased about the network and wanting to make a difference. Agatha and I always wondered. She was like a comet, blazing through life. She never talked about her deeper feelings, not even to me. She'd never have kept a diary."

They sat in silence for a moment. Lily lifted her chin. "You must go now, Eva."

"I can't leave you with Meyers, Lily. Others have died because of me, other men besides Mahoney."

"It doesn't matter. Agatha tried to tell me. I understand now. Your staying will only complicate the story. You must save yourself, Eva. For me, and for Agatha. Can you manage?"

The two women stood and regarded each other, knowing what saving herself would involve for Eva.

"Where will you go?" Lily asked.

"To a border motel first. I abandoned a friend there. Then to bed. Beyond that, I'm not sure. And you?"

"To France, if Marc will have me. Will I see you again?"

"Perhaps."

She walked across the room, and paused in the doorway, looking back at Lily. "When Meyers asks why you waited so long to notify the police, tell him the phones were out of order."

She smiled briefly, and was gone.

Epilogue

THE LETTER

Monday, October 11, France

The light was trembling and golden, the air fragrant with the scent of harvested grapes and ripe corn fields. Lily was sitting on the terrace, looking out over the meadow, trying to name the blue of the sky. Madonna blue, she decided, as flawlessly blue as the painted cloak of the Virgin in the ancient stone church in Jeanine's village near Dieulefit.

Lily's arms and legs were bronzed and her hair streaked by the late-summer sun. It had grown longer since her arrival in August, the curls more unruly than ever. She twisted one now in her fingers and then looked up as Marc approached her, placing one hand on her shoulder.

"Can I help?" she asked.

Jeanine was sequestered in the kitchen, preparing a Thanksgiving Day feast for the misplaced Canadian. She'd left her husband, her father, and her brother in charge of the baby, and firmly ordered Lily outside to dream. Only Lily didn't feel misplaced. She felt as if she'd come home.

"No, you can't help. It's worth my life to let you into that kitchen. Jeanine wants the meal to be a surprise." He sat down beside her. "Lily, there's a postman here from Dieulefit. He has a registered letter from Toronto addressed to you and you must sign for it."

"But how? No one knows I'm here."

"One person would have known, Lily. My guess is that this has to do with Agatha's estate." He extended a hand to help her up and they walked around the house to the front entrance where the mail carrier was patiently waiting.

"*Bonjour, Mademoiselle Ross. Cette lettre est pour vous, mais il faut remplir cette fiche.*"

Lily took the form, ticked the appropriate boxes and scrawled her signature across the bottom. "*Merci, Monsieur.*" Both curious and apprehensive, she handed back the official acknowledgement of receipt.

"*Bien, le voici. Au revoir.*"

They waved him goodbye, the letter heavy in Lily's hands, and strolled back to the terrace. Marc saw the memory of pain in her eyes and moved discreetly away.

Lily turned the letter over, carefully easing open the flap, her mind filled with the memory of Agatha's face as she had first seen it in the doorway of her Rosedale home a few months and a lifetime ago. Eva had warned her not to look at Agatha's body and she had not. She remembered her as she was, a figure of grace and dignity. A smaller, thinner envelope fell into her lap, addressed in fountain pen, in the elegant script of a generation that had studied penmanship. It read simply: *Lily Ross, Confidential.*

She picked up the covering letter first and scanned it. Then read it again in disbelief.

> *Dear Ms. Ross,*
>
> *Please find enclosed a confidential document which we are forwarding to you, as instructed by the last will and testament of the late Agatha Elizabeth Quinn.*
>
> *We are also informing you at this time that you have been named by the same testament as one of the heirs of the estate in the amount of 12.4 million dollars. In addition, Mrs. Quinn has stipulated that you may remove any personal items and/or fixtures from her principal residence that you may wish to keep, after which time the house and property will be sold and the proceeds distributed to various women's shelters in Toronto.*
>
> *Upon your return to Canada, please contact our office at your earliest convenience. One of our representatives will be pleased to assist you in making the necessary arrangements.*

Lily's hands were shaking as she put aside the official letter, scarcely noticing the *yours truly*, the signature, or the name of the law firm, scarcely believing in its authenticity. *There must be some mistake,* she thought, *some explanation.*

She stared at Agatha's letter, the black ink stark against the cream parchment. *Tell me, Agatha, what have you done?*

She clasped the note to her breast, as if she could once more touch its writer, and then heard, more than read, its farewell words.

Jan Rehner

My dear Lily,

Please do not be shocked. Listen to me, one last time.

Everyone waits for the phone call in the middle of the night, the one that constricts your heart and renders you helpless. Mine came on a brilliantly sunny day.

A police officer called to say she had found Hayley, dazed on the side of the road, beaten and sexually assaulted. Then Bonnie came into my arms and told me all she could endure remembering. It wasn't simply that the world was askew for a time. It was fundamentally changed. Nothing would ever be the same again, not for Hayley, and not for those of us who survived.

From that instant, I can trace myriad threads of light and darkness. The brightness comes from Bonnie, whom I trust you now know as Eva, from the network, from the lives redeemed and saved, and from the gradual resurgence of joy, made all the more poignant by the knowledge of its fragility.

I need not speak of the darkness, irrational and evil, for it has brushed you as well. It is also, sometimes, irresistible. One must not linger in its shadows lest the soul absorb its blackness.

And so, my dear, I am placing my faith in you and your own special gift of capturing light. Eva has been too long wrestling the darkness, and I fear her goodness will be drained unless she is set free. Like you, she must reinvent herself. I do not underestimate her ability to do so, nor yours.

We once spoke together of choices. That is my true legacy to you, Lily. Perhaps I was arrogant to take my choices into my own hands. But I did not take them lightly and I feel no self-recrimination. Perhaps I am arrogant still, for I am placing the network and its considerable resources in your hands to lead, disband, or reshape, however you please. There are women who will help you, should you choose to stay, and none who will blame you, should you not wish the burden.

*I can see your serious brow wrinkling even as I write
these words. You must not worry about Eva. I long ago
provided for her needs, those, at least, within my power.*

*And why you, Lily Ross? Because there are leaps of faith
everywhere, if only we believe. Do what you will with a
full heart, and my blessing.*

The note was signed simply, *Agatha.*

Lily held it in her hands for a long time, her face wet with tears,
until Jeanine came to find her.

"The letter," she asked gently, "it's really from Agatha?"

"Yes."

"She was an impossible woman. I always liked her."

"Me, too."

Lily folded the letter carefully and slipped it into her pocket. As
she crossed the terrace, glad of company and the festive house, she
thought for a moment of Eva, and wondered where she was, and if
she shared the same untroubled sky.

Jan Rehner has published poetry, literary criticism, a feminist analysis of infertility, and a text on critical thinking. *Just Murder* is her first mystery novel. She lives in Toronto and teaches humanities and writing at York University.